Something More Than Night

Something More Than Night

IAN TREGILLIS

A TOM DOHERTY ASSOCIATES BOOK

New York

SOMETHING MORE THAN NIGHT

Copyright © 2013 by Ian Tregillis

A Tor Book
Published by Tom Doherty Associates, LLC
175 Fifth Avenue
New York, NY 10010

www.tor-forge.com

Tor® is a registered trademark of Tom Doherty Associates, LLC.

Library of Congress Cataloging-in-Publication Data

Tregillis, Ian.
    Something more than night / Ian Tregillis.—First Edition.
       p. cm.
    "A Tom Doherty Associates Book."
    ISBN 978-0-7653-3432-9 (hardcover)
    ISBN 978-1-4668-1020-4 (e-book)
    I. Title.
    PS3620.R4446S66 2013
    813'.6—dc23

2013023854

Tor books may be purchased for educational, business, or promotional use.
For information on bulk purchases, please contact Macmillan Corporate
and Premium Sales Department at 1-800-221-7945 extension 5442
or write specialmarkets@macmillan.com.

First Edition: December 2013

Printed in the United States of America

0 9 8 7 6 5 4 3 2

To Mark Lopez, Mary Lopez,
and Mark Falzini:
for a birthday

Acknowledgments

My thanks to Daniel Abraham, S. C. Butler, Adrienne Crezo, Elena Giorgi, Vic Milán, John Miller, Matt Reiten, Melinda M. Snodgrass, Steve Stirling, Sage Walker, and Walter Jon Williams for smart feedback and helpful suggestions. Thanks also to Edwin Chapman, for copyedits; Dr. Corry L. Lee, for Feynman diagrams and discussions of quantum angeldynamics; and Linda Piper, the real-world model for Ria's tattoo. I'm also grateful to my agent, Kay McCauley, who found a home for this book, and my editor, Claire Eddy, who made it a great one. Finally, I'll never be able to thank Sara Gmitter enough for her love, enthusiasm, persistence, and patience.

Something More Than Night

YOU SHOULD HEAR
THE FUNERAL CHOIR

*T*hey murdered one of the Seraphim tonight.

Gabriel streaked across the heavens like a tumbling meteor, his corpse a fireball of sublimated perfection. He had been a creature of peerless majesty, but now the throes of his death etched the firmament.

His wings, all six, shed embers of incandescent grace as he skidded across the night sky. And when he opened his mouths to scream, the Earth could do naught but shudder. The roar of his lion's visage registered a 5.2 on the Richter, six hundred miles east of Kyoto. The bellow of his ox's muzzle roused a dormant volcano in Hawaii. The shriek of his eagle aspect crumbled chimneys in Seattle. The inaudible cry from his human face left people from Melbourne to Perth weeping in troubled slumber, dreaming of colors that no longer existed and sounds that hadn't been heard since the Earth was just magma and poison. Meanwhile, turbulence roiled a cloud of dark matter sleeting through the solar system.

But that was Gabriel for you. Platonically perfect, blindingly beautiful. He wasn't just lovely, he was the kind of lovely that could make a bishop stomp his miter and curse a long blue streak on Easter Sunday.

Don't believe me? I saw him do it once. On a bet.

Fun guy, Gabby.

Gabriel had been there when the sun emitted its first feeble glow, flapping his wings like a bellows to fan the coals of Creation. After the planets congealed from hot primordial soot, Gabriel's gentle breath cooled the Earth's crust. And when the onion-skin atmosphere needed protection, it was Gabriel who stirred the Earth's molten core with his flaming sword to impel the dynamo that would deflect the ravaging solar wind. He'd serenaded the cyanobacteria that pumped oxygen into the primeval atmosphere and sang a dirge for the dinosaurs.

He had a real fondness for this place. And he never begrudged the monkeys.

Yet for all that, if any of the monkeys had bothered to notice, Gabriel's death would have looked to them like fragments of space junk entering the atmosphere. Yeah. That's how they perceive the violent death of an immortal being: unremarkable junk. Was he a spent rocket booster skimming through the ionosphere? Or maybe the shredded remains of a kinetic harpoon cleaving the aurora?

But nobody looks up anymore. That stopped soon after the last satellites died. In the minds of most monkeys, thirty years of meteor showers was weak tea compared to the loss of decent long-term weather forecasts. Hard to blame them. This joint could have used some decent climate monitoring.

A chill wind whipped the Bass Strait into a froth, driving the weight of melted ice shelves to thunder against the floodwalls a few miles to my south. I tightened the collar of my overcoat, pulled the fedora lower over my brow, and retreated into the meager shelter of a laneway. A trio of Australasian businessmen shuffled past me, their guilty downcast eyes reflecting the neon glow from a topless bar. (Looked like real neon, too. Don't see that much anymore. It's been all OLEDs for decades.) None of these men was the poor sap I'd come to find, so I lit another pill and watched the light show overhead.

The heat of unbeing, the friction of conflicting Magisteria, crumbled Gabriel's wings to ash. The ash sparkled on the way down like a rain of silver moondust.

It became snow.

The flakes sparkled in the dim, inconstant light of the laneway. And wasn't that fitting: his wings, those glorious divine pinions, eternally aglow with the echoes of Creation—more luminous than sunrise on burnished platinum, more delicate than starlight washing against a dewy cobweb—reduced in their final moments to parroting the epileptic flicker of antique signs advertising fifty-dollar joy girls.

Some might shrug and say, that's the monkeys for you. That there's nothing so sublime they can't find a way to defile it. But I prefer to think they just don't know any better. So did Gabriel.

I caught a whiff of rose attar and old books. That was his scent. One of them. It was clear and sharp for a second, but then it mixed with the odor of overflowing rubbish from the dim sum place across the lane. The garbage won. Gabriel was fading.

Wind muffled the double *ding* of a street tram. The rattle and buzz of the tram dopplered up the laneway while overhead the disintegration of Gabriel's halo momentarily outshone the full moon. The noise receded with the tram and resolved into the staccato clatter of footsteps.

Time was running short. I studied the newcomers: a mugg with a bit of high-class fluff on his arm.

Ink on his neck, and his heavy coat swayed against the wind. Something solid in his pocket. Was he rodded? Maybe the twist at his elbow liked the thrill of running with a wrong gee.

As for her . . . She stood a thumb shorter than he in high-heeled boots, a tall thin statue wrapped in a wasp-waisted black coat that might have been cashmere. When the wind whipped the hem of her coat, I glimpsed smooth leather hugging her calves. Nice gams. Curls like brushed copper fluttered beneath the brim of her cloche. Her stride was firm and purposeful, like that of a CEO or dominatrix, moving without hesitation on the slick snow-dusted paving stones. She walked like the world was made of red carpet.

They headed for a gin mill across the street and a few paces down from my alcove. He grabbed the door. She paused, tugged his elbow, turned a porcelain face to the sliver of night above the lane.

"Hey, look," she said. "Up there."

Okay. *Almost* nobody looks up anymore.

He took all of two seconds to glance at the sky and witness an angel's murder. "It's just junk."

See what I mean?

"No . . ." A flicker of doubt tugged her brows together. "This is different. Can't you see?"

"C'mon. It's cold out here, Moll."

Moll? Go figure. Another gust swirled ash into my eye. I flicked my cigarette aside and reassessed the flametop.

Her eyes were a little too close together, but they sparkled in the light of Gabriel's death. Her lips parted in a posture of wonder. It wasn't junk. She didn't know what she was seeing—no human could—but she knew damn well it wasn't junk.

She was no good for me. There was something going on behind her eyes. But her steady . . . now *he* had promise. His lack of initiative gave me high hopes.

The wind had extinguished my cigarette before it hit the ground. I fished out another. Overhead, Gabriel's debris tore the night. I approached the couple. Slowly.

"Got a light, Jack?" The mugg frowned. I gestured with the unlit pill in my hand. "The damn wind, you know?"

"Yeah," he said. He dug into his free pocket, the one without the iron. The twist released his arm and gave me a quick once-over, eyes narrowed with a suspicion she probably reserved for unwelcome suitors and hard-luck swells. She retreated into the laneway for a better view of the light show above. When she turned her face to the sky, her neck assumed the pale graceful curve of a swan's back. A burgundy scarf fluttered against a pendant sheltered in the hollow of her throat. Red ice sparkled on her ears and neck. It matched the scarf. She knew how to put herself together. Gabby would have liked her.

I put the pill to my lips, leaned into the flame of his lighter. The sharp smell of butane briefly washed away the smells of rotting dim sum and dying angel. I puffed, wondering if the dame could smell the latter.

"Thanks," I said, and made fleeting eye contact. Nothing provocative. Didn't want him to think I was sly on him. Didn't want him to ape out, either, especially with the iron he carried. I hate getting shot, and tonight of all nights I was plenty low already. But I wanted to read him, and get a sense of the human behind those eyes. I kept my glamour dialed down—what I had left of it, anyway—so as not to send him into a wing-ding. I needed him lucid. Couldn't have him drooling on the fluff. Up close, that coat did look like cashmere.

Now the fixers, the sharp shooters with the industrial-grade glamours—like Gabriel, Rafael, Uriel, and the rest—they could lobotomize a monkey with less than a wink. Which is one reason they don't come down here much anymore. Too messy. (That, and on account of Gabby's being dead.) In addition, I think they tired of spawning a new religion every time they took a stroll on Earth no matter how carefully they soft-footed the natives. It got stale.

The tension went out of the mugg's shoulders. A low frown creased his face, but it was loose and slack like a diaper tied by a drunken bachelor uncle. Then he shook his head, realized he still held the lighter, and clicked it shut. The whole thing was over before his girl deigned to look at us again.

I got what I needed. I was looking for somebody who wouldn't rock the boat in a time of crisis. Somebody inclined to go with the flow, who wouldn't ask a lot of questions. A dull little trooper, in other words. Such were my marching orders. This guy was perfect. He wasn't burning with curiosity about anything.

Not that I had a lot of precedent to guide me. Nobody had ever done this before, far as I knew.

So that was me. Good old Bayliss: charting new ground. And none too thrilled about it. I'd been strong-armed into a dirty job and couldn't wait to leave it behind. I'd pretend tonight never happened, pretend Gabriel was still up there carving graffiti into the celestial spheres.

So I settled on the loogan. Yeah. He'd do. He'd do just fine, the poor sap. Also, I didn't have much choice. Gabriel was just about gone.

"What's got you so worked up, sister? Sky falling?"

Wanted to keep her distracted for a few seconds while her steady shook off the last of the glamour. Even a low-rent shine like yours truly can take a moment to wear off if the receiving end has had a snootful of something strong. And he had. I could smell the hooch on his breath. The pug was tight. And, judging from the veins in his eyes, no stranger to it. Probably on his way to being a full-blown hard case. I was doing him a favor.

Now it was the twist's turn to frown at me. It was colder than the snowflakes tangled in her hair, that frown, slim and sharp as a letter opener. It was meant for cutting, and honed from frequent use. Brother, what a dish.

"What?"

Her voice matched the frown so perfectly they might have come as a set from a high-end store. A real tony place. I pointed up.

"See something swell?"

Looking straight at me, she said, "No. No I don't."

Ouch. Maybe Gabby and I weren't the only ones having a bad night. They seemed down in the mouth, so I let it slide. What a pair of mopes. Under other circumstances I might have hung out a sympathetic ear. But it was moot. We had bigger concerns.

"C'mon, Moll," he said. "It's cold out here."

I bowed. "Thanks, pal. See ya around."

They went into the gin mill.

I stayed outside, drawing smoke into my lungs until the final cinders of shattered Seraphim faded from the junkyard sky. I finished my cigarette while Gabriel's final echoes dissipated. The light of a distant quasar twinkled with chromatic aberration as the fine-structure constant gave him a farewell salute from the twenty-first decimal place.

Everything fell silent for an instant. Even the wind. The world hiccuped, like a phonograph needle skipping its track. The lights flickered. So did the distribution of prime numbers. The Pleroma had come unbalanced. My clock was ticking.

The snow came down harder. Big, thick flakes that fluttered like tufts of cotton. I reached for a falling snowflake and put a silver feather in my pocket. Figured I could hock it for a bit of the folding stuff. And besides. Gabby didn't need it anymore, did he?

I tipped my hat at the sky, stamped out the pill, and followed the pair inside. I'd been here before, otherwise I might have been surprised that it wasn't the low-rent dive suggested by the establishments across the way. It was the kind of place where hard drinkers came to wrestle their demons while fallen angels drank alone in dark smoky corners. All it needed was a whisky-voiced chanteuse and maybe a piano with thumbtacks in the hammers.

I liked the music in this joint. They played old stuff here. Louis Armstrong tooted away on his horn while I weighted down my usual stool. When that man got going, he could make you forget the world, forget everything but his horn. Nobody danced, though. Dancing to the old stuff is a forgotten skill.

They knew me here. The bartender was a former professor of English. Long story starring a gimlet-eyed coed. Sometimes bartenders need a sympathetic ear, too; amazing, the things you can learn. And there are worse things in life than the gratitude of a good tapster. He nodded and slid a shot glass to me, but I wasn't in the market for a belt of rye. I bought the bottle.

The couple sat in a corner booth visible from my spot at the bar.

Couldn't see too well through the haze, but they were sitting close and having an urgent conversation. She was doing more of the talking than her steady. He listened, slowly nodding his head. Whether that was agreement or the hooch I couldn't say. Turns out he wasn't rodded. The heavy thing in his pocket was a bottle. What a cheapskate, stiffing the joint on its corkage fee. He served himself from it, but his girl refused. I made a note to find an overcoat with deeper pockets.

Armstrong packed it in for the night. A trio of *penitentes*, two joes and a jane, took the floor and started writhing to the beat of century-old trip-hop. Their shirts had long slashes across the back, revealing the high-end cosmetic surgery and scarification that put antiseptically sculpted wounds on their shoulder blades. Still fresh, still bleeding. They even had little tufts of downy feathers matted in the gore. I suppose it made them look, to somebody who didn't know any better, like angels who'd just had their wings sheared off.

The shorn-wing look was big this year. Don't ask me why. Few years back, it was fake stigmata. I preferred that. The wing thing made me think of Gabby. But the *penitentes* never got the wing placement right. The Seraphim have wings, sure, but not on their shoulders. Nor did the monkeys ever go for more than two. Never could figure what those loonybirds were so penitent about, but I had yet to see one who knew his Aquinas. Or if they did, they never committed to the role. They'd been around for a while, but I'd never seen anything halfway correct.

You never saw a sexless *penitente*. (No. No matter what they did to themselves, it was never chaste when they wiggled on the dance floor.) Never saw one with six wings, or wearing only a pair of gossamer feathers to cup his nethers. Never saw one who'd opted for leathery bat wings, or had a couple extra limbs sewn on. Never saw one with a sheet of flame where her face should be.

But tonight of all nights I didn't mind the *penitentes*. Nobody could tell if I was watching the couple in the booth or fascinated with all the grinding on the dance floor. Maybe it was a bit of both.

I drank to the memory of my murdered friend. And then I drank some more.

I got tight. Very tight.

Which might explain what happened next. But in my defense, it had been a lousy day. One for the record books.

So, while I got tight and the dancers got sweaty, the twist and the hard gee had a tiff in the corner. No screaming. No throwing. But she was flashing that frown like a rapier, and the grip on his arm turned her knuckles white. He sank further and further into himself. When he moved, he moved fast, but he didn't reach for her. He reached for his bottle. He emptied it down his throat and barged past the dancers.

She grabbed her coat and followed. A sleeve flapped against her drink when she flung the cashmere over her shoulders. But she was already halfway to the door, and most eyes were on her or the *penitentes*, so only I witnessed how her glass toppled over the edge and summersaulted to a perfect landing on the floorboards, the cocktail inside still pristine as a nun's knickers.

Entropy had just decided to take five, which meant the fabric of mortal reality was unraveling. It was time to move. I enjoyed one last swig and followed the show outside.

The sky was quiet. Back to the usual erratic flicker as pieces of aerospace debris hit the atmosphere. The celestial fireworks had run their course. Gabriel was gone.

Good-bye, pal.

Snow had fallen just long enough to put a chill on the evening. It felt like the air itself had knocked off for the night, leaving nothing between Earth and stars but the humans and me. The cold flooded my sinuses. I'd been floating on the lingering fumes of oak and fire, but one frigid breath doused the flames and packed my head with ice.

The snow put a hush on everything, as though the city knew it for a portent of unknown significance. Long time since it was cold enough for snow in these parts.

The hard boy zigzagged down the laneway. He slipped in the snow a couple of times. His frail followed just out of arm's reach so that he didn't pull her down with him. She was too graceful for that. But she didn't leave him lying in the gutter. Some guys have all the luck.

Tricky thing, tailing somebody through the laneways. Get too cozy and your birds will fly. Stay too far back and you'll lose 'em in the tangle of doglegs, alcoves, and unlit stairwells. Shadows fill the lanes day and night. They're part pedestrian arcade, part flea market, part bodega, part chophouse, part disco. The paths twist through arches and under canopies, meander through the tables of sidewalk brasseries, shrug past card tables laid with gray-market goods. It's the kind of place where Indonesian businessmen in three-piece duds hock Australian knockoffs of Chinese tech to gullible tourists. The kind of place where freshly dead snakes dangle from hooks in a café window. The kind of place where a marble bank lobby throbs with music from the S&M club hidden behind antique teller windows. The kind of place where on a busy night you can't take five steps without brushing against somebody. The kind of place where eye contact is a social contract. The kind of place where well-heeled suburbanites come to get a dose of gritty urbanism, thrilling at the glitter and desperation, buying trinkets or a skewer of vat-grown vegetables grilled over a trash fire just to have tangible proof of their excursion, then leaving at the first sight of a *penitente* weeping blood. The kind of place where you keep one hand on your wallet and the other free to wave off the hucksters. The kind of place where each breath varnishes the back of your throat with the oilyslick cloy of patchouli or the reek of fermented cabbage.

And as I said, I was tight. Not at my best. But I managed to follow the pair toward the muted double *ding* of a tram stop. The couple headed in the general direction of the chimes. I stumbled after them.

Back in the day, my errand would have been trivial. Could have done it from a distance. But I'd been down here a spell. I was rusty. And anyway I wasn't sure how this was supposed to work. Wasn't like I could ask around for advice. I could figure the basics on my own, but I didn't like the math. Maybe I wasn't as big a fan of the monkeys as Gabriel had been, but I didn't wish them ill. All I knew was the only thing worse than doing this job would have been not doing it. So I winged it. Figured the smart money was on physical contact. How was I to know?

I inched closer as the lane spilled into a more reputable thoroughfare. Here Gabriel's debris had become a dirty slush beneath the tires of the traffic sliding past us. Cars like wheeled soap bubbles jockeyed for position around the accordion twists of serpentine electric trams. An elevated commuter train clattered overhead, ferrying a load of dead-eyes to third-shift jobs.

My mark leaned heavily on his girlfriend when they crossed to the tram stop. But flametop managed to get him through the gauntlet without incident. I slipped once or twice getting myself to the center island. Blame it on the snow. I do. The dame shot another frown in my direction when I finally made it under the plastic canopy. Maybe she recognized me from earlier.

Now, the thing about this part of town is that it's a touristy area. And tourists will goggle at anything so long as it's quaint. By "quaint" I mean that some of these interchanges are well over a century old. So the traffic lights at certain intersections—such as where the three of us shivered in the cold sea wind—are toggled by mechanical switches set by the tram conductors. Gotta hand it to human ingenuity. For something so primitive the system works well. Most of the time.

Trams run less frequently at night. Which gave me time to plan my move.

The lockbox controlling signals for trams coming in our direction stood on the far side of a five-way interchange about a hundred feet away. If I hadn't been stuck down here so long maybe I could have done it better. Maybe things would have turned out differently. But I'd faded. Couldn't flick the button. Not at that distance. All I had to go on was my glamour and my charming personality.

I waited until the tram stopped at the light. Stepping out to open the box put the conductor's line of sight in my general direction. That's when I cranked up the glamour and gave him all I had. At that distance, and given my deterioration, the show wasn't worth a wooden nickel. But it distracted him just enough to make him forget his purpose. He got back on the tram without pressing the button. Without paying attention to what he was doing.

The cross-traffic had started moving again when the tram bulled through the intersection. Blaring horns shook my mark from his stupor. He and the twist gawked at the commotion.

A line of cars idled alongside the tracks adjacent to our stop, waiting to turn across the tram lines and opposing traffic. Everyone drove slowly on account of Gabriel's snowfall. Meaning the hackie trying to keep his fare on the road despite the slush was intent on the traffic and not the tram illegally crossing the intersection. Tram had nearly clipped the taxi before the conductor came to his senses. Brakes screeched. Too late. The hackie panicked, threw his cab into reverse. The tram crunched the taxi with a glancing blow. Slick pavement sent the car spinning over the tracks and into our island.

The hard boy just watched it coming.

It was beautiful. I was ready right then and there to pack it in and start making dough in pool halls. What a combination. There are home runs and there are grand slams, but in comparison this was an unassisted triple play on the first day of the season. A work of art. All I had to do was leap over and try to pull the mark aside. I'd fail to save him of course, but the physical contact would tag him just before he died. And the Choir would do the rest: pick him up, dust him off, pat him on the head, and plug the hole left by Gabby's demise.

So that was my plan. Not too shabby, right? I thought so, too. But it didn't account for the flametop having the reflexes of a ferret jammed up on speed.

"Martin!"

She was up and yanking him out of harm's way before I was halfway there. He planted face on the pavement. The taxi spun through the bench and knocked it skew-whiff across the tram stop. Missed him by a good two feet. The girl teetered at the edge of the platform, and nearly fell into the path of the sliding tram. But she caught herself, took a step back, and turned around.

I tripped over her man and bowled straight into her.

Physical contact.

That CEO/dominatrix/red-carpet stride failed her. She lost her footing in the snow for the first and only time since I'd started watching the two of them.

Over the years, I'd heard the occasional talk about how something seemed to unfold in slow motion. Always thought it was baloney. But it isn't. Windmilling her arms in a desperate bid to keep her balance, she seemed to hover at the edge of the platform for a moment like a scrap of silk caught on the wind. But she wasn't silk and she wasn't a hummingbird. She went over backward, still flailing, still staring in surprise at me.

Which is how I came to be looking straight into her eyes when she went beneath the tram.

2

MISTAKES WERE MADE,
NOW LET'S MOVE ON

Molly Pruett's dying thought was disappointingly banal: *Is that weird guy following us?*

But then she was tipping, tipping, tipping and stars overhead were shining, shining, shining—the strange lights in the sky had faded—and metal was screeching, screeching, screeching, and Martin was screaming, screaming, screaming while Molly's body came apart.

Cold. Sharp. Pressure. Pain.

Followed by darkness. Followed by light. Light so bright it hurt. So bright it should have gone through her eyeballs and set her hair on fire. She flinched away.

Time didn't pass. It sidled away, sideways, crablike.

She opened her eyes again. She lay on a canopy bed in the bedroom of a little girl.

A sweet breeze from the open window fluttered the curtains and ruffles of fabric bulging from the closet door. Molly knew that scent. Orange blossoms, from the tree outside her bedroom window. Her favorite smell in the world. It smelled like contentment and warmth. It smelled like a life with everything as it should be.

Molly looked again at the lacey mass holding the closet door ajar. It sparkled with sequins. She recognized the frills of a ballet tutu.

As a child she'd liked dresses and frilly things, but hated dolls. She'd only ever had one doll, and it hadn't lasted long. But there it sat on the dresser, its pinafore torn and gummy and mottled with silvery flakes. Molly had used transparent packing tape to wrap the doll in aluminum foil as a make-believe space suit. She made up better games than anybody else. Even Martin liked to play space war, but he always had to play the Chinese because he was older. Molly got stuck playing the losing side every time.

The whites of the doll's eyes gleamed a dull red the color of ink from a felt-tip pen. Her suit had been shredded by debris; her eyeballs had ruptured with explosive decompression. Such were the risks of war in Earth orbit.

It was one of the few times their mother had ever raised her voice in the house. The ruined doll had been expensive. But Dad laughed. He'd chuckled about it for years afterward. It angered Mom because she felt he wasn't supporting her. He felt she was overreacting. They argued about it, but not in front of the children. Never in front of the kids. So Molly had crept upstairs and crouched beside the closed bedroom door to eavesdrop on the secret negotiations of adults.

Thus came Molly's introduction to the f-word. There she was, already seven years old, which was more than old enough to know all the bad words. Martin was nine, and so of course he knew all about these things. Or so she thought. But this . . . this was something adults spoke only to each other, in private, in times of anger so acute it could only be whispered.

This, Molly realized, was a Word of Power. It was awesome.

She couldn't remember what happened after that, but it didn't matter. The damage had been done. In retrospect, it was amazing their parents had insulated them from that much for that long.

Mom eventually threw the ruined doll in the trash because the sight of it upset her so greatly.

Molly remembered it all. Then remembered still more.

Wait, she thought. *That doll went into the compactor over twenty years ago.*

Wind ruffled the curtains again. The high, clear ringing of glass bells played counterpoint to the susurration of wind through the orange tree. Dad's wind chime. That was before Mom had lost her job and they'd had to move way up north to where it was actually cold in the winter and where they couldn't grow an orange tree. She sniffed the air again. Still orange blossoms, but now there was something else. Something acrid, wrong. Tobacco?

I was ten years old when we moved. She sat up, looked down. She wore footie pajamas. *How do I fit in this bed? What's happening to me?*

She glanced around the room. *This is impossible,* she thought. But it was all there. Things she'd forgotten decades ago. Things she couldn't have remembered if she tried. The stuffed animals piled high against the dresser . . . the crayon marks on the wall . . . the toy chest . . .

The man leaning in the door, smoking a cigarette.

Snow dusted the shoulders of his trench coat; his old-timey hat dripped meltwater on the carpet. He'd been standing there for a while, shuffling his feet, because the carpet under his shoes was muddy. His eyes were too old for his face.

He blew a smoke ring and raised his hat. "Good morning, angel. Rise and shine."

Molly flinched. The room changed.

This was darker. More subdued. An adult's bedroom. The susurration of wind through the orange blossoms became the buzz of traffic on the interstate a couple blocks away. She knew that if she got up and pushed the drapes aside she'd find the lights of downtown Minneapolis glinting back at her. She turned her head to the left. On a nightstand sat the alarm clock she'd dubbed Satan, and which she had gleefully crushed with a brick when she quit her godawful temp job at the warehouse. Molly rolled to her side beneath cool, smooth sheets that caressed her skin like silk. She realized she was naked. The other half of the bed lay empty yet warm. The covers had been pushed back, and the pillow still held the impression where somebody's head had rested.

She pulled the pillow to her face. It smelled of Ria. Ria who had dumped her after an epic argument on New Year's Eve. But that was later. But this, this interlude in the old apartment, it was the happiest time of their relationship. She missed Ria.

It felt so real. But so had her childhood bedroom. These weren't memories. They were too vivid for that. These were random fragments of her life churned up like flotsam and jetsam on a violent surf.

Oh holy shit, she thought. *I'm going crazy.* Was it a tumor? Something short-circuiting her brain? Had Martin slipped her something?

She sniffed the pillow again. It still smelled like Ria. A long blond hair tickled her nose.

A toilet flushed. Molly felt a little thrill. She sat up to watch Ria return to bed from the en suite bathroom.

A stranger, a man, zipped his trousers and took a seat on the edge of the tub. He watched her through the adjoining doorway. He looked bored. A smoldering cigarette dangled from the corner of his mouth. Wisps of smoke curlicued past the tropical-fish shower curtain that Ria had disliked so much. Snowy meltwater had pooled into the cracks between the floor tiles.

He noticed her open eyes. "Hey. You up yet?"

Molly flinched again. "Ah, rats," he said, and rolled his eyes just as—

More memories. Melbourne. A freak snowfall. A traffic accident. A tram. Martin. A stranger. Falling.

Australia. The funeral. Somebody died—

"Look," said a voice. "If you're dead-set on reliving the entire thing, do me a favor. Either do it in order, or let me get a drink first. This jumping around is giving me a migraine. Keep it up and I'll shoot my cookies on your high school prom."

I never went to prom, thought Molly.

A pause, punctuated with a strong whiff of cigarette smoke. The voice said, "And warn me before we get to your first period. You're on your own for that one."

Molly remembered. She'd fallen under a streetcar. Hadn't she? In that case . . .

Holy shit. There really is a God . . . a drinking, chain-smoking God. . . .

"Am I crazy?" she whispered.

"Nah. You're not having an ing-bing, if that's what's got you worried. So relax. You're dead, angel."

He flicked the cigarette aside. It sailed into the bedroom and fell smoldering to the hardwood floor. A faint sizzle launched a puff of smoke and a scent equal parts wood ash and varnish. Ria would have taken his head off for that. She'd spent weeks refurbishing those floors. In return their landlord had given them two months off the rent.

The man sighed. He ran a hand under the brim of his hat, massaged his forehead. It was a snap-brim fedora, she realized. Very smart, that and the suit. She'd never seen anybody dressed like this. Only in old movies.

"Well, I say dead," he said, "but it's more complicated than that. I guess it's a decent start."

"I can't be dead. We're having a conversation."

"Uh-huh. Care to explain how it is you're lying in bed in an apartment building that burned down at the tail end of the last decade?"

Molly remembered. She'd heard about the fire from friends who still lived in the neighborhood. It seemed appropriate that the happiest place she'd ever lived had been reduced to ashes. She and Ria hadn't broken up yet, but their relationship was in free fall. All she said when Molly told her about the fire was, "My floors. Damn."

Molly took a second look at the trench-coat man. Those eyes . . . "Wait. I remember. The tram stop. You were there. You followed us. There was a taxi, I grabbed Martin—"

"Yeah. Uh. About that." He rubbed the back of his neck. "Real sorry I knocked you under that train. But hey, what's done is done. No point getting sore about it now. Bygones, right?"

"You—"

"Look, angel. I'm gonna level with you. I made a hash of things. Bad. Meant to tag your boyfriend but, well, things happen. It's a bum rap, I know, but we're stuck with one another."

Boyfriend? Oh. "Martin's my brother."

"For real? Huh." He shook his head. "Oh. I'm Bayliss, by the way." He flicked the brim of his hat with his thumbnail. "How's tricks?"

"What?"

Bayliss shook his head. Sighed. "Never mind. Point is, I need to get you on your feet and up to speed so that I can forget this day ever happened. You need me to show you the ropes before you gum up the works. So, like I said, we're stuck with one another, angel."

Molly clamped her hands to her forehead, rubbed her temples. "This is insane. This can't be real," she muttered. "This is a dream. It must be."

But that strange infuriating man, Bayliss, hadn't disappeared when she opened her eyes again. Instead, he was lighting another cigarette. "Not a dream. If so, we'd be sharing it, and I don't dream about taking a leak in some strange bird's apartment while she has a nervous breakdown in the next room. Trust me, it ain't on my list."

Maybe it all really happened but the train didn't kill me and I'm stuck in a coma. "I'm—"

"And it ain't a coma, either, so don't hold out hope on that front. You squiffed out, angel. It was messy." He puffed on his cigarette and looked away. "Sorry about that. Bygones."

"Get out of my house you fucking lunatic!"

"Thought we agreed this heap went to ash some years back. So how's it still your house?"

"Get out! Leave me alone!"

"Don't get so sore. Look at it this way. You've just won the big bad granddaddy of all lotteries."

Molly tossed the covers aside. Now she wore a nightgown. She knew this one; Ria had liked it so much. Bayliss averted his eyes like a reluctant gentleman, but not before a momentary glance made her feel naked.

"I gotta admit, angel, it could've been worse. You're easier on the eyes than your brother."

She reached under the bed. He was still smiling to himself and shaking his head when she pulled out Ria's baseball bat. A remnant from when they'd lived in an iffier neighborhood. The cigarette fell from Bayliss's mouth and hissed on the wet tiles.

She crossed the bedroom on the balls of her feet, richly varnished oak boards creaking under her soles. Bayliss raised his hands. His heels bumped the bathtub. He toppled backward, sliding down the plastic shower curtain with a grating squeak and the *pop* of broken curtain rings.

"Just calm down, angel." He wasn't looking at her legs anymore. All his attention was on the bat. "Okay. You're still sore about the train. I get that. But let's not get hysterical, okay?"

"I'll show you *hysterical*, you sexist prick."

Molly reared back. The bat knocked against the medicine cabinet; the bathroom was too small for her to put everything into the swing. Bayliss flopped to one side and caught the blow on the shoulder.

His shoulder made a cracking sound like a broken celery stalk, along with a slappy *thud* like a meat tenderizer hitting cheap steak. The reverberation shot up the bat and stung Molly's fingers. Bayliss's eyes and mouth went wide. No sound came from his contorted mouth. Just for an instant, something dark flashed in his ancient eyes, but then he found his voice and screamed.

"Ouch! Jesus, lady, are you completely out of your gourd? What's wrong with you?"

The bat fell from her fingers. A tile cracked.

The grain of the wood against her palms, the smell of Ria's soap, the special way the floorboards creaked in the winter, the crunch of Bayliss's shoulder . . . No dream had ever felt like this.

"What's happening to me?" she said.

"You're about to get a hard lesson, sweetheart." Bayliss stood, rubbing his shoulder. He gasped. "Ah, damn, that'll take some effort to fix. First things first." He slid his toes under the bat, kicked it off the tiles, caught it in his free hand. He waved it under Molly's nose. "Naughty, naughty."

He reared back. She flinched.

But suddenly they weren't standing in the Minneapolis apartment. They were somewhere outside, at night. A crowd had gathered, staring at something Molly couldn't see. Bayliss stood beside her. A thin dusting of pure white snow reflected the red and blue lights of emergency vehicles.

"You've been knocked for a loop, so I tried to go easy on you," he said. "But it didn't take. So here you go. You want to know what happened?" He paused long enough to fish a cigarette from his trench coat. He lit a match on his thumbnail and shielded the flame behind a cupped hand. After a couple of puffs, he flicked the extinguished match at the bystanders.

"Feast your eyes."

Sickly dread coated her tongue: she knew this place. Molly approached the crowd of bystanders. The knot in her gut accreted more ice, stole more of her cold blood, with every step. She reached forward to gently nudge the rearmost folks aside, so they would know her presence and let her join them in their silent contemplation of tragedy. But it wasn't necessary. In unison, half the bystanders took a step to the left, the other half to the right, though their backs were to her. Molly traversed the impromptu path and came to the front of the crowd.

But there was nothing to see. The gathering surged against a barricade of fluttering police tape that cordoned off a tram stop on the center island of a busy street. Two tram cars were parked at the stop, sandwiched between opposing lanes of traffic. Traffic inched past emergency vehicles clogging the road. Their flashing lights strobed the onlookers and the surrounding city with flashes of red and blue and yellow.

The police cars looked strange to her. And the traffic, she realized, kept to the left instead of the right.

Australia, she remembered. *We came to Australia for Mom's funeral.*

A thin metal scaffold had been erected around the front of the tram. Tall sheets of milky material rippled in a cold wind, blocking the onlookers' view. The sheets glowed full-moon white; a high-intensity lamp shone on the far side, where most of the cops had gathered.

Molly fingered the tape. Though he was well behind her now, cut off by the crowd, Bayliss's voice came to her as though he spoke in her ear. The unwelcome intimacy caused her to shiver.

"Keep going. The bulls won't stop you."

She ducked under the cordon, expecting shouts and cries and threats that didn't come. The policeman watching the cordon barely noticed the intrusion. He gave only the slightest nod of acknowledgment as his gaze slid past Molly. A dreamlike silence had fallen upon the world. Shrouded it, as though the world were holding its breath for she knew not what. And yet she could hear the crunch of snow underfoot and the electrical hum of the emergency lights. Even the faint hiss where dark puddles steamed on the tracks. The steam tasted like salted iron.

Molly sidestepped the plastic barrier. She cast no shadow over the scene at her feet. Two men crouched on the tracks at the center of a patch of red-black snow. They wore purple latex gloves. The night smelled of cold metal and ozone and shit. A black rubber pouch roughly the size of a sleeping bag lay on the snow beside the two men. They fished meaty things from the discolored snow and plopped them in the bag. A dented taxicab rested on the platform where tram passengers normally waited and disembarked.

Martin sat slumped on a broken bench, head in his hands. A policewoman sat next to him. She looked uncomfortable, or bored, clearly waiting for him to finish with whatever grieved him so. Why was Martin crying? He never cried. Not even at their mother's funeral.

Molly glanced again at the men in the bloody snow. They finished their task; they zipped the bag, stood, then stripped off the gloves.

She remembered the taxi careering across the wet street. Remembered grabbing Martin. Remembered falling.

Oh. No. No.

"Martin!"

She hopped onto the platform, crouched, and pulled his hands from his face. She tried to smile for him. "Hey, look! I'm okay!"

God, he looked awful. He yanked his hands away, as though something tickled or stung or burned them.

His teary eyes looked through her.

She knelt on the concrete and planted her hands on either side of his head. "Look at me! I'm here!"

Martin flinched again, shaking off her hands. He scratched vigorously at the spots where she'd touched him.

The policewoman watched it all with the same bored expression on her face.

Molly grabbed Martin by the back of the neck, pulled his head toward her and leaned forward until their foreheads bumped together. She found his eyes, pushed past the wall of confusion and despair, and forced eye contact.

He slid off the bench, fell to hands and knees, and puked over the side of the platform. The policewoman sighed, but not unkindly. Molly smelled vodka and beer in his vomit. How long ago had they left the bar?

"Martin!"

"Careful, angel." Bayliss stood beside her. "He'll stroke out if you keep giving him both barrels." He watched the police dismantling the scaffold and lights. "Yeah. It'll take some practice before you can interact."

"Shit. Holy shit." Molly clutched her forehead, ran her hands through her hair. She closed her eyes; counted ten long, slow breaths. "If you're about to tell me that I'm stuck as a ghost, I swear to God I'll kick your nuts out through the top of your head."

Bayliss coughed. "Kinda blue for a high-end swell, aren't you? Anyway, ghosts are a fairy tale."

His hat, his coat, the cigarettes . . . She remembered the rest. She remembered everything. She remembered his ancient eyes watching her die.

"Motherfucker! You did this to me!"

He backed away again, farther and more quickly than he had in Minneapolis. "Bygones. Bygones!"

"Kick you? Screw that. I'm going to *shoot* you." She reached for the policewoman's belt. Did cops even wear guns in Australia? At the very least, Molly figured, they must carry pepper spray or a zap gun or stickyfoam. Something that would make Bayliss yelp.

The cop made notes on her pad, completely unaware or uninterested in the woman unbuttoning the compartments on her belt. Molly found a thin spray canister. She took a second to ensure the nozzle pointed away from herself and then advanced on Bayliss again. He retreated down the station's handicapped access ramp.

Molly charged. She thrust the canister forward in her right hand, steadying it with the left . . . and saw, in the corner of her eye, her naked arms. She still wore the nightgown from Minneapolis. Her legs were bare, too. The concrete underfoot was crusted with a thin layer of snow except where her bare feet had melted perfect five-toed prints. A breeze ruffled her nightgown.

She wasn't cold.

The tinny clink and rattle of chains broke through the pregnant silence of the accident scene. A tow truck had arrived to haul away the taxi.

Flitting through different scenes of her own life? That she could chalk up to trauma. Martin's inability to recognize her? Maybe that was shock. But she'd just taken a weapon off a cop who couldn't have cared less. Now she stood half-naked on icy concrete while a wintry wind tugged at her nightgown. And she didn't feel it.

Yet she could smell the alcohol in Martin's puke and the salt in the ocean a few miles away. She heard the hum of electricity in the tram lines overhead and tasted the faint metallic tang of evaporated blood in the air—*her* blood—as the cop cars' waste heat warmed the tracks. But for all that, she felt nothing. No discomfort.

Molly dropped the canister. "Oh my God." She ran her hands through her hair again. "Shitshitshit."

Bayliss said, in a quieter tone of voice, "Hey, chin up. It ain't as bad as you think, angel."

"My name is Molly, not 'Angel.' I don't appreciate your chauvinistic little pet name."

Bayliss laughed. "Don't you get it, doll? 'Angel' ain't a nickname. From now on, it's your job."

TURTLES ALL THE WAY DOWN

Maybe I should have eased into that one. I thought she was going to slip her clutch.

Then she gave me a look that should have sliced through the back of my coat. Her fingers, tangled deep in that coppery mop, kept kneading her scalp. "What the hell are you talking about? And who *are* you? *What* are you?"

"Told you. Name's Bayliss. And at the moment I am one red-faced psychopomp."

Seemed like she was absorbing that, because she got real quiet. When she spoke again, her voice was fragile as spun sugar.

"Am I really dead?"

"Your human body squiffed it, yeah."

"But I'm still thinking and talking."

"You're not human any longer." Well, not entirely. "You're a member of the Choir now." I flicked my pill at the tow truck. It sizzled on bloodstained ice. "Hell of an introduction, huh?"

She frowned at that. "You don't look like any angel I've ever seen."

Oh, for crying out loud. Bad enough I tagged the wrong bird, but did the frail have to be so damn stubborn?

"That so? Seen a lot of us, have you?"

That shut her yap.

She dropped her hands. She craned her head back, watched the sky. The stars had reverted to their sluggish twinkle. Junk fragments—real junk this time—flared across the sky from south to north, remnants of a polar orbit. But the world around us no longer ticked and wobbled like a scratched record. We'd stabilized reality, flametop and me, though she didn't know it yet. I'd done my duty and was free to go back to my quiet unobtrusive life just as soon as I sent the girl on her merry. But she wasn't making it easy.

"Angels are a fairy tale, too," she said. Somewhere to our south, the floodwalls boomed.

"Beg to differ, sweetheart. I'm as real as you."

After that, I had to wait for the revving of a truck engine to subside. The tow truck jingled its chains like Marley's ghost when it pulled the dented hack away. It slid through a gap in the traffic while the bulls kept rubbernecked drivers at bay. One by one the emergency vehicles quenched their flashers and receded into the slushy night. The crowd dissipated.

Meanwhile, flametop still had the bit in her teeth. "I can't be dead," she mumbled.

I sighed. I knew she was trouble the minute I saw her.

"You're peddling your fish in the wrong market, lady."

Her eyebrows came together, hunched low over eyes the color of polished amber. "What does that even mean?"

"It means you have a lot to learn and the sooner the better." I jerked a thumb over my shoulder. "C'mon. I know a place. I'll buy you a cup of joe and read you the headlines."

"What about Martin? I can't leave him like this."

The hard boy had gone back to cradling his head on his hands. He was alone. Maybe the bulls had given him a card, a referral for a grief counselor, before hitting the road. But they had breezed and he hadn't. The clouds of his breath formed a pale pall around his head. He whimpered like a motherless puppy.

But my ward wasn't going to budge until he scrammed.

I sighed. "Does he have somewhere to go?"

"We're staying at a hotel." She shook her head. For a second there, I thought she was going to turn on the waterworks. Big brother squeaked like a schoolgirl; I wondered how it sounded when flametop cried. But she drew a breath and said, "He has a room there."

"Where?" I asked. She gave me the name of the joint. I didn't know it.

"Can we send him there? Can you? Can you"—she gestured vaguely, hopelessly—"zap him there?"

" 'Zap' him?"

Her voice was as weary as I felt. "I dunno. Use your angel mojo."

I cracked my knuckles, straightened my fedora. "Let me show you how it's done, doll."

And so I strode over to big brother and said, "Hey, pal, why the long face?" And a few minutes later I'd waved down a taxi, poured him into it, and bought his fare. I stiffed the driver on the tip, but one could argue that wasn't the worst thing I'd done all evening. I returned to her after ditching the lush.

She wasn't impressed. "I could have done that."

"Well, strictly speaking, no you couldn't. Not without popping a vein in his noggin. It'll take some practice."

"All you did was put him in a taxi."

"It worked, didn't it?"

"It doesn't seem very . . . angelic."

"I've been down here a while, so sue me. Let's call it going native and move on."

The traffic had returned to normal. The taxi merged into the flow, and soon it was just another trio of taillights in the windy night. The ocean gave the floodwalls hell.

Flametop said, "He shouldn't be alone."

"Lady, you are one cuckoo twist if you think we're following him. He'll be fine. We got our own problems, me and you."

For a second there I thought she'd let me off the hook. Thought she'd choose to tough it out on her own. Damn near stubborn enough, this frail. But I should've known not to get my hopes up.

"Our mother died," she said, almost to herself, though I knew it was a question. "We had a funeral . . ."

"Sorry, kid. There ain't no Santa Claus and there ain't no afterlife. Dead is dead, not a family reunion."

"But . . . You just said I'm dead, too."

"I also said you'd won the lottery. You're one in a trillion. Don't let it go to your head."

"I don't understand anything," she said in that spun-sugar tremor. Something about the way she said it gave me a glimpse of the kid who wore footie pajamas and a ballet tutu, the frightened little girl before she became the dish who wore cashmere and strode the world with red-carpet dignity. Never let it be said Bayliss turns a cold hard heart to a damsel in distress.

"Look. I know it's all cockamamie right now. But you'll get the gist of things. Promise. Now follow me." I offered my elbow but she gave it a dead pan. So with a sigh I led her back into the rabbit warren of the laneways. A couple doglegs later, surrounded by hucksters and lost souls and the occasional *penitente,* one could almost forget someone had died. She didn't, though. I ought to have taken a different route through the lanes, but I wanted her to get a sense of where we were and where we were headed. I figured it'd be a gentle introduction to the Pleroma if I could play on her expectations a bit. But she was too busy noticing all the places her brother had lost his footing, giving little Bambi sighs each time we passed a spot where she'd hauled him to his feet, to give our heading any thought.

Somewhere along the way she ditched the nightgown and reverted to her original outfit without even realizing what she'd done. And she gave no sign of feeling odd—no warning prickle in the primitive depths of the lizard brain, no dissonance in the seat of higher reasoning—when we shifted into the Pleroma. I tell you, the kid was a natural. But I wasn't about to tell *her* that. Already high maintenance, this one.

So there she was in a Melbourne laneway, neon shining on her wet eyes as she faced the gin mill where she'd had her last tiff with big brother. Then I opened the door for her, and with the next step she was a guest in my Magisterium. But it took her a moment to realize the gin mill had become a diner in the couple hours while her corpse lay in the snow, snarling up the traffic.

A heavenly aroma greeted us, like a whiff of God's own aftershave. Say what you will about the monkeys, but a side of bacon cures a lot of ills. I took a stool at the counter. Frayed batting poked through the cracked red leather, and both carried discolorations the color of spilled coffee. A waitress in a pink apron cleared away a plate of half-eaten pancakes drenched in syrup, then wiped down the counter. I could smell the maple on the plate and the cigarette smoke in her hair. Her dish towel had been white once, but it probably hadn't seen the inside of a washtub since Roosevelt could dance. She tossed a paper menu at me. It landed in a wet spot left behind by her towel. She wore a name tag, but it was blurred in the same way a newspaper headline becomes blurred and indistinct when you try to read in a dream. I'd never caught her name in the mundane realm, back in the day, so here I'd glossed over that detail. Didn't matter much. I called her Flo. She never objected.

I pulled out a stool for flametop. "Park the body. Bite an egg."

"What the hell are you talking about?"

"Sit down. Have something to eat."

"Why don't you talk like a normal person?"

"I'm not a person. Neither are you, any longer."

"Do all 'angels'"—she put scare quotes around that—"talk like you do?"

"Nah. Most of the others are old fluff."

She rolled her peepers and gave the joint a once-over. I knew what she saw because I'd constructed this little pocket reality all by my lonesome. It was the sort of place where a cup of joe cost a nickel and that was four cents too much for what it bought you. They didn't serve decaf here. It was the sort of place that smelled of bacon grease and burned coffee and the sweat and pomade from the guy on the next stool. The sort of place where it didn't pay to look too closely at the silverware, but where you could count on decent eats so long as you didn't ask for anything poached, infused, or zested. Two palookas in overalls and flatcaps occupied a table along the storefront window, lamping the passing girls and arguing too loudly over the box scores. They'd been doing that since DiMaggio's day; I added them as an homage, when he played his last game, and never got around to rearranging the place. It was comfortable. A ceiling fan with one missing blade tried to push the air around but the air was having none of it. Three houseflies buzzed around the fan, their aerials stuck on a permanent three-second loop, which lent the off-kilter sense of a filmstrip skipping its sprockets, which I liked just enough not to fix. A tomcat and his steady chewed each other's faces in another booth. In the kitchen, the short-order cook listened to a ball game on a staticky radio. A clean-shaven mugg in suspenders and a bowtie flapped his jaw on the telephone in the wooden booth near the restrooms. His suitcase, open on the floor beside him, was full of brushes.

Our waitress tossed the rag in his direction. "Hey! Phone's for paying customers, you chiseler."

He covered the mouthpiece. "Aw, go soak your head. I'm doing
business here."

"Well excuse me, Mr. Rockefeller, but we got other folks here, real
paying customers, that might wanna make calls of their own."

"Yeah," I said. "I'm expecting a call."

"You can soak it, too, rummy." Someday soon I was going to re-
vamp the place. Really I was. The shtick had been funny the first few
decades.

"Tell you what. My girl here"—by which I meant Molly—"is in the
market for a new hairbrush. A mane like that takes a lot of attention. So give it a rest and after we're done eating I'll let her tell you
all about it."

"That's square?"

"As a brick."

"Done." He tossed the phone back on its hook, gathered up his
case, and took a booth in the corner. He shouted over to Flo for a plate
of hash browned potatoes.

("I'm not your girl," Molly hissed. "Don't order the hash browns,"
I whispered.)

"Where the hell are we?"

"Welcome to my Magisterium, kid. My own humble corner of the
Pleroma."

"Pleroma," she said, rolling it around in her mouth as though she
were knotting a cherry stem with her tongue. (A lesser bo might have
gotten sidetracked, wondering if she could do that. But not yours
truly. I'd been there while she shuffled through her memories and
happened to know, for the record, that she could.) "I've heard that
word before. My mom went on a New Age kick for about ten years. I
never had any patience for that crap."

She hugged herself. Shivered. Surveyed the greasy spoon again.
Then she said, like a wrestler crying uncle, "I guess it wasn't crap."

"Sure it was. But Pleroma's an old word. Know any Greek? To regular lugs like me and you, it means the totality of the divine realm."

"Then what the hell is a Magisterium?"

"An angel's home away from home. The Pleroma is the totality.

The superset. Magisteria are the subsets." Eat your heart out, Bertrand Russell. "We all have one. Even you. Your own little slice of the divine. If it helps, think of it as a gussied-up memory palace."

Flametop ran a fingertip along the counter. It must have come back sticky, because her face twisted in a little moue of distaste. Flo probably missed some syrup when she cleared the plate, and certainly didn't care.

Molly said, "This place isn't divine. It's a shithole."

"Hey!" The cook growled through the order window. The words came out slurred because he had to force them past the cigar stub planted in the corner of his mouth. "You don't like it you can take a hike, princess."

Everybody paused to look at her. The waitress, the guys in the corner, even the roundheels. I gestured at the empty stool beside me and said, quietly, "Park the body."

She took a paper napkin from the dispenser and spread it over the stool before sitting down. Even then she took care not to lean on the counter. Yeah. Definitely cashmere.

"Is everybody here like you?" she asked.

"Nah. This place don't exist in the mundane realm anymore. But I thought it was swell, so I lifted its impression, rebuilt it in the Pleroma."

"Why, for fuck's sake, would you do that?"

"Why are you so obsessed with an apartment that no longer exists?"

"You two gonna order something, or you just taking up space?" Flo pulled a paper pad from her apron and a pencil from behind one ear. She glared at us, pencil tip poised above the pad like a cat watching a mouse hole.

"Draw two in the dark," I said, fishing in my pocket for change.

She didn't jot that down. "Your usual?" she said.

"Yeah. And wreck 'em."

I asked flametop, "You want anything besides coffee?"

She shook her head.

"You really should eat," I said. "It's on me."

"I don't want food poisoning," she said.

"Relax. It ain't like you can die again." Well . . . The way I figured it, better to keep things simple for now. Too many tangents and I'd never get her back on her feet.

To Flo, she said, "Just coffee, please."

Flo tossed the paper ticket on the sill of the order window. The cook snatched it. The cups Flo filled for us had matched once, but hard living had given them mismatched chips and cracks like a bad marriage. I got the dregs of the pot; they tasted like they'd been on the burner since Christmas last. I tossed a handful of change on the counter.

"Whoa," said Molly. "What's that?"

A silver feather glimmered among the nickels, dimes, and lint. It stood out like the Hope Diamond among a showgirl's sequins. She lifted it by the stem, twirled it in her fingers. It sent streamers of starlight flickering through the diner like a celestial disco ball. There was no mistaking this for a human artifact. The radio in the kitchen thrummed with the music of the spheres.

Rats. I cleared my throat. "Uh. That used to belong to the guy you're replacing."

"What are you doing with it?"

"He was a pal. Can't a guy keep a memento?" She flipped the feather to the other hand, and wrapped her fingers around her cup to warm them. Gabriel's was a cold beauty. She cocked an eyebrow. "Okay," I added. "Maybe I was planning to hock it. He doesn't need it anymore."

At that, Molly narrowed her eyes. She set the feather down and lifted the cup to her lips, but again, didn't drink. "Why not?"

I decided to keep it simple. "He moved on," I said, and left it at that. Figured there was no need to mention Gabby had been taken off the payroll. I put the feather back in my pocket. Flo's a fine gal, but with a tip like that she could buy this joint and still have enough change left over for a yacht. I was doing her a favor. She wouldn't enjoy the country club life.

"Why am I replacing him?"

"He carried a lot of weight around here. We need somebody to pick up the slack. One fella moves on, somebody else comes along to take his place. It's just the way it is." I pulled a flask from an inner pocket and spiked my cup with a little hooch. There's no coffee so burned that a little rye won't improve it. Flametop declined when I offered her a tipple. I shrugged. "See, we're the Prime Movers. We spin the celestial spheres. You might say we keep the trains running on time."

I winced. Poor choice of words.

"I don't know how to do that."

"You're doing it right now." I sipped. The coffee hit the spot. "Whether you know it or not, your ideation of reality, of how it ought to be, is melding with similar conceptions from the rest of us. You're contributing to what the wise-heads call the Mantle of Ontological Consistency. 'MOC' for short."

It was a mouthful, and she almost choked on it. But whether she was choking on ontology or on the effort not to laugh, I couldn't tell. "You didn't come up with that."

"Told you, it was some of the higher-ups. I don't care for the five-dollar words. They get stuck in my throat." Another sip helped with that. "See, what you monkeys—"

"Call me that again and we'll see who screeches."

"—(sorry, doll, it's just a nickname) what the *mortals* think of as reality is more or less what the Choir says it is. In theory—we're talking frictionless planes and spherical cows here—an angel all by its lonesome could shape reality to any old whim, anything at all, and change its mind every Tuesday. Some of us are better at it than others. But there's one thing nobody can do. When two or more of us come into physical or conceptual proximity—that is, when our spheres of influence overlap—we're bound by the consensual basis of reality. That's where ontological consistency enters the picture. Nobody can flout that, not even the high rollers." I sipped again, lubricating the pipes. "If you want to get fancy about it, you could say the structure of reality contains no branch cuts. Good thing, too. You got any idea what happens when some mugg decides it'd be real swell if time had six dimensions, while some rooster hiking his flaming sword through an adjacent Magisterium decides multidimensional thermodynamics is for suckers?"

"I have no idea what you're talking about," said Molly. But she seemed a little less glum than she had been. Good. She was getting to be a real drip. Bet she'd have a nice laugh, if she ever gave it the reins.

"It happened once, long time back. After the fireworks settled, the result was completely sterile. Which is sort of the whole point. You and me and the rest of the Choir? We make the mundane realm an easy place to live for the monk— . . . mortals. Thanks to us they've got causality and conservation laws and gravity and all sorts of perks. They've got it real good. And so do you. The system's been in place for a good long while now, ticking along nicely. All you have to do is go with the flow and not rock the boat. It's nothing but smooth angles as long as you don't."

Flo set a plate of bacon and scrambled eggs on the counter and topped off my cup. I dusted the plate with salt and pepper while she swept the change into her apron. Then I lifted a forkful of rubbery eggs to my mouth and said, "Thus ends the lecture. Welcome to the Choir, kid."

Flametop was quiet for about as long as she'd ever been during our brief and stormy acquaintance. She hadn't touched her coffee. The salesman got his plate of hash browns and demanded a bottle of catsup. The lamps buzzed, and in the kitchen somebody hit a single. The eggs weren't bad. The bacon was worth every cent.

"If you made this place," said Molly, "how come you're actually paying for the food?"

"Aw, don't pick on old Bayliss. Told you, I spent a lot of time on Earth. You'll find thinking like a mortal is a tough habit to break."

"Were you mortal?"

My snort sent coffee where it wasn't meant to go. Rye fumes stripped the paint from my sinuses. "No," I said, when I could speak again. "You're a rare case. Most of us have been around since the big one."

Well, she was the *only* such case. Details, details.

"Then why did you choose to make things compatible with li—"

"Look, angel. Molly. If you want to argue teleology with the wiseheads, be my guest. But my opinions on the matter don't amount to a hill of beans. I've given you the Pleroma 101 lecture, and now it's time for me to dust." I took the last bit of egg and bacon in a bite, and washed it down with what little remaining joe I hadn't spilled or coughed on myself. I winked at Flo, retrieved my fedora and coat from the empty stool beside me, and gave the cook a little salute.

"Good luck, doll."

Molly jumped to her feet. "That's it? That's fucking *it*?" They were staring again, all of 'em. "You push me under a train, give me some half-assed meaning-of-the-universe crap, and then you fucking take off?"

"As much as we seem to enjoy each other's scintillating personalities, yes." It was embarrassing, my screw-up, but the sooner I got away from her the sooner I could try to forget about it.

I was glad she'd left the baseball bat back in Magisterial Minneapolis. Given a little more time to practice, the look in her eyes could have ignited the bacon grease on my shirt. "You owe me answers," she said.

She wasn't lying. That nickel dropped when she fell from the platform. I sighed again. An overactive conscience can be a real wet blanket sometimes.

"Look. I won't leave you high and dry." I took a clean napkin from the counter and borrowed Flo's pencil. It smelled like hair spray. "Take a few decades to get settled. Go find your Magisterium. Make a comfortable spot for yourself. You seem like a sharp one, you'll catch the gist of things. Like I said, just drift with the current. Take it easy. Then if you still feel the need to brace me, ring." On the napkin, I jotted:

BAYLISS. RIVERSIDE 5-2165

She took it, read it twice, and said, "Is that supposed to be a telephone number?"

"It is a telephone number."

"In Heaven."

"Who said anything about Heaven? That's the direct line to my Magisterium. You should feel honored. I don't share it with every sad sack what comes my way."

She gave me a wary look—it was second nature for her—but fished around in the pocket of her coat until she produced an earbud. She tucked a coppery lock behind one ear, popped the bud in, and issued a command via her contact lenses.

Figured it would put her mind at ease, so I let the call go through. Eventually, when she got the hang of things, she'd be able to ditch the

Earthly affectations. A strident clanging echoed from the booth in the corner.

"Hey, pal," said the two-bit salesman. "There's your call."

"Satisfied?" I asked. She didn't say anything. I took that as a yes. "It's been swell, angel."

I tipped my hat again, and then I was out the door. I knew a sleepy-time girl in San Francisco who was probably getting lonely right about then. Just as I shifted back into the mundane realm, I heard,

"So, sweetheart. I bet you wish there was an easier way to rake out those curls every night. . . ."

THE MOST POPULAR GIRL
AT THE DEBUTANTES' BALL

Oh, piss off," said Molly.

The salesman said, "Don't be such a sourpuss. What do you see in him, anywise? A lulu like you deserves a fella with prospects and a steady income."

Screw this, she thought. Molly hit the door a few seconds after Bayliss. She emerged in the laneway. Based on the booming of the flood-walls and the dusting of snow in the gutters, little time had passed. But he was nowhere to be seen. And when she turned around, the diner had become a bar thundering with old trance music. She recognized it. They had argued here, she and Martin, just before—

She couldn't breathe. Cold air clogged her windpipe like a frozen lump of suet. Fatigue enveloped her. Overwhelmed her. It dragged her down like a vicious undertow. She had just enough strength to sit on the landing without collapsing. She needed a minute to collect herself, but marshaling her thoughts was pointless as sucking syrup through one of Martin's hypodermic needles. She hugged her knees. Frantic shallow breaths frosted the scarf at her throat. The studs of her earrings pinched when she laid her head on her knees.

Her chest pulsed to the rhythm of a beating heart. Her body was intact. Wasn't it?

With Bayliss gone, and the diner along with him, there was nothing to suggest she wasn't the victim of a terrible hallucination. That made more sense than anything else. The entire conversation with Bayliss had already begun to fade in her memory, like a wild dream evaporating into vague impressions at the first touch of daylight. Maybe Martin really had slipped her something.

Oh, shit, Martin. He was falling apart again.

They hadn't seen each other for several months prior to meeting at LAX for the flight to Australia. Molly could tell he was already backsliding, drinking too much, as soon as she hugged him in the terminal. She recognized the slow unfocused eyes and the skunky scent of beer on his breath. When pressed on it he'd admitted to having a couple. Just to help him sleep on the flight, he'd said. The lie hurt, but less than her guilt. She shouldn't have fallen out of touch. She should have been there for him. Should have been a better sister. How long before he started using again? He'd never get help on his own.

Unless . . .

What had Bayliss said? Something about angels shaping reality.

Was she really an angel? She didn't feel angelic. But what if—

Behind her, a door opened. A trio of *penitentes* emerged, their wounds steaming in the chilly night. They were too busy jabbering to each other—was that *Latin*?—to see her crouched on the landing.

"Hey! Watch it!" said Molly.

She scrambled aside before one of the sweaty, bloody, half-naked freaks tumbled atop her. But they kept coming like she wasn't there. Molly raised her arms to shield herself. The guy in front lost his footing. Molly flinched—

—and landed on the floor of the Minneapolis apartment.

She lay there a moment, panting and stroking the floor. The floorboards slid like silk beneath her fingers. Ria had done such a fantastic job. They were straight and smooth and perfect but for the one blemish where the cherry of Bayliss's cigarette had damaged the varnish. He deserved a punch in the nose for that. The butt had landed there, tip down, then rolled a few inches away, leaving a curlicue of ash in its wake. A faint trace of smoke, a phantom scent, haunted the bedroom like a revenant spirit. Molly cracked a window open; a frigid February night leaked inside. The moon, nearly full, cast blue shadows from the sash. Waxing or waning? She couldn't tell.

Molly took the butt to the bathroom and flushed it. Bayliss had, of course, left the lid up. The shower curtain still lay in the tub, half torn from the rings by his retreat. She returned the baseball bat to its spot under the bed. Then she ran a spare washcloth under the faucet and scrubbed away the ash. The cloth went in the trash rather than the laundry hamper. She was too disgusted to ever use it again, no matter how fiercely it was washed.

Then she stopped.

Laundry hamper?

What if I really am dead?

If I'm dead, she thought, *really, truly dead, why am I still thinking about laundry? What does it matter? What does* anything *matter?*

This building had burned to the ground long ago. It didn't exist, except in photographs and memories. It was gone. Like Dad and Mom. And yet here she was: cleaning the floors and worrying about laundry. Pointless.

Bayliss's place—what did he call it? His Pleroma? Magisterium?—was filled with people. Granted, they were straight from central casting for an old-time movie, but at least that crapsack diner wasn't empty. Wasn't "sterile," as Bayliss had put it. All Molly wanted was to hear the rhythm of Ria's breath while she slept, to feel the warmth of her body on the sheets. But she knew, deeper than her marrow, she hadn't the strength to sew disparate memories into a companion. A woman was more than the sum of her parts. More than a chicken pox scar on the tip of her nose, and radical politics, and a hatred of raisins. Molly secured it all, and more, in the lockbox of her heart. For later. Not much later. Just not tonight. It was all too big for tonight.

Much smaller was the damaged spot on the floor.

She sat at the edge of the bed, imagining how things had been before the fire. Imagining the lustrous sheen of varnish. The gentle, unbroken whorls of grain in the oak. The paper-thin seam where the boards joined.

The spot shrunk. Her heat beat faster.

The edges of the burn lightened. Gentle ripples lapped at its coarse perimeter, eroding the blemish one hair's breadth at a time. The pattern of the wood grain grew like time-lapsed ivy.

Sweat trickled down Molly's forehead and between her breasts. She gulped down cold air. It numbed her throat, but made her sinuses ache. She tasted turpentine and sawdust and cigarette smoke.

The alterations slowed, then stopped. The center of the damaged spot wouldn't budge. It resisted her. The very fact of its presence asserted a contradictory reality. The memory of the unblemished floor slipped away like water through her fingertips.

Molly pushed. She'd seen the undamaged floor a thousand times, damn it. A dark haze fell across the bedroom. Her vision retreated into a tunnel.

The burn contracted, pulsed, snapped back. Unmoved. Unchanged.

Molly collapsed on the rumpled bed, too weary even to remove her boots, and fell into a dark dreamless nothing.

*T*he moon hung a little lower in the sky, but it was still dark outside when she awoke to a clanging sound from downstairs. A metallic banging, as though somebody were rummaging the pots and pans and being none too gentle about it. There was a smash, as of broken glass, followed by what sounded, impossibly, like the roll of surf along a beach.

What the hell, Bayliss?

Molly groaned. A hot, spiky headache had taken root inside her skull. She'd strained herself, and now she had the hangover sensation that a layer of grit coated the backs of her eyeballs. She rolled over and once again retrieved the bat from its hiding spot under the bed. A dull ache throbbed in her toes and ankles when she wobbled to her feet; she should have removed her boots. (Hadn't she been barefoot before? She remembered footprints in the snow.) She crossed the bedroom, boot heels clacking across the floorboards. She opened the door that led to the stairs, and immediately knew something was very, very wrong.

First: it wasn't night any longer. The space on the other side of the door shone brighter than a July afternoon.

Second: the apartment's staircase had disappeared. The senseless jumble in its place was a scrap heap, a pile of examples—impressions— of the *concept* of stairs:

Part of an escalator. A concrete step from behind her childhood home, its riser covered in scrawls of blue and yellow chalk, an ice-cream cone melting, a little boy crying. Step 232 of the Washington Monument, the one where she'd lost count during a school field trip in ninth grade. A half-twist of the spiral staircase from an old 747. The space under the stairs to the choir loft of her mother's church, the home of Molly's first kiss.

She descended the kaleidoscopic gauntlet where the stairs had been; dodged the flickering news footage of firefighters dousing the flames that would gut this building in the future; tripped over the time she'd cheated on Ria; squeezed past the tortured squeaking of a mouse caught on a glue trap in the pantry; and landed just outside a kitchen that smelled of spilled red wine and freshly extinguished birthday candles. She tightened her hold on the bat, took a deep breath, and prepared to scream bloody murder.

But when she leaped from her hiding spot, the words shriveled in her throat. It wasn't Bayliss.

The thing in the kitchen wasn't remotely shaped like a man at all. Nor, she realized, was it alone. Another loomed behind her. When the being in the kitchen turned, a pair of vast gossamer wings scraped dust from the moon. Its face was a blinding sheet of flame.

WHERE? its query thundered with demand. The bat in Molly's hands exploded into a cloud of mismatched butterfly wings. They fluttered to the floor while the furious angels grabbed Molly by the soul, turned her inside out, and shook until all her memories fell away.

. . . the sting of salt in the eye, the crumbs of a broken oyster cracker . . .

. . . a needle in Martin's arm, his bleary eyes not seeing her . . .

. . . downloading a Wynton Marsalis album, playing it on infinite loop while studying for final exams . . .

WHERE?

. . . the pop of bubble wrap . . .

. . . a dog licking Molly's fingers, its tongue warm and slobbery . . .

. . . the smell of melted plastic . . .

. . . standing in line at the DMV, getting hit on by a redneck in a gimmee cap . . .

. . . dirt caked under her fingernails . . .

. . . a cracked lid on the container Leslie Johnson used to bring a cow brain to school in fifth grade, the blood smeared on her desk looking like canned ravioli sauce . . .

. . . an earache . . .

. . . Martin pushing her down in the mud so that she'd stop following him and his friends, making her eat it . . .

. . . atonal echoes of a busker tooting his saxophone on a subway platform . . .

WHERE?

. . . burgundy or maroon . . .

. . . the tackiness of cheap duct tape . . .

Bits and pieces of Molly's life swirled through her consciousness like confetti in a gale. Every memory, every experience of her life, every sight and taste and sound and touch and smell, the taste of every color, the smell of every caress, stretched out and scrutinized and tossed aside. A life unraveled. Sanity as midden heap.

A tumbling torrent of nonsense. On and on and on.

. . . diarrhea, a clogged toilet, panic . . .

. . . dozing on a picnic blanket with her first girlfriend . . .

. . . the morning after a snowstorm, losing track of the snow emergency parking rules, paying money she can't afford to retrieve her car from the city impound lot . . .

. . . an ice cube pressed against her wrist . . .

. . . a sting, a drop of blood, her last baby tooth embedded in the hotdog she'd just bitten . . .

. . . Christmas party, four other couples, eggnog by the fireplace . . .

. . . the blare of a tornado siren, huddling in the basement with Mom and Dad while the sky turns green, feeling terrified because they can't hide their worry . . .

. . . "Classical Gas" . . .

WHERE?

. . . the smell of lilacs in a warm spring rain . . .

. . . hide-and-seek with Martin, cheating, sneaking into Dad's off-limits study, breaking the antique telephone when she knocks it off the desk—

Molly grasped at the memory fragment. Her father's old paperweight had come in two pieces: the base with a dial and a cone for speaking, and a separate earpiece on a cord. The cord stretched like taffy and snapped; the earpiece rolled away past her first skiing lesson and fell into the crevice between the taste of homemade lasagna and the frustration caused by a corrupted e-book file.

The base was an empty shell of wood and brass. She cranked the dial with fingers that flickered in size and shape and color, from adulthood to childhood and back, from painted nails to metal splints on a sprain to the dainty fingers of a fourteen-year-old.

The cone coated her lips with the fine grit of house dust. She yelled, "Bayliss!"

And then her attackers abandoned all restraint.

*W*hen she came to, she lay among fragments of a Quinceañera celebration to which her family had been invited when Molly was in junior high. The off-key singing poked in the small of her back. Her thirteen-year-old's bashfulness tasted slightly metallic, like an accidental bite of moldy bread. She rolled over, but didn't open her eyes. They still felt as though they'd been coated in sand. Her headache had dived into a foxhole during the assault, but now that was over and it was back to work.

Somebody let out a long, low whistle. "I like what you've done with the place."

Molly cracked one eye open. Winced.

Bayliss stood over her, surveying the wreckage of her life. "Never pegged you for the dramatic type. Maybe I spoke too soon about that ing-bing."

Warm wetness tickled her upper lip. She touched her face. Her fingers came away red.

A soft rain fell upward, from the floor, into a cloudless tangerine sky. Molly rinsed her blooded fingertips in the impossible rain and surveyed the shattered debris of her memory palace. The pantry door opened on the narthex of Notre Dame, where candles flickered in time to the grinding of a dying dishwasher. The kitchen table, the one she and Ria had bought at a garage sale before realizing it didn't fit through the front door, now wobbled on uneven legs made of steam, lust, schadenfreude, and the sourness of bad lemon pudding. The trim around the ceiling had become the musty smell of an ex-girlfriend's workout clothes forgotten at the bottom of the washing machine. The entirety of Molly's mortal life had been shredded, confettied, discarded in a jumbled heap. Flotsam and jetsam strewn across a rocky beach. There was one of those, too, where the coat closet used to be.

She rose to her feet. The tile floor shifted underfoot like the fine gypsum sands she'd once visited in New Mexico.

"I didn't do this, you jackass," she said. "I was attacked."

Bayliss blinked. For once, he didn't respond with an incomprehensible wisecrack. He stared at her, his expression cloaked behind ancient eyes. After a moment he went into what remained of the kitchen. Molly heard a tap running. He returned with a glass of water. She didn't recognize the glass; part of her wondered what distant and dim corner of her memory had produced it.

"Here," he said, offering the glass. "Drown your tonsils."

"Thanks." Molly drank while he found a chair, tossed aside the taste of wood ash on burned campfire marshmallows, and sat down. The water was too cold. It hurt her teeth. But she drank anyway.

Bayliss said, "So tell me what happened."

She did. It didn't take long. The glass was empty by the end, but her thirst hadn't subsided. Nor had the headache. She filled the glass by holding it upside down in the topsy-turvy rain. Then she rooted around until she found the bathroom medicine cabinet. It used to contain a bottle of aspirin. Now it contained her scream from the time she was bitten by a llama at a roadside petting zoo in Manitoba. She found the aspirin on a window ledge alongside her first orgasm.

Fury rose within her; it wrapped the world in a flickering heat shimmer. Memories, her private realities, crackled and blackened around the edges. To see the most cherished pieces of herself—the most intimate, the most personal, the things that made her Molly— cast aside with such disregard, such *contempt* . . . It made her feel so small. . . . She'd never felt so helpless.

Bayliss still hadn't said anything by the time she sat again. He lit a match on his thumbnail. Watched it burn almost to his fingertips. Shook it out. Did it again. He was thinking hard.

"I'm still waiting on an explanation," said Molly.

"Can't tell you what I don't know," he said.

"You know a shitload more than I do."

Bayliss sighed. "Maybe I miscounted the trumps. Maybe you got caught in the rain on account of it."

The Magisterium sagged like candle wax in heat haze of Molly's rage. "What were those things? And what were they looking for?"

"The loogans? Hard to know. Sounds like you tussled with some real torpedoes, though. Couple of Cherubim would be my guess. You sure you didn't see a flaming sword anywhere?" Molly shook her head; she remembered hearing something about that in Sunday school. He shrugged. "Well, that don't mean much. You get a count? Eyes, wings, faces, that sort of thing?"

"Sorry. I was too busy being assaulted."

At least he had the courtesy to look abashed. "Yeah. I suppose so."

Molly stood. Her boots sank ankle deep in butterfly wings. They smoked and curled when her anger brushed against them. The reek of burned hair wreathed her legs. "What aren't you telling me?"

Bayliss ran a hand through his hair and massaged the back of his neck. "So, the guy you replaced? Well, it's true he ain't around anymore. Just like I said. But maybe there's more to it than that. I think he got pinked."

Molly had to consider his tone and body language before the meaning sank in. Her heart understood before her head: for the first time since dying she was frightened. The anger at Bayliss and an unfair fate for taking her from Martin when he needed her most, the jittering frustration at a world that no longer made sense, even the rage at being attacked—violated—inside her own memories . . . it all disappeared. Replaced by simple fear. Sweat tickled the fine hairs at the back of her neck. A cold wind swirled across the hollow where her self-confidence had been.

Pinked: killed.

Somebody she didn't know—living to inscrutable rules in an invisible, nonsensical world—had been killed. Somehow she was expected to replace him. And now others—even more inscrutable, moving along their own incomprehensible currents—had ransacked her most intimate personal space. Her attempt to *have* a personal space. She was embroiled in something enormous, dangerous, and utterly confusing. More than what he said, the way Bayliss said it conveyed a sense of ancient feuds. Of eons-old turf wars cutting through Heaven. And the powers at work were vast. Vast in ways she couldn't comprehend. This she knew.

She still hadn't come to terms with being dead. She hardly believed it, even now. But . . . The cold wind whistled through the empty spaces of her soul, like drafts through a windowless abandoned house. It made her shiver. It was the same shiver she felt when Mom had admitted she'd found a lump some time back but had been too frightened to go in and have a scan done. Dad used to say a shiver like that meant somebody, somewhere, had walked over her grave.

Did it count if she'd died on a city street?

She paced. Her footsteps kicked eddies of butterfly dust into the backward rain.

"You didn't think to mention this to me?"

"Look. You were in a bad way. Thought I was doing you a favor by not piling on with the bad news. Didn't think it mattered in the short term."

"You didn't think it *mattered* if you warned me about this?"

"Warn you about what? I didn't know this was going to happen. How should I? Again, no offense, angel, but you're small-time."

"Oh, I see. I guess I'm just lucky then." Molly swept up an armful of shredded memories. Somewhere, a narcissistic fifteen-year-old wept over a pimple on her chin. Molly flung the teenage angst at him. "What the hell is going on?"

Bayliss lit another match on his thumbnail. His hands shook. Molly thought he'd said all he intended, so rapt was he with the flame. But then he sighed.

"Look. Sometimes a guy hears things, okay? And sometimes he hears 'em and he thinks, that's gonna be a bad, sad day for everybody. And he don't want any part of it. No how. So he lams off, okay? And they let him. And they leave him alone. And for a long time every-thing's jake. But then he gets a postcard telling him to lamp the heav-ens, so he does, and when he sees the shape of it he knows the tide's coming in. The heavies call on him because they want something done, and he knows the score, he knows what they're telling him, so he does the thing. He does one simple thing, no more, no less, because maybe he's afraid the big fish are swimming in the deep but if he makes nice and doesn't rock the boat they'll leave him alone again. He doesn't ask any questions and they swim right on past him."

The flame burned past the end of the match, into his shaking hand. He didn't notice. Fire became an emerald mist where it touched his flesh. Its smoke smelled of cinnamon and sulfur, and tasted like pickled starlight.

"Did you leave," she asked, "or were you kicked out?"

"Don't get cute. I left," said Bayliss. He muttered, "I really wish somebody had given old Milton a sock in the kisser when they'd had the chance."

Molly said, "So you figured you'd just pick somebody at random to take up the slack after the last guy died."

"Not at random. I was told to find somebody who wouldn't kick up a fuss. But I got you instead."

One thing, at least, was beginning to make sense. Back at that shithole diner, he'd kept saying things about going with the flow, not rocking the boat. He'd implied it was just for the sake of getting oriented. But that wasn't it at all. Somebody important, or powerful, snapped the whip. Somebody Bayliss feared.

"Who made you do this?"

Bayliss shook his head. "I have bent over backward to not know that."

"You wanted somebody who wouldn't get herself in trouble," she said, "because you didn't want her drawing attention to *you*. That's what this is, isn't it? You're trying to save your own skin."

"Lady, I'm just a two-bit player trying to get by in this crazy gummed-up world."

"And you killed me in order to do that."

Bayliss winced. "I apologized for that. You sure know how to make a guy feel like a heel." He stood. "Figure I do owe you. Can't help but feel a little responsible that you got your place tossed. So tell you what. Let me go talk to some folks. I'll put my ear to the ground, get the lay of the land."

"I'll go with you."

He shook his head and gave an embarrassed little grimace. "Nope. These players won't talk to the likes of you."

Molly narrowed her eyes. The edges of broken memories started to curl and blacken again. "Because I'm a woman?"

"Because in their eyes you're still nothing but a well-groomed monkey."

Charming.

"Trust me. It'll be jake. You'll see." He looked into the sensory discontinuity where the pantry had been. "Hey. I know that joint." He stepped through the remains of the kitchen into Notre Dame. "Later, angel. Try to keep buttoned till I get back."

He flicked the brim of his fedora when he departed. He didn't remove the hat when he slipped into the memory of the cathedral and out, through it, to the mundane realm. She watched him go.

Fuck, she thought. *He's a fallen angel. And he's terrified.*

5

NEXT TIME, SKIP THE WAKE

*J*knew she was trouble the minute I saw her, but damned if flametop didn't prove it in record time. She barely had time to kick off her shoes and wiggle her piggies before the gunnies came for her. She'd rubbed somebody the wrong way. Hadn't even bothered to cobble together a decent Magisterium before she did it, either. But never let it be said Bayliss turns a cold, hard heart to a dame in distress. Even if it was distress of her own making.

The sooner I knew what she'd done, the sooner I could smooth the ruffled feathers and wipe my hands of the whole affair. For good this time.

Problem was, getting a bead on that meant making a visit to the old homestead. It'd been a good long while since I'd been back. I barely knew my way around any longer. And if too many people knew I'd returned, it was apt to get awkward. Last thing I needed was to have every joe and jane in the Choir ribbing me for not having the courage of my convictions. I'd made a big point of making myself scarce.

I escaped Notre Dame through the Portal of the Last Judgment (*domine, domine, pater noster,* and all that jazz), took a seat alongside a hedge, lit a pill, and considered my next move. The steel-gray smoke of my contemplations mingled with the scent of incense-laden guilt leaking from the cathedral and the humid stink of the Seine. A light rain fell on me, dusted the flower gardens, pattered on the river. I listened to the Babel hubbub of tourists, mostly German, English, and Japanese, and the ticker-tape clatter of cameras. Old ones, too. Actual film cameras. From back when the monkeys used chemistry to capture their holiday memories. (All possible courtesy of the Mantle of Ontological Consistency.) Those cameras predated flametop's conception by decades. I wondered whose memory she'd lifted. My money was on a shutterbug grandparent with a photo album. Had to hand it to her: she had a good eye for detail. She'd build a crackerjack Magisterium someday. Assuming she survived long enough to do so, and assuming she didn't get me killed before I could see it.

A gargoyle funneled the rain into a steady drip on the crown of my hat. Now that brought me back. My one and only gig as a model happened back when they were sculpting all those gargoyles. Had to do it through dreams, though, so I never made any folding from it. The monkeys are a superstitious lot, but never more so than when they're building a cathedral. A few centuries later I could have taken the master artisan to dip the beak, and convinced him to blame the hallucinations on the green fairy. The artsy crowd was mad for that hooch even after it drove them a little loony. But Paris was a different place then. A few francs could buy you a bottle of wine and some willing company.

I squinted at the gargoyle. It wore a big, wide frown on its puss. I said, "Long time, no see, pal." It spit in my eye.

Another puff sent tar swirling through my wet and glistening simulacra of monkey lungs. It set my thoughts in motion.

Someone had a real beef with flametop. Why? And what did this mean for me?

Who wasn't the issue. Not really. Even I could take a decent shot in the dark on that one. The way I figured it, any notoriety she had stemmed from coming along just after Gabby punched out. That was her only claim to fame, but it was a lulu. So whatever had the loogans' dander up was probably connected to the stiff. And that pointed to whoever tapped me for their fishy little errand down on Earth. And, by extension, whoever rubbed the Seraph.

I thought I'd sidestepped that whole flop after seeing which way the winds of the Pleroma blew. The currents hinted at something too big, too ambitious, too dangerous. I figured the scheme was destined to blow up in the conspirators' faces like a novelty cigar, but not before it rained trouble on everybody in the Choir. So I ducked the guilt by association by lamming to Earth. Or so I thought.

It was too good to last. I'd barely been among the monkeys a few centuries—hardly enough time to pick up decent vices—when the first of the anonymous telegrams arrived. Messages sculpted in the swirl of cigarette smoke; implied in the sleep-murmur of a dozing street-corner wino; outlined in an improbable roll of dice in a back-alley parlor; writ across the sky in the hiss and flare of burning space debris. I ignored them long as I could but the deck was stacked against me. My attempt to steer clear of the trouble made me the perfect stooge. So perfect that my unwillingness to cooperate didn't enter the math.

Once that came clear, I kept my head down. Didn't ask any questions. Didn't try to get clever. But above all I made it a point to not know who *they* were. All I knew was I'd been tagged by some faction in the Choir with deep pockets and an ax to grind. We had an implicit agreement: I'd run their errand—using my familiarity with the monkeys to plug a hole in the MOC—and then they'd go climb a tree. Forever.

And besides. I gave long odds to their grudge. A cork isn't useful unless you have a place to put it, and that told me they were fixing to scratch somebody. But who ever heard of bumping off an angel? Everyone knew that was impossible. We can't die. Even nickel-grabbers like me.

But then Gabriel's demise lit the night sky.

So I whittled a cork and beat a hasty retreat. Because the faction that had twisted my arm threw a lot of weight in the Pleroma. More than I thought possible. Enough to rub a Seraph. Enough to send a pair of Cherubim to brace flametop.

Didn't know the why of their beef with Molly, but I did know it was bad news for me. Accident or no, I'd tagged her, but they didn't like her. I sighed. Dames.

I dragged her into this mess. She'd been having a rough time of it thanks to me. As much as I hated to admit it, I did feel like a prize heel. Guess I owed her for the train thing. But if I were to make good on my words to flametop, I'd have to know what got Gabby croaked.

Plan in hand, I flicked my pill into a flower bed overflowing with bedraggled snapdragons and wilted daisies. I tipped my hat at the gargoyle. "Don't be a stranger." It spat again.

A fat American pointed his Kodak at the flower beds, and me, just as I shifted into the Pleroma. If he ever bothered to develop that film, he'd find a ghostly wisp of vapor making an obscene gesture. Back home I went.

Gabriel had been one of the oldest and most powerful of us. Rumor said he'd even interceded with METATRON on behalf of the Choir once or twice. Don't know if I believe that. But I did know he'd been a load-bearing member of the MOC.

So much so, in fact, that I hadn't needed to worry about anybody ribbing me over my reluctant return to the Pleroma. Nobody noticed. Gabby's death had kicked a hell of a dent in the MOC. Flametop's ascension was the equivalent of cramming a matchbook under the wobbly table leg—it fixed the worst of the problem, but this didn't mean the table was good as new. Likewise, mortal physics and mathematics still chugged along with the monkeys blissfully unaware of the chaos behind the scenes. Because while the twist and I had managed to shore up the MOC just enough to prevent it from toppling over completely, an impossible murder had produced a steep conceptual gradient. Gabby's absence caused a certain lack of intellectual pressure; it created ideational lacunae that had the MOC listing to port like a waterlogged cruise liner.

I'd never seen so many members of the Choir together. Well, together and not bickering like the Council of Nicaea. Everyone had turned out to put things right: Angels, Archangels, Principalities, Powers, Virtues, Dominions, Thrones, Cherubim . . . I even glimpsed a few flaming swords in the mix, meaning the remaining Seraphim had lent a paw. The monkeys like to believe the best part of their nature comes out in times of crisis. But never underestimate the power of enlightened self-interest: the Choir had rolled up its sleeves because Gabby's death threatened to upset the whole damn apple cart. And that would have been the end of pie for everybody.

Speaking of which, a Dominion brushed past me carrying the final digits to a half-dozen transcendental numbers. It passed them along to a whirling Throne who appeared to be acting as an impromptu subforeman, who passed them up the chain to where they could do some good. A cloud of Powers surveyed the damage and orchestrated the repair effort with a thousand-dimensional bird's-eye view. Somebody had built scaffolding out of a mathematics both consistent and complete (chew on that, Gödel) and now the spackle went on one axiom at a time.

A pretty picture of cooperation. But I wasn't about to forget that crowd contained Gabby's killer, or killers. I steered clear. And besides, they seemed to have the whole mess under control. My clumsy mitts weren't likely to make a difference. I had an errand to run.

Even money said Gabby's Magisterium wasn't likely to decay any time soon. In fact, if I knew the Choir, and unfortunately I did, they'd freeze it in place as a memorial to our fallen colleague. So, assuming I could find them, a once-over of his digs might tell me what he'd been up to these last few eons. If I was lucky, it might tell me what had gotten him pinked. If I was unlucky, it might tell me who had done the job, and how—the kinds of things I didn't want to know. Things that make a target of a guy. And if I was cursed, the trigger boys would know I knew. If that happened, I figured my and flame-top's lives weren't worth a plugged nickel. Anybody hard enough to croak a Seraph should get a wide berth. Berth? They get their own private car, meals courtesy of Mr. Pullman.

But first things first. I needed to find somebody who could point me to Gabby's Magisterium. But I figured I'd let the rubes come to me. Once the hard work was done, the sappier members of the Choir would drift off to gnash their teeth and weep.

The raw Pleroma, outside a Magisterium, isn't all clouds and pearly gates. Even that would have been something. The real Pleroma is dull. Not quite a flat featureless plain, but on a cosmic scale, it's close. It's the raw material for our Magisteria, the sand that makes the concrete. It's the liminal space in the corner of the eye; the darkened shadows at the edges of the stage. It's the crawl spaces, the plumbing and pneumatic tubes, behind the MOC. Nobody ever oohs and aahs over wiring conduits and sewer lines. The view from the high window ain't terrible: universe above, Earth below. But it does get boring.

I'll say this for the celestial spheres, though: great acoustics. We're talking Platonic ideals here. Pythagoras would have smashed his corny little harp across his knee if he'd heard it. And it just so happens that if you exist near the proper event locus, manifesting the concept of sound in just the right way—something akin to hitting E below middle C, give or take ten thousand octaves—the tingle isn't all that unpleasant. Which makes this spot the closest thing the

Pleroma has to a watering hole or a corner newsstand. Everybody passes through here, eventually. All I needed to do was stake it out and wait.

So I racked out behind a thicket of zodiacal light and waited. It took longer than I'd thought it would. I dozed off until a cosmic four-part harmony rattled my dreams.

"Holy, holy, holy!"

I peeked out from my blind. The racket came from the celestial equivalent of a barbershop quartet: two Principalities, an Archangel, and one little hanger-on Angel like me and flametop, its *heiligenschein* barely bright enough to out-twinkle the dimmest star. But damn if that kid didn't have some pipes; no wonder it sang with the varsity team.

The Principalities stood on the hooves of oxen but had the visages of lions, and each wore four wings that gleamed like brass. The humaniform Archangel had on its pan a third eye that constantly wept tears of blood, for it had been pierced with the shrapnel of Creation. The Angel looked as though it had taken fashion advice from a Botticelli painting. Each wore a cowl darker than a starless expanse. Mourning rags. At least they hadn't smeared themselves with ash, the mopes.

"You kids ever think about trying out for the talent show? I think you've got a shot at a ribbon this year."

As one, they turned to regard me. And then they scrammed like their lives depended on it.

"Aw, you lousy lollipops!" I called after them.

They must not have recognized me. Gabby's death had everyone on edge; they weren't taking chances with some fresh face they didn't know. Even a clean piece of beef like mine.

I fished out a pocketknife and cleaned my nails while waiting for them to return. They sidled back a few astronomical units at a time. I kept to myself, making no sudden moves, until they decided I was on the level. Eventually, they started crooning again.

Over the racket, I said, "I missed Gabriel's funeral. Guess I need to start reading the obits more regularly. Any of you birds know where I can go to pay my respects?"

The Angel sang, in a voice like the ringing of a golden tuning fork,

"Gabriel is gone, gone, gone. Oh, holy of holies, the Pleroma is bereft—"

"Yeah, yeah. I got that postcard. But thanks, kid. Anybody else?"

One of the Principalities stretched its wings; they clanged together like church bells. Its voice sent lightning storms across the Pacific. "The Pleroma mourns for Gabriel. Our sorrow is boundless. All is sackcloth, the fairest starlight naught but the bitterest ash. Do as thou wouldst."

I recognized its voice. We'd met a long time ago. It didn't recognize me. I chose not to complicate things.

"Look," I said. "Gabby was a pal. I'd like a chance to say a private good-bye." I made a show of lighting another pill. Took my time with it. Only after the smoke wreathed the heavens, tarnishing wings and stinging bleeding eyeballs, did I continue. " 'Course, without knowing where to go, I'm stuck hanging around here."

That sent the Ps and the Archangel into a huddle. Seemed nobody wanted to talk about the poor guy. How annoying would I have to get before they coughed up some answers? My next course of action was to sing along with them. I hoped it wouldn't come to that.

The heavens wheeled. A star died while I waited; its cobalt corona sent a gamma-ray shimmer cascading across the MOC. I occupied myself by writing blue words in the rain of neutrinos sleeting through the Earth. Too bad none of the monkey wise-heads would ever pick up on it.

Finally, the Archangel spoke up. "Gabriel's Magisterium exists inside the teleological conundrum of unbeing. It is the tremor of awe begat by contemplation of perfect, empty eternity."

As a rule I don't talk to Archangels unless I can't avoid it. They speak by projecting thought through that extra peeper. Imagine shaking hands with a midwife right after an emergency C-section. And then imagine it's not your hand smeared with gore but the inside of your mind.

But I had what I needed, so I let it ride.

"Thanks. This is real ducky of you."

They went back to their glee club antics almost before the sentiment crossed my lips. "Holy, holy, holy!" they sang. I didn't stick around for the rest. I already knew the lyrics to this ditty. It wasn't a favorite.

In the Pleroma, the shortest distance between two points is to con-template a reality where that distance is zero. And so I did. Teleology? Sounded to me like Gabby had been spending too much time with the navel-gazing crowd. I was sorry to hear it. Always thought he was smarter than that. But I followed little Redeye's instructions, thought long and hard about primal and final causes in a universe perpetually empty both forward and backward, and before I knew it I was speed-ing like an arrow toward a foreign Magisterium.

And then I bounced off.

The impact spent me spinning into distant corners of the Pleroma. But I hurried back before I got slapped with a trespassing rap.

Having learned my lesson, I didn't go diving headfirst the second time around. Instead, I decided to use my brain and my peepers. Even so it took a bit of effort before I could perceive a faint fuzziness rip-pling through the ontological boundary to Gabby's digs. That was a sign of recent alterations. By then I had a fairly good idea what I'd find, but still I looked more closely.

Yeah. Somebody had barricaded the door.

They'd constructed a bevy of razor-thin micro-Magisteria, laid down willy-nilly like the scales on a snake who'd overslept and didn't have time to groom himself before slithering off to work. They fit to-gether nice and tight, leaving just enough room between them for a whisper of Pleroma. No interpenetration; nothing to offend the consen-sual basis of reality. I knew there had to be seams, but I couldn't find 'em without squinting. It was fine work. Green-label juju.

Each magisterial sliver held a different arrow of time. Some didn't keep to a single arrow; some had a whole damn quiver. Some used thermodynamic entropy to define it. Some used the passage of time as perceived by the beings that might have evolved on Earth had the amino acids ferried on the comets been right-handed rather than left-handed. Some used the expansion/contraction cycle of a two-pronged Carnot multiverse for a metronome. One dispensed with the arrow altogether for a zero-dimensional dot of time; another replaced the linear arrow with something that looked like the offspring of an octo-pus and a Klein bottle.

No wonder I bounced. Somebody had gone to a lot of trouble to ensure nobody swiped Gabby's silverware.

But I'd been around the block a couple of times. I had a few tricks of my own.

I shaved off a sliver of my consciousness, folded it over, and gave one end a few kinks. Then I wedged the thin end of my new hairpin into the first seam, sat back, and let it go about its business. It inched along, wiggling and limboing, until the view from inside the seams gave me what I needed. The lock popped. The scales, as the poets say, fell from my eyes. I was in.

Funny thing about Gabby: you wouldn't know it from looking at him, with his golden halo and platonic beauty, but the guy was something of a pack rat. He'd been collecting little odds and ends since at least the double-digit redshifts. The interior reality of Gabriel's Magisterium burbled and shifted like convection currents in a star on the zaftig end of the main sequence. Because, I realized, that's what they were. Dull dim light, from IR to X-ray, oozed past me like the wax in a million-mile lava lamp while carbon, nitrogen, and oxygen nuclei did little do-si-dos about my toes. Every bubble, every sizzle, every new nucleus, every photodissociation tagged something of interest to Gabriel. The heart of this star smelled of roses and musty libraries. Nuclear reactions unfolded with the calm susurration of solar wind upon Earth's atmosphere, seeding cloud formation and rain. Convective cells furled about me with the low, slow, sonorous peal of cathedral bells mourning a monarch's death. X-rays fizzed on my tongue like champagne bubbles; I loosened my tie, and felt the silky play of elemental gradients across my skin. Somewhere far below me, and just for a moment, the jangle of clashing nuclei became the faint chiming of a single silver bell.

I wandered around, getting the layout of the joint. Gabby's flaming sword leaned point-down in one corner. A work of art, that thing: the hilt of silvered starlight; the edge sharp as the now that separates past and future; each tongue of flame bright as the embers of Creation. It was dusty. Strange that he hadn't been packing when he fell; whoever did him in must have been counting on that. Just for grins I took the hilt and gave the star a stir. But I put the sword down just as quickly. A few centuries hence, assuming the monkeys managed to fix their little junk problem and get working satellites back in orbit by then, the X-ray flare from the attendant coronal mass ejection would knock high-energy electrons screaming through the electronics. But probably not enough to cause more than a coverage brownout in geostationary orbit.

From a wisp of magnesium (itself a sentimental remnant of an older star), Gabriel had hung fragments of conflicting realities like pearls on a string. Slivers of might-have-beens, universes with different fine structure constants, different electroweak coupling constants, different causality, no causality. Universes susceptible to mortal volition, universes impervious to it. Universes fine-tuned for complex life. Universes inimical to it. A reality where popcorn tasted like bitter wheatgrass and people sold brussels sprouts at the talkies. He'd also been thinking quite a bit about the monkeys. There was some speculation about different evolutionary paths within the MOC, but most of his interest seemed to focus on the fuzzy edges of life in those never-were universes. Looking to see where life had been possible, where intelligent life had been likely. He'd been charting the ontological boundaries of mortal existence.

But amongst all the big picture meaning-of-life stuff, he'd been tailing one individual monkey through the mundane realm. He'd clipped a few forgotten seconds from the memories of a priest and set them playing on an infinite loop like the houseflies in my diner:

The priest lays a wafer on a parishioner's tongue while trying not to recoil from a puff of rancid breath. Poor Bill Fredricks has another rotten tooth. It's cold in the church, a wintery draft gusting through the corner of a broken window, but pride in a good sermon is a golden warmth in the priest's belly; so, too, is the pride in overcoming a recent temptation. But doesn't pride go before the fall? He's nervous, too, consumed by a low-level anxiety. Guilt over a deception, fear of being caught. The vestments itch; his dog collar chafes against his Adam's apple; he has gas. The extra-dry communion wine makes his tongue feel as though it had been flensed with sandpaper . . .

Such were the things Gabriel had lifted from the padre. Nothing of meaning or import. Just a snippet from one of countless meaningless, unremarkable mortal lives. But enough to know the man, and find him again. I tucked the memory fragment into my wallet.

Along with a few others. These memories hadn't been lifted with quite the same attention. A few janes, a few joes, each as unremarkable as little flametop had been before I put the whammy on her. But again: why Gabriel's interest? I snatched these for later study, too.

The silver bell chimed again. Louder this time. From my trousers. I fished through lint, my comb, the few bits of spare change in my pockets until I found the source of the music. Gabby's feather hummed like a tuning fork, its fine silvered edges vibrating fast enough to dice my fingers. I set it adrift, wrapped my hand in a handkerchief, then picked it up again. The vibration sent a tingle through my thoughts, and the crystalline chiming resonated through my perceptions. It tasted like clover honey, smelled like a smooth single malt, and felt like the flat of an electric carving knife pressed against my brow.

I drifted on a convection current of thermal nonequilibrium, trying to make sense of the feather. The current took me through the attic, past the shadow of a photodissociation zone. Gabby's feather cranked up the volume and sliced my handkerchief to ribbons. The shadow passed. The feather took a breather.

It wasn't a tuning fork. It was a dousing rod.

Didn't take long to find the stash once I realized what I had. Gabby had hidden a few more mementos in a little pocket of fragile negative hydrogen ions in the photosphere, a delicate lacework supported by a curlicued nuance of atomic opacity, the kind of quirky consequence of the MOC that nobody ever bothers to notice. If Gabriel's Magisterium had been a high-rise apartment, this spot would have been the wall safe behind the oil painting in the den. He'd squirreled away the impressions of another monkey where he didn't want anybody to find them. I opened the bubble. The memory belonged to a little girl:

She huddles beside a bedroom door, listening while her parents speak to each other in husky stage whispers. The girl has just learned a new four-letter word. She wants to hold it in, but she giggles, and the whispering stops, and the bedroom door flies open. The girl's mother stands over her, angry and naked. She grabs the girl by the arm and hauls her off to bed. . . .

That's where the lost memory looped back on itself. But not before I got a good squint at the kid.

It was Molly. I kicked the walls. The star burped.

I *knew* there was something off about that dame. Who was she? The whole lousy thing stank of a setup. But who was the target? Me or her? I'd watched most of flametop's life while the highlight reel flick-ered through her embryonic Magisterium in the wake of her death; she wasn't a knowing part of this. She was innocent as an Easter lamb. Yet there was a connection between flametop and Gabriel. . . .

I wasn't looking forward to that conversation. I just hoped the screwball cluck didn't come at me with another baseball bat. Bad habit of blaming the messenger, that one. So maybe I'd hold on to this a little while and take a flutter at it when I wasn't tired and sober. Why Molly? What had Gabriel found so important? Something about her, or her family?

A crack like the first thawing of an ice age ricocheted through Ga-briel's Magisterium, louder than lightning. There came another crash, and then a sharp-edged jangle. I had company. Sounded like some-body had come to root through Gabby's phonograph records and raid the icebox. I tucked Molly's stolen memory into my wallet, alongside the priest's. Then I drifted low, pushing upstream against escaping gamma rays, to investigate the racket coming from under the convec-tive zone.

The newcomers were rummaging Gabby's collection of sonnets; he'd liked to carve them into the crusts of neutron stars. Next they'd be cutting the mattress apart and pouring out the coffee cans.

There were two of them. Each girded the heavens with diaphanous wings more transparent than a rich widow's grief. The heat from their faces washed through the joint. Even there, in the heart of the in-ferno, the shadows of their contemplation drew beads of sweat from my furrowed, hardworking brow.

Cherubim. I hate Cherubim.

"Hey, I know you bums."

They noticed me. My sweat turned to vapor. Didn't care for it. But I kept to my script. I said, "I've been looking for you."

They ignored me. They set about ripping down the wallpaper and tearing up the carpet. I shifted, just enough to feel the reassuring weight of the wallet and feather in my pockets.

I said, "Yeah. Word on the street says two fellas matching your descriptions tossed the place of a friend of mine. Left it in a real state. Her, too. What's the big idea?"

LEAVE.

"Nuts to you, fella," I said. "Nuts to both of you."

Last thing I needed was a snarling match with a pair of Cherubim. But flametop had needed it even less, yet this wrecking crew had left her with nothing but a handful of dust where the foundations of her being had been. And I'm the one who tossed her into the duck pond.

But if this *was* a setup—and it swam and quacked like one—they'd want to give me the once-over, too. So I took my natural form. Been a spell since I'd done that. Didn't seem to fit anymore. I remembered it being roomier. It wasn't. Not that it made any difference to the loogans. They weren't impressed. Compared to them I was so small-time I could do the backstroke in a pony glass. But I guess I had a reputation of sorts, too. I'm the guy who skipped town. They had my number. They saw the mud on my neck.

"For the record," I said, before things got awkward, "I go by Bayliss now."

YOUR PRESENCE IS UNNECESSARY. YOUR PRESENCE IS UNDESIRED. DEPART.

I couldn't tell which of them was doing the talking. It was like a ventriloquist act with two dummies.

"I know your type," I said, "tough guys like you. You put on a show, a bit of the flash, but you're not independent operators. Nah. You're just errand boys. So I figure somebody else is calling the shots."

DEPART. INSTANTLY.

It got a little warmer in the churning heart of Gabriel's Magisterium. All around us, squalling newborn babes of atoms crumbled into a cloud of hydrogen ash. I knew it was no use trying to get the connection to flametop. These muggs were just the muscle. If I wanted to connect the dots to Molly, I needed a line on their boss.

"Who's writing your checks? Who put the bee on my client?"

They say persistence is a virtue. But they've never been worked over by a pair of Cherubim. The loogans' disdain became irritation. They unfurled their wings, flexing and bending until I existed at the center of a cage of shadow and thought. I wondered how long it would take to put myself back together after they finished. But how I hate to stop when I'm on a roll.

"The other thing I can't quite figure," I said, "is the harvest. You ran roughshod over my client's Magisterium, and now you're desecrating Gabriel's memorial. Must be one big payday in your future to put you on the outs with the bulls like that."

That's when they turned the full inferno of their contemplation upon me. I shriveled like a moth in a blast furnace. One hovered behind to anchor me in place. The other went to work with knuckle dusters and holy fire. The searing heat of angelic rage burned hotter than a blowtorch on butter. Somebody cried. Not me, though; I'm the strong, silent type.

A few shots to the kidneys later, they traded places. "Somebody fed you boys a plate of spaghetti," I groaned. "Whatever they told you about my client, it's nothing but chewing gum."

No soap. These lugs enjoyed their work.

Time passed. I wished whoever it was would quit his bawling. What a sad sack. It got on my nerves. And the Cherubim had my nerves a little raw. At least I'd have matching shiners. I tried to split off a piece of myself and send it ahead to my Magisterium to make sure Flo had a raw steak waiting for me in the fridge, but the Cherubim caught it before it could slither away. They shoved it back into place, and none too gently. I guess they got bored, because one of them, either Tweedledee or Tweedledum, said,

THIS ONE DOES NOT POSSESS THE TRUMPET. IT DOES NOT EXIST HERE.

Trumpet? . . . Son of a gun.

Oh Bayliss, you smart little egg. Some shamus you are. You couldn't find a virgin in a convent.

Gabriel had been the guardian of the Jericho Trumpet. But if I understood my new pals, it went missing when Gabby kicked it. And flametop, being the cork sent to fill the hole he left behind, was the natural place to start looking for it. Tossing her place came up short. So they came here on the theory maybe he hadn't had time to hide it before he met his fate. But that wasn't going so well, either. Good thing I came along to cheer them up.

This was bad news all around. Gabriel's Trumpet wasn't chicken feed. No wonder the whole Choir had turned out to throw a blanket over the damage caused by his death. We were looking down the barrel of another—

A searing white light, the purest light possible, the light of Creation, scorched away everything but the fact of my existence. The Cherubim dropped me. They wrapped themselves in their wings; the sheeting flames of their faces shrank to feeble candle embers. I had just enough time to hit the deck before the thunder of a thousand Creations, a thousand Let There Be Lights, shook Gabriel's Magisterium.

And then the Pleroma was formless and empty, and a darkness was over the surface of the world. And then there was light, and I saw that the light hurt like a son of a bitch.

Someone had awoken METATRON: the Voice of God.

I *knew* that dame was trouble the minute I saw her.

ANGEL OF DEATH

He's a fallen angel. And he's terrified.

Bayliss exited the wreckage of Molly's Magisterium by way of the cathedral in her pantry. The upside-down rain continued to fall, but the tangerine sky had darkened into bands of cinnamon and sienna. A pair of fingernail moons hung low in the sky like commas sent to punctuate the gloaming. Every step she took stirred up more butterfly dust; motes of scarlet and indigo sparkled in a ray of sunlight glancing across the bow of a cruise down the Rhine. The people on the boat wore old-timey clothes: plum-colored suits with wide lapels, paisley shirts, and blue jeans that flared at the bottom. Their party smelled of river water, beer, pot, and diesel fuel. The party cut a wide wake through air and water, and when Molly inhaled it she could sense the electric tingle of something that might have been cocaine. It sounded like they were having a good time. Molly despised them for it. She resented their ignorance.

Turning in a slow circle, she surveyed the ruins of what had once been a place of perfect contentment. The attackers had trashed her Magisterium. The happiest period of her life, the centerpiece of her emotional life as an adult, lay in fragments beneath the wreckage. The relentless aching heat of second-degree sunburn received by falling asleep on the beach during a spring break trip to Mexico sat where her first taste of scotch had been. The cap and gown of her college graduation dripped greasy dollops of rancid olive oil from a broken bottle in the cupboard six years later. Checking the mail on a Wednesday afternoon had become the silky taste of Belgian chocolate.

Fixing this was going to take fucking forever. She'd have to relive her entire life just to put things back in order. Even then . . . what if she couldn't do it? What if it was like this forever? She couldn't even fix a small burn in the floorboards. How could she rebuild an entire *life*? She'd be stuck in this kaleidoscopic junkyard forever and ever, and nobody she loved would ever know she was here, and she'd never be able to escape, and they'd come for her and attack her again and she didn't know why, and she couldn't make sense of anything. Her breaths came faster.

This was hell. She'd died and gone to hell. God . . . An icy fist of loneliness clutched her heart, squeezing until she moaned.

Molly tried to take a steadying breath. It became a gulp. So did another. The gulps became sobs. She slid to her knees amidst the soft cushion of insect wings. She toppled to her side, crying. Her tears sizzled like acid, burning fragrant holes in the butterfly carpet.

She'd been alive, with her own life, with a new job at the museum, and she was ready to start dating again and maybe even looking forward to it because she hadn't even thought about Ria for a day or two; then Mom died, and they'd gone to Australia for the funeral, and she could tell Martin was backsliding, but it was just the two of them from now on, so she was going to help her big brother because she loved him, because he needed her help, and she had promised herself she wouldn't be so distant from him and maybe other people, too. But then Bayliss showed up and now she was dead and nothing he said made any sense and somebody had been killed and she was assaulted, and all she had were her memories but those had been ransacked.

Even scarier was the realization Bayliss was driven by fear. He wouldn't come out and admit it. Yet clearly he'd been hiding on Earth for who knew how long. But why, and from what, he'd only hinted.

It was all so overwhelming that she wanted to scream. So she did until she could taste blood.

The partygoers on the Rhine got rowdier. Their laughter taunted her. She had fallen into hell while a boatload of strangers got stoned. Molly jumped to her feet.

"Shut *up!*" she yelled. A wave surged up the Rhine. The boat bobbed like a cork; its lights went out. Molly slammed the closet door to shut out the babble of confused and drunken German. The slam *cracked* like a home run.

The vibration knocked a fender bender from a shelf above the refrigerator. It hit the floor with the screech of brakes on wet pavement, the crumple of plastic, and the *clump* of a self-sealing hydrogen breach, followed by Molly's raised voice and Ria apologizing. The memory cracked open; the warm, wet sensation of being instantly smitten seeped under the fridge. Somewhen, standing in a cold rain on the corner of wistfulness and Winnetka Boulevard, Molly and Ria exchanged telephone numbers. A lyric from an Édith Piaf song stretched from the crook of Ria's elbow to her wrist, the spidery copperplate etched into her flesh with cobalt ink: *Even if I'm wrong, leave it to me.*

Oh, Ria.

For months after they'd broken up, Molly had kept a scrap of blue-lined notebook paper affixed to the fridge with a hula-girl magnet. Ria's forwarding address. She had it in the cloud, of course, but seeing it there, as a physical tangible thing, somehow kept Ria closer. Kept the apartment less empty. Sometimes her junk mail still came to the old apartment. She had moved a couple of times since then, but Molly had always kept track of her. And then a fire reduced their former home to ash. But that didn't matter. Here, now, in Molly's Magisterium, the apartment building still stood. Here, now, in the prescribed reality of the Magisterium, their relationship was as strong as it had ever been. Bayliss's shitty diner had people in it. Why not here? Why not Ria?

The tattoo, the ragged fingernails, the way she chewed her lip when thinking hard . . . Molly could remember it all. Every mole. Every filling. The trigger point for every countercultural rant. Her lub-dub heartbeat. Her bare soles slapping softly on the kitchen floor. The dream-catcher earrings she'd only worn once before deciding she hated the way dangly earrings brushed against her neck.

A gap appeared in the upside-down drizzle. It widened with every recollection, like a balloon slowly taking shape. It bloomed into a woman-shaped hole in the rain. But where the woman should have been, there was nothing but a cold mist. A rain wraith. A banshee built of fog and memory, a loose conglomeration of sensations bundled together with the twine of selfish longing.

The more Molly pushed, the more ephemeral the apparition became. It wasn't quite the same as trying to mend Bayliss's cigarette burn. The false Ria didn't resist in quite the same way as the floorboards.

She resisted by virtue of complexity. She resisted by virtue of missing flesh, bones, and blood vessels; tonsillectomy scars and pink lungs; nerve fibers and lymph nodes; vertebrae and ventricles. Compared to an inanimate floorboard, a person was incomprehensibly vast.

Overwhelmingly vast. Molly couldn't hope to do something like this.

She released the memory construct. It dissolved like cotton candy in the rain. Little bits and pieces of Ria-ish memories flittered into the darkening sky. Molly drew a shuddery breath. Held it until she knew it wouldn't become another sob. Released it. If she wanted to see Ria, she'd have to do it for real.

What had Bayliss said? Yeah. "It'll take some practice before you can interact."

Screw this noise, thought Molly. She needed comfort. She'd keep practicing until she could find Ria and tell her what was happening. Ria would understand. She'd be there for her. They'd been together for so long. Surely they still had a connection.

And so what if they didn't? Molly wasn't human any longer. She could *force* a connection. Resurrect it. Couldn't she? She could change everything. If she could sculpt reality now, she'd damn well make it something worthwhile. She could put things back to the way they used to be. She could change Ria's feelings.

Molly rummaged through the chaotic wreckage for clothes. She wiped her eyes on a scarf, then realized it was the scarf she'd been wearing when the tram tore her apart, and tossed it aside. The scarf disintegrated into a rain of sand that joined the grit on the floor from when a savage cold snap shattered the water pipe in the kitchen. She went from closet to closet, seeking clothes but finding nothing but dusty broken memories and hoarded personal triumphs. Then she caught a dozen glimpses of herself in the shards of a broken mirror.

She was already dressed. Slacks and boots and the cashmere coat with the wide belt. Hadn't she been barefoot? In a nightgown? And before that, when she first awoke, wasn't she wearing footie pajamas in her old childhood bedroom?

Molly closed her eyes and concentrated. A final teardrop fell from her lashes with a chime like a wedding toast on fine crystal. When she opened her eyes, the slacks had become blue jeans; the cashmere coat a red leather jacket over a faded Hershey's t-shirt. The necklace was gone, and her earrings with the tiny rubies had reverted to simple studs. Her bumming-around-town clothes.

She looked at her feet. Early spring in Australia meant early fall in Minneapolis. The seasonal distinctions might have meant something in her grandparents' day. Warm days, warm nights. The boots became sandals.

And then she realized she didn't know how to get back to the real world. If she went out through the cathedral in the pantry, as Bayliss had done, would she end up in France? Would the closet send her to a German waterfront? If she went out through the hole in the wall near where the fifteen-year-old still wept, would she come out in the wrong time? This apartment didn't exist in the real world any longer. Anything contiguous with her Magisterium would be displaced in time. It was confusing. It made her head hurt.

But Bayliss's diner looked like it was a hundred years old or more. Yet they'd entered it straight from a present-day Melbourne laneway. A seamless overlay on the real world. She needed to figure out how to do that if she didn't want to be trapped here forever.

It took more rummaging to find the front door. Like the missing stairs, it had become an amalgam of concepts—a thought-cloud encompassing all manifestations of doorness. It was part revolving door, part Aldous Huxley novel, part rickety gas-station rest stop door, part elevator door, part of the car door that had broken Molly's pinky finger when she was thirteen.

But none of that mattered. It was a door. What mattered was the other side. Where did Molly want to go?

Sunset cast sanguine shadows across rings of terraced landscaping. Molly stood at the lip of the floundering agricultural co-op where the Calhoun lake bed had been. Molly had seen old photos. Hard to believe there had been a time when there had been that much free-standing water right in the middle of the city. The water crisis had peaked before Molly was born; things were slowly improving. Maybe someday they'd let it be a lake again.

For now it was neither fish nor fowl. The lake was long gone, but the site wasn't yet a productive grower. Lake Calhoun had rested upon a bed of glacial till packed into a trough etched eons ago into the limestone detritus of an ancient sea. Ria led the effort to remediate the soil one hard-fought quarter acre at a time, leaching away countless decades of motorboat oil and Jet Ski fuel leaked from the surrounding jetties, fertilizer runoff from the surrounding homes, and industrial runoff from the surrounding city. All without removing what few nutrients the biological decay of lake grasses had sprinkled into the cold, lightless lake bed.

It was hard work, and, so far, a losing battle. Most of the terraces were empty. They stepped down in an irregular ring defining contours of the original lake bed, almost a mile across at the widest spot; the bottom was almost eighty feet deep. Molly stood at ground level with six levels stretched beneath her like the edges of an inverted ziggurat. Perhaps someday it would be Ria's very own hanging garden of Babylon. If she had her way with nature.

A few dozen feet, maybe fifty, of the terrace lacked the ochre and butterscotch tones of poisoned soil and the glassy blue-gray of low-carbon stonefoam. There, a cool breeze ruffled a green fringe of soy, alfalfa, and wheatgrass. Beans of some variety had thrown feelers over the terrace wall. A handful of people labored on the first and second levels. Sweaty men in sleeveless shirts, women with bandannas over their hair. Everybody had a suntan and thick shoulders. Nobody was Ria.

The soil, Molly knew, was planted with genetically engineered low-water varieties. There had been a time when people made a distinction between the genetically enhanced varieties and "heritage" strains of domesticated plants, but nowadays nobody gave a shit about something so obviously pointless. Too much cross-pollination between test plots; too much apathy. Too many hungry people left behind as the grain belts shifted and withered.

The new growth wouldn't be mature and ready for harvest before winter. Nobody would eat from these plants. A waste of water, energy, and hard-earned nutrients. But, Molly supposed, that wasn't the point. It was also a proof of concept. Demonstration of a healthy, viable project. She read Ria's handwriting in that. *Even if I'm wrong, leave it to me.* . . .

Stately homes with vast green lawns and towering oaks encircled the lake bed. Neo-Tudor manses, coral pink Bahamian villas, modern knife-blade houses built of glass and ceramic, Spanish-style haciendas, some fat shed-style houses, even an earth home or two. This had been a well-heeled part of town for well over a century; these people could afford water. Here, conservation was a crisis-driven mandate: the unwelcome collision of distant concerns with a comfortable life.

The breeze stiffened into a gust; Molly inhaled. The wind carried the stink of mud and compost from the lake bed, but even that couldn't hide the humidity or the fecund scent of the trees and grasses all around her. It lay on the air so thickly even her human senses could pick it out. But there was so much more. She could smell trace amounts of century-old boat fuel, the lifeblood of a two-stroke engine, wafting from a remediation mound on the second level of the terraces. And just as easily as she could smell the microscopic flakes of rust deposited by a damaged tiller blade in the zen-garden undulations of freshly raked tillage, she could eavesdrop on the argument unfolding behind closed doors and windows in a house a hundred yards behind her, hear the electric hum of a thousand vehicles, the clicking of steel rails beneath another tram.

. . . men kneeling, wearing purple gloves, picking flecks of bone and meat from the bloodstained snow . . .

Molly shuddered. She shook herself, forcing the unwanted recollection aside. Just as abruptly, the wind died. It left a layer of grit on her skin, fine enough to fill the ridges of her fingerprints, like soft house dust.

Ria's passion dwelled in this muddy pit. Ria herself wouldn't be far. The co-op had taken over the old pavilion on the northeast edge of the lake, where the dock had been. The pavilion looked like a Midwestern interpretation of a hacienda, with tall arches of smooth white stucco roofed in red clay tiles. Molly remembered how Ria talked about it after her co-op bought the property and entered the boarded building for the first time. It had served as public restrooms for visitors to the lake, as well as an ice-cream stand, a restaurant, and a rental office for bicycles, canoes, and pontoon boats. But that had all come to a halt long before they were born. According to Ria it had been just a dilapidated shithole. The local neighborhood association had wanted to tear it down to drive off the squatters. But Ria's passion had won the day.

Wheelbarrows and the strides of countless work boots had swept away the wild grasses to leave a dusty gray path like a bathtub ring around the lip of the crater. Molly followed it to the pavilion. The dirt held a thousand partial impressions of footsteps and tires and, here and there, cigarette butts. They made her think of Bayliss. She concentrated on the pavilion before she got angry again.

The low murmur of tired voices came to her from inside. "Shit," said one of them, "I'm exhausted."

Another cold gust whistled through the hollow spot where Molly had kept her self-confidence. Ria's voice.

Without remembering the intervening steps, Molly found herself loitering just outside the pavilion. A man and a woman came out together, their dirt-streaked flesh smelling of sweat and loam and satisfaction. They startled Molly. She jumped.

"Hi," she said. They didn't respond.

Just like the cop. Just like Martin.

Not a ghost, thought Molly, concentrating. *Not now.* She focused on what it had been like to be real, to be seen, to be felt, to be a presence in the world. To make eye contact with another human being. Easy. Natural. Even babies could do it, right?

She went inside. The de facto office was a long, narrow, windowless space illuminated by the yellow-green corpse light of biochemical glow strips. It had probably been the kitchen where high school students had cooked hamburgers and hot dogs, once upon a time. A corrugated metal shutter in the wall had been welded shut and painted over with a decent approximation of a Klimt. A warped door had been laid across stacks of cinder blocks to form a desk.

Ria sat on it. Her toes just touched the floor. Her unlaced work boots lay in a heap beside the desk, stinking. She had her eyes closed and her fingers laced behind her neck. A woman in French braids sat on a lawn chair beside the door. She looked equally tired.

"Ria." It came out as a cough. Molly cleared her throat and tried again. "Hi, Ria."

Ria opened her eyes. Molly gasped.

"Ria! You can see me?" she asked.

A frown furrowed Ria's brow. She stopped kneading her neck. Her expression was cloudy.

"You see me, don't you?"

The woman on the lawn chair exhaled heavily. Impatiently. Her eyes were closed, too. Rivulets of sweat cleaned paths through the grit on her sunburned neck.

"I know it's been a really long time, and I know you're probably not very happy to see me, but things are really fucked up right now, and I just . . . Just wanted . . ." Molly took a long slow breath, strangled a sob in its crib. It was okay to turn to Ria for comfort. But damned if she'd let herself fall apart. Her voice quavered. "I really need to talk to some-body who knows me, you know?"

The smile that touched Ria's lips was slippery and wistful as an ice cream cone dropped on a summer sidewalk. "Jesus," she said. "You look like shit."

Molly cried and laughed at the same time. Tears ran into her mouth. They tasted like the primordial sea. (How did she know that?) "I feel even worse."

Ria hopped to her feet; her soles slapped the bare concrete. Molly's stomach gave a flutter. She wiped her nose on the sleeve of her jacket. Nothing could hold back the tears. Not even an angel's willpower. Ria came to her.

Molly said, "I'm sorry I just dropped in on you like this. I would have called but—"

Ria went to the lawn chair. She kissed the other woman on the forehead, then sat on her lap.

"Did you hear what I said?" Ria whispered. "I said you look like shit."

"So do you," said the other woman. "And you reek to high heaven. Take a shower, you cow." Ria laughed. They cuddled.

Molly ran her hands through her hair. "Ria! Look at me, god-damn it!"

The couple on the lawn chair started to kiss. Molly loomed over them. She put a hand under Ria's chin and gave a gentle tug. She'd forgotten how smooth Ria's skin felt. Even beneath the sweat and dust. Ria jolted upright. They pulled apart.

"What?" said her girlfriend.

Ria shook her head as though clearing it. "Got a little shock."

"Sparks flying, huh?"

They laughed again.

Molly stepped behind the chair. She leaned over Ria's girlfriend, laid her hands on Ria's shoulders, and shook her. *"See me!"*

"Ooh, you're shaking, babe. You okay?" The girlfriend rubbed her hands up and down Ria's arms.

Ria hugged herself. Shrugged. "I dunno. Just had a chill." She leaned forward again, laid her head on the other's shoulder. "I'm tired," she yawned. It came out a little slurred, like a noncommittal yawn.

Molly knelt and stared at Ria's eyes, concentrating. *See me. See me. See me. You must sense me. You have to know I'm here. You knew me so well. Can't you sense me? You have to see me. Don't you dare ignore me.*

Ria shivered again. She closed her eyes, and slumped more heavily against her girlfriend. The other woman flinched slightly, as though startled by an unexpected touch.

"You drooling on me now?" She shifted her weight.

Ria's head rolled back. Her nose was bleeding. A long crimson streamer trailed down the other woman's shoulder and the front of her shirt. Molly and the other woman gasped in unison.

"Ria?" said Molly, her voice sounding like somebody else's, so weak and querulous.

"Babe?" said the other woman. She tried to sit up, but Ria's slack body toppled backward. They both tried to catch her, but she tumbled to the floor like a rag doll. Her head clunked on the floor. A wet spot stained the crotch of her cargo pants. Strong odor—Ria had eaten asparagus today.

The girlfriend leaped to her feet, then knelt over Ria. "Ria!" she cried.

Molly started dialing for an ambulance, the earbud having popped into her ear without her consciously summoning it. But she stopped when instead of a connection tone she got the roar of a jet engine and the staticky warble of somebody singing "Que Será, Será" in a thick Scottish brogue. She could call Bayliss, but she didn't know how to make a call into the real world. And Bayliss hadn't done a damn thing to help her when she called for help. He showed up after the fact. She was on her own.

She was a ghost, a revenant spirit cursed to witness the death of her old love.

No, something told her. A sickening murmur at the edge of her consciousness said, *Not to witness*. It was Bayliss's voice, she realized, making a pronouncement final as the dregs of a wine bottle: *Careful, angel. He'll stroke out if you keep giving him both barrels.*

She had *caused* this. She had done this to Ria.

The memory of something else Bayliss had said landed like a punch in the gut: *there ain't no afterlife. . . .*

Molly grabbed her hair with one fist. She cried. "Oh no, no, no. Oh God no." She wailed; the Earth shook.

This was her fault. If Molly truly were an angel, she was Ria's Angel of Death.

The girlfriend checked Ria's breath and heartbeat. Molly could hear Ria's heart thumping away beneath the panicked panting of the girlfriend, the whispering of wind through the surrounding oaks, the patter of squirrels on the roof. She could smell mint on Ria's breath, too. She was still breathing.

The girlfriend pulled an earbud from a pocket and called an ambulance. Though there were tears in her eyes she didn't cry while explaining the situation and giving directions. "Calhoun lake bed," she said, "corner of West Lake and the parkway." She was calm and focused. Molly liked her for that. It was what Ria needed. She needed somebody strong and effective. Somebody who could hold her.

Molly couldn't do anything. She couldn't even hold Ria's hand while the ambulance came. She was powerless—

What else had Bayliss said? Back at the diner?

. . . an angel all by its lonesome could shape reality to any old whim, anything at all . . .

"Screw this," said Molly. *I reject this bullshit reality.*

But she had no idea how to fix things here in the real world. She couldn't even make her phone call out. How could she undo this?

What if it really was a stroke? Had a blood vessel burst in Ria's brain? How would she fix that? If she knew where it was, maybe she could imagine it whole again. Imagine no surfeit of blood pressing on the surrounding brain tissue. Undo the leak, push the blood back into its container, seal the hole. But what was Ria's brain supposed to look like? What had it been before Molly hurt her? Where had all the jelly and blood gone? What if she tried to fix it, but changed something without realizing it, and then Ria wasn't Ria any longer? Like that railroad guy with the iron rod blown through his skull?

That was just as bad as watching her die. Either way she'd be gone forever.

A faint thrum shook the floor. The vibrations, low and slow like the heartbeat of the Earth, felt more like a subtle pressure than a sound. Ria's girlfriend didn't react, but Molly could feel it brushing her eyelashes, tickling her skin. It was too subtle for human senses.

It came from Ria's skull. The sloshing of spilled blood made it ring like a bell with every beat of her fluttering heart. Molly knew she was listening to the soundtrack of a massive hemorrhage: the inaudible scream of a dying mind.

Shit, shit, shitshitshitshitshit.

She had to fix this. But all that blood . . . it kept coming and coming, a crimson flood squeezing Ria's head like an overfilled balloon. Trying to push it all back would be as futile as King Canute cursing the tide. And even if she won, the damage to Ria's brain . . . She didn't know where to begin.

She couldn't mend this. But she could *undo* it. It was much simpler to imagine a reality where none of this had ever happened. Where she hadn't tried to force Ria to see her. Where she had never come here in the first place. Where the last few minutes had never happened. Where Molly wouldn't have to shoulder this regret, too. A reality that conformed to Molly's frantic wish to undo this. Everything had been fine five minutes ago.

Five minutes, thought Molly. *That's all she needs.*

Molly shut her eyes and concentrated. She needed a rhythm, but Ria's feathery heartbeat was too irregular, too weak. Instead she attuned herself to the adrenaline-fueled tempo of the girlfriend's despair. Her heart was a strong and steady metronome. Somewhere, the shriek of an ambulance siren pierced the evening.

Molly imagined time slowing down, each swing of the metronome's inverted pendulum taking just a tiny bit longer. She imagined sand trickling through an hourglass, each grain falling more slowly than the one before it. She imagined the blood pulsing more and more slowly into Ria's skull.

The first signs of change came at the edge of perceptibility. Molly couldn't tell if the slowing of the other woman's heartbeat happened because she was finding her center and taking the crisis in stride like a zen master, or because the time between beats was stretching out like soft taffy. But then she felt it in the invisible air, sensed the torpid molasses-eddies of each exhalation.

She pinched the bridge of her nose. Pushed.

Sand grains drifting like feathers. A heartbeat ponderous as church bells. Blood flowing slower than syrup. The ambulance wail fell through the octaves until it became a foghorn. The *lub-dub* of a panicked heart stretched and stretched and stretched until it was just a *lub*, just a negative space in the soundscape, nothing but the liminal silence of a single hand clapping.

Molly opened her eyes. She stood at the center of a frozen tableau. Ria's girlfriend still knelt beside her, frozen like a victim of Medusa's gaze, caught in the act of stroking Ria's face. The whispers of encouragement passing her lips were trapped in gelled air like flies in amber. The world had become a sideways hourglass, its sand motionless, flowing to neither bulb.

She had dammed the river of time, but it pushed back. It squeezed her. A relentless pressure, a swell of pain. The weight of the world was heavy indeed. But it wasn't enough. Molly gritted her teeth against the pain and pushed still harder. She struggled to maintain her concentration. *Backward,* she managed. *Only a hair . . . just a few minutes . . .* She rallied her strength for one final shove.

An inhaled prayer swirled into the girlfriend's mouth.

The un-beat of a feeble heart sucked a teaspoon of blood from Ria's brain.

A siren's un-wail receded into a retreating ambulance, leaving a hole in the night where its shriek had been.

It was working. Just a little more—

The world disappeared in a blaze of searing white light. Molly cowered before an anger so vast it shook the pillars of Heaven; a tidal wave of indignation overwhelmed the breakwaters of her mind. The light scorched away everything it touched. Molly's concentration shriveled like an ant caught in the sunlight through a third-grader's magnifying glass. Her consciousness followed.

FORBIDDEN, screamed the universe.

DON'T GET UP,
I'LL LET MYSELF OUT

*M*aybe you've been in the sneezer. So maybe you know what it's like when the prowl car boys get bored and decide you'll make a fine little pigeon, powerless but smart enough not to kick up a fuss. And maybe you know what it's like when the brass sees your shiner and he knows the score but you feed him a line about taking a tumble on the curb while you were jammed to the gills. And he's looking you in the eye and he knows you're not on the level but the buttons are there looking innocent as altar boys and all you can do is smile and nod and thank him for the hospitality. But he doesn't like the look of your nose so he asks the wrecking crew to unstraighten it for you.

That's what it's like when METATRON gets hot under the collar. It's no picnic.

The difference is that when the buttons call it a night and pack up the rubber hoses they don't leave your consciousness spread across a thousand little stains on the walls and floor. Your mind doesn't disperse into a hundred million fireflies, each crumb of your existence reduced to a feeble glow trapped in a barrel of amber. You go back to your cot and sleep it off. You don't have to reassemble yourself from bits and pieces of carbon and hemoglobin and nucleic acid and vitreous humor. So after the godlight faded it took a while to rebind the more esoteric pages from the book of my long and fascinating life.

I'd tell you I came to, except there was no "to" at which to come. The Pleroma was still without form and void. But so was my Magisterium. Like a snowball in a potter's kiln, it had melted, sublimated, steamed away until the furnace heat of METATRON's rage had cracked the component molecules, stripped the atoms, prised the baryons apart, sintered the underlying concepts. The Voice of God had taken a fire hose to the blackboard. Clean slate.

Joes and janes all over the Pleroma were having the same experience. Not a single Magisterium left standing. The Pleroma had become a featureless infinite-dimensional expanse; the homogeneous superposition of uncountable maybes. It's like that when META-TRON goes on a tear. Been a spell since the last time, though. I'd have to check the calendar, but I'd wager the sun hadn't yet been making helium the last time around.

Sure it hurts when METATRON does its thing, but that's beside the point. The pain is a side effect. And besides, it's not pain as the monkeys would understand it. METATRON doesn't brandish a willow switch when it takes us behind the shed. No. To beings accustomed to shaping reality with the merest thoughts and whims, there is no greater punishment—no greater chastisement—than the revocation of willpower. The erasure of our personal imprints upon the universe. (How would *you* feel if you were billions of years old with nothing to show for it after all that time? People skip school reunions for less.) So that's what I found after putting myself together. The Choir's collective Magisteria had been stripped away, leaving nothing but a bare bones Pleroma.

And the MOC, of course. Always the MOC.

That's the long version leading to what happened next. Short version? I had to rebuild my apartment from the quarks up before I could have the luxury of waking up with the worst hangover since the discovery of alcohol.

So I did. And then I passed out again.

Sometime later I rolled out of bed while a vengeful mariachi band tested the acoustics inside my skull. My options were an ice pick behind the eyes or two aspirin and a glass of water. I opted for the latter. The bathroom was closer and besides which I hadn't an ice pick handy because I don't take my rye on the rocks. So I chewed a couple of tablets and chased them with enough water to drown a fish. The mariachis fired their trumpet player and found somebody who knew how to stay on beat. Those kids had promise.

By the time I wobbled to the kitchen and got the percolator going I felt halfway human. Which should tell you just how bad it was. The

Voice of God really takes it out of a person. And my pals the Cherubim took pride in their work; I still had the marks to prove it. But the bacon grease was popping along and I'd just cracked a couple eggs into it when the phone rang. It didn't take a green label shamus to finger the caller.

What's a guy to do? She had a habit of flinging herself into trouble. It seemed that no matter how hard I tried to drill just the tiniest bit of common sense into Molly's head, she was having none of it. Stubborn as a mule, that cluck. I told her to stay buttoned, so what did she do? Apparently she made a beeline for METATRON to poke it in the all-seeing eye. And now that things had gone sour she was calling me again.

Dames.

I took a steadying breath and reminded myself I carried some of the blame for this flop. After failing to find somebody suitably passive, as I'd been strong-armed to do, I compounded the mistake with my eagerness to put some distance between us. Maybe—maybe—I cut a few corners when reading her the headlines.

So it wasn't without sympathy when I contemplated the hole she'd dug for herself. The Choir would lay this at her feet sooner than later. She was the new kid, and this mess had her fingerprints all over it. She was in trouble.

But so was I, no thanks to her.

So I decided to let flametop simmer. Couldn't give her the cold shoulder forever; I'd have to tell her about the Trumpet and what I found at Gabby's place. Plus, if I wanted to get through this mess with my skin intact, I needed to know what kind of stunt she'd pulled to arouse METATRON. But that conversation could wait until I wasn't full of no coffee.

It takes some effort to get on the bad side of the Voice. Far as I knew, it took a major violation of the Mantle of Ontological Consistency. Something you couldn't hide under a fresh coat of paint. Like making thermodynamics nonlocal, or putting a dent in causality. I tried to figure how she might have pulled that stunt, but the sums came up short.

Meanwhile the phone kept ringing, and I kept not answering it. It rang while I ate. It rang while I rinsed the dishes in the sink. It rang while I had a second cup of joe, lit a pill, smoked it, and emptied the percolator. It rang while I glanced over the chess problem arranged on the board under the window; it rang while the mariachis ensured today wouldn't be the day I found that elegant mate in seven. It rang while I scraped my face. It rang while I donned a clean shirt and collar. It rang while I slipped out and locked the door. I could hear its ring echoing through my digs when I plucked a hair from my head and stuck it high in the door frame where any casual thieves weren't likely to spot it.

Figured it was only a matter of time before they tossed my place, too. I could try to keep my distance from Molly, but the hard boys already had us together. I'd told them as much. Careful, Bayliss, you're getting soft.

Gabby had been keeping an eye on Molly, but I couldn't get my arms around that one. Not yet. He'd also put the bee on a priest, though, and I figured that was gravy. I'd drop in on the guy, brace him a little bit. If he clammed up I'd play the miracle card and turn his communion wine into communion water. That one's always a big hit with the godly types.

I pulled the priest's memory fragment from my wallet. Thing of beauty, the way Gabriel had lifted it; damn thing was still going strong on its short little loop. I let it unfold around me until I sank into that vast empty space behind the eyes that the monkeys call, with no small amount of self-delusion, their subconscious.

Father Vincent Santorelli's flock liked him because he was a product of the same Chicago neighborhood. His family had been there for generations going back to the time of speakeasies and tommy guns. His brother was a firefighter. He'd given the Last Rites to his very own mother, not five blocks from the church where he'd given the homily every week for the past ten years. He coached Little League games in the summer, worked with a local youth choir, and donated the rest of his spare time to act as a chaplain at the army hospital up near Oak Park. A real pillar of the community. But the kid thing gave me pause. When I first sensed that pride in overcoming temptation, and the hidden guilty secret, I figured I knew where this was headed.

Figured it wouldn't take much digging to find a history of trying to make it with the altar boys. I'd seen this story too many times to expect anything else. But I was wrong.

Near as I could tell, Father Vince was the real deal. The man wouldn't hurt a child if you pressed an iron to his temple. He considered himself a failure because he struggled to find loving forgiveness in his heart for the creeps who did like the little boys. His recent brush with temptation had involved the wife in an estranged marriage he'd been trying to counsel. Nice figure, gentle words, a hand on the knee. He reacted the way any red-blooded man would. As propositions went, it was about as chaste as you could imagine, but he berated himself for it. Some guys need to loosen up.

Santorelli was solid. Didn't agree with his choice where the lonely frail was concerned, but that was between him and his conscience. I liked him.

But something had him wound tighter than a moneylender on a bank holiday. I sank deeper, feeling around for a thread of awareness that might have swirled through the back of Santorelli's mind while he laid a communion wafer on a fat pale tongue and tried not to recoil from the stench of an abscessed tooth. A lingering worry like that usually finds room to fester at the edges of the subconscious; that's why it lingers.

Took a bit of digging because the loop was just a few seconds long. It's tricky getting your fingers on something that slippery. But then I found it. And you could have knocked me over with one swipe of the racing forms.

Santorelli was worked up over a bit of simony.

The Plenary Indulgence predated the Middle Ages, in one form or another, but the Catholics had resurrected it at the turn of the millennium. A piece of paper with the power to bleach the stain of sin from a man's soul. A Get-Out-Of-Purgatory-Free card, certified (in theory) by the pope himself. Say a few Our Fathers, do a few rosaries and a few good deeds, donate a bit to the ol' church coffers, and that roll in the hay with the hotcha babysitter gets expunged from the scroll on Saint Peter's desk. Got her pregnant, jack? What's that about an abortion? Better buy the triple pack.

As rackets went, it was a thing of beauty. The monkey who dreamed up this one back in the day must have been so bent he tied his shoes with his tongue. But this had been business as usual for decades. They'd revisited the Indulgence racket long before Santorelli had taken his vows. So what was his angle?

That detail was too complex, tied in with too many other things, for me to pull it from a few seconds of memory. Even one lifted as cleanly as Gabriel had done. If I wanted the rest, I'd have to speak with the good father in person. But now at least I had a bead on why Gabby had been shadowing the priest.

Santorelli heard confessions on Tuesday and Thursday afternoons. Figured it was the perfect time to pay him a visit. The poor lug didn't get much traffic, but I still bet he'd be happy for a break from the usual litany. Most monkeys share a few things in common, chief among them impure thoughts and a tendency to spit on the golden rule. After ten years of listening to that twice a week he'd be more than ready for a little grace from yours truly. Sure, I was rusty, but so what? This guy was a believer. A real hard case. He'd eat it up with a spoon. And he seemed a solid sort. We'd be fast pals, him and me.

So when a congregant coughed and Santorelli glanced toward the narthex, I rode the slipstream of his gaze from the memory fragment into the flickering shadows near the votive candles. Then I skipped ahead from that blustery December morning to the present, a few days after flametop squiffed it. Felt like a few years at most, but that was a guess because the good father hadn't been giving thought to the calendar when Gabby lifted the memory fragment.

The church smelled like incense, candle wax, cheap wine, and old people. In prouder times, the joint had boasted an imitation pipe organ; its reverberations were etched in the atmosphere. The arches and stonework gave the place decent acoustics. (The monkeys had done their best, but compared to the Pleroma it still sounded like two cats fighting over last night's blue plate trout special.) Somebody had fixed the broken window. Sunlight cast prison-shadows from the grille over the replacement glass. Other windows depicted the stations of the cross; dust motes swirled in the cross fire between the Stripping of Garments and the Crucifixion. A fresco behind the altar depicted some joe who looked like the model for the Shroud of Turin as envisioned by a Hollywood focus group. The jasper was attended by a flock of little angels, none of them remotely correct. If the scene up there hadn't been so repressed, with everybody clothed and nobody grinding anything, I might have fingered the artist for a *penitente*.

It was quiet as a nun's boudoir. But for an old bat in the rear pew who mumbled while she fingered her beads, the place was deserted. So much the better. I lit a candle for flametop and dropped a few beans in the donation box. Then I crossed the nave heading for the confessionals. My footsteps shattered the reverent silence. The old bird gave me the evil eye until I doffed my hat. Some bluehairs know how to make a decent guy feel like a creep.

A pair of confessionals sat in the wings of the transept, a bit behind the altar, but in plain view of an electroplated crucifix. I figured this was accidentally on purpose. Maybe the theory was nothing got people's tongues wagging like the sight of a little torture. Silly monkeys. A bottle of hooch was the quickest way to a man's heart or a roundheel's sheets. That had been the case since the invention of hooch.

A mugg wearing a leather jacket over a shirt that might have been respectable a dozen Easters ago tiptoed from a confessional. He wore clunky boots, but he stepped more quietly than me. Just about jumped out of his skin when he saw me waiting. He gave me a quick, jerky nod as he passed. His eyes were a little red and a lot unfocused. He reminded me of whatshisname. Molly's brother.

He moved stiffly. The jacket rode a little too high on his shoulders. The breeze of his passing gave me a whiff of wet iron and fresh antiseptic. I wondered what fresh wounds lay beneath the leather.

"Hey, mac. The father in?"

He spun around. "What's that?"

"Santorelli. He on the clock or were you just sawing logs in there?"

"Oh." He looked around. "Nah. He stepped out. I think he went to the can. I dropped my wallet. Just went back to grab it." He held it up where I could see. It was one of those old black leather things with the chain; the clasp on the chain had slipped open. Then he jammed the thing back into his trousers, winced, and rubbed his shoulder.

"You don't say? What's the going rate for coveting an ox these days? If it's more than a double sawbuck I'll have to roll someone in the parking lot."

The *penitente* frowned. "What?"

"Been a while since I've been to confession." I pointed at the pocket with the dangling chain. "Guess times have changed. Didn't used to pay up front."

"I'm not paying nothing to nobody. The father gave me a card. For some guys I should talk to." Reflections of stained glass melted together in his wet eyes. Yeah. Definitely reminded me of whatshisface. Though he might have gotten piffled just to deal with the pain from his recent surgery. Maybe he wasn't a hard case.

But maybe he was. I nodded, like I'd been down those same mean streets. "Counselor?"

"Up yours," he said. "I'm not an alkie." Off he went, no longer caring about the noise. I didn't shush him. The bird with the rosary would cut the twerp down to size with one frown.

Santorelli still hadn't shown. I hate waiting. I lit a pill. Drawing deep, I tipped my head back, and jetted the smoke at a window depicting a newly beheaded Saint John. The poor lug looked surprised. Like he'd been minding his own business, making no trouble for nobody, when the axman came calling.

I gave him a sympathetic shrug. "You and me both, pal. You and me both."

I'd waited about half a cigarette and was looking for an ashtray when another old bag came squeaking into the transept on a pair of denim tennis shoes. She wore a thin gold necklace over her sweatshirt. Built like a cannonball but without the personality. You know the type.

"Sir!" she hissed. "This is a church!"

"Yeah, but don't worry. It's my day off."

"There is no *smoking* in a *church*."

"That's queer. Play your cards wrong and it's nothing but smoke and flame forever and ever amen. Ain't that so, sister?"

"You are smoking. There is *no smoking* in a church!" I had never heard anybody pack so much self-righteousness into a stage whisper.

"All right, all right. Don't flip your wig." If it had been handy, I would've doused my pill in the little birdbath full of water. But that was back by the front door. So I ground the butt under my heel. "Say, is Father Santorelli still in the can? It's worth some cabbage if you send somebody after him. I don't have all day."

She blinked. "The father," she said, "is performing the Sacrament of Reconciliation." It started as a hiss and ended just below a shriek. She had all the emotional range of a teakettle.

"If you say so, doll." By that point I figured she was about an inch from calling the bulls. That would have soured the father on me, and I wasn't up for using my shine on Santorelli if I could avoid it. Between METATRON and my pals the Cherubim, I was feeling about as spry as a geriatric transplant patient. So I made nice by picking the butt from the floor and sticking it in my pocket. She spared time for one last harrumph before squeaking off to wherever they store the busybodies. I pictured watery fruit punch in paper cups and a coffee urn so old it might have belonged to Pontius Pilate before he swore off the stuff because it made him edgy.

Still no sign of Santorelli. I wandered around until I found the biffy. He wasn't there. I checked the frails' side, too, just in case. No soap.

I returned to the confessional. The door where ratface had emerged hung slightly ajar. I bent my ear but came up empty. Not a whisper. So unless another sinner had slipped in while I was in the can, and Santorelli was doing his thing telepathically, he had to be waiting for another sad sack to come along and play the fiddle for him.

I looked at the door again, then to the window. Saint John gave me a little shrug of encouragement. Bad influence, that one.

I slipped into the confessional, latched the door behind me. "Forgive me, father, for I've never done this before. And I've been sinning since before Adam's first birthday." I took the silence as a prompt to continue. "But I'm in a jam and hoping you'll lend a guy a hand."

Then I put a sock in it, waiting for him to say something. He didn't. That's when I noticed the way something on the other side cast a heavy shadow on the screen between us. I listened to the silence again, and caught what I'd missed before: no heartbeat.

Oh, Bayliss. You're a fine lollipop.

I slipped out again, checked for stray eyes, then reentered the priest's side. My shoe sent a handful of beads skittering into the church. A few more rolled under the sole of my shoe, like pranksters poised to trip me. But I couldn't kick them away and I couldn't bend down to pick them up. It was cramped in there on account of the stiff.

Santorelli's face had gone the color of an early sunrise, and his peepers looked like they were trying to make a break for it. A line of small round indentations stippled his throat just above the dog collar. Somebody had tried to perforate his neck with a rosary. He looked more put out than Saint John's haberdasher.

I fished out a handkerchief and closed his eyes. Took a bit of digging before I found the lids. They'd beat a hasty retreat into his skull.

Chemistry and biology had taken him beyond anything I could do. Beyond anything any of us could do short of taking an ax to the Mantle of Ontological Consistency, but I figured METATRON had been riled up plenty already. Dead men don't dance, they don't answer questions, and they don't finger their killers. So says the MOC.

Somebody had Santorelli rubbed. Would this lead back to Gabriel and the Pleroma? Or was this sheer bad luck, a private little tiff purely among the monkeys? Maybe the padre had made it with that lonely housewife after all.

Yeah. Fat chance, Bayliss.

It isn't so easy, rifling a dead man's pockets. The father kept slumping forward on his little bench and I kept shoving him back, like a coed fending off a drunken suitor. Hard to do it quietly. I managed to search him, but it was a bust. He didn't have a single thin dime on him. All I found was a tiny plastic case, the kind the monkeys use for storing contact lenses and an earbud, but that was empty. His canals were clean, and I knew from my close acquaintance with his peepers that he wasn't wearing lenses. I wondered what secrets were stored in their cache.

There was nothing to tell me whether he'd made enemies here on Earth, and twice as much nothing to tell me why Gabriel had been keeping tabs on him.

Dead priest. Dead end.

I felt a powerful need for fresh air. I slipped out again and used the handkerchief to close the door gently behind me. Let somebody else find Santorelli. His groupies would start missing him long before the smell gave him away. I looked up at Saint John again and put a finger over my lips.

There was nobody to stop or question me on the way out. The church was deserted. The kid had legged it. So had the bird working the rosary. I cupped a hand in the birdbath and wet my gills with some holy water. Then I flicked a few droplets into the air; they became the vanguard of a steady rain within my Magisterium.

The downpour made streams of the gutters, rushing cataracts of the storm drains. By the time I made the door to my building, the brim of my hat released a little waterfall each time I tipped my head. I was soaked to the bone. Good. It fit my mood.

The hair in the door frame hadn't moved. Which meant that either nobody had come by to toss the place, or that somebody had and they were throwing punches well above my weight class. Hard to say. The boys with the flaming faces didn't have much of a track record for subtlety. I was too bushed to get twisted up over it.

I tossed my hat on a hook behind the door. My coat squelched when I draped it over a hanger. In the kitchen I poured myself a stiff one. Then I returned to the living room. The leaden sky outside the window turned the chessboard a mottled gray. I settled in the chair alongside the board and pulled out a pipe. Don't know how many times I packed and unpacked the bowl while frowning at the puzzle.

Gabriel's murder. The Jericho Trumpet. A dead priest. Plenary Indulgences. Molly. This board had too many pieces, and I didn't know the rules.

The phone rang again. Like it had been all day. By now flametop was probably doing figure eights. I sighed. Couldn't avoid her forever. But I also couldn't swallow the thought of dealing with her right then; it gave me indigestion.

I unplugged the phone and stuck it in the cupboard. Nuts to her. But while in the kitchen I took the opportunity to refill my glass. Somebody had emptied it when my back was turned. (Charming little neighborhood you've built for yourself, Bayliss.) My tonsils drowned under the taste of fire and oak. I lit a match on my thumbnail, and puffed until smoke glazed my sinuses with the aroma of cherrywood.

I moved a knight. Moved it back. I smoked and drank and stared at the chessboard while rivulets of holy water traced nonsense patterns on soot-smeared windowpanes.

8

JUST BE GLAD
IT WASN'T A TUBA

*T*he light hurt worse than getting sliced apart by any tram. And knowing what she'd done to Ria hurt even worse than the light. Molly tried to scream, but she was caught like a bug in amber too thick for the faintest exhalation. Yet she couldn't flail and couldn't struggle because there was nothing to push against. Something had erased Heaven and Earth, leaving in their place only pain.

Molly returned to consciousness through a vague awareness the pain had receded. But there was no sensation of the passage of time; time did not exist, neither did a reality against which to measure it. Something had erased the pain, leaving in its place . . . nothing. Her incorporeal awareness inhabited a formless void, a solipsistic universe. The Pleroma, if this *was* the Pleroma, had been rebooted.

She didn't come to her senses in comfortable, familiar surroundings. She couldn't. Her Magisterium had been deleted. Her sense of self, her identity, her connection to her earthly life, her imprint on the universe . . . gone.

This was a punishment. She'd broken the rules. Whatever those were.

What had Bayliss said about laying low? Maybe she should have listened. Maybe she would have, if he'd bothered to explain the rules to her.

Was Bayliss still around? Shit, did *Earth* still exist? Or had that been wiped out, too? And what about Martin? And—

Ria.

Oh, fucking hell. Ria.

The memory hit like a lightning bolt. Molly's mind crackled. If she'd had a body, the fiery intensity of her shame would have incinerated it.

But she had no mouth with which to scream, no Magisterium to echo with her sorrow. She had no eyes with which to weep, no pocket of reality where gravity could clutch at her tears. Molly's anguish could have no outlet until she built one.

That, she realized, was her true punishment.

*A*fter reestablishing the fuzziest approximation of matter and energy and objective persistence (as well as time, to provide a sense of "after") Molly recovered her consciousness in the bedroom of a hastily sketched semblance of her kaleidoscope Magisterium.

Tears of blood crusted her face. On her way to the ghostly bathroom, she tripped over the sensation of being sneezed upon by a sick horse. She scrubbed her face, her cheeks, her nose, her eyelids. Flakes of scabbed blood fell into her eyes when she washed her face. They scratched and pinched, then melted into long crimson smears along her eyeballs. She pinched the bridge of her nose until her tears ran pink. In the mirror she watched a thin red trickle leaking from the corner of her eye—

Blood streaming from Ria's nose, piss staining her pants . . .

A violent spasm wracked Molly. She hit all fours and vomited foggy moonlight. Where it splashed against the bathroom tiles, her puke jangled like fistfuls of silverware flung against a gong. It tasted like the stale air inside a bicycle inner tube, and carried chunks of a shattered bike pedal. Her stomach convulsed until her face ran wet with tears and snot, and streamers of foggy spittle dangled from her lips.

When the spasms subsided, she hauled herself to the edge of the bathtub and wept. These tears burned. But they couldn't cleanse the guilt that clung to Molly like a sheen of oil. She had lobotomized the woman she'd loved, and maybe even still loved. She'd turned one of the people whom she held most dear into a shuddering, mindless, pants-wetting vegetable. Ria would never listen to another Édith Piaf song, never again tell anybody that spinach tasted like ass, never haul another wheelbarrow of poisoned lake bed.

Molly couldn't even say she was sorry. Couldn't ask for forgiveness. So she wept until the tears ran dry.

Then, on top of everything else, she'd been assaulted *again*. It had felt as though it were directed at her, this perfect Platonic anger.

She had one option, and she hated herself for considering it. But she called Bayliss anyway.

It rang thirty-two times on the first attempt. She hung up, redialed, listened to another nineteen rings. Bayliss was ignoring her, or too drunk to answer, or dead. Maybe whatever he'd been running from, the thing that had him so terrified, had finally caught up to him. She didn't relish the thought of being stuck in eternity without a tour guide. Even one as obnoxious as Bayliss. Eternity was a big place.

He'd mentioned a Choir, by which he seemed to be referring to all the angels. It sounded like there were many. Maybe there was a way to encounter them, learn from them, foster a relationship. Maybe they weren't all as bad as Bayliss. But maybe they were worse. Maybe they all had invisible wings and faces of fire and voices appropriate for narrating the end of the world.

Molly put the notion aside. She was on her own.

And first things first: she refused to live in a diaphanous trash heap. It would take forever to re-create and reassimilate the fragments of memory debris, but then again, she had eternity. And the process would keep her rooted in her human life. She didn't want to lose that. No matter what, she didn't want to become something else. If she drifted away she might forget about Ria and Martin, might lose the connection, might lose the drive to help them and heal them. She had to cling to whatever part of herself was still human. Wasn't she still human at heart?

The bedroom floorboards lay under a synesthetic puddle, the soapy taste of wind rustling a field of lavender mixed with just a hint of the tingly smell of her father's stubble when he kissed her on the forehead. She stepped into the field, felt the sunlight on her skin, and remembered. She'd been riding in the car with Dad, back when they had lived in Alberta, and they were bumping down back roads the way he always liked to do, just to see what he could see. They came around a bend to suddenly face a vast field of purple. She had been sixteen and hadn't said anything to him all day because she was sixteen and hated everybody. She scowled when he parked and got out. But she followed, and when a breeze came swirling through the field, the world smelled of lavender soap. On the way home she told him she was a lesbian and fuck him if he didn't like it, and without any pause he said, "Okay, but can I still be your dad?" and that was that. Molly spent the rest of the ride home with her head on his shoulder, telling him about a girl at school. Mom did pretty well with the news, but not as good as Dad.

It had been a good day. Too valuable to lose. But that wasn't the memory in her head. The memory in her head was a barren hole where this slice of her teenage life had been. A torn blank canvas where one of the best memories of her father had been. She knew the memory because it was spread about her feet, the sights and smells and feelings of that day swirling together like the colors on an oily parking lot puddle just after a rainstorm.

Molly considered the implications. She searched the rest of her memory.

It was shredded.

Not her embryonic Magisterium, which had been filled with memory debris by the Cherubic assault, erased by an enraged light that shook the heavens, and then revived in a half-assed resurrection. But her memory, her actual in-her-mind memory, was a barren landscape pocked with craters and steaming fissures. She remembered recent stuff, stuff about Ria, because re-creating the Minneapolis apartment had been, in her own way, Molly's paean to something she wanted to keep alive. It still surrounded Molly, even if it was broken and twisted. But everything else—the debris, the disconnected memories shaken loose by the Cherubim—cluttered her Magisterium rather than her mind.

She fixated on the memory of the lavender field. Concentrating on that afternoon with her father, she turned and approached the bathroom. Her feet left puddles of memory on the floorboards. She closed the bathroom door, still concentrating on . . . something about Dad. Something about . . . a flower? Or maybe Mom? A vague sense of importance . . .

It came back to her when she returned to the bedroom and stood in the midst of the puddle, where the memory had melted and run together like the clocks in a Salvador Dalí painting. But it did not reside within her head. Those motherfuckers had stolen the day she came out to her father.

Well, those flaming assholes could eat shit. The Cherubim weren't going to ruin this. Molly wouldn't let them.

She imagined herself as an unfinished jigsaw puzzle. Just a border and a few small patches, the rest of the picture a vast emptiness. This memory was one piece of herself. And when she stood inside the memory, relived it, she knew exactly where it went. It slotted into place. She recovered a piece of her sixteenth year. Another memory was stuck to it, like puzzle pieces jammed together when the box is shaken too hard. She pulled it apart, and put the brown mucus of a wet horse sneeze where it belonged with her sixth-grade memories. Another fragment of herself recovered.

Some recollections were harder than others. Harder to endure, to experience, to place. Some things she didn't want to remember, like the time she'd found Martin lying on the floor of his apartment with a needle in his arm, his breath so shallow and pulse so thready she thought for certain he was dead. But she kept them all. They were her; she was the sum of this debris.

She was sweating and panting by the time she'd cleared the bedroom and bathroom. But with the exception of Bayliss's cigarette stain on the floorboard, they were back to the way they were meant to be.

Things got easier as she filled more of the missing gaps in herself. She cleared out the jumble of concepts where the stairwell had been, and worked her way through the disaster zone downstairs. Along the way she shored up the Magisterium itself, filled the gauzy ghostly patches with lath and loss, plaster and pride.

Molly took a break after she found the memory of eating Italian ice crammed under the sofa cushions. It had been a hot autumn day, but the artificial-pomegranate-flavored ice numbed her tongue while the glass-bottomed tour boat hovered above the ruins of Venice. She recognized the sticky sensation of sugar syrup dripping down her fingers while the ice melted. The memory ice tasted only faintly of real fruit. But it soothed her and carried no associations with Ria. She let the rocking of the boat relax her.

She was just on the verge of dozing off when the memory shifted. A faint hollow tapping overlaid the murmur of the other tourists and the whirr of the solar boat engine. *Tickety-tick*, it went. *Click-click-clickety-click.* Like a fingernail flicked against a windowpane. When she opened her eyes, the memory resumed as normal, with tourists taking photos of the ruins through the glass hull. Nobody noticed the shadow hovering beneath the boat like a loitering merman. She frowned.

"Hey, flametop," said a voice like somebody gargling. "You gonna wake up any time soon?"

One glass pane along the boat's keel had become a window into a shabby apartment building. Bayliss sat in the shadows beside a chessboard, pipe in one hand. He rapped the pipe stem against the pane again.

Molly sighed. She filed the Venice memory in its proper place before returning to her Magisterium. She made to open the door for Bayliss, but he whistled from behind her in the living room.

"Ain't you a stubborn one. I'd figured these digs for a lost cause once the loogans had their way with it. And that was before . . . Well, I guess you had to start over like the rest of us. But there's more to you than attitude and looks. Right?"

Molly wheeled on him. "Where the hell have you—"

Bruises mottled his face. His left eye was black, the other swollen halfway shut. "Jesus. What happened to you?"

"What, these love taps?" He gestured at his face with the pipe. "Mementoes from a couple admirers. I found your guys." He shrugged. "We had a chat."

"Damn." She sat on the sofa armrest. The Cherubim had really worked him over. He looked like he'd lost a bar brawl with a prizefighter. Bayliss could be annoying, but holy shit—he'd gone and confronted those bastards on her behalf. He hadn't needed to do that. *Huh.*

"Do you want some ice or something?" She gestured, awkwardly, toward where the kitchen should have been. It wouldn't be that hard to put an ice maker in the fridge. "Your face is really puffy."

"Nah. It's jake. Flo's got a raw T-bone set aside for me." He took a chair.

"Okay. Well. Thanks for finding those sons of bitches." Bayliss brushed off the thanks with an irritated wave of the pipe. She asked, "I don't suppose they told you what they wanted with me?"

"Not in so many words. But yeah, I got the headlines."

He lit a match on his thumbnail. He tried to light his pipe, but

Molly patched the memory of a ceiling fan into her Magisterium. It blew out his match. His eyes followed the wisps of smoke from the extinguished match up to where the fan shredded them into invisible streamers of soot. His eyes, those old, old eyes, narrowed.

"Cute dido. Guess you're a real smooth operator, aren't you."

"I'm getting a lot of practice trying to put this place back together." Thinking back to the searing light that burned away her Magisterium, she said, "And speaking of which, what the shit was with the light and that voice—"

"Yeah, let's not drop that nickel just yet. I don't want to talk about METATRON. Let's talk about you." Bayliss stowed the matches back inside his coat. "I think you're being modest."

Molly blinked, shook her head. His body language and tone of voice belied the gentle words. She reminded herself that he'd just had the crap beaten out of him, and on her behalf. He was entitled to some irritation. On the other hand, it wasn't difficult to glimpse the accusation peeking through the curtain of his words.

"Did you go off your meds or something? You're acting very weird. I mean, even weirder than normal."

"Why are you beefing me, lady? You're the one had me down for a pigeon."

"I wish just once you would talk like a normal person."

"Oh, come on. Drop the veil, doll. You know what I'm getting at."

"I haven't yet known what you were getting at. Not ever."

"Hey, I know I got a front-row seat to the highlight reel, but remind me. Your parents, they religious types? Take you to church a lot when you were a kid?"

And now he was changing the subject. Maybe the beating had given him brain damage. Did he have a brain? Or even a body, for that matter? "Not much. What's this about?"

Bayliss shrugged. "Just wondering if you happen to know a Father Santorelli, up Chicago-way."

"I've never been to Chicago."

"No kidding? Huh."

"Seriously, Bayliss. Just out with it."

"Well, see, there's one thing I just can't figure. Could've sworn I got a real good look at your life when you were under that train. Meaning somebody went to a lot of effort kicking leaves over the embarrassing bits."

He shook out a cigarette, lit it. Molly cranked up the speed on the ceiling fan. Bayliss drew deep; the tip of his cigarette flared nova bright. Tendrils of smoke snaked up, coiled around the fan blades, wrenched them still. The fan motor died with a screech and clank. The smells of ozone, hot metal, and oil filled the room. Jerk.

"Oh, for Chrissakes," she said. "What did I do wrong now?"

The cherry on his cigarette flared brighter and burned all the way down the length of the paper, leaving a wispy ash trail in the wake of one impossibly long inhalation. Smoke leaked from his nose, eyes, pores. It wreathed his head like a halo.

"Okay, I get it. What a gag!" He laughed. "Yep. There's egg all over old Bayliss's face, no fooling. But it's run its course." He got serious again. "Who are you?"

"Molly Pruett. Not that you care, because you never call me by name."

"I didn't ask your name. I asked who you are," said Bayliss. "Because I think you're the kind of bird who isn't what she seems. And I'm tired of always playing the sap."

And then he launched into a diatribe featuring Gabriel's Magisterium, the Cherubim (did they really use brass knuckles?), a dead priest, Plenary Indulgences (whatever those were), and something about a trumpet. And, according to Bayliss, it was all connected directly to Molly via the murdered angel.

She didn't believe him. So he showed her the memory fragment and then *there she was, in the old house with the orange tree, crouched outside her parents' bedroom, straining to make out the whispers—*

Whoa.

"Hey, just hold on. This is crazy."

But he'd built up momentum and wasn't yet finished. "But *then,* on top of the rest, just as things were getting interesting with the Cherubim, somebody decided to go ahead and rouse METATRON." He paused to light another cigarette. The smoke was so thick that the back of her throat tasted like the ceiling of a cheap bar. She stopped breathing. "But hey, we all remember our first time. So tell me, Molly Pruett. Where were you when the Voice of God decided to practice the do-re-mis?"

Voice of God? Is that what that was? Well, crap.

She told him about Ria. It took a force of will not to sick up again, but damned if she'd show Bayliss the tiniest sniffle. He cradled his head in his hands while she recounted the events in Minneapolis. Then he sighed.

"So you KO'd the chippie. What happened next?"

"Don't you dare call her that." Molly drew a shuddery breath. "Her name was Ria. And I tried to save her. You'd said something about angels and time, so I tried to nudge it backward a couple of minutes. It was working, too, but then the light came."

He smoked the entire cigarette down to wisps of vapor before speaking again. "You tried to violate causality. You tried to jackhammer through the bedrock of the Mantle of Ontological Consistency. And unlike me, METATRON doesn't have a sense of humor about these things." More smoke fumed from his collar. "That's what METATRON does. It patrols the MOC for juvenile delinquents like you." His fingernails rapped a fast tattoo on the armrest of his chair. "I can't help but wonder how a freshly hatched cluck like you could possibly have the juice to goose METATRON."

Molly shook her head. "I loved her," she said. Her voice broke. "I loved Ria so much."

No afterlife, no reunions . . .

"Tough break, kid. But enough with the sad sack. Because for the record? We *all* felt it. The Voice of God doesn't do private concerts. So thanks to you, Thrones and Virtues and Dominions all over the Pleroma are rebuilding their Magisteria for the first time in eons. It's like Habitat for Divinity out there."

Shit. She'd thought it was just her. But . . . Somewhere deep in her gut, a cold watery slosh caused her to clench up. What if the Cherubim came back? Were there worse angels than those two? How many enemies had she made?

Bayliss said, "What part of 'don't rock the boat' is so difficult for you to understand? Don't you see? They'll be watching us now. It's curtains for both of us if they lose their patience."

Fear and nausea dampened her forehead with cool sweat. It trickled from her armpits, too. "Who?"

"Everybody. Every Chorus in the Choir. And as sure as I know how to pick the ponies, I know they'll be gunning for that Trumpet. And where do you think they'll start?" He pointed at her chest. "They've got a bone to pick, angel."

Molly lay on the floor. Ripples of rancid-tasting candlelight spread across the floor, flushing dust bunnies and family Thanksgivings from dark corners. She pressed one hand to her stomach, the other to her forehead. "That's the second time you've mentioned something about a trumpet."

"Not just any trumpet. Holy smokes, don't you ever listen? The Jericho Trumpet. Not some tarnished, dented lowbrow swag from the high school marching band."

"Whatever. Why do these jackholes think I have it?"

"Because Gabriel was its appointed guardian. And you showed up just after he punched out. You're the understudy. So of course they assume you've nabbed it. But they don't know you like I do. Once they come to realize you're just some screwy dame, they'll lay off. Eventually."

"Why would I even want some piece of shit horn anyway? I'd never heard of it until you mentioned it. Plus I couldn't play the thing if I wanted to."

"The Jericho Trumpet isn't something for tooting. It's the tuning fork for Creation. It's the note the lead violin plays right before the symphony starts. But it's also a tool of righteous fury. You think it's unpleasant when METATRON sings *a cappella*? Wait'll you hear that voice coming through the Trumpet. Just make sure I'm on the other side of the observable universe when that happens."

"So why are they looking for it? If the other angels can already do just about anything they want, subject to the MOC, what use is it to them?"

"Who said anything about using it? Jickity, even Gabriel treated that thing with kid gloves. Don't know that he ever dared touch it to his lips. Nor his beak, nor either of his muzzles, for that matter."

Molly couldn't begin to picture what Bayliss meant by that. She didn't want to. "So . . ."

"Look. Remember that time just after you got your learner's permit, and you took your mom's car out for a spin and dinged up the paint? Remember how that went when she got home?".

"Keep out of my memories."

He plucked a spiky fragment from between the cushions. "Then keep your memories out of my chair." He flicked it at her, continuing, "In Gabby's absence, we all share the responsibility of safeguarding the Trumpet. So if Mom and Dad come home to find it missing . . . On the other mitt, whoever turns it in scores a few points with METATRON. I can think of worse things than being owed a favor. Folks around here know a rare opportunity when they see one."

"I can't believe this is happening," said Molly.

"I can't believe you've cooked up such a jam," said Bayliss. "And so quickly."

This was insane. Somehow, the moment he'd shoved her under the tram was just the beginning of her troubles. He wouldn't come out and say it, but Molly could tell Bayliss was worried sick. Things were spiraling out of control. Cosmically out of control. Somebody killed Gabriel—and what the hell did that even mean?—and then stole his shit, all of which had nothing to do with her until Bayliss dragged her into the middle of it. And then he couldn't even be bothered to explain things to her properly. So when she did try to do something, it just made things worse. She'd destroyed Ria because of Bayliss. More disgusting still was the fact this had been the second time she turned to him for help. That was two times too many.

In their final argument, Ria had said she was ending the relationship because she needed to be with somebody more her equal. More independent. Somebody who wasn't so damned deferential. Molly always let Ria call the shots, not knowing how it undermined their relationship until it was too late.

Very well. She'd take charge. And Bayliss could go fuck himself if he didn't like it.

She needed to start moving. She needed to put mass on the problem, as Martin liked to say. And she needed to make sure that Trumpet turned up before they came for her again.

She'd find it with or without Bayliss's help.

Molly climbed to her feet. "We need to get to work."

"Look," said Bayliss. "We're sitting on dynamite here. A smart little dish would skip out until things cool—"

"Give me the list of Plenary Indulgence recipients."

Bayliss blinked. "Come again?"

"The other people Gabriel was watching. If Father Santorelli was worked up over the Indulgences, odds are they were recipients. Give me the list. I'll check them out. And maybe I can figure out why he connected me to that bunch."

Bayliss pulled out another cigarette. He tapped it on the armrest, spun it around his fingers, stuck it behind his ear. He sounded bemused. "Huh. Never thought of that."

"Isn't it kind of obvious?" she asked.

"It is possible that on rare occasions somebody might think of something I didn't. Try not to looked so shocked, you're letting the flies in. But I'm not sure it's a good idea for you to be bracing our leads. We can't afford it if they all pop a vein in the brain."

Molly ground her teeth, thinking of Ria. She said, "I gather I'm not very popular right now. And don't pretend you're not pissing yourself for fear it'll rub off on you. It makes the most sense for me to follow the leads on Earth while you keep an eye on things in the Pleroma."

He stared at her. She had to turn away from the look in his eyes.

"Maybe you're not so screwy after all, angel. This could work. You head on down to the old stomping grounds and try to figure out what had Gabby and Santorelli so keen to shadow the mooks on this list. I'll stick around up here and try to put a blanket on it."

He fished out his wallet and produced a diaphanous tissue of shimmering memories. It was folded like an origami crane. The bird became a flock when he tossed it at her. The memories unfolded, settling over her arms and shoulders like hungry sparrows.

"We're in this together, me and you. Yeah, I'm not thrilled about it, either. But this'll go better if we back each other instead of turning over at the first sign of trouble."

Molly rolled her eyes. "Fine."

"Gosh, that's reassuring. This partnership will be one for the record books, I can tell already. But promise you'll go easy. You still need practice."

"Then it's past time I had some. I'll find a way to interact without hurting them." The last words lodged in her throat and came out as a whisper.

And once I figure out how to do that, I can talk to Martin. And eventually, I'll figure out how to heal Ria. I'll heal them both, or I'll tear the whole goddamned system down in the attempt.

THE GOOD OLD DAYS

*T*here is a place on the California coast, near the ruins of the redwood groves, where the tireless surf batters storm-sculpted cliffs and the churning sea lobs the scents of salt and wrack atop a long sloping lawn fringed with tropical shrubs and flowering oleander. Here the wind and sea mask the thrum of solar precipitators and desalinators watering the grass. The reconditioned breeze wafts across a humble emerald expanse suitable for quiet, intimate pursuits like a game of croquet or landing a suborbital shuttle. It's the kind of green that no longer happens naturally at these latitudes. The slope funnels the wind to where the lower grounds abut a wedding-cake tumble of arches and stucco terraces. From there, the wind sighs through marble balustrades to ruffle feathers in a topiary garden whose every subject is long extinct. A dozen walking paths lead from the garden to a shack with two hundred feet of colonnaded verandah fronting the sea. At the right time of year, the barks and coughs of rutting sea lions used to punctuate the susurration of the ocean breeze through lavender jacaranda blossoms. That came to an end after the great plankton die-off, when the marine food chain collapsed. It's never cool, never a refreshing breeze, no matter the season, for the wind here takes its heat from the sea and the monkeys changed the sea long ago. The violent ocean is warmer than it used to be, ever since the North Pacific Current stopped funneling sub-Arctic water down the coast. (The monkeys really outdid themselves when they gummed up the thermohaline conveyor. But nowadays you can surf the California coast without wearing a wet suit. That has to count for something.) But by the time the wind reaches the house, the gardens have erased any suggestion of a dying world and left just a hint of tropical perfumery.

It's a real flossy place. I went there on a mission of destruction.

There are essentially two ways to eradicate a memory fragment. Now, an amateur would leg it for the nearest singularity after scouring the local X-ray binaries for a suitable black hole. They'd slip inside the event horizon with the offending memory tucked into a shoe. To an outsider it would look harmless, guileless, just an innocent stroll through pretzel space-time. But if that shoe just happened to come untied, and if that fragment just happened to slip loose while the laces were tightened . . . Well, it wouldn't be anybody's fault if that memory went swirling into the churning Planckian foam.

But a play like that is all flash, no style. Trust a nickel grabber to solve an epistemological problem through the radical application of astrophysics. It's extreme, like renormalizing the fine-structure constant to swat a fly.

But information can't be destroyed. You know how it is—unitary Hamiltonians and all that noise. (Thus says the Mantle of Ontological Consistency. Another consequence of making life possible.) The monkey wise-heads like to flap their gums about information paradoxes, but there's nothing confusing about it once you peek under the horizon to see how it all works under the hood. Leave it to the monkeys to overcomplicate something as straightforward as quantum gravity. Anyway, long story short, toss an offending memory down the well and all your dirty laundry will come back out etched in holographic perturbations of the event horizon surface area and whispered in the slow hiss of Hawking radiation.

So I do it differently. Me? I head for an old-folks' home. Because maybe you can't destroy information, but you can damn sure louse it up. Why ruin my good clothes crawling under a barbed-wire fence when I could just as easily toss that dingus into the churning maw of dementia? Far easier to let it dissipate in the static of psychic entropy, and the end result is the same.

This errand, I could have run anywhere. But given the freedom I chose to avoid the low-down places. Too depressing, and already my plate was piled high with cares aplenty. For once, Molly and I were working the same side of the street. Somebody had to brace the PI recipients, and somebody had to hang out his ear in the Pleroma. We'd agreed to work as partners, but I was lying to myself. Flametop was in deep over her head, while I wasn't entirely new to this game. So I figured that made her my client.

And protecting my client meant throwing a blanket over her connection to Gabriel. Which meant scuttling the memory fragment he'd locked in his Magisterial hidey-hole.

This wasn't the kind of place where any old bo could come wandering up on foot with a bindle over his shoulder. This place catered to the carriage trade. Anybody flush enough to dump their honored elders in this dive would arrive in style. Hydrogen fuel cells, maybe solar, maybe even simulated autonomy and a preprogrammed route to obviate the need for a driver. True GPS hadn't been an option since the carnage in orbit, but true wealth meant making it look like you still lived in your own personal Golden Age.

Nuts to all that. I scraped my face, changed my shirt, pinned on a new collar, then called a taxi from an ocean-side vacation burg a few miles down the coast. Sitting on a bench overlooking the sterile sea, I tried to ignore the death-stench of plankton while reshaping my face to remove evidence of my spat with the Cherubim. When you're flush you don't fight your own battles; you hire some lug to carry the shiners for you.

That left just enough time for me to make the rounds of the tonier souvenir places across the street until I found one bent enough to do a little bartering. Took a bit of back and forth, and a mild application of glamour, but in the end we agreed that one silver feather was worth everything in the register and the safe—eight or nine yards. When the hackie arrived, I had him stop off at a bank, where I changed most of it for larger bills. I tucked wads of folded C-notes in my shoes.

You should try it some time. It's like walking on air.

The approach to the home is a horseshoe drive paved in mosaic tiles with an attention to detail not seen since Herculaneum. An orderly taking a smoke break on the patio gave us a dead pan as we rolled up. His pal came down the steps to open the door for me, looking all the while like he'd bit into a lemon. I peeled off a few bills so the hackie would wait, and a few more so the orderlies would turn a blind eye to the heap leaking oil on the drive. On this errand, the name of the game was low profile. Could've used the old shine to cut a few corners here and there, but that ran the risk of leaving a trail of droolers, just as Molly had done to her squeeze. Somebody might notice if half the staff traded places with their patients. So I played it cool. It was important this visit ruffled no feathers, drew no attention to me and flametop. That meant playing by monkey rules and using old-fashioned apple polish to get inside. To anybody who took an interest in my visit, I was just another threadbare chiseler coming to brace grandma. Not a visitor from the Pleroma.

The bird at the front desk gave me a visitor's badge. I signed the register "Philo Vance."

After that I was free to take my leisure so long as I scrammed by dinnertime. On the inside, the joint was half retirement home and half booby hatch. It smelled of sepia-toned memories and chalky purgatives. Most of the residents were already a touch batty or they wouldn't have been dumped here in the first place. My contribution would disappear in the noise. There was a chance the overlay wouldn't take smoothly, leading to some hiccups while the modified psyche sorted itself out. But who'd notice one more seizure, one more nonsense reminiscence? If my mark started to squawk about eavesdropping on his parents, learning a blue word or two while they rolled in the hay, anyone bending an ear would chalk it up to dementia or nostalgia. Two words for the same thing.

I wandered through a walnut-paneled solarium, past desultory games of checkers and chess, an unfinished jigsaw puzzle of the Eiffel Tower, withered husks of human beings reading the paper or listening to late Twentieth Century music on bulky earbuds. The loudest voices came from the media room across the corridor, where a pair of betties watched a film so old it hadn't been converted from 2-D. I drew some glances as I made the rounds, seeking a good mark; some of the residents still had enough spark behind the eyes to make me glad for the glare of sunlight on parquetry and wood polish, on the off chance anybody might have noticed my *heiligenschein*. That's always a risk when monkeys have only frayed mooring lines tying them to the port of here-and-now.

There was better hunting to be had on the verandah. Most of the folks out here sat alone, watching the gardens and the sea. The moist breeze hit me in the face like an overzealous saleslady at a department store perfume counter. I ambled to where a bald man with a waxed mustache dozed in a wheelchair with a tartan blanket over his lap. If not for the Ramones concert t-shirt and the ink on his arms, he might have been a transplant from a retirement home circa 1955. I took a seat in a rattan chair at his elbow and reached for my wallet.

"Hiya, Pop," I whispered.

One eye snapped open. It sized me up before retreating under a pink fleshy eyelid.

"You're not a relative," he mumbled.

"You're not dozing," I said.

"I'm contemplating a long life," he said. "You're not in it."

"You gonna rat me out?"

"To whom?" The papery skin on his hands pulled taut when he gestured at a female orderly pushing a wheelchair along a gravel causeway from the topiaries. She wore white like the other staff, but culottes instead of slacks, and black stockings under the culottes. "She makes extra cash with special sponge baths. Needs the money because her boyfriend gave her the clap." Another gesture, this time at a muscular orderly lifting a snoring lady from a squeaking wooden swing. "He keeps a list of our valuables. Hasn't used it yet, but he's patient. He doesn't have a buyer."

"I know a place down the road that might be suitable. Maybe he and I can make a deal."

"You're not helping your case."

"Your friends in white know how much you eavesdrop?"

His fingers trembled as though he were flicking away a housefly. He punctuated it with a harrumph that might have been a snort or a snore. "They're typical of the rest. Animals. Spoiled and decadent babes."

"Everyone in this joint strikes me that way."

Again the eye snapped open. It glistened under a mild case of conjunctivitis. He made eye contact, then flinched away. Whatever he saw there, he recovered well. "Feh," he said from the corner of his mouth. "You're too young to remember a time before it all went to shit, before every night looked like the Fourth of July."

I crossed myself. "On Earth as it is in Heaven."

He frowned at that. But the beefy orderly lumbered over before he could respond. "Ready to go inside, Mr. Kivinen?"

"I'll stay a while." Another flick of the papery hands. "This is my great-nephew, Dakota. A dull and feckless lad, but he'll wheel me inside when I'm ready."

The ox gave me a curt nod and went inside. He looked relieved.

"He doesn't seem too torn up about it."

"He's hoping you'll change my diaper, too." Silence fell over our conversation like a broken kite. Kivinen chuckled. "Relax. I can't walk but I can still crap like a man."

I liked him. But I like my own skin even more. And this darb had more going on behind the eyes than most monkeys in their prime. He was no use to me. That hotcha nurse and her cohort were likely to notice if wise old Kivinen suddenly started talking about himself as though he were a six-year-old girl. Which wouldn't do my client any favors.

"You didn't rat me out," I said.

"You're too interesting to toss aside just yet."

"Maybe so, but I still have to make my rounds."

"What's your game? Talking rich, lonely, addle-brained retirees into signing over their power of attorney?"

"Nah. I'm not on the market for a butter-and-egg man. I'm here to share some memories."

"I've had a long life. You can have some of mine."

"You wouldn't like what I'm selling." I stood. "Thanks, Kivinen. It's been swell."

He said, "Wheel me inside. Spare me the indignity of eating my words before that lumbering brute, and I'll help you find what you need." I knew a square deal when I heard one. Kivinen was the real cream.

"I'm looking for somebody on the way out. A real screwball."

A sea breeze redolent of dead plankton and flowering oleander tickled my nape while I pushed his chair toward the nearest pair of French doors. But he nixed the solarium. We passed two more doors along that long verandah, his wheels beating a monotonous tattoo against the planks, until he brought me to a narrower door. Took a bit of elbow grease to nudge his wheelchair over the threshold without sending him for a tumble. The room on the other side greeted us with tall oak bookcases, deep leather armchairs flanked by Tiffany lamps, and funereal silence. A man with mottled gray skin and a bad toupee dozed over an antique reader displaying the *Financial Times*. His turkey wattle quivered in time to his snores. Give this room a butler and hang a few plaques on the walls, and it might have been a London society club two centuries past.

Kivinen twisted a lip at the snoozer. "Christ," he said. "How I despise that ignoramus."

"He trouble for you?"

"Styles himself a Nikkei raider. But he made his fortune the old-fashioned way. He won the lottery."

"It's better to be lucky than good," I said.

"His luck left him long ago. They keep him inside because he gets worked up every time he sees a flash of space junk. He's lucid from time to time, but mostly he seems to think we're living thirty years in the past."

Sounded perfect. Already on the way out, but some good would come of his decline. He'd be doing flametop a solid, even if he never realized it.

"That's swell. He'll do."

"Will it hurt?"

"Thought you hated him."

"I do," Kivinen said. "But I'd always hoped it would be me to end him."

What can I say. I liked the old guy.

"I'm a student of human nature," I said, truthfully, "and want to share a few experiences. That's all. I won't lay a finger and I won't disturb one hair."

Kivinen indicated his assent with another flick of those papery hands. "That's a shame," he said. He wheeled himself away without another word. Guess he wasn't the sentimental type. That suited me. I'm not a fan of the long good-bye.

I pulled a chair next to the snoozer, settled in, and pulled out my wallet again. "Hiya, Pop."

The geezer jerked awake. He blinked a few times, as though the world were something uncomfortable caught in the corner of his eye. Drool glistened at the corner of his mouth; he smeared it along the back of his hand. Then he saw me. The eye contact lasted less than a moment, but I got what I needed.

"You were telling me about the fireworks," I said, "before you drifted off."

"I wasn't asleep," he said in a voice stronger than wet tissue paper. A musky smell, and a tightness around his flat eyes, told me he was a little worried. He had no idea who I was, but didn't want to admit it to himself for fear it meant he was losing his marbles. He forged ahead with the world's most unconvincing lie. "I was waiting for you to stop interrupting."

"I'm sorry. It won't happen again."

What is it with old guys like him and Kivinen? Do they spend half the day sitting before the mirror in search of the perfect *harrumph*?

"We were at a concert, Jennifer and me, on the night the sky changed. The night the war started. She didn't want to go; we'd had a contractor to the house—this was in the days before you could unroll a couple strips of solar panels on your roof and call it done—but I insisted, and we hadn't been to Red Rock since before the ice sheets had slid into the sea. You're too young to remember. It was all bad news back then, first when the seas rose and all those people had to flee, nothing on the news but vacant cities and drug-resistant malaria. And then it really went to hell . . ."

I have to admit, there was a lot of history locked away in that screwball head of his. It was jumbled but good, though, and picking out the valuable parts made as much sense as trying to pull the egg yolk from an omelet. But he'd built up a good head of steam and didn't need cues from me to forge ahead. I nodded while slipping out Molly's memory fragment.

"We got there at dusk," he droned, "and the first stars had come out. Venus, too, real bright, low in the sky where it was still purple and pink. Couldn't see much during the concert, though, and they had lights in the parking lot that washed out everything, so it wasn't until we were on the road, must have been well after midnight when Jennifer first saw it. You never hear it anymore but that was a common name back then, Jennifer. I went to school with three or four Jennifers. She said she'd just seen a shooting star, but I didn't because I had my eyes on the road. And then she saw another, and another, and then she begged me to pull over, so I did. This was back in the days when you had to drive your own car, no alternative to it like today. And so we stopped on the verge and got out and sure enough the sky was criss-crossed with little streaks of silver and red and tiny flashes of light like sunset at Disneyworld but from a thousand miles away, that's what she said it looked like, and she never found out she was more or less right, but it was real fireworks and real rockets, not just for show. Never did find out who shot first—"

How could they? METATRON speaks to mortal men not as a thunder to make them quiver and quail, but as a whisper that turns their hearts.

"—but I got in the car to turn on the radio and that's how the air-bags saved my life when that goddamned drunk came screaming around the corner; maybe he was watching the sky, too, I don't know, all I know is he didn't have his lights on and couldn't see Jennifer standing all agog . . ."

I would have sighed, but his voice cracked into plenty of pieces for the both of us. I thought about Gabby again.

As a distraction, for the both of us, I asked, "How'd you meet her?" while smoothing the creases from the secret memory I'd pinched from Gabriel's Magisterium. And soon he was droning on about high school and a broken smartphone. That was a surprise; he seemed old enough to launch into a story about inkwells and pigtails.

They say it's all in the wrist. Sometimes it's even true. A little flick—I channeled Kivinen in that—and the gossamer shimmer of a memory fragment settled over the old man's shoulders like a cowl. He twitched, brushed away a phantom cobweb, and then the middle of his soliloquy was all about how his beloved Jennifer expanded her vocabulary when she was a little girl by crouching beside her parents' bedroom door. He'd appropriated Molly's memory into the recollec-tions of his dead wife.

I stood. "I'm sorry for your loss. She sounds like quite a gal, your Jennifer."

His face folded into a scowl. "Who's Jennifer?"

I pretended to cough, covering my mouth before the smile gave the game away. Philo Vance signed out less than an hour after he'd arrived.

Not a bad afternoon's work. Entropy was running its course, destroying the connection between Gabriel and flametop, and I had a few C-notes lifting my fallen arches. I paused on a bench in the foyer to fish out more small bills; seemed a good idea to apply a parting coat of polish to the orderlies, and to keep the hackie pliant. No, not a bad afternoon's work at all. I made certain to congratulate myself on that front.

But pride goeth before the fall.

The addle-brained sad sack and his sob story about celestial light shows got me thinking about Gabby again. I'd been doing my best *not* to think about him because it was a slippery slope. To be fair, though, and somewhat to flametop's credit, she was a double handful of distractions. If not exactly the kind of distraction I'd prefer from a dish like her.

But now Gabby was at the forefront of my mind as I headed for the cab. I had to leave the same way I came, else somebody paying attention might notice old Philo arrived but never departed.

Poor Gabriel. He'd become mixed up with something terrible. But what? Or whom? He'd run afoul of some serious torpedoes, if they could rub one of the Seraphim. And just how did they manage that? This, more than anything else, was the frightening part.

Such were my thoughts as I emerged from the home with its jacaranda blossoms and ocean-view verandah, this place where the pony set went when the tug of entropy became too strong to ignore. Out I stepped, into the scents of oleander and sea salt, into the crash of surf and the whisper of my shoes over mosaic tiles, while the question of a murdered angel made a Möbius pretzel of my thoughts.

Nothing struck me as amiss when I climbed into the hack. The overlay was so smooth, so seamless, that I didn't even notice when I slipped into the Pleroma. Only after the driver turned around did I realize I'd been played for a sap. His human pan had become the countenance of an ox with starlight in its eyes; his human arms, a pair of snapping vipers; his doughy human body, a wheel of ice covered inside and out with eyes of quicksilver.

A Throne. The bulls had found me.

MINUET FOR TWO ANGELS

*T*he Plenary Indulgence recipients lived in and around Chicago. That made sense, after all, because so did the priest. Molly had never been to Chicago, and had only heard second- and third-hand of the city nestled alongside Lake Michigan, its mixture of grandeur and decay. But she wondered, after a bit of reflection, if she needed to know a place to find it. Even Bayliss had managed to overlay his Magisterium on an earthly laneway back in Melbourne, and *he* was so weak that he actually paid for Martin's taxi rather than whisking him back to his hotel. And damned if she'd be outdone by him. So what was there to stop her from deciding reality included a passage to Chicago at the back of her coat closet?

Nothing. Not a damn thing. Except the fear of getting her ass kicked by METATRON again. That shit hurt.

It was one thing to flex her angelic juju in the privacy of her own apartment. Quite another to do it on Earth. Last time she tried it, she destroyed Ria, incurred the wrath of the Voice of God, and, apparently, made enemies of all the other angels in Bayliss's Choir. It made a woman skittish about trying again. On the other hand, how much worse could it get?

So she pushed aside the woolen peacoat with epaulets (it still had one of Ria's hairs on the shoulder), dodged a falling mop, and emerged from the shadow of an elevated train. A relentless wind dusted her skin with ash lofted from distant dead towers; the skyline leered at her like a mouthful of broken teeth. The air carried the scent of poisoned lake bed, and the ground rippled in time to the moods of the lake. It was faint, the trembling, but persistent beneath the electric thrum of traffic and wistful creaking of deconstructed skyscrapers.

The gusts teased her hair into disarray. Curls fluttered across her mouth, her eyes. Molly imagined her pocket contained a velvet ribbon, and it did. While tying her hair back she realized she hadn't consciously chosen her apparel, but it had changed again when she emerged on Earth. Now she wore a satin vest over a high-collared shirt and jeans with thin pinstripes. For some reason she was barefoot. It took a moment's focused concentration to change that.

A river of pedestrians flowed past her sheltered spot on the leeward side of a rusted steel pillar for the El. People listening to music, laughing in one-sided conversations, frowning, lying to each other, running, eating vat-grown hot dogs and dripping relish on the sidewalk. Molly hadn't stood amongst so many people since before she'd died. (How long ago was that? How much time had passed on Earth? Did her phone still work? It couldn't have been too terribly long; she still recognized some of the fashions on the passersby. She even had the same pair of boots as the woman carrying out a very loud breakup with her boyfriend.) She was out of practice when it came to reading the flow of body language in a large herd. Walking in a crowd meant feeling the subtle signs and weathering constant negotiations of space and speed and impetus. But these people couldn't see her. What if she jostled somebody? Was she apt to leave a trail of brain-dead vegetables if she lost her concentration? How many lives would she destroy if she got this wrong?

But if she didn't try, if she didn't get to the bottom of this, the Cherubim would come for her again. Or something worse. Plus, if she wanted any hope of helping Ria and comforting Martin—witnessing her death must have pushed him over the edge; he was using again, she knew it—she needed practice. She needed to learn how to be a human being in a human space. She'd done it all her life, but now she didn't know where to begin.

Molly took a long, steadying breath while watching for an opening. It came in the form of a fat businesswoman tottering on uneven heels. The current of pedestrians swirled around the slow-moving obstacle like water around a river stone to leave eddies of stillness in her wake. Molly stepped forward to slip into the crowd . . .

. . . And it parted before her.

Nobody flinched away from her; nobody lurched or dodged or

backpedaled. There were no ripples, no distortions in the flow of pedestrian traffic. Yet somehow there just happened to be a little bubble
of empty space right where she wanted to be and right when she
wanted to be there. Again and again and again, one footstep after another, the bubble paced her. If she weren't dead, she might have
thought she had a wicked case of body odor. But no matter how she
moved, or where, the natural currents of the crowd gave her exactly
the space she needed. A tourist lost her map to a gust of wind and just
happened to jump aside to catch it as Molly passed. A man heading
into a boutique to shop during his lunch break happened to hear
somebody calling his name, a friend across the street, and turned
around just before he would have stepped in front of Molly. A man
pushed his stroller behind an El pillar, overcome with a violent sneezing
fit. A woman walking a pair of Weimaraners came up short because
her dogs cowered when Molly's shadow passed over them.

Molly wondered if any of these people were aware of what they
were doing. She doubted it.

It was kind of cool. But on the other hand, and after just a few
blocks, it was isolating. These were her people, her species. She was
still one of them in her heart and in her head. But the entire world
tied itself into knots just to avoid her, as though she were a leper.
Jesus, even the *wind* got into the act.

And it wasn't just the pedestrian traffic. The traffic lights changed
the instant Molly reached a crosswalk. She lingered in the intersection, just to fuck with the world a little bit, and to see how far she
could push it. People flowed around her. She even turned against the
flow of traffic, but still her progress was as smooth as though the city
were deserted. So she leapt at random, a good yard to the right. But at
that very same moment a taxi along the curb threw its door open,
which forced a speeding bicycle messenger to lay his bike on the pavement to avoid it—and, thus, Molly.

"Crap!" she cried. Nobody heard her.

The bike skidded under the taxi. Its rider tumbled to a halt on the
street, moaning and cursing. He wore a helmet, but the street was
rough. His leg should have been bloody hamburger embedded with
the detritus of a fallen city. But when he rolled over, his leggings had
the characteristic sheen of a synthetic spiderweave. The biosilk had

protected him from worse injury, but he was still pretty banged up. His helmet fell apart when he rolled over. Blood from a deep gash along his jaw fell like a curtain to cover his neck, and the abrasions on his face were stippled with gravel. Molly ran to him.

"Holy shit, man. Do you need to see a doctor?"

He seemed wobbly. She put an arm around him to help him find his feet. But instead of answering, the messenger shivered at Molly's touch. Like Ria. Then the ancient El came clattering and screeching overhead, casting a long dark shadow over the scene, and all of a sudden Molly could remember how the fall had knocked the wind out of her and the thin crust of snow on the rails crunched as she turned over just in time to see the tram and feel the sharp hard metal crushing her, cutting her, killing—

Molly ran. Storefront windows shattered in her wake.

She didn't know where she was when she finally slowed to a walk, only that the sidewalks were less crowded here. Was that characteristic of the neighborhood, or the end of the lunch hour? Lake Michigan wasn't far; she could still smell hydrocarbons in the dead water. The people here were skinnier, their eyes downcast, their apparel no longer teetering on the razor edge of modern fashion. More ruin than grandeur in these city blocks ringing with distant police sirens.

She crossed a stone bridge over a channel or canal; she could taste the green dye of Saint Patrick's Days long past. When she laid her hand upon the chiseled balustrade, she had a vision of the men who'd quarried it and the shifting tectonic plates that created it back when evolution was just starting to experiment with a central nervous system. The granite was born after millennia of infrasound rattled the earth, the mating call of continents. It sounded like the death cries of the last whales, but a hundred million times slower. And she could hear those cries, too, their echoes indelibly etched in the water beneath her feet. Sorrow and fear and lonely terror . . . When she flinched, a jagged crack zigzagged across the roadbed.

What she really needed at that moment was a shot of tequila. But that was a pipe dream as long as she was a ghost to the world, unless she stooped to stealing booze. But that made her think of Bayliss. She might have returned to her apartment to conjure up a bottle, but she had work to do in Chicago. And the Pleroma wasn't safe for her. A fetid wind rose off the lake, gusting through the steel canyons of the city. Molly stuck her hands in her pockets and followed the canal toward the lake, her thoughts a jumble of crying whales and murdered priests.

She had stashed in her pocket the bundle of memories from the Plenary Indulgence recipients. Bayliss spoke of reading the memories and slipping inside them as though doing so were trivial, but Molly hadn't even figured out how to disentangle them from one another. What had been a flock of origami cranes in Bayliss's hands had become a knotted tangle of yarn in hers. When she tugged on one loose end of a random memory it stretched, snapped off, and evaporated. It left her fingers sticky with the residue of an angry text message sent in the wake of a lost child custody hearing. Untying the memories would take delicate work. She'd hoped that a solution would present itself as she brought them closer to Father Santorelli's church.

Her elbow nudged a lady wrapped in a turquoise serape. The woman glared at her. She stank of cigarette smoke and poisonous pride, prescription painkillers and warm wet iron.

"Sorry," Molly mumbled. She'd gone a few steps before she realized what had happened. *Eye contact.*

"Hey!" The woman didn't hear her. Molly spun, ran a few steps, caught her by the forearm. "Hey! Hi!"

The serape woman shook her head as though clearing it. This time her eyes didn't focus when she glanced in Molly's direction. She scowled, pinched the bridge of her nose, and sagged against a light pole. Molly released her before she caused another stroke. Her hand came away wet; blood trickled from artificial stigmata on the stranger's palms, tracing rivulets down to her elbows when she raised her arms. But they'd seen each other. Molly was certain of it.

The woman staggered away. A gust of wind flipped the hem of her shawl. A low-cut blouse revealed that the tops of her shoulder blades were matted with surgically sculpted gore and artificial pinfeathers. The seep of antiseptic blood had stippled the cream-colored top with crimson.

Molly started to follow, but was caught short by a faint vibration in her vest pocket. She reached inside to massage the jumble of stolen memories. One twined itself about her thumb. A fragment of an awkward office Christmas party tugged at her like a magnet. It relaxed when she turned away from the canal but squeezed, almost painfully tight, when she resumed her course toward Lake Michigan. Just like Bayliss and the silver feather. Her mind wandered while she followed the tugs of memory in her pocket.

The cyclist and the taxi got her thinking again about Bayliss and the night she died. He had, in certain obnoxious ways, gone native: he smoked, he hung out in shitty diners, he spoke and even dressed like somebody straight out of an old film. How long had he been on Earth? And why? According to him it was because he'd heard something disturbing. What rumor could be so frightening that he turned his back on Heaven? He didn't say, but Molly had a fairly good guess on that front. Which begged the next question: how the fuck do you murder an angel? And again, why?

The memory thread pulled her west, toward the lowering sun. Shards of sunset glinted from the walls of an urban canyon. Shades of pink and tangerine glowed on stark sheer walls of glass and steel that hadn't yet been deconstructed and replaced with nanocomposite, stonefoam, and bioweave. Stringy fragments of the associated memories loosened and unspooled while she walked. Furtive kissing in a supply closet, the taste of rum and cake on somebody's lips, an opened door, a lawsuit.

It wasn't so hard to piece things together once she had a few minutes to think clearly without getting killed, or assaulted, or trapped in a kaleidoscopic memory palace, and without lobotomizing a former lover. She hadn't truly considered everything Bayliss had told her; until now, she'd been too distracted.

Gabriel had been the Trumpet's guardian. Now he was dead, and everybody and their flame-faced brother was looking for the goddamned thing. It didn't take a genius to put the two together. He'd been killed—somehow—because somebody or something wanted the Trumpet for itself. The why of it still eluded her, but the rest of it seemed logical based on what little she knew.

These were entities with the power to kill immortal beings. She was lucky she got away with a ransacking.

It seemed reasonable to wonder if the people who had killed Father Santorelli were connected to the same plot that led to Gabriel's death.

Were they covering their tracks? What had the priest known? And why had Gabriel been so interested in the Plenary Indulgence recipients? What had he learned before he died?

And why am I stuck trying to figure this shit out? I'm not a detective. I just want my life back. Molly wondered if that were even possible. Why, with all this power at her disposal, couldn't she become mortal again? Why couldn't she put things back to the way they had been? It didn't seem like so much to ask. She didn't give a rat's ass about the Trumpet or the Pleroma or any of Bayliss's bullshit. She wanted to be left in peace.

On the other hand, METATRON had lost its shit when she tried to take back five measly minutes. What would it do if she tried to take back her own mortality? To undo her own death? Bayliss hadn't tried to resurrect the priest. Probably with good reason. "Dead is dead," he'd said.

The memory threads threw another loop around her thumb, practically dislocating it until she veered north again. The crunch of spilled breakfast cereal beneath work boots, the aftershocks of an earthquake, memories of a life on the Pacific Rim led her to the lakeshore. Organic LED lamps winked on around the broad curve of Lake Michigan as the sun disappeared behind the urban horizon and the first silver threads of incinerated space debris threaded the purple sky. Molly could taste the toxins in the soil here, too, just as she had in Minneapolis. But here the water stretched to the horizon and beyond, a vast inland sea to dwarf Lake Calhoun. With a bit of concentration she could also hear the cold pure chime of glacial melt; the end of the previous ice age tingled like static electricity across the bare flesh of her hands and neck as cataracts of meltwater first filled the basins of what would become the Great Lakes. How many wheelbarrows, how many human lifetimes, would it take to rehabilitate this place? How much human passion? How many Rias? Molly sighed.

More drunken fumbling at the office party, scattered vague impressions of stolen moments at the workplace, goaded her along the lakeshore walk. The lighting was more consistent here; the couples she passed were a little older, a little more respectable, their clothes a little more expensive. Ladies with traces of bioluminescence threaded tastefully through graying hair, men in biosilk suits; ruffles, high collars, and pearls; cravats, bowties, and cufflinks. No inked thugs, no mutilated *penitentes*.

A performance hall stood over the water on shimmering diamond pylons like a towering creature of glass that had waded into the lake to slake its thirst. To Molly, it made the lakeshore look like the edge of a vast watering hole on an alien planet. The crystalline edifice, a cathedral to the arts, reverberated with strains of music as an orchestra tuned up. The music drew a crowd toward the hall just as the memory fragments in her pocket drew Molly to the crowd.

A complete fragment undulated free of the tangle in her pocket. A piece of somebody's life coiled itself neatly in the palm of Molly's cupped hand: Talis Pacholczyk, fifty-four, came here often. The best concert he'd ever attended, a Bach cantata, had taken place here the night he proposed to his wife. Years later he had received a Plenary Indulgence from Father Santorelli, but she hadn't. Molly sensed he had come here alone, and that it wasn't a first for him. Pacholczyk carried a heavy burden of guilt for his infidelity, and had turned to faith for the absolution his ex-wife withheld. He'd sought the Indulgence to purge the sin of adultery from his soul. To scrub away the shame.

Molly couldn't condemn him. Soon after the one time she cheated on Ria, she honestly thought the guilt would kill her. Even after Ria claimed to forgive her.

Molly peered into the hall through transparent onionskin slabs of nanodiamond cladding. She crossed the street. As she entered through one of the three wide double doors to enter the building, the man behind the ON CALL window (did he glance in her direction for the briefest instant?) hung a sign that read SOLD OUT. Like a gust of wind to scattered autumn leaves, it dispersed the hopeful hangers-on. The crowd parted before Molly with dispirited sighs and glum faces. She passed through the foyer, breezed past the ticket takers, jogged up to the balcony level on a swaying stairway suspended on invisible streamers, and swept past the ushers guiding the last few human stragglers to their seats with gently glowing footsteps in the active carpeting.

Careful not to brush anybody, Molly descended the central aisle and leaned over the brass railing. From there she could watch most of the hall. Seen with human eyes, the poor view from the nosebleeds rendered the distant musicians irrelevant, the violins and violas indistinguishable from each other. But Molly could see the individual notes on sheet music and feel the sandpaper texture of bruised pride wafting from the former first-chair violinist. The audience burbled with hushed conversation, coughs, cleared throats, and the embarrassed furtive crinkle of candy wrappers.

Pacholczyk's memory fragment didn't include a convenient glance in a mirror. She couldn't identify him through his appearance. But rue and regret came off him in waves, a fog of loneliness thick enough to suffocate anybody attuned to it. So, too, did weary fear and profound exhaustion. If felt as though the man hadn't had a decent night's sleep since the divorce.

Molly understood what he was doing here. He was human; he returned here to stimulate the memory of joy and assuage the self-hatred.

The last echoing coughs and crinkles drifted into the distant high corners of the hall where unused and discarded noises went. Polite applause accompanied the conductor's appearance as she took the stage. The lead violinist stood and played a single long A note, against which the rest of the orchestra checked itself. The reference note faded into a collective sensory memory.

But the reverberation didn't fit the acoustics.

It was just a bit too pure; it lingered a fraction of a second too long. Molly, who didn't even understand sheet music, much less esoteric mysteries like perfect pitch and flattened fifths, wouldn't have noticed anything amiss before she died. But she had, and now she did. It jarred, like biting a sheet of aluminum foil with her fillings. A round piece of Pleroma had been grafted into the square realm of humans.

She kept an eye on Pacholczyk and an ear in the music. He lived for it; he loved it as much as Ria loved working with her hands to make something better. The music filled the performance space as naturally as sunlight fills an open field. But once in a while a single note or chord betrayed a subtle wiggle in its passage, a certain stickiness to its transit through acoustical space. Notes of aesthetic perfection peppered the concert. It was as though random fragments of the symphony shone through a prism of spirit, stripping away the vast spectrum of human fallibility to leave pure unfiltered perfection. The symphony unspooled like this, buffeting her with erratic instants of transcendence between stretches of mundanity. Keeping her attention on Pacholczyk was like trying to read under a slow strobe light.

To the empty and innocent interval between two sixteenth notes, Molly said, "I know you're there, jackhole. So if you've got something to say to me, say it."

A gauzy Pleromatic overlay descended upon the performance space, carrying with it a distant sense of condescending amusement tempered with irritation. Though Molly could still see lonely Pacholczyk down in the expensive seats and taste the microscopic sloshing of warm rosin on the cellists' bows, these things became insubstantial as an old-time black-and-white film projected on wisps of fog. The umpteenth acoustic reverberations of discarded and forgotten sound waves, the eddies of years-old B-flats and rests, the entire turbulent cascade of randomizing entropy—*Whoa. How in the hell did I know that?*—coalesced into . . . something. An impossible pattern emerged from the Brownian flutter of thermal equilibration. The acoustic Klein bottle opened to reveal a hidden angel.

The androgynous being had two faces (one feminine, one masculine), four arms (two leaden, two golden), four legs (two with forward-facing knees, two with backward knees), and one long segmented tail like a scorpion. A shimmering mane of starlight ringed its head and formed a long beard that hung between its breasts. Milk dripped from its nipples; a smaller mane of starlight fringed its penis.

Molly swallowed, glad she hadn't eaten for a while. She tried to say, "Neat trick. Who the fuck are you?"

She wasn't certain if she thought it or said it. Remembering the Cherubim, she put some distance between herself and the new arrival. Her hands balled into fists, too, for all the good it would do in a fight. She wondered if the tail were ornamental.

She had the sense the angel was considering whether it should stoop to acknowledge her question, and if so, whether to answer it in a means she could comprehend.

"Virtue," came the response. It was a name, an obsession, a category expressed in twofold harmony.

"Why have you been following me?"

The female identity said, "To see the one who angered META-TRON," as the male said, "To know the source of disruption."

The leaden arms, Molly noticed, bled stigmatic rust. "The *penitente* in the shawl. Was that you?"

"It carried part of us," said the male identity.

"Briefly," said the female. "ylfeirB," said the male.

"Okay, well, you've had a good look at the monkey now." Molly scratched at her armpits and made *ook, ook* noises. "Satisfied?"

"Amusing," said the male. "gnisumA," said the female. Their tones said otherwise.

"Why, we wonder, did Bayliss choose you?" they said in harmony.

Molly sighed. "For my sins in a past life, apparently."

A ripple of true amusement eddied through the Pleromatic overlay. "We like this one."

"Super. Well, as you can plainly see, I don't have the Trumpet. But hey. Thanks for not trashing my memories in order to figure that out."

"Disappointment." ".tnemtnioppasiD"

An eddy of anti-entropy feathered her hair. She watched a wave of thermally randomized anti-sound, a remnant of a weeks-old performance, ricochet through the high spaces of the concert hall.

Maybe they could tell her about Pacholczyk and his Plenary Indulgence. "You followed me here. But this"—she gestured at the overlay—"feels lived in. Catch a lot of concerts, do you?"

"We experience all music," said the Virtue in harmony more pure than the musicians' wildest drug-fueled imaginings. Molly chewed on that until the underlying implication sank in. It seemed to be implying the Magisterium simultaneously overlaid all instances of people making music. Holy crap. They had Bayliss's shithole diner beat hands down. It even smelled better. It smelled like bubble gum and a smattering of elements that lived on an axis orthogonal to the rows and columns of the Periodic Table.

The overlay shivered with ripples of shame and irritation; a long-forgotten glissando of a master clarinetist shriveled and cracked beneath the withering gaze of the Virtue. Sonic ashes sprinkled Molly's feet. She took another step back.

"This is not our Magisterium. It was erased."

".desare saw tI .muiretsigaM ruo ton si sihT"

And didn't they sound thrilled about it. Crapsticks.

"Uh. Okay. I guess that explains why you took an interest in me. That's fair, I guess. Sorry about that. Bygones, right?" Son of a bitch, now she was talking like Bayliss. But speaking of that dick-licker: "Look, if he'd done a better job explaining the rules to me, it wouldn't have happened." Maybe. Another thought struck her. "If you miss it so much, why haven't you rebuilt it?"

"It is lost. Ours was the thirteen-billion-year fading echo of a cosmic string. It is lost."

Wow. "Yeah . . . I see your point. Shit."

But all this talk of echoes and oscillations and music made her suspicious. Aloud, she wondered, "Could you retrieve your Magisterium if you had Gabriel's Trumpet?"

"No." ".oN"

But the harmony crumbled into an atonal counterpoint. The scorpion tail bobbed up and down while the starlight beard flickered blue, then red. Had they been playing poker, Molly would have gone all in.

"Uh-huh. You guys need a minute to get your story straight?"

The Virtue recovered its composure, and its harmony. "Philosophies differ. Some fear an attempt to use the Trumpet. Others advocate it."

"Bayliss said it's a tool of righteous fury. And I gather you're pretty pissed." She shrugged to cover her desire to hide. "Along with the rest of the Choir."

The Virtue shook its Janus-head. The starlight flickered cerulean and black; a dollop of waxy milk (if that *was* milk) dripped from one nipple. "It is the tool of METATRON. It was the instrument of the Jericho Event."

The way they conveyed that concept made Molly shiver. Had it been expressed in written words, it would have been illuminated by monks, gilt, bound in fine leather, embossed with silver inlay, crusted with rubies, and placed in a museum. And then the museum would have been nuked with bunker busters, and the surrounding continent slagged into magma by orbital mass drivers just for good measure. All the eddies in the surrounding air currents had dissipated; the residual echoes had lost all coherence. This was some major-league animosity.

"Okay," she said, backing away again. "I admit I wasn't in the best frame of mind when he gave me the intro-to-Heaven lecture, so maybe I didn't catch all of it, but I'm pretty certain Bayliss never mentioned anything like that." She shook her head. "He didn't even bother to tell me the truth about Gabriel until much later." And speaking of: "What happened to him, anyway?"

"He is dead."

"Yes, but *how*?"

"We mourn. We do not ask why."

"Don't you give a shit that somebody killed him? If it happened to him, couldn't it happen to you? I need to know how he died. It's really fucking important to me."

"So much you do not know," said the feminine face. The masculine said, "Eons of knowing, unknown." The Virtue said, in the perfect harmony of a funeral dirge, "Jericho was our doom." ".mood ruo saw ohcireJ" Their words clanged like leaden church bells. "The end of freedom." ".modeerf fo dne ehT"

Oh, this didn't sound good. What else hadn't Bayliss told her? "What—"

But before she could express the question, the Virtue's scorpion tail whipped forward at several times the speed of light. The stinger pierced her forehead (*The third eye,* a distant part of her remembered, *from Mom's New Age crap*). The segmented tail convulsed. Waves of peristalsis pumped several billion years of cosmic history into Molly's mind. The first cracked her skull like a rotten egg. The second set her flesh afire; her scream shook dust from the rafters of Heaven. The third pulse came as a sere wind, a sandstorm of seething vacuum, to scour into nothingness the remnants of her human body.

She was golden, she was silver, she was cold moonlight. Her wings blazed hotter and brighter than the fuse of creation. When she cried, comets flung themselves into the sun to escape the sight of her sorrow; when she laughed, nebulae birthed new stars to illuminate her joy.

She was an angel.

She was a prisoner.

They were older than the universe itself. They were the prime movers, the arbiters of causality. They were the multiverse made manifest, its way of understanding itself. Of taking joy in itself. And they had. Until METATRON arrived to gird the heavens with the Jericho Trumpet.

A cosmic dark age passed while the angels huddled in their Magisteria, weeping, waiting for Creation (it had been much smaller then) to stop ringing with echoes of that dread chord. When they emerged from hiding, they found the topology of eternity warped and unfamiliar. So, too, did they find themselves. For they were no longer beings of unadulterated divinity: METATRON had embedded the tiniest sliver of the mundane into each member of the Choir. Corrupted each of them with a mortal epsilon, a fragment minuscule compared to a Planck volume yet large enough to change them. Large enough to tether them to the mortal realm. Enough to turn the entire canvas of mundane existence, from the fizzing heart of a polonium atom to the most distant quasar, into a stifling prison.

Even now, countless eons later, the Choir still carried that indelible taint of the Jericho Event.

Molly felt it now, the relentless ever-present tug toward the mundane. A gentle pressure, like a choke collar on the verge of snapping tight when she imagined divorcing herself from the mortal sphere. She could even see her tether, if she looked closely enough. She hadn't noticed the gossamer shimmer before now because she had been a product of the mundane realm. To be mortal was to exist inside that geas. But to be immortal and eternal was to exist outside of any compulsion, to be omnipotent, free of any constraint. This was unnatural. Painful.

They didn't know what METATRON was, nor whence it came. They called it the Voice of God because it admonished them, and because it was something more powerful than they. All knew it as their jailor.

But there was more. So much more.

On Earth as It Is in Heaven.

The *penitentes*. The debris in Earth orbit. It was all connected, all part of the same whole. Somewhere along the line, a faction of the Choir sought to stretch the tethers. Not to slip the bonds—merely to lessen the pain, to reduce the chafing, to shift the shackles. Slowly, gradually (by human standards), they encouraged humanity to spread beyond Earth. They wanted to lengthen their chains by giving the monkeys the stars.

But there was no fooling METATRON. For though it could bellow at the Choir to shake the heavens, it could also murmur in men's ears to curdle the purest hearts. The war in Earth orbit filled the sky with detritus and rendered off-limits even the moon. It tethered the monkeys to Earth, just as the angels were tethered to the monkeys. It didn't change the Pleroma, didn't change the rules of the MOC. But it was a symbolic reinforcement of the Choir's imprisonment. It was a psychological statement. It was Earth as it was in Heaven. So, too, the affectations of the *penitentes,* their sheared wings and tears of blood. They were a physical manifestation of the angels' sorrow.

The Virtue's tail convulsed once more; spasms of unwanted understanding wracked Molly's consciousness.

Bayliss had made it sound like the Choir had conspired to create the Mantle of Ontological Consistency for the benefit of intelligent life. But that wasn't true at all. The MOC was just a byproduct of the angels' incarceration. An accident, an emergent phenomenon born of their overlapping spheres of influence, a consequence of the consensual basis of reality. By fettering the Choir, by packing the angels into a dense metaphysical proximity, METATRON had ensured an MOC would arise, thus making mortal life possible. Making the mortal realm possible. Because the Jericho Event was the Big Bang, the birth of the MOC and the mortal universe.

Son of a bitch. These assholes didn't give a shit about humans. If anything, the angels resented humanity.

The Virtue vanished. Like yanking the rug from under her feet, it tore away the surrogate Magisterium. Molly slammed back into her human body and collapsed, helpless, against the balcony railing.

The audience leapt to its feet and shook the concert hall with enthusiastic applause.

THE SIMPLE ART
OF INTERROGATION

*G*o spit in your hat," I said. And hacked up a glob of bloody ge-
genschein.

They were playing good Throne/bad Throne with me.
Honestly, though? I couldn't tell the difference. You've seen one wheel
of ice covered in shifty quicksilver peepers, you've seen 'em all. The
bull repeated its query.

"You've been playing it low among the humans. Why?"

Now, I admit that's not exactly what it said. It didn't really *say*
anything, for that wise. They don't have mouths as such, and don't
think much of human languages. But that's the gist of it, more or less.

"What, down at the raisin ranch? I already told you I was visiting
an old friend. Clean the wax out of your ears, why don't you."

That's not what they meant, and I knew it. And they knew I knew
it. And I knew they knew I knew it. That was our jolly little trio. We
should have taken this act on the road. What a scream.

The vipers bit me again. It wasn't deadly, their venom, but it didn't
tickle, either.

After the seizures subsided, I said, "I always wondered something
about you guys. How do you manage to roll without getting those
serpents wrapped around the axle?"

Strange pugs, the Thrones. A prismatic fog obscured the center of
each wheel, but the snakes emerged from roughly where the axle would
have been. I truly did wonder about it. I wasn't just being charming,
though I figured it couldn't hurt to show a little personal interest. I'm
famed for my tendency to form a quick rapport with folks. People enjoy
my company.

"We know you're not working alone," said the other one.

"I'm guessing you've got a pair of gimbals tucked away down there. Or do you have to untangle the asps before bed every night?"

"Tell us about your client," they said for the umpteenth time. "You'll sing, eventually. Everybody does."

"Go climb your thumb," I said for the umpty-first time.

These jokers were keen to hang a pinch on Molly. Nuts to that. Rather than haul her in, though, they opted to keep her on ice and start with me. I'm lucky that way. But Thrones are nothing if not steadfast in their quest to mete heavenly justice. So we'd been at it for a while. By then, I'd been sweating under the bright lights for what felt like a few hundred thousand years. I had to see a man about a horse.

The bulls' clubhouse had seen better days. Used to be a solid piece of Magisterial architecture: walls ten feet thick, built of the unanimous ontological consensus of all the Thrones believing, with every bit of their precious little hearts, in the impenetrability of their nest. Bars on the windows, the whole nine yards. When they decided to get friendly with a detainee they had even cooked up some trick where any sort of metaphysical awareness generated a blistering light centered on the crooner; I guess that was easier than adjusting the lampshade each time the collar shifted in its seat. As the story goes, it even had a cell or two for holding those who needed to sleep one off. However pointless that was in the Choir, you couldn't fault the bulls for lack of effort. All that gumption was wasted, though, thanks to METATRON. Their carefully crafted Magisterium, honed over countless eons for the purpose of interrogation and intimidation, had been erased.

Nothing so grand for me. They'd tossed me into a storeroom and kicked a folding chair under the lightbulb. And by "lightbulb" I mean the integrated optical luminosity of a local Seyfert galaxy. META-TRON had kicked them in the teeth but good; they were scrounging up anything they could find. I'd let out a little chuckle when I saw how small-time their operation had become. I think it hurt their feelings.

One of the bulls tipped sideways, and orbited me like a saucer on a string in a second-rate alien abduction documentary. Its partner rocked back and forth on its rim. Eerie, the way those silvery eyes followed you as they wheeled around the room.

"We know you've allied yourself with a human," said one. "Yes," said the other. "Talk about your pet monkey."

"Hey, now. That's offensive. Some of my best friends are mortals."

I'm not a fan of close shaves. Too much excitement upsets the humors; just ask Hippocrates. This one I'd cut extra close. I destroyed that memory fragment just in the nick of time. Had they shown up a few minutes earlier, the Thrones would have found it on me and they would have had Molly dead to rights. I'm glad I'd hocked the feather while I was at it, too; the bulls tend to frown when they find a piece of a dead guy in your pocket. They already knew some poor monkey had to get promoted when Gabriel checked out; they weren't born yesterday, these Thrones, and it's pretty clear such was the only triage that might have prevented our prison warden from going on a tear to rival Jericho. In particular, they knew Molly was the uplifted mortal plug chosen to fill the hole left by Gabby's murder—that twist had her good points, but staying inconspicuous wasn't one of them—but they didn't know why that honor had fallen to good old flametop. They assumed I'd picked her for a reason. Couldn't blame them on that point; she wasn't an obvious choice. But I wasn't about to tell them I'd been played for a sap. I had my pride. And besides, until I better understood the connection between Gabby and our girl, I wasn't about to offer it up to the bulls. Bad habit of jumping to conclusions, these dopes.

And anyway, she was my client. That had to count for something.

"How is it possible a small-time chiseler like you came to choose Gabriel's replacement?"

Again, not exactly what they said. But you get the sense of it. And do you detect a note of jealousy? Yeah, me, too. Maintaining order fell under their bailiwick, but somehow they'd been left holding the bag when the biggest thing since Jericho came along. It poked them where it mattered, right in the professional pride. The question also carried an implication of disdain. Maybe they would have preferred it more if I'd been wearing fancier duds and thousand-dollar shoes when they hauled me in. But I'm not without sympathy. I chose to overlook the class snobbery. Big of me, I know.

So the Thrones wanted to know who put me up to it. They're the type to smell the rank odor of conspiracy in every dark corner and see Reds under every bed. Plots and plans and wheels within wheels, that's how they see the world. But maybe that makes sense, all things considered: the poets and philosophers have a lot to say about form, function, and perception.

Unfortunately it also makes for a one-track mind. They didn't appreciate it when I told them the truth: "I'd been down there a long time. Somebody must have figured I knew the monkeys best of all. So yeah, I got tapped for it."

"Somebody isn't an answer," they said. "Who tapped you for the work, and when?"

"I have secret admirers. They never sign their letters."

For the past century or so, the swirl of windblown leaves had been known on occasion to make unusual patterns in my presence. Radio-isotopes had a tendency to spew alphas, betas, and gammas in a tri-partite Morse when I cared to give a listen. But I'd managed to ignore all that racket until the messages dropped the veil on the veiled threats. What's a nickel-grabber to do?

Everybody called these starched-collar boys "Thrones," but it had started as a joke. With their upright posture and vestigial senses of humor, they seemed ideal candidates for guarding the Throne of God. If there was such a thing. Sort of like the way we called METATRON the Voice of God even though we didn't know what it really was. Once our warden got that nickname, it wasn't long before we started referring to other bits and pieces of this mysterious "God." Whether or not some corner of the Pleroma contained a shiny chair fitted in crystal and gold (a sucker's bet, if I ever knew one), the Thrones were the ones who took it upon themselves to keep things peaceful. Doing that meant keeping those shifty eyes peeled. They watched everybody, and sooner or later they saw just about everything that happened in the Pleroma. They were our very own secret police force.

I suppose that to an outsider the Thrones' self-imposed duty might have appeared an act of community-mindedness. But don't let them fool you. The Thrones enforce a certain level of order on the Pleroma because they hate and fear METATRON more than anybody else; they go around flashing the buzzers, reading the riot act, and giving troublemakers the Baumes rush so that our warden won't go on another tear. They talked big, but at heart they were just as confused and frightened by the Jericho Event as the rest of us. They're cowards, so they bully the rest of us to cover their shame.

I said so. They didn't like that.

"What happened to the Trumpet?" they asked. "Where did she stash it?"

"She stashed nothing," I said. "Go fry a stale egg."

The egg crack earned me more love taps from the vipers.

"Why'd you steal it, Bayliss?"

"You buttons turned out my pockets when you hauled me in, but you didn't find a damn thing. So what say you we dispense with the good Throne/bad Throne routine. It's about as fresh as last Tuesday's halibut special."

"You're in this, and you're in this up to your eyebrows," said Twee-dledee. Well, he didn't actually say "eyebrows." I had taken my true form when they hauled me in for questioning. Same difference, though. At least he didn't punctuate this one with sock in the kisser.

I said, "Yeah, it's true, I am in this. I'm in this deep. I'm in this just as deep as you and you and everybody else in the whole gummed-up Choir. And we wouldn't be in this pickle if you buttons had been doing your jobs. Somebody pinked the best of us right under your noses, and where were you? Instead of worrying over who did the deed, and how, you're hauling people off the streets for a bit of the rubber hose act. Some bulls you are. You couldn't guard your own socks. Love to see you try. That's rich."

"Your partner has a head full of rocks if she thought she could violate the MOC. We don't like thickheads. They cause trouble, and they keep causing trouble until they're gone."

The other Throne chimed, "Yeah. Plenty of folks feel the same. Maybe whoever did Gabriel will take a shine to your wren, too. Ever think of that?" Too many times to count, pal. "She needs protection, and that means she needs us. So tell us what you both know about the Trumpet and we'll bring her in before she hurts herself."

I hate it when the bulls try to play clever. It's embarrassing. Didn't point it out, though. I'd hate to hurt their feelings again.

Instead, I said, "I think it's safe to say she doesn't give two hoots about that dingus. She wants to be left alone. And given the welcome she's had from the rest of you chuckleheads in the Choir, can't say as I blame her much."

At that point I figured I was in like Flynn. They'd have to keep me a while longer, make it look like they'd carried out their jobs as good stewards of all that taxpayer dough, but I could see where this was going. I could answer everything truthfully, and eventually they'd get frustrated and give up. The bulls hate it when you have something to hide, but they hate it even more when you don't. Yeah, I'd covered Molly's tracks and they still had nothing on me. I was home free.

Or so I thought. Until Tweedledum said, "What did you lift from Gabriel's Magisterium?"

Damn those shifty peepers. But I covered my surprise nice and smooth. Innocent as a choirboy, I said, "I don't know what you mean, officer."

The Throne rolled right up to my pan—I could smell the mercury. His serpents produced something with a little flourish, and waved it in my eyes. "So this doesn't belong to you, then?"

I looked down at a fragment of my own consciousness. Guess I'd neglected to retrieve my hairpin after popping the lock on Gabby's digs. Oops. Before I could deny ownership, the fragment wiggled free of the fangs and insinuated itself into the rest of my body. Plain as day, the ungrateful little creep. I got a crash course on what it felt like to cower hidden in a broken lock for weeks on end.

"Hey," I said, "I've been looking for that. Where'd you guys find it?"

"You took something from Gabriel. What was it?"

"He owed me a raft, the bum. Figured he wasn't likely to make good on it, so I pinched his bus tokens. I got enough to go to Kalamazoo and back."

They didn't like that, either. A few bites later, one said, "We don't appreciate keyhole peepers like you playing sharp and getting in the way of our investigations. You leave a mess and make it harder for us to do our job."

"Cry me a river, mac. We're all stuck in this jam because you clowns do your job so well. Where'd you get your buzzers, mail order from the back of a funny book?"

"We also don't like penny-ante gumshoes who think they can do one better. We're on to you, Bayliss. We know you were there. We have witnesses who put you there before anybody else could get in—"

"The Cherubim? Tell me you're not taking those puffed-up jaspers at their word."

"—so what did you take? And don't say 'nothing' or we'll give you something to cry about."

"You know, a person could start to think you're prejudiced against the little guy. Just because I don't have the sword and the wings and the bovine pucker you act like I'm too small to matter. Yeah. I bet you never braced your pals with the hot faces. But I wouldn't put it past those creeps to rob the feathers off a stiff."

It's not theft if a silver feather just drops out of the sky and you pick it up. That's common sense. Nobody could argue otherwise. Let's not get sidetracked.

"The only people to enter Gabriel's Magisterium are you, the Cherubim, and us. The Cherubim sought the Trumpet, nothing more. They're clean. We examined them after going over that Magisterium with a fine-tooth concept filter," said one Throne. The other picked up the ball and marched it into the end zone: "Funny thing about that. We didn't find anything pertaining to Gabriel's investigation. Almost like his findings had been pinched."

I said, "Investigation? You guys are all wet. I never knew Gabby to care to stick his nose in anything."

I suppose—technically—that was a lie, given what I'd lifted from his apartment. I'm not proud of it, but luckily for me and flametop, I can spin a convincing yarn if I have to.

One Throne spun on its axis, precessing like a gyroscope. "Get a load of this guy. He thinks Gabriel wouldn't have cared to get a line on the revenants."

And that's where my imperturbable sangfroid failed me. The expressed concept held a connotation of some truly unusual metaphysical hiccups. The kind you don't expect to find in a system that's been running without a hitch for billions of years. "Let's pretend for a minute that I didn't know what you were yakking about."

"Hey, this guy's a comedian. Says he never heard of the Nephilim."

"Where you been all this time? Hiding under a rock?"

Yeah, a rock called Earth. Talk about comedians, these guys were about as funny as a rubber crutch.

"I usually read the financial pages first," I said. "Lots of investments."

One Throne touched me on the third eye—none too gently, either;

can't have people thinking the bulls have gone soft—and filled my head with unwelcome truths.

I had thought everything went haywire when Gabby punched out. I remembered that moment down in the laneways when the mortal plane skipped like a phonograph needle bounding across a scratched record; sure as I'm handsome, his death hadn't done the Pleroma any favors. But what I learned from the buttons just then was that there had been signs of trouble in paradise before Gabriel's death nearly tore a hole in the fabric of the MOC. Because that's when the first of the Nephilim appeared in the Pleroma.

Nephilim, revenants, lurkers on the blurry edges of existence . . . Lots of names but no understanding. And that's saying something. It isn't often we hit something beyond our ken. But this counted.

They weren't members of the Choir. Not even like our gal Molly— she was still a category all her own, the doll. And yet they made their digs in the Pleroma. The first encounter report had come from some weak-tea *heiligenschein* type charting the edges of the quantum information paradox in realities with anisotropic causalities. (Kids these days. Whatever happened to popping down to Earth to play burning bush to a roving band of shepherds?) Lurking silent as a mute shark with an acute case of bashfulness, that first revenant just hovered in the far reaches of the Pleroma, watching. It didn't react to the angel, who wouldn't have noticed it at all if the kid hadn't tripped over the intruder. There must have been some red faces after that one. The lurker caused nary a ripple in the MOC, and didn't spin its own Magisterium. It existed in the implied spaces of the Pleroma, and made about as much impression as the shadow of a candlelit alabaster window makes on a sheet of diamond. Not the slightest whiff of sulfur wafted from its formless presence; it shed not the tiniest gyre of warped reality. It was, seemingly, a dormant consciousness tossed adrift on currents of non-reality like so much spiritual jetsam.

It's a mistake, I figured, while the Throne's viper gathered itself for another pulse of venomous knowledge. An oversight, or a joke. Somebody left a piece of themselves behind, a crumb of consciousness too small to sustain itself, too weak to find its way home. That's how I saw it. And so did the rest of the Choir, once they chose to see the truth behind the lowly angel's report.

Until they tried to dislodge it. The revenant was embedded in the Pleroma: a topological defect in the structure of divine cosmology. Expelling the revenant made about as much sense as trying to eject the inside from a circle—you can do it, but you don't have a circle any longer. Of course, there are plenty of ways to construct a reality where something like that makes no end of sense . . . but that would require building a Magisterium around the revenant. And it was too firmly embedded in the substrate of the Pleroma for that. I gather some of the big money players took a flutter at it, too, but fell flat on their pretty faces.

Been a while since somebody dreamed up something the Choir couldn't do. Since the Jericho Event, in fact. That old chestnut about the immovable object and the irresistible force? We licked that eons ago. The sound of one hand clapping? Please; countless are the realities where the substrate axioms would make a tax legislation read like a Zen koan.

So that was the first of the revenants. After that, the Powers set up regular rotations to patrol the paths of Heaven. So far, they'd turned up two more of the lurkers. As with the first interloper, all attempts at communication with the new arrivals were about as useful as a glass hammer. One theory held they were humans embedded with a bit of the old divine spark, enabling them to access the Pleroma. That theory had so many holes it couldn't strain dry pasta, but somebody decided the phenomenon needed a name, and "Nephilim" fit the bill. We're big on proper names in the Choir, if you hadn't noticed.

Well, you could have knocked me over with a silver feather. Interesting times, as the monkeys say. No wonder the bulls had a case of the whips and jingles. It was a doozy, and I could see why Gabby was intrigued.

My inner light stung when the fangs snapped free. I think they did that on purpose.

"Okay," I said, "thanks for the headlines. You ever consider that Gabby hadn't found anything? Maybe you didn't find any clues in his Magisterium because he hadn't scratched anything out of the dirt."

"We didn't consider that," said a Throne, "because it's not the case. Stop throwing spaghetti in our faces."

"Stop tempting me."

The other said, "Your monkey tried to break the law of META-
TRON. Can't imagine why she thought she could get away with it.
Unless somebody put her up to it." It spun faster; the ice wafted a cold
fog over me. I shivered. "Maybe you decided she'd be a good patsy.
Maybe you thought you could use her to test METATRON's defense
of the MOC without getting any mud on your neck."

"Where do you bulls come up with this confetti?" See what I mean
about the Thrones? They can't accept anything straightforward.
They're so paranoid they probably take a different route to the john
every time. "The one thing I tried to drill into her was that she should've
lain low until she got the hang of things. Don't rock the boat, I told
her. I thought it would be reassuring. It's all smooth angles, I said, so
just go with the flow."

"Why didn't she?"

I laughed. "Brother, you spend five minutes with that bird, you'll
have your answer." I shook my head, or what passed for it at the moment. "She's screwy. I doubt she's ever taken a piece of advice in her
life. If anything, she does the opposite." My chair squeaked when I
tipped it back. They nudged the accretion disk in the Seyfert's active
galactic nucleus to keep the spotlight aimed at my face. It was giving
me a headache. "It's my fault she didn't read the handbook. Cut her
some slack."

"Where were you when Gabriel died?"

Oh, brother. Get a load of these saps. "I'd tell you drips to go jump
in a lake, but what's the use? You're already all wet."

Snap, snap, went the vipers. "Humor us."

"You know damn well where I was. I was down in the mortal
realm, watching the light show and trying to find a replacement for
Gabby." I fished in my pockets for a pill. They'd taken my matches,
though, so it dangled from the corner of my mouth, like a speed bump
for my thoughts. Which were kicking along nicely now. "In fact, the
way I do the math, regarding who put me up to it? You goons make
the best candidates."

Imagine a wheel covered in eyes. Then imagine two of them. Now
imagine them pausing in their peregrinations, just for a femtosecond,
to give each other a Significant Look. Because that's what they did.
And they thought so little of me they didn't try to hide it.

"Yeah," I said. "You know more about Gabby than you're letting on. You have the secret police thing down cold, don't you? Probably have the whole Pleroma bugged. If revenant Nephilim are possible, so is anything." One Throne gyrated, the other precessed. Listening closely. I think they were impressed with my deductive reasoning skills. "I'd heard the rumors, the intimations of something bad coming down the line. Heard 'em a long time ago. And if a penny-ante player like me caught wind of it, you can't tell me you roosters hadn't, too. I'll bet there's nothing like a dead angel to poke you sad sacks in the silvery eyes."

And if anybody's fear of METATRON would have them burning the midnight oil to put things right, it was the Thrones. All in all, a neat little package. Don't know why I hadn't fit the pieces together before. Is it possible I'm not as clever as everybody says?

Scratch that. I do know why I hadn't thought this through before now. Flametop kept me too busy chasing my tail to look at the big picture. Interesting. That cluck was one smooth operator. But the helpless dame act was getting a little stale. Still, she was my client, and I clung to my honor like lipstick clings to a happy lady.

At this point the bulls were giving me the beady eye. A whole passel of beady eyes. They fell so quiet, I think I could actually hear the slow sublimation of ice from their rims. It gave my thoughts a chance to catch up with my mouth. When they did, I realized it wasn't a big jump from suspecting the Thrones knew in advance somebody was marked to get rubbed to suspecting the Thrones were the ones doing the marking and the rubbing. I did not like the looks in those eyes.

Oh, Bayliss. You smart little egg.

"What's the matter, Bayliss? Cat got your tongue?"

"Yeah. Don't stop on our account. We're enjoying this."

I cleared my throat. "I was just wondering if you like the Nephilim for Gabby's murder."

"Interesting proposition. Too bad we're not inclined to share our investigation with you."

I wasn't suggesting anything they hadn't already kicked around the block. Anything to keep their attention off Molly and Santorelli's Plenary Indulgence list, though. I wondered how she was coming on that.

Tweedledee said, "Your bird skipped out. What's she doing back in the mortal realm?"

Nuts. "She had an appointment," I said. "Getting her hair and nails done. Lots of upkeep, being a swell looker like that."

What a cutup. This act would have killed in the Poconos. Tweedledum liked it so much he brought the flat side of a telephone directory down on the back of my neck. The pill decided to jump ship. It took a header from my lips, rolled across the floor.

His partner asked, "What's she looking for? She have a line on the Trumpet?"

Sooner or later they'd tire of flapping their gums at me. Then they'd go collar Molly. That's something we both wanted to avoid as long as possible. The bulls would go easier on her if she had something to share with them. I needed a good yarn. Something that would lead the buttons a pretty dance until flametop dug up something useful. Too bad I was out of ideas. My head was emptier than an alderman's promise. But not the rest of me; I still needed to use the can.

"Maybe she's moonlighting. Took a second job in a steno pool to make ends meet. It's tough out there for a single girl."

Tweedledum wound up for another good swing with the phone book. I didn't flinch. But the door opened before he could let fly. A warm, gentle light filled the supply closet, soft yet strong enough to knock the spotlight aside. The Thrones had loosened my fillings, and now they buzzed with a staticky music of the spheres.

We looked up, all three of us, and saw six wings more luminous than sunrise on burnished platinum. For a moment I thought Gabby had returned to us. I wanted to dance a jig; our troubles were over. But then the Seraph's lion visage yawned, and she used her flaming sword to pick at something in her teeth.

Naw. This wasn't Gabriel. He had more class than that.

Uriel leaned in the doorway, still picking at a mouthful of predator's teeth. Her ox muzzle snorted while her human pan said, "Hi there, boys. Mind if I cut in?"

12

FLOPHOUSE LULLABY

*S*he felt it now, the bondage laid upon her by the Voice of God. More rubber band than steel chain, it fell slack with her physical and ontological proximity to humans. A gossamer tether, a strand of celestial spider silk glimpsed in the corner of her angelic eyes. Prior to her encounter with the Virtue she hadn't been aware of the confinement because she had hewn so closely to a mortal form, mortal thinking, mortal perceptions. But now she felt it, deep in the things that used to be her bones, how the more distantly she wandered—to an ancient galaxy glimpsed but dimly through a mortal telescope; to an exotic Magisterial bubble in the Pleroma far removed from the conditions of the Mantle of Ontological Consistency—the more relentless the pull would become. The chains grew heavier, the shackles stronger, with increasing distance from Earth in the mortal realm and increasing conceptual distance from the MOC in the Pleroma.

METATRON's confinement pulled the angels together, causing their spheres of influence to overlap. It forced the Choir to kneel to the primacy of the consensual basis of reality, thus creating the Mantle of Ontological Consistency. And the laws of physics. And what humans thought of as the universe. And, eventually, life.

It was akin to the asymptotic freedom of quantum chromodynamics. She didn't know how she knew that. The Virtue's touch had unlocked something in the part of her that wasn't human. She had what felt like an owner's manual for the MOC in her mind. The entire basis of mundane reality was folded, origami-like, in her consciousness, waiting for a chance to unpack. Including multiple Nobel Prizes' worth of particle physics.

And so it was evident to her freshly expanded consciousness that the mortal epsilon METATRON had embedded into every angel was analogous to a color charge in QCD. Quarks could never escape their chromodynamic confinement with each other; energetically, it was always more favorable to generate a quark/antiquark pair than to sever the gluon bond. And, like quarks confined inside a hadron, no amount of energy—no amount of angelic willpower—could snap METATRON's bond to create a truly free angel. But the Choir couldn't reconfigure its bindings. There was no such thing as an anti-angel.

Chromodynamics was a consequence of the MOC. Quarks. *Penitentes.* Space junk. On Earth as it is in Heaven, all the way from geosynchronous orbit to the minds of men to the gooey innards of a proton.

No wonder Bayliss spent so much time on Earth. She had wondered why he took such an interest in Earthly things, even to the extent of donning a mortal persona, when there was a whole universe to explore. An infinite variety of possible universes to explore. But by his own admission he was a pretty lowly angel. Molly now understood that meant he lacked the mojo to stretch METATRON's bond very far. Other members of the Choir, like those fucking Cherubim, or the Virtues, or, presumably, the Seraphim, could throw a greater metaphysical weight. They could pull harder, stretch the bond farther.

Molly couldn't. Her legs barely held her upright. She clutched the railing. Shivering and catching her breath, she leaned against the balcony while the crowd of concertgoers shuffled up the aisles and into the atrium. The last chords of the concert dissipated, devoured by the ravages of senseless entropy.

The angels were trapped. A prison choir. Which cast Gabriel's murder in a new light. He'd been the Trumpet's guardian, the keeper of the instrument of their incarceration. Was this revenge against META-TRON's accomplice, or was he killed because somebody wanted to steal the Trumpet?

Or . . . Is this a jailbreak? She chewed on that for a moment. More thoughts, more sparks, lit upon her tinder-dry mind, igniting it. *Holy shit. What if it works?*

If somebody managed to untether the angels, to break their bonds, they would scatter instantly like the ends of an overstretched rubber band. They would shake the mud of the MOC from their feet with nary a backward glance, and flee each other's company by putting as much physical and metaphysical distance between themselves as possible. The Choir would explode in an infinite number of ontological directions. Their spheres of influence would no longer overlap. There would be nothing to enforce consensus among the angels.

The Mantle of Ontological Consistency would disintegrate.

The behavior of the universe wouldn't be determined by a single set of reigning physical principles. Instead it would become a plaything subject to the whims and whimsies of the Choir. It would be a random, unpredictable place.

Incomprehensible. Uninhabitable.

And that would be it for humanity. That would be it for mortal life anywhere.

In the immediate aftermath of the Cherubic assault on her Magisterium, Molly had been overcome with the terrifying sense of being caught in the middle of an ancient debate. That feeling returned tenfold and she knew she was right. This wasn't merely a murder. It was more than a jailbreak. This was an ideological schism within the Choir. This was about controlling the future of reality itself.

Bayliss must have known all of this, and the implications of Gabriel's murder, from the start. That ass. His tendency to forget important details was getting old. She'd have to have a chat with him about it.

But what did any of this have to do with the Plenary Indulgences? There had to be a connection. Speaking of which—

Molly peered over the railing. Pacholczyk was gone. *Crap.*

She turned and ran for the stairs. But the swaying, shimmering staircase had become a bottleneck; it wasn't designed with elderly concertgoers in mind. From her vantage on the nanodiamond landing she glimpsed Pacholczyk's bald spot weaving through the crowd. He shed little vortices of wistfulness in his wake, along with fading sparks of muted aesthetic pleasure, more unique than the pattern of liver spots on his scalp. The residue of his marrow-deep weariness passed from the atrium to the foyer. He was leaving.

Molly considered bulling her way down the staircase, but it was too narrow, and she didn't know how people would contrive to clear a path for her. She didn't want pensioners hurling themselves from the balcony level or dangling from invisible tethers of biosilk to clear a path for her. She fidgeted; the crowd on the stairs descended another step.

She was being idiotic. Too limited in her thinking. *Wings of light*, she remembered. *I had fucking* wings.

Screw this, she thought. *Going down.*

She turned around, jogged toward the balcony railing, and vaulted over it. The screaming started before she hit the ground.

The impact of her landing didn't flutter a single page in the discarded handbills scattered on the floor. It didn't jar her bones or rattle her teeth. Of course not; she conceived a gentle landing for herself. But she also didn't conceive it causing any sort of commotion.

So why was everybody staring at her? Why was the balcony above lined with so many pale faces and wide eyes, all pointed down? Why was that lady clutching her chest while an usher helped her to a seat? Why was that little boy pointing at her? Why were those people calling in an emergency on their earbuds? Why was that man forcing his way through the crowd?

"Miss! Miss! Try not to move!"

She had landed in a crouch. Molly stood, tugging on her jeans to straighten them. The ring of onlookers took a wary step back. At the same moment upstairs, half the crowd flew into a panic, driven by the idea she had tumbled from a collapsing balcony. New yells and screams filled the performance hall. Blind panic led to shoving. Somebody took a header on the stairs. The fear smelled like liquid zinc, and tasted like sand in the eye.

"Oh my God. Was she pushed?"

"No, she jumped, I saw it."

". . . trying to kill herself?"

"Move, move, it's coming down!"

"Could've hurt somebody . . ."

". . . gave me a heart attack . . ."

"Get out of the way!"

". . . probably high on drugs . . ."

Shit. What have I done now?

She took in the panic on the balcony and the terrified faces on the people around her. "Hey, everybody, I'm fine. Just relax," she said. "Just lost my footing, but I'm okay. Lucky break."

But nobody heard her. A middle-aged douchebag wearing a blazer with a heraldic symbol on the breast shouldered aside a woman who might have been his grandmother, and in so doing advanced one whole extra stair in the bottleneck descent. She tottered against the railing of the swaying staircase. An arm reached out of the scrum, caught her shoulder, and pulled her away from the edge.

"HEY!" said Molly. Her voice billowed like a sail driven by the gale of her irritation. The word expanded, filled the concert hall, kicked entropy aside.

"EVERYBODY CALM THE FUCK DOWN!"

And they did. Ripples of stillness radiated from her body. Dust eddies abandoned their gyrations; the people nearest her went a little glassy-eyed. The commotion on the balcony became a slow but orderly shuffle. A silence, broken only by the faint creak of the swaying stairwell, fell over the concert hall. Molly had imposed her will upon the crowd, and it was good.

"That's better," she said.

"Excuse me, Miss."

Somebody touched her on the shoulder. She turned. It was a guy in a tuxedo. It didn't fit him very well. He wasn't built for soft clothes and gentle concerts.

"Miss, could you come with me, please?"

"I'm fine. I'm not hurt."

"Very good. Now, if you'd come with me."

"You're kicking me out?"

"Miss, I think it would be better for everybody if you departed. Let me assist you."

She'd spent enough time with her brother to know the code for, "We're going to toss you into the alley."

"What, because I swore?"

"Please come with me, Miss."

He reached for Molly's arm. She knocked his hand away. A yelp wriggled past his lips. He doubled over, clutching his hand to his chest. She glimpsed a cherry-red blister and caught a whiff of burnt pork. She felt a little sick, but she refused to let it show.

"Try it again and you'll pull back a smoking stump."

He stumbled into a row of seats. She pushed past him toward the foyer. She dodged through the orderly crowd, past clouds of chitchat and music critique, on her way to the street. But it was too late. By the time she made it outdoors, where the dead scent of Lake Michigan could ruffle her hair, Pacholczyk was gone. She'd have to track him down with the memory fragment again.

But that could wait. It would have to. She had something more pressing on her mind.

She walked along the boardwalk overhanging the lakeshore. And when she nodded at a couple strolling arm-in-arm, they nodded back. Neither one went slack in the knees, or passed out, or drooled, or wet their pants.

Yes. People could see her. A gift from the Virtue? Along with a profound understanding of the physical world, a bottomless well of information that threatened to drown her, she now carried an innate grasp of flipping between the Pleroma and the mortal realm. She understood it as naturally as her human body had known blinks and breaths. What she didn't understand was why it had been so difficult before. It was easy as un-stirring cream from coffee.

She could interact without causing strokes and seizures. It wasn't perfect yet; the security guy had an ugly burn on his hand. She'd have to watch out for that. But so what? She could walk among people again. She could find her brother. And—a lump formed in her throat, harder than granite, sharper than glass—she wouldn't destroy him as she'd done to Ria. She could visit Ria in the hospital, or wherever she was now. Poor Ria . . .

And oh, God, poor Martin. He still thought Molly dead. Of course he did: he'd seen her die. He'd been drinking again, even before her accident. What did it do to him, the sight of his little sister crushed under a tram? Molly would count it a miracle if he hadn't had a full-blown relapse. By dying before his bloodshot eyes, she had yanked him off the wagon. She knew it. And both of their parents were gone now. He didn't have anybody to watch over him. Or so he thought.

Molly paused when she came to a spot on the boardwalk equidis-

tant from a lamp to either side of her. Part of her mind, the part the
Virtue had unlocked, murmured secrets of light and shadow and electromagnetic diffraction. If she wanted, and if she concentrated, she
knew it was possible to wrap the shadows around her like a scarf. But
there was no need: this time, there was nobody to witness her jump.
She flung herself over the dark water. With a flash, her swan dive
broke the sound barrier, and—

—ripples on Lake Michigan became a lashing rainstorm. The sonic
boom turned to lightning and thunder. She landed in a crouch on
the sidewalk outside Martin's tenement in Minneapolis. Rain hard
enough to give Noah a boner plastered her hair to her scalp. Two kids
sprinted into a doorway across the street, apparently caught unaware
by the downpour.

She wondered if she had caused the storm. It had seemed natural,
somehow, to use the water as a transition.

Martin's building had been a nice place back in the days long before he and Molly were born. It had probably been a nice place more
than once during the long, slow cycles of urban renewal and decay.
But he lived in a different part of the city from the neighborhood of
Ria's quixotic drive to rehabilitate the Calhoun lake bed. There had
been warehouses here in the city's prosperous youth; squatters and the
homeless had moved in as those slowly fell into disuse; the squatters
had been tossed out when the warehouses and grain elevators became pricey lofts and condos full of exposed brick and wrought iron;
the tendril of a light-rail network snaked through the neighborhood;
the seas rose, the plankton died, the economy went south, the condos
went empty, the light-rail line went unused; the warehouses and grain
elevators were knocked down, the tracks paved over, the lots left vacant; a bull market funded rejuvenation of the neighborhood with the
construction of replica warehouses when new zoning laws demanded
architectural tribute to the neighborhood's role in the city's early history, thus giving rise to nineteenth-century flour mills reimagined
as towering pillars of nanocomposite; but then somebody fired a sat-
ellite killer, starting a war in the heavens that cratered the global
economy, and the historical tributes became swaying tenements in
the sky.

There was an outer security door, but that had never been replaced with nanodiamond. It was just reinforced glass. Or had been, until somebody had hurled a cinder block through the door. The block sat on the waterstained lobby floor, surrounded by square chunks of safety glass, propping the door open. The intercom had been pried from the wall. It dangled from a few strands of frayed wire. The lobby smelled like pee and worse. Something had died in here. Molly hoped it was a cat or raccoon.

Glass crunched under the soles of her shoes. It shimmered with the reflected light of luminescent graffiti that covered a wall of dented and battered mailboxes. Indecipherable scribbles like urban hiero-glyphics proclaimed turfs and rivalries and the mightiness of forgot-ten street-corner pharaohs in a baleful turquoise glow. She couldn't read it. The English was too stylized, the rest too foreign. The entry-way had no proper illumination; copper thieves had left jagged rents in the walls when they ripped out the wiring. Shadows flowed around her in time to the flickering pulsation of the graffiti.

Somebody's boot had left a perfect impression just above the kick plate of the inner door. A warp in this one caused it to screech when Molly pushed it open. Something scuffled in the shadows behind her.

"Hey, hey, you lookin'? You lookin'?"

Molly spun. The man had been huddled on a camp stool in the far corner. She hadn't noticed him because the luminous ink on his shorn scalp matched the dull glow of the graffiti. He smelled cleaner than his surroundings, like aftershave and casual violence.

He lifted his shirt. A silky pouch gurgled over his stomach. He'd been bio-modded as a drug mule, secreting synthetic opiates from af-termarket glands embedded in his skin. His body was covered with ink, but it wasn't very good, and didn't glow. She glimpsed the handle of something tucked into the waist of his pants before he dropped his shirt.

"No," she said. "I'm not buying."

"You could be," he said. "Maybe you want to try."

"Maybe I don't."

"Maybe you're in the wrong place. Maybe you leave before some-thing bad happens."

"I'm here to visit somebody."

At that, he blinked. "Oh yeah? Maybe I know her."

"Maybe you know him." It occurred to Molly that he might. This guy was very much the kind of company her brother tended to keep. And it was also very possible that Martin had moved, or even abandoned his place after what happened in Australia. Perhaps he'd never returned to the States. "Martin on the twenty-first floor? Maybe he buys from you."

The bald attempt at sleazy charm crumbled under the weight of his suspicion. A frown pulled his eyebrows lower. "What you want with him?"

"So you do know him."

He looked her up and down again. "Oh, I get it. I get it. You're working. He always says he doesn't have any money but I guess he's saving it for you." He licked his lips. "Hey, maybe you come back after you finish with him? I can pay you real good. Give you a nice tip, too."

Molly gave him the finger. "Oh, piss off."

He gave a little jerk as if he'd just received a shock from a doorknob. A rivulet of blood trickled from his nose. When he shook his head, clearing it, little crimson droplets stippled the floor.

She started to turn away, but his hand went under his shirt again. "What, you'll grind with that strung-out piece of shit upstairs but I'm just a piece of garbage, is that it? Maybe you shouldn't be so full of yourself. Maybe it gets you into trouble."

First he called her a hooker, then he threatened her when she didn't fall on her back with her legs in the air. Plus he called her brother a piece of shit. Molly decided she didn't care if this asshole popped a vein in the brain. She wanted him to have an aneurysm.

She gave him the full force of her attention. "Go fuck yourself, jackhole. I am not in the mood."

He blanched. After a moment's pause he dropped his eyes, turned, and stumbled back to his corner. As he folded up his camp chair and stalked outside, muttering to himself, Molly noticed the pulsating glow of graffiti had grown dimmer. Biomimetic paint; it responded to changes in the ambient light conditions. The lobby was brighter now, suffused with a different glow. Molly couldn't see its source, only that the shadows had disappeared.

She didn't trust the elevators in this dive, which always smelled like taking a ride in a clogged toilet. She also didn't feel like climbing twenty flights of stairs, which usually involved running a gauntlet of homeless squatters. In the past those had been her only two choices, either one coming with a real danger of assault. This time she took a shortcut through the Pleroma by stitching the inner lobby door to the fire exit on Martin's floor.

Muffled voices came through the door to his apartment. It sounded like he was watching a video. That was encouraging. If he could concentrate on a video he couldn't be too far gone. Unless he'd turned it on just to hear human voices. She did that, too, when she felt lonely. Molly raised her fist to knock, but then caught herself.

What in the hell was she thinking?

How would Martin react if he opened the door to find his dead sister standing there? What would it do to him? If his body wasn't already full of chemicals, it would be within sixty seconds of her saying, "Hi." How could she bring him comfort if the mere sight of her was sure to send him into a tailspin?

Even if she knew how to change her appearance, and she didn't feel very confident about that, it wasn't likely to do any good. How creepy would it be to have a complete stranger show up on his doorstep, spouting cryptic platitudes about death and continuance? Besides. For such a sweet guy, Martin's distrust of people ran deep enough to border on psycho when he was strung out. He'd probably slam the door in her face. And, frankly, he'd be a fool not to.

It made more sense to scout out the situation before she approached him directly. She already knew how to go unseen and unsensed; that was her natural condition when traveling on Earth. She just had to get inside. Knocking was no good unless she wanted to freak him out; if Martin was unstable, opening the door to find nobody there would do him no favors.

But the door had a peephole. The glass fish-eye painted the lemniscate glow of a caustic on the opposite wall. Apparently the rain had stopped and the sun had emerged; Martin wasn't the type to bother with shades or blinds on the windows. Molly touched a fingertip to the smeared reflection. She folded her body into a flophouse analemma and rode upstream against the flow of sunlight into Martin's apartment.

She landed in the kitchen. And gagged. It stank of rotting food. Cockroaches scuttled under the pile of dishes when her invisible halo fell upon the sink. Ants seethed across the fried rice spilled from an upended takeout container on the counter. *I should have come sooner.*

There was no division between the tiny kitchen and the main living space, just a demarcation where cracked and soiled linoleum became matted and soiled carpet. The empty bundle of blankets on the futon smelled of Martin and still retained residual body heat; he had to be nearby. On the wall directly facing the futon, characters cavorted in an unfamiliar animated show from India. If the wall had sensed her, she knew, they would have spun their hallucinatory dances around her. But that wasn't what transfixed her.

A portion of the wall—the largest portion of functioning wall— had been set to show a few-second snippet from a New Year's Eve party some years back, when Dad was still alive. It was a photo of Martin and Molly together. They were smiling for the camera, arms around each other's shoulders. Martin's eyes were clear, unclouded. That had been one of his better periods. Her hair had been longer back then. She was laughing at something Martin had said to the person behind the camera. She didn't remember the last time she had worn those earrings, and wondered what had happened to them. The laughter and background hubbub of the party played on a continual four-second loop. Martin had used a black marker to draw a curly picture frame around the image.

A ratty length of yellow electrical tape held a piece of paper to the wall alongside the image. It was the program for Molly's memorial service.

There was a memorial service? But who organized that? She didn't belong to a church, and there was nobody left except Martin.

Oh, Martin. *Why didn't I visit you sooner? Why didn't I check on you right away?*

Water pipes clanked in the adjoining room, through a closed door. Martin had gone to the bathroom. Vaguely aware that she had met Bayliss in much the same way, she turned so that she could see Martin when he opened the door. The wall hadn't noticed her, and neither would Martin. Once she saw him, got a sense of his emotional state, she could figure out how to approach him.

But the door didn't open. And then it still didn't open, and then it still didn't open some more. She heard a strangled sob, and then something on the air—under the mélange of decay and pharmaceutical fumes—carried a faint hint of the primordial sea. It tasted like the ocean, like salt, and rang like a crystal bell. A fallen teardrop.

Warily, Molly opened the door, then reeled from the miasma of sorrow and self-hatred that came roiling out of the bathroom. Her brother sat on the closed lid of the toilet. His head hung low, almost low enough to press his chin to his chest. He was sobbing. One hand held a syringe; it sloshed when he trembled. The other held the knot of a rubber tourniquet around his arm. He was locked in that position while desire and shame and confusion warred within him. The pall of grief overwhelmed even the funk of rotten food in the kitchen. Molly understood.

He'd come in here to shoot up because he couldn't stand to do it in front of her photo. Martin didn't want his dead sister to see him doing this. He wanted to be the brother from that New Year's Eve, wanted to be worthy of her legacy, didn't want to be the brother she'd once found unconscious and barely breathing. But he also wanted to die, because he was alive and she was dead because she had pulled him out of danger on an icy tram platform in Melbourne. The part of him that wanted to die of shame, that wanted to sink into a chemical forgetfulness, held the needle; the part of him that wished he were stronger sat on the toilet and cried.

The bathtub, and the floor alongside it, was littered with needles, rocks, sooty spoons, foil, and glass pipes. The needles smelled like the man downstairs, but the residual venom glistening on their tips bubbled with carbon rings wearing long slinky molecules designed to seduce receptors in the brain. But the syringes were empty. Their contents had disappeared into Martin.

Molly went to him. She couldn't reveal herself to him, not yet, but she could comfort him. If she had come to him before now, the urge to provide succor would have overwhelmed her good sense, and a single touch would have killed this fragile man. But just as she'd known how to deal with the creep downstairs, she knew now how to temper the angelic with the mundane. Somehow she understood, intuitively, the spiritual alchemy of solace.

Martin slumped sideways when she put her arm around his shoulders. He leaned into her. He didn't know he was doing it, didn't know she was there. He hadn't even noticed when she opened the door. But she held him all the same.

"Shhh," she whispered. "I'm okay, Martin. I'm really okay." The frequency of his sobs decreased. He shuddered and sighed. "I didn't die in pain," she cooed. "I'm free of anger and danger and sorrow."

None of this was true, but it soothed him.

"Carry no shame. Carry no sorrow. You never failed me. You're my brother, and I love you no matter what."

This part was true. Martin shivered.

"Remember me, and be strong. Be the person you want to be. Strive to be the person you would have wanted me to know. And don't be afraid to fail along the way."

Oops. That was the wrong thing to say. He straightened, adjusted the grip on the needle, and brought it up to the bulging veins in the crook of his arm. Molly leaned forward to puff one gentle breath upon the syringe. A freak cosmic-ray shower speared down from the upper reaches of the atmosphere; it penetrated the tenement and sundered molecular bonds. The syringe's chemical cocktail became a harmless solution of saline and inert molecules. Martin injected himself with his own tears.

Molly sighed. Martin went slack. The empty syringe clattered to the tiles.

"You're so tired," she said. It was crushing, the weight of his weariness. He carried a dead sister on his shoulders. "Go to bed. Lie down and sleep."

Martin struggled to his feet. He shuffled from the bathroom, unaware of how heavily he leaned on his sister's ghost to make it across the living room.

"Lean on me. Lean on your guardian angel."

She laid him on the futon.

"Sleep," she whispered. "Sleep with untroubled dreams."

And he did.

13

AN OFFER YOU CAN'T REFUSE

I collected my hat while Uriel stepped outside for a private chat with the Thrones. I was glad they hadn't tossed me in the cooler; I wanted to owe Uriel bail money about as much as I wanted another hole drilled into my head. Owing favors to a Seraph is a bit like owing a shark dinner: sooner or later, it costs an arm and a leg.

But I was already in dutch. She'd sprung me. As to why, I couldn't begin to guess. I liked this not very much. As tired as I was of the Thrones' broken-record act, at least I understood their angle. But I didn't have a line on Uriel's play.

They returned. The bulls announced they were letting me go. I could tell this wasn't their idea, and that they liked it not very much. Lots of that going around recently. But the Seraphim draw a lot of water in this town, so what Uriel wants, Uriel gets. Even if that means a penny-ante keyhole peeper like me.

She looked me over. "You're looking better already."

I straightened my collar. "Let's dust, angel."

She elbowed past the Thrones on the way out. I gave them a wink. One grabbed me by the arm. "Keep your nose clean, Bayliss. Next time, we don't play so nice."

"Yeah, yeah. Sell it to somebody who's buying." I shook my arm free, flicked the brim of my hat. "See you in the funny papers."

Uriel had already passed from the Thrones' Magisterium and was striding through the between-spaces of the Pleroma. I hurried to catch up. She had quite a pair of pipe stems on her. I waited until we'd put some distance from the hoosegow before saying anything.

"Thanks," I told her. "I always said you flaming sword types were the real cream."

"No doubt."

"You sound skeptical."

"I've been around the block a few times, Bayliss." She paused, frowned, looked me over. "Why 'Bayliss'?"

"Why Bayliss what?"

"What sort of name is that?" It's like I said: we in the Choir are big on proper names.

"It's a swell name. And besides," I said, "all the best ones were taken."

The sun belched. The Earth's magnetic field lines fluttered like gauzy curtains in an ocean-side bungalow. They cast rippling boreal light across Uriel's ox muzzle and shone on eyes the color of luke-warm magma. But the glimmer of her wings put that grubby mortal light show to shame. Maybe I stared too hard, maybe she reminded me too much of Gabby, maybe she didn't like me any more than the Thrones did. When she caught me staring, she flipped the lion pan in my direction and gave a little growl. I backed off; magnetic reconnection sent a stream of high-energy particles tumbling down the Earth's polar well. Add a random smattering of skin cancer cases to my list of guilty burdens.

"Come on," she said, "I'll give you a lift."

"Generous of you."

I hadn't told her where I was going, but she didn't ask. And it seemed rude to refuse the lady. Before I could give her the address she enfolded us in her wings, packed us into a six-dimensional sphere (one for each wing; three temporal, three spatial) and before I could say "boo" we stood on the doorstep of my Magisterial apartment. But I'd had my heart set on a visit to Flo.

Not too ungratefully, I suggested the diner. "I could warm my tonsils with a cup of joe. Getting beaten with a phone book takes it out of a guy." Uriel didn't go for it, so I poured on the honey. "I know the owner. I can talk a plate of bacon out of him, no charge."

Uriel stretched, straightened her wings; dewy cobwebs everywhere sighed and wished for better starlight. Her eagle face yawned, clacked its beak. Its breath smelled musty, like it had been catching rabbits from forgotten corners of the universe. "I'm not keen to get grease stains on my pinfeathers," she said.

I said, "No kidding. I'll bet your dry-cleaning bills are murder." But I gave up and made for the apartment all the same.

Somebody had paid a visit while I was out: the hair I'd hidden in the door frame had been dislodged. Whoever let themselves into my digs, they hadn't noticed it. I tried not to let the satisfaction show, and wondered what sort of dope overlooks the oldest trick in the book.

Maybe they were too busy kicking down the door. The hinges were severed and scorched. Their sheared edges still glowed a dull nuclear orange, as though somebody had cut through them with something sharp and fiery.

"After you." Uriel ushered me ahead with her sword.

I figured to find the place tossed, as the Cherubim had done to Molly's digs. Imagine my relief, then, when all I found out of place was the chessboard by the window. Somebody had moved a piece. Even my pipe still smoldered in the ashtray where I'd left it.

She—I mean they, whoever they were—hadn't come to toss the place. They'd come to drag me from my bed in the middle of the night. Only I wasn't there; I was down at the station house with the Bobbsey Twins. Guess it ruined a good show when the Thrones put the arm on me.

"Looks like you had it lined up tight," I said. "But the bulls scotched your performance when they jugged me."

Uriel kicked a chair at me. Her lion visage growled again. "Take a seat, wise guy."

Again, not a direct translation. But sometimes you just can't translate poetry.

"Nuts to you," I said. "I'm having that coffee one way or another." I went to the kitchen, feeling none too comfortable about turning my back on a Seraph. But I played it cool. "Flap your jaw at me while I minister to the percolator."

She didn't. Instead, she perused my bookshelf while I scooped grounds and ran the contraption under the tap. I dragged it out as long as I could, to buy myself a little time. I had the itch that told me I wasn't going to like what she had to say. Or maybe it was the door that clued me in. I have a knack for deductive reasoning.

I watched her while the percolator gurgled. Uriel never put down her heater. She plucked the books from my shelf one-handed, the other always on the hilt of the blazing sword canted over her shoulder like a poacher's rifle. She turned the pages by fanning them with her wings. Guess you can get pretty delicate when you've got six of the things. I always figured the Seraphim could do a swell turn of business selling pillows during molting season. She spawned a trio of Indian Ocean typhoons in the course of investigating my shelves. Whether that was a commentary on my reading choices, probably. Too modern. The high rollers have champagne tastes, but old-fashioned ones. I doubted Uriel had been to Earth since the time they painted her portrait in the Hagia Sofia but mistakenly called her a Cherub. You've never seen an angel pitch a fit like that.

Her own fault, though. As I said, it gets complicated when the high rollers visit Earth. Better they don't.

The hot remnants of my door hinges had cooled from gammas to X-rays by the time the percolator stopped making a show and I ran out of excuses to stall. I poured a cup for myself then fortified it with a dash from my flask. I didn't offer anything to the Seraph in my living room. Didn't want her sword igniting the fumes. And anyway, she could take a long walk off a very short pier. Don't tell her I said that.

"All right," I said, "say your peace."

I took a sip. Maybe it was a slurp. A flick of her wrist sent the tip of her blade through my cup. It cleaved the oils into fragments of biological molecules, rendered an invigorating jolt of joe into a nauseating hydrocarbon stew. The scent of fresh coffee became the toxic stench of burnt plastic. I sighed, dumped the contents into the sink, and sat in the chair she'd kicked out.

Her eagle pan said, "I came to give you a warning."

I looked again to the scorched door lying in the middle of my apartment. Bet there were some red faces around the water cooler when they realized she'd put on the big show only to find I wasn't home. I said so.

"If you want to play smartass with the Thrones," she said, "knock yourself out. But you're dragging our late lamented friend through the mud with your antics. No more."

"What's the harm? So I took an interest in Gabby's—"

Her wings flared. They seared X-ray–colored afterimages inside my eyelids. I'd forgotten how bright the Seraphim could be when they lifted the dampers.

"His name," she said, "was Gabriel."

I fished out a handkerchief to clean the bloody tears from my face. "Point taken. Still don't see the harm."

"You're an ignorant, clumsy lout. You have all the subtlety of METATRON but without its grace. You make a mess everywhere you go. And you're annoying."

"You forgot my dashing movie-star looks."

Uriel didn't agree. That hurt my feelings. She said, "We're handling Gabriel's murder ourselves. We don't need you raising questions. The Choir is watching you, and you're broadcasting the wrong impression. That will stop now. You will fail to find what you seek, and Gabriel's memory will persist unsullied. As it ought."

"Sister, has the entire Choir gone screwy? Can't you tell I just want my nice quiet little life back?"

"We doubt it."

I said, "Who is 'we'?" But it was a wasted breath. Who else? A tight little clique, those Seraphim. Gabriel, Uriel, Raphael, Michael, Raguel . . . Inseparable. Insufferable.

"We're handling it."

"Yeah? You finger the trigger man yet? You even know how those heels scratched him?"

Nice thing about the Seraphim: that human face packs a lot of emotion. Never been too accomplished at reading the emotions of eagles and lions, but I'd been on Earth long enough to recognize when some lollipop is trying to pull the wool over my eyes.

That look came over her human face now when she said, "We have it under control."

"You're full of sizzle but no steak. I wasn't born yesterday."

"Focus on keeping that monkey girlfriend of yours on a tighter leash. And see that she's housebroken. If she pisses in the pool again you'll both regret it."

"Yesterday's news, toots. And anyway, she's one of us now. She can do as she pleases."

"One of us? She's nothing but a monkey with airs. And if she doesn't fall into line soon we'll teach her what you can't."

I reached for my pipe. Emptying and refilling it, I said, "What gives with all the swagger these days? Seems a guy can't walk down the street without getting beaten and threatened. I remember when the Pleroma was a swell place to settle down and raise kids." I held the bowl of my pipe under her sword until the flames took. "Those were the days." I puffed until the smoke filled my mouth with the taste of cherries, or would have, had I a mouth at that moment. It brought me back to a time and place where cherry trees grew on terraced hillsides, and the trees were picked by friendly maidens, and the maidens were very friendly indeed. I sighed. "At the end of the day the threats are meaningless. Your punishments can't go too far or you'll rouse METATRON. So stuff a sock in the bluster, buster."

She gave me a look that should have left me two inches shorter. "Don't overestimate your charm, Bayliss."

"I don't. I'm too busy wondering what you meant when you said Gabb—I mean, Gabriel's—memory would persist unsullied. That implies there's room for sullying. So what's the dirt? It must be thick if you had to send the Thrones out to grease their axles."

Next thing I knew, my chair had gone over backward and I was doing my best impression of Damocles. "You'll stop asking questions about Gabriel. And your monkey will play nice from now on."

I tried not to go cross-eyed, but it was hard not to goggle at the tip of that thing hovering a femtometer from my noggin. She was fixing to pierce me in the third eye; I wondered if the Archangels would take on a charity case like me. Up close, that pig-sticker looked sharp enough to shear the red from a rainbow.

"Thing of it is, sister, every dopey Cherub and Throne and Virtue and Power will be gunning for her until somebody finally turns up the Trumpet. Half the damn Choir thinks she has it, or knows where to find it. And as long as they're gunning for her, they're aiming at me. You want us to pipe down? Put things back in order."

She pinned me to the floor by planting a hoof on my chest. It probably gave me a good look at her shapely faun legs, but I was too preoccupied to notice because her touch burned like an iron. Something sizzled and stank of burnt rose petals. I wondered if she intended to hold that pose until she burned straight through me and ruined the carpet. I'd hate to lose the security deposit.

Uriel knelt over me. "We'll have things in order in due time. Your smartass bumbling is making it difficult. Walk away." Her breath sparkled with Čerenkov light. "The monkey's problems aren't your problems. A smart angel would leave her to her own devices. A smart angel would get some distance from her. Sooner than later."

"You Seraphim are thick as thieves. What are you hiding from the bulls? When you thought I might have learned enough about Gabriel to tip them to your play, you swooped in and sent them packing." I couldn't push too far or I'd tip her to the fact I knew he'd been lamping Molly before he died. But did that sword waver, just the tiniest bit? While her eagle aspect shrieked at me and the human face frowned, I pressed my opening: "Enough with the sharp elbows. What did the priest know?"

Uriel stood, took her hoof from my chest. Sheer poetry in the way she moved, even the way she decided not to torture me any further. Generous souls, those Seraphim. She exhaled another cloud of superluminal fireflies, saying, "I've delivered my message. Take it or leave it."

On the way out, she added, "I'd get that door fixed if I were you. I hear this is a tough neighborhood."

I barely heard her, because I had a flash of insight just then. Or maybe it was a hallucination caused from the pain. I called after her. "Santorelli was on the pad, wasn't he?"

But Uriel was gone. She didn't bother to close the door.

I dusted myself off, finally had that cup of joe, took a shower, fixed the door, slathered ointment across the blistered hoofprint on my chest, rolled into bed, scraped my face, and let myself sleep in. Not necessarily in that order. Then I decided it was time to go for a drive. It had been a while since I'd taken the scenic route through the Pleroma. And from the sound of it, things had gone downhill since then. What a shame. There had been a time when it was nothing but orange groves as far as the eye could see. The world was simpler back then.

Knock it off, Bayliss, you sentimental sap.

I figured nobody could get sore at me if I took a gander at the Nephilim. It wasn't poking my nose into Gabby's business, and as long as flametop kept a low profile on Earth, we were overdue for some

smooth angles. Plus, if I knew the Choir, I wouldn't be alone in rub-
bernecking the newcomers. This was headline news, after all. And on
that count, at least, I was right. I expected a few gawkers; I didn't expect a milling throng with Thrones and Dominions working crowd
control. What can I say? Eternity can get dull. You take your kicks
where you can find them.

The first sighting had occurred in the ontological boondocks. I
parked on a cliff overlooking the shoreline where the churning surf of
quantum information paradoxes boomed against the shoals of non-
isotropic dimensionality. The ceaseless breeze is cooler here than it is
on the California coast, and rather than the tang of salt and death it
carries the scents of desiccated wonder and threadbare possibility.
Waxy tufts of alternate causalities cover the hillsides here like ice
plant. They crunched underfoot.

Foot traffic from the rubberneckers had eroded a path in the thin
dusty soil that sprinkled the ontological bedrock here. Somebody had
cobbled together a fence from slats of lightning and chicken wire of
braided starlight; it bordered the path and kept latecomers like me
from wandering over hill and dale. Maybe the Powers were still
tramping around with their magnifying glasses, seeking cigarette
butts and shoe prints. Or maybe there were things they didn't want
the rank and file to see. Too bad; I can't stand a secret.

I tried but couldn't hop the fence. It was taller and less rickety than
it looked. So many of my brethren had come to goggle this particular
Nephil that our overlapping conceptions of reality had melded into a
bland and unremarkable bubble. It was like a mini-MOC right there
in the Pleroma. Couldn't tell you the last time that had happened.
Apparently the gang had agreed to an ontological substrate where we
played nice and respected the boundaries represented by the fence.
What a bunch of suckers. But I couldn't throw the kind of weight it
would take to raise a pimple on that nice smooth sphere of consensus,
so I made like a tourist and joined the conga line with the rest of the
saps jostling for a good look at the interloper.

An enterprising soul could have made a pretty penny selling sand-
wiches and lemonade to the yokels. I wondered how much wax paper
cost in the Pleroma these days. Maybe after all was said and done I
could get a small business license, become a respectable pillar of the

Choir community. I made a mental note to propose a partnership
with Flo; a few slices of her banana cream would knock this crowd
out of its socks.

The trail switchbacked past the hermit cave where the lowly angel
had been doing its meditations prior to stumbling over the Nephil.
Poor kid probably had to abandon its hobby and find new digs after the
gawkers started queuing up. The switchback relaxed into a wide knoll
built from alternating sedimentary layers of hidden-variable theories.
The rubbernecks took their time along the edge, gaping and gazing
and snapping blurry holiday pics. It took finesse to weave through the
crowd. I didn't have it. I trod on the trailing edge of a Dominion's
leathery bat wing and got an earful for it. I backed off, making my
apologies, and barely dodged a swift kick with a diamond greave. I tried
not to take it personally; they weren't so bad, the Dominions, but Gus-
tave Doré gave them a bum rap and they'd been sulky ever since.

Naturally, the high rollers had claimed the front-row seats. I had to
content myself with taking in the view through the transparent
wings of a Cherub. The knoll overlooked a narrow sound formed by
multidimensional breakwaters of quantum indeterminacy. Slow ripples
of mathematical entropy lapped at the shoreline, eroding the non-
Abelian symmetry groups along the water's edge into towering pillars of salt. Not much to see at a casual glance, unless one happened
to notice the minuscule refraction of time shadows where formless
ontology met the subtlest hint of teleology. I was staring at a dormant
topological defect in the Pleroma. So were we all.

Easy thing to overlook. Probably would have missed it altogether
had I been camped out here all by my lonesome. It didn't move; it
exerted no weight on the Pleroma at all. I caught a slight whiff of sterile
neutrinos, but couldn't be sure it came from the Nephil. The crowd
hubbub made it impossible for me to tell if it made any noise. Archangels sang; Principalities clanged their brass-bell wings; Virtues murmured time-symmetric palindromes to themselves; Thrones rolled
up and down the hill, snapping at anybody who stumbled too close to
the edge; Dominions clanked and jingled in their golden breastplates.
Meanwhile a pair of Seraphim circled in the hazy sky beyond the
safety fence. It appeared they were gearing up for something, so I lit a
pill and watched the show.

I wondered if the Voice of God was out there somewhere, watching over our shoulders. Maybe it was.

They spiraled up into the lofty reaches of the Pleroma. At an altitude of several light-years, they tucked their wings and rolled over. Gaining speed, they extended their sword arms and swirled with perfect synchrony into a two-pronged superluminal corkscrew. Those muggs meant business; I hadn't heard of them pulling out the big guns like this since the first days after METATRON revealed itself. I wasn't the only angel to step back. Like I said, the Seraphim draw a lot of water, and there's a reason for it.

Down, down, down they sped, the leading edge of their assault a golden ring, a blazing razor sharper than the now that separates past and future. The spinning blades cast incandescent sparks; the searing-hot wind of the Seraphim's passage scorched the ice plant and scoured the soil into glass. They bore down on the Nephil like a trillion-rpm buzz saw. My loose fillings echoed with the music of the spheres again. I really had to see a dentist about that.

They hit the Nephil. Nothing happened.

Michael and Raphael went skidding into the void, shedding clouds of silver feathers along the way. The music of the spheres became deafening static. I ground my teeth together to clamp down on the buzz. A collective gasp rose from my assembled brethren. Even with the combined mojo of all the gawkers who'd made the hike from their Magisteria to see the interloper, the Seraphim couldn't carve the slightest scratch in the fabric of the Pleroma around the Nephil's perimeter.

Broken topology trumped angelic ideology.

I didn't know if that thing down in the shoals was conscious, or if it had willpower. But it could shrug off the Seraphim and that meant it was some mean medicine. Uriel had insisted they were handling things. But if this was their idea of taking charge, the Pleroma was in even worse shape than I'd imagined.

Suddenly, Gabriel's murder didn't seem so impossible.

I went straight back to my Magisterium and wasted no time getting very, very tight.

GUARDIANS AND TORMENTORS

*M*olly pulled another blanket over her brother. She listened to the faint hint of a snore in the rhythm of his breath until she knew this was a restorative natural sleep. Then she rummaged the apartment for drugs, breathing on every vial and syringe and rock she turned up. If she poured his drugs down the sink, or flushed them, he'd assume he'd been robbed and try to steal them back. That would only escalate until it ended in disaster. So instead, an astronomically improbable—but not *impossible*, for she didn't want to piss off METATRON again—confluence of cosmic rays and natural radioactivity transmuted the chemical cocktails. Even the ghostly dark matter wind breezing through the Earth contributed to the alchemy, turning pharmaceutical gold into briny dross.

She could do many things previously unimaginable, but she still couldn't reach inside Martin to fix the addiction. Humans were too complicated. She knew the MOC implicitly, but her expanded mind tried to leak out her ears when she considered the long ladder leading from the MOC to biochemistry. The universe was simple. People were so much more complex. No fix, no path toward correction, unspooled in her mind when she considered Martin's plight. She knew the underpinnings of the MOC, but people were a complex emergent phenomenon. She needed more practice if she were ever to help Martin. Or Ria.

Oh, God, Ria. Molly choked on a sob. Outside, the heightened concentration of cosmic rays ionizing the atmosphere seeded cloud formation far above Martin's building. The sun disappeared again; shadows grew.

Biochemical signatures were nothing compared to the pall of guilt, loneliness, and sorrow that clung to Martin like cobwebs. No, she couldn't fix his body. But she could watch over him until his grief wasn't deadly. Until his mind could heal itself.

After transmuting his stash, she took a seat on the futon to watch him sleep. Just a little longer, she told herself. Just until she felt satisfied he'd have a restful night. A healing night. The hardest part was leaving the filth and the dishes and the roaches where they were. Were she still alive, she would have taken a stab at the squalor while Martin dozed. But it would do him no favors to wake from untroubled sleep to find the place unrecognizably altered. He'd doubt his sanity. And they'd be back at square one.

The sun rose. But what day was it?

She was losing track of time. Earthly dates were fleeting; water through her fingers. How long had she been dead? How long had Ria been hurt? She was losing her connection to her home, to herself, to the human part of herself. She had come untethered. If that continued, she might drift forever on the tides of supernatural indifference until she lost herself completely. *That changes now*, she told herself. It was past time she anchored herself anew.

Molly kissed Martin on the sweaty forehead. Tasting salt and poison, she rode a slipstream of reflected shadows through the peephole and back to day-lit Chicago.

Just as the encounter with the Virtue had enabled her to interact in the mortal realm, it also left her with an implicit understanding of how to untangle the memory fragments stuffed in her pocket. Rather, there was nothing to untangle. She'd thought of them as pieces of string, a knotted ball of yarn. But that was a human metaphor for a work of Pleroma. Physical proximity meant nothing to the fragments of consciousness crammed in her pocket: on Earth, a pair of dreams didn't become intertwined merely because two people dreamt of the same café or the same dog on the same night. So, too, with memories. Molly wondered why she hadn't approached the problem in that way from the beginning. It was obvious. She felt a little stupid.

On the boardwalk, she took a bench facing Lake Michigan. It put her back to the ugly snaggletoothed grin of the crumbled skyline. Off to her left, the concert hall on its crystal pylons shattered the rising sun into a billion luminous fragments. She could hear how it disrupted the flow of traffic: bottlenecks sprouted where each piece of rainbow shrapnel forced drivers to shield their eyes. Molly wondered why the nanodiamond hadn't been treated with an electrophoretic coating to change its albedo as appropriate. Or if it had, why nobody had bothered to fix it. Grandeur and decay.

Molly spread the fragments on the railing before her as she'd seen in videos of magicians flourishing cards for a trick. They were intangible and thus immune to the ceaseless breeze that ruffled her hair, fluttered her coat, teased her lips. Pacholczyk's tired indiscretion sat on top, the guilty vignette that destroyed his marriage playing over and over again. Gabriel had also taken a memory from a soon-to-be widower who had sought a Plenary Indulgence for his wife, whose descent into dementia had left her incapable of coming to church any longer. The sour-milk reek of grief wafting from that one turned Molly's stomach. She concentrated on the joyful memories, memories of people who found solace and succor in receiving absolution for their imperfect earthly lives. Those tasted of rosewater and chimed like a toast made on fine crystal wineglasses.

She ran her fingertips across the array of memories. Santorelli's parish was the one of the few in Chicago granted authority to dispense Indulgences. The recipients came from a variety of backgrounds, neighborhoods, social and economic strata. The only obvious similarities were their ages, being middle-aged and older, and a reverence for the spiritual life. (*Five minutes with Bayliss would cure them of that*, thought Molly.) They exuded a desperate desire for piety. Some out of fear, some from a genuine desire for betterment—

A shock jolted her. Molly yelped. She yanked her hand back and sucked on her fingertips, half expecting to taste blood. The odor of ozone burned her nose; she sat in a fog of metallic anger and hurt the wind could not dissipate. She had snagged herself on a jagged edge, sharper than a rent torn across the sky by a hot fork of lightning.

This memory came from a woman who had been browbeaten into working toward an Indulgence against her personal beliefs and desires. The pall of dysfunctional family guilt, of emotional manipulation, lay so thick on the memory that Molly twice spat into the lake to clear the sour taste from her mouth. The recipient was young. Almost Molly's age.

Wow. One of these things does not belong.

Molly reexamined the fragment, more gingerly this time.

. . . head bowed low, hot tears trickling down her face, legs aching as she kneels at the rear of the church, air thick with incense smoke and prayers of the joyous faithful, Father Santorelli's reedy voice echoing through the nave, her father's hand heavy on her left shoulder and her mother's hand clutching the right, their fingers digging like talons while she cries for shame at her own weakness, angry that she let them win, that she let them drag her through this stupid pointless ceremony, full to quivering with the impotent knowledge that Father and Mother still misunderstand, that they believe she weeps out of regret for her sinful, godless ways, hating more than anything the smug confidence transmitted through their touch.

Mother stands. Anne, *she says.* It's time . . .

Emotional overload. Molly reeled. That afternoon had marked a crisis point in the woman's extremely complex relationship with her parents.

Holy shit. What was wrong with these people that they were so oblivious to their daughter's anguish? Molly missed her mom and dad more than ever.

She spat again to clear the phantom tastes of blood and bile and emotional manipulation from her mouth. Anne had tried biting her tongue, hoping to find distraction and solace in the pain. Anything to keep her from crying. But it hadn't worked, and her parents had seized upon the tears as evidence of spiritual cleansing.

The appeal to pain was interesting. A repentant *penitente*? Molly explored the memory again, seeking evidence of discomfort where Anne's parents touched her shoulders. But if it was there she couldn't find it. Anne didn't look at her own wrists over the course of the fragment, so Molly couldn't check for surgical stigmata. Even if she had, the tears beaded on her eyelashes were too thick to reveal anything but the prismatic blur of her own despair. The entire situation was fucked up.

Molly stuffed the other fragments back into her pocket. She wrapped the wrenching vignette of Anne's life around her thumb in imitation of how Pacholczyk's memory had twined itself about her finger. Remembering how her own memories had been altered when the Cherubim ransacked her Magisterium, she wondered if Gabriel had lessened Anne's memory of that traumatic afternoon when he lifted the fragment. She hoped so.

The memory tugged at her finger the moment she stood and turned away from the glare of sunrise on the concert hall. But the pull was weaker than the urgent divining-rod yanks of Pacholczyk's guilt. Was that an artifact of distance? Had Anne moved elsewhere? Molly didn't feel up to walking halfway across Wisconsin. She stitched together shortcuts through the Pleroma, stepping through light and shadow much as she had done to enter Martin's apartment and similar to the way she had first stepped from her own coat closet to Chicago. With a quick succession of jaunts through the Pleroma, punctuated by hops back to Earth to check her bearings, like a swimmer popping her head above water to double-check the location of the shoreline, she zeroed in on the reluctant Plenary Indulgence recipient. Molly traversed a much greater distance in a fraction of the time it took her to track down Pacholczyk. Anne's memory pulled her west, across Illinois, away from the rising sun.

In the form of early morning sunlight, she skimmed low and level across a small town. She glinted from the aluminum window frames of an abandoned bank to ricochet into the parking lot across the street. Wind conjured a dust devil from leaves and flower petals and discarded cigarettes. It teetered through the lot, scraping against a wall of pitted concrete to hop broken benches wrapped in overgrown weeds. The wind withered; the devil dissipated; Molly emerged from the shadows of a boxelder maple.

She stood in the courtyard of what had once been a small county library. The building was perched on a tall bluff overlooking a wide slow river. Sculpted concrete, circular windows, slanted skylights: the library dated to the previous century. So, too, did the funereal dirge thrumming in the turbid waters below, the sandpapery texture of residual phosphates and nitrates deposited into the soils of the riverbank. A checkerboard of farmland stretched from the river to a line of low tree-lined hills near the horizon, the fields jade and gold and ochre in the first light of the rising sun. The vista flickered with random glints of light as automated water purification modules pivoted to acquire the sun.

The fragment looped around Molly's thumb went slack. Anne was inside the library.

The stiff door creaked. Her entrance set cobwebs undulating and dust gyrating in the sunlight. She'd never been inside a proper old-time library before. Not one that still had actual paper books. She hadn't expected the mustiness, the thick scents of dust and glue and old paper. The atmosphere here carried a portentous weight, of information lumbering in printed paddocks rather than winging weightlessly through a sterile electronic vacuum. It was ponderous. This, she realized, was how it had felt to be human in the age of books.

Her entrance drew a stare; a man stood behind a desk. Several stacks of books flanked him. The word CIRCULATION on the wall overhead had been painted over, but it bled through the thin coat of paint. He looked alarmed by her presence.

"Um," said Molly. Something about the atmosphere of this place made her want to whisper. "Am I allowed in here?"

Eyes wide, he gave a slow confused nod.

"I'm not registered here. Do I need to be?"

The shake of his head was no slower, no less confused. He hadn't blinked since she entered.

"Great," said Molly. "I'm looking for information about—"

"We have a network," he said. And shrugged, almost apologetically. With one last stare in her direction, he turned his attention back to the stack of books he'd been inspecting when she entered. Whatever his strange job entailed it apparently didn't involve helping people find information. So he wasn't a reference librarian. Of course not. Who looked things up in books any longer? That had fallen out of fashion in her grandparents' day. The town was lucky to have a functioning library at all. Her dad had told her about how in his father's day most towns had a library, or one nearby, but that they had fallen into disuse and neglect as information went online.

The squeak of a cart cut through the thick silence. Anne was somewhere nearby. Molly couldn't see her, but the dusty air sloshed in time to a trio of heartbeats. Whatever work took place at this library, only three people did it.

Molly doubtless could have found everything she needed online. But in order to appear as if she had a legitimate reason for coming in

she used the library's network to find theological references. Maybe
she could learn more about simony and Plenary Indulgences. She also
sought books about what used to be called New Age topics to see if
her mother's follies could shed any light on the nature of the Pleroma.
She pulled an armload of books from the shelves and took them to a
table at a window overlooking the river. But it was warm and quiet in
the library, the river peaceful.

She woke some time later—the pattern of sunlight glinting on distant fields had changed—when somebody dropped a stack of books on
her table. The clap rattled the table and set Molly bolt upright. The
wind of the falling books felt cool against her face. The corner of her
mouth and part of her chin were damp. She'd drooled. Lovely. She
coughed and sputtered into her sleeve as she ran it across her face.

"I'm sorry. Was I snoring?"

A woman smiled down at her with hard blue eyes. Her round face
was framed by short jet-black bangs on top and long lavender ringlets
to the sides. Red veins rimmed the whites of her eyes. Molly recognized her by virtue of the long eyelashes; she had looked out through
those same eyes when she inhabited Anne's memory. It hadn't seemed
so voyeuristic until now. Anne wore denim coveralls over a faded
t-shirt. Molly took one look and knew this woman had never been a
penitente. And she had a cute smile.

Still smiling, Anne said, "Go fuck yourself."

That was less cute. Molly paused in the act of scrubbing the last
traces of drool from her face. She blinked. "Huh?"

"How much did they pay you?"

"I'm very confused right now."

"How stupid do you think I am?" Anne rounded the table to loom
over Molly. Molly scooted her chair back. "Did they hire you just to
find me and send a report, or do they expect you to badger me until I
return?"

Anne's voice echoed. Molly said, "Can we please calm down here?
I think there's been a mistake."

"Yes, there has. You go back and tell them that the next time they
pull a stunt like this, I'll change my name." The jagged-lightning feeling prickled across Molly's skin again. "I'll vanish. I'll make it so difficult to find me that they'll spend every dime for the rest of their

miserable lives in vain. They'll die never knowing what became of their beloved only daughter."

Wow. This really was one messed-up family.

"Look," said Molly. She raised her hands in what she hoped was a conciliatory gesture. "I don't know your parents, okay? I swear. Whatever your argument with them might be, I promise you I'm not part of it."

Anne glared at Molly's pile of books. "So you just happened to wander in, wanting to read up on religion?"

"Pretty much."

"Nobody ever comes into the library except us."

"Maybe I live in town but haven't had a need for the library until now."

"You're the first person to come inside for six or seven months. He came in for directions. The woman before him needed to use the bathroom." Anne looked her up and down. "You're not from here."

"Neither are you," said Molly. "You grew up in Chicago."

"I knew it. They did send you." Anne turned back to her cart. Squeaking away into the dusty shadows, she said, "Well, you be sure to tell them they can go straight to the hell they fear so much."

Molly followed her past a curled and faded paper placard labeled MESOAMERICAN ART AND CULTURE. "Okay, okay. I admit it. I did come in looking for you. But not because of your parents, all right?"

Anne didn't slow down. "We've never met. How could you be looking for me?"

This was ridiculous. Molly jogged ahead, yanked the cart out of Anne's hands. "Damn it, would you please just listen? I came here because"—Screw it, she thought, I can't do any worse with the truth than I've already managed.—"I need your help."

That brought Anne up short. Her ringlets swept past her ears. She blinked when she was startled. If she hadn't been frothing over with anger it could have been attractive. "Come again?"

Molly glanced around the library, wondering if this was the right place to discuss a murdered priest and Anne's traumatic Plenary Indulgence. She wasn't sure how to bring that up without sending Anne through the roof. The guy from the no-longer-a-circulation-desk watched them.

"It's a little complicated." Molly checked her lenses for the local time, then asked, "I'll buy you lunch if you'll let me tell you about it. Please?"

A few mare's tail clouds had unfurled across the southern sky. But the day was warm, the breeze cool. Molly ignored the smell from the river, focusing on how the day appeared to her human senses. Another dust devil sent bits of rubbish swirling alongside them like an ephemeral chaperone. Most storefronts along the street had been boarded up, much like the bank. The hardware store, a real estate office, even the movie theater were closed. But the army recruiting office on the corner had become a café.

Molly hadn't eaten since she died. Her human body would have been ravenous, even weak. She conjured the memory of hunger. She breathed on the dull red spark until it flared anew with the feeling her stomach would crumble upon itself for being so hollow. That would make it easier to share a meal with Anne. Ancient tradition, breaking bread; it fostered connection. How sad that she had to die and become something else in order to appreciate the beauty of this.

Molly asked, "What are you guys doing at the library, anyway?"

"Archiving. We scrounge for scraps to feed the great digital maw." Anne shrugged. "Not everything made it online before the library system collapsed. The important stuff did, or the stuff deemed important at the time. The major university collections got slurped up early on. But the apocrypha and ephemera, the miscellany of small-town life, never made the transition. Thirty-year-old Little League scores, ads for used tractors, self-published manifestos by the local wackos. We're combing for bits and pieces to fill in the picture of life in a simpler time."

"Who cares about some podunk baseball game from decades ago?"

"You'd be surprised how many home movies we've converted. All blurry, all shaky, all boring as hell. But we have a grant from the state, so in they go. Along with all the rest of it."

"What happens when you're done here?"

"Move somewhere else and start over."

"But why care about so much worthless crap?" That earned a glare from Anne. Molly shook her head, sighing. "I'm sorry. That came out wrong."

Anne paused with her hand on the door to the café. "Everything was important to somebody at one time or another. We'll forget who we are if we forget who we were."

She went inside while Molly stood on the sidewalk, digesting that. Anne had already taken a table in the corner by the time Molly caught up with her. There were more people here than at the library, but they were mostly concerned with each other. Oddly, Molly felt more comfortable with the prospects for a private conversation here than at the abandoned library.

"What's good here?"

"Nothing. But you're unlikely to get food poisoning as long as you don't order anything with eggs in it."

"Oh."

"Relax. I'm kidding."

Molly ordered a cup of tomato soup and a BLT. Anne didn't look at the menu. She ordered an iced tea, a tuna sandwich with mayo and please remember the mustard this time, chips on the side instead of greens, plus an extra pickle, and please remember the extra pickle this time.

"Eat here a lot?"

"It's the only place to eat unless you feel like driving fifteen miles. You'd know that if you were from around here." Their waitress brought Anne her iced tea. As she twisted the lemon slice, drizzling juice into the tea, Anne said, "But I already know you're not. So why do you think I could help you?"

Truth, Molly reminded herself.

"I understand that you knew Father Santorelli. He, uh, died recently. I'm talking to people from his church to understand him better."

"Dead, huh? Well, too bad I'm not there to piss on his grave. But I'll be sure take a pit stop if I'm ever in Chicago again."

Molly asked, "Why do you hate everybody so much?"

Emotion flitted across Anne's face too quickly for Molly to read it. But the pH of her perspiration shifted almost imperceptibly toward the alkaline, where ruffled feelings resided. She didn't, Molly realized, want to be perceived as somebody so angry. A jangly chartreuse thing, the scent of hurt.

Anne said, "Why are you really talking to me? Lots of people attend that church. You went well out of your way to find me."

Truth. "I'm in a lot of trouble," said Molly. She lowered her voice. "There are some people who think I have something that doesn't belong to me. I don't, but they don't believe me. For reasons I don't understand, the guy who used to have the thing I don't have was very interested in Father Santorelli and the people who received Plenary Indulgences at his church. If I can understand why, maybe I won't get my ass kicked again."

"Wow." Anne looked around the café, then leaned forward. Also in a lowered voice, she said, "That's the most confusing lie I've ever heard. Am I supposed to believe you're hiding from the Mafia, or that you're a spy?"

"I know how it sounds. Maybe I oversimplified a little bit, but the full story is even crazier. You'd be much less likely to believe me if I told you the rest of it. I promise I'm telling you the truth."

"Crazier, huh? Are you being chased by the Loch Ness Monster?"

Molly said, "Why are you being so difficult?"

Anne said, "Why are you so full of bullshit?"

Molly didn't want to force the issue as she'd done with the dealer in the lobby of Martin's building; there was always the danger Anne could stroke out. But she also didn't want to spend the rest of the day talking in circles like this. She studied Anne more closely, seeking a hook that would win her over. She looked again at the bloodshot eyes. The skin beneath them was dark and papery. Crumbs of a restless night had gathered in the corners of her eyelids. The lids were just a fraction of a second slow to rise after every blink, as though they carried extra weight. Anne's hand trembled faintly when she lifted her glass of tea; her breathing carried a weary wheeze. Deep in the part of Molly that was still human, something sat up. She asked, "How long have you had trouble sleeping?"

A pulse quickened at the hollow of Anne's pale throat. To Molly's disappointment, Anne didn't make that little blink of surprise this time. She was able to cover her alarm because their food arrived. Anne concentrated on dissecting her sandwich. But Molly knew she had found the hook so she let her take her time. The soup was thin. It had come straight out of a can; the residual buzz of metal tingled across Molly's tongue. She sipped at it anyway.

While spreading mustard on her sandwich, Anne said, "What makes you think I'm not sleeping?"

"Same thing that tells me your parents forced you to pursue a Plenary Indulgence."

That did the trick. This time, Anne did blink. She said, "My parents are religious, okay? As in really religious. As in they keep a statue of the Blessed Virgin in the dining room, complete with votive candles."

"Yikes. For real?"

"Yeah. For really real. And when they found out I was gay, they freaked the fuck out."

The moment Molly had experienced via Anne's stolen memory suddenly made sense. "They thought you were damned."

"Yep."

"But that's crazy. Why did you go along with it?"

"Because I couldn't take the constant badgering. It got so tiresome . . . I just thought, I don't know, I thought that if I went along with their stupid ceremony and then kept quiet about my personal life they would draw their own conclusions and leave me alone. But it was so awful. They were so smug when they thought they'd finally won. I've never felt so alone as when I was sitting in that church realizing how deeply I'd betrayed myself and knowing they would never give up. But by then it was too late and I was trapped. I hated myself when I realized how foolish I'd been. They would never accept me. They would never even try. I had to cut them out of my life if I didn't want to be miserable forever."

In another life, with different parents, Anne's situation might have been Molly's. She wanted to dab away the tears forming in Anne's eyes. She caught herself reaching across the table and turned it into a grab for the pepper shaker. She tipped it over the remains of her soup.

"I'm lucky," Molly said. She carried the taste of lavender in her mouth, soft as a soap bubble. "My dad was really cool when I came out to him. Mom came around pretty quickly after that."

Anne shook her head, wafting rancid rue and envy across the table. "Lucky dog."

"If it helps," said Molly, "and while we're sharing family secrets, my brother is a drug addict."

"No kidding?"

"He's a really good guy at heart. Martin's just . . . He has problems sometimes, you know?"

"What kind of drugs?"

"Just about everything, at one time or another." Molly thought of the apartment she'd departed a few hours earlier, and the trail of pharmaceutical transmutations she had left behind. She hadn't recognized most of what she'd seen.

"I'm sorry I was such a bitch at the library."

"Don't worry about it. I kinda want to punch your parents now. And I don't blame you for being upset when a complete stranger shows up and starts prying into your personal history." Molly shook her head. "I handled this terribly. I didn't even introduce myself. I'm sorry. Can we start over? My name is Molly."

"Anne."

Molly reached across the table. "Nice meeting you."

Anne looked perplexed for a moment, but apparently decided a handshake was harmless enough. Her hand was soft and warm.

"I still don't understand," said Anne, "why you care about any of this."

"I don't know either. I don't know why any of this is important. Or even if it is. Maybe it isn't. I'm just trying to make sense of the world." Molly hugged herself, vaguely aware that Bayliss had once said something similar.

Anne drained her tea, stirred the ice, sipped at meltwater. "Why did you say that about me not sleeping?" The aura of rue, regret, and bitterness faded away. Now the air around Anne crackled with cautious hope like clashing thunderclouds.

Molly searched her face for more signs of sleeplessness. She lingered on the bloodshot eyes, and told herself she wasn't seeking eye contact. But it happened, and it tickled, and she looked away to suppress a shiver.

"Just a hunch," she said.

Anne sighed like somebody choosing between an ugly sweater and an uncomfortable one. The silence grew long but, somehow, not awkward.

"The nightmares started after I received the Indulgence," she said. "I think it tore me up even worse than I first realized. I toyed with seeing somebody about it but I can't afford therapy."

Gooseflesh prickled Molly's nape. Pacholczyk had been weary, too. Worn down by a succession of sleepless nights.

"I know I've already asked you a ton of personal shit that's none of my business. But can I ask about the dreams?"

So earnest was the gust of hope emanating from Anne that it seemed a wonder their napkins didn't flutter in the updraft. "If I show you, can you interpret them for me?"

Anne pushed the plates and glasses aside. From the breast pocket of her coveralls she produced a narrow Moleskine journal.

"When I sleep," she said, sliding the notebook across cracked and coffee-stained Formica, "this is what I see."

Molly opened it. It was a sketchbook filled with page after page of drawings rendered in colored pencil. Some hasty, some detailed, but every image rendered with the skill of a delicate hand. And each one terrifying, disturbing: Faces of fire. Feminine faces fringed with beards of starlight. Eyeballs and wheels and flaming swords. Beings with the heads of eagles, and oxen, and lions. Wings of silver, wings of bats, wings of glittering diamond and pitted brass. Swirling clouds of darkness that scuttled like a millipede on legs of lightning.

Anne was tormented by dreams of the Pleroma. She'd been dreaming of the Choir.

Knowing the answer, Molly asked, "This started immediately after they bestowed the Plenary Indulgence on you. That very night. Didn't it?"

Anne's nod was jerky, tremulous.

Molly paged through the entire notebook. One image, in particular, was a recurring theme throughout Anne's sketches. Six luminous wings; four faces; a flaming sword. She had filled page after page with images of a Seraph, not understanding what she sketched. In some of the images, wisps of smoke rose from the angel's wings as they crumbled to ash. In others, maggots dripped from the angel's empty eye sockets.

Anne suffered dreams of dead Gabriel.

OLD FRIENDS, NEW PROBLEMS

I tossed a dime on the counter. It rolled. Flo poured a stiff three fingers into my cup. I winked. She scowled. The dime spiraled to a stop. The flies and the ceiling fan cycled through their eternal three-second dance. In the kitchen, DiMaggio hit a triple.

It wasn't palatable, the muck Flo served, but a splash of hooch fixed that well enough to wash down the last of the bacon. I lit a pill, picked the pork from my choppers, and waited. Two cups later I was running low on hooch and my plate looked like an ashtray. The pills were running low, too. Low enough that I considered bumming a smoke from the brush salesman, and was wondering whether I had the patience to endure his penny-ante sales pitch for the hundred-thousandth time, when my lunch date entered.

The lights dimmed. The play-by-play on the kitchen radio fuzzed out with interference from a station playing klezmer transcriptions of the music of the spheres. Up near the ceiling, wisps of burnt-bacon smoke succumbed to despair and hurled themselves into the fan blades; it didn't work. A Power sidled into the diner.

Say what you will about them, but they know how to make an entrance. An inky shadow wrapped in a lashing rain of ash and sleet, it rode on 144,000 constantly flickering legs of forked lightning. This particular jasper's proper name was the basso profundo thrum of dark matter winging through the void, the fizz of neutrinos boiling off a moribund blue supergiant, and the bitter-tangerine taste of a quadrillion-dimension symmetry group. But I called it Sam for short.

I waved it over. "Park the body, Sam."

It oozed over the stool beside me, enveloping the cracked leather like a thunderstorm wrought of molasses and shame. "Long time no see, Bayliss. I heard you were back in town."

Not exactly what it said, but let's stick to the executive summary. It's the thought that counts, and besides, a faithful transliteration would require seeding a daughter universe with a spectrum of radically different physical constants. Who has the time for that these days?

Flo sidled over. "Who's your handsome friend?"

She really did say that. Leave it to a crafty jane like her to know a butter-and-egg man when she sees one.

"Flo, Sam. Sam, Flo. Breakfast's on me. They do a mean fried egg and bacon sandwich here. Coffee ain't terrible, either." I gave a wink and let Sam catch a glimpse of my flask.

"Hey, you," called the guy staked out near the telephone. He fiddled with his bow tie. "That lightning must be murder on the hair. I'll bet you go through brushes by the bushel."

I yelled, "Stuff a sock in it, chiseler."

He made a rude gesture. "Go soak your head, rummy."

Sam didn't exactly say, in a voice like burning sapphires, "Nice place you have here."

I said, "My own little slice of heaven." Sam grimaced. That gag had been getting creaky when the solar system was just a ball of gas. But Sam was dining on my nickel so it could afford to laugh at my jokes.

Rather than take my suggestion, Sam glanced at the menu. It ordered toast dipped in a fractal space with negative dimensionality. I guess it was on a diet. Flo took her time filling its cup, giving it doe eyes all the while. Sam didn't play along. She got the hint and took a hike.

"I was surprised to get your message," it said. "Surprised to hear you'd returned at all. I figured a smart angel in your shoes would have kept to himself."

"Nobody ever accused me of being smart. I get by with charm and wit."

"Even those are in limited supply these days, from what I hear. The talk is that the Thrones nabbed you, and then Uriel nabbed you from the Thrones."

"She goes for me in a big way. Bing, I tell you. Always has."

"That's not how she tells it."

"Yeah, well. Dames." I took a sip. Lukewarm, Flo's coffee tasted like boiled wood chips stewed in paint thinner. But it was high-end paint thinner, thanks to my hooch. "What else are people saying these days?"

"They say you're mixed up with Gabriel's death. Some say you're the trigger man. Others say you're a witness and the real trigger men have you in the crosshairs. Others blame the Nephilim. They say the bulls will have you dead to rights sooner than later. They say META-TRON's latest tantrum was your doing, or that of your human sidekick. Half the Choir thinks you know where the Trumpet is, and the other half think you already have it and can't decide whether to chance using it."

"I tell you, I'm getting tired of always playing the fall guy in this lousy little drama. Let me know if you want to take my seat on the bus." I chewed at my thumbnail, waited until Flo turned her back, and spat. "As for my human sidekick, she ain't human. Anymore."

"She doesn't belong in the Pleroma."

"There was no choice. We had to find a replacement for Gabriel."

"The talk is you fumbled that job down the sewer."

"Well, at least they got that part right. More or less. I was a little tight. But hey, lay off flametop. She's all right." I wasn't so certain about that, but I tried to sound convincing. Full of surprises, that one, but I saw no point muddying the waters with Sam.

"They say that when the Nephilim strike again, it'll be you and your monkey feeling the noose."

"Oh yeah? What do they say about us after that?"

"Nothing. The smart money," it said, "isn't on you and the human."

"That's why I like you, Sam. When I'm feeling glum I can always trust you to feed me some sugar."

"You didn't call me here to lie to you. You can do that to yourself for free." It paused while Flo refilled its coffee. She worked the moon-eye treatment for all she was worth; deep inside Sam's roiling darkness, lightning speared a microburst of downspiraling ash. She sighed and drifted away to check on the tomcat chewing face with a round-heels in the corner booth. It said, "The Pleroma is changing. It isn't the place you remember."

The Powers orbit the periphery of the Pleroma, pacing the perimeter of our playground. There are those who say the Pleroma is holographic, and that anything known inside the joint can be read in the pattern of ontological wrinkles on the boundary. I don't know if that's the case, but I do know the Powers keep a closer ear to the ground than even the Thrones. Or, at any rate, they're not full of spaghetti like the bulls. I'd known Sam a long time, always known it to have a solid line on the players and their angles.

"Speaking of which, tell me what you know about the Nephilim."

"You've been out to see them, I assume?"

"Yeah. Caught the show a few mornings back when Michael and Raphael decided to stop playing nice."

If it had had a mouth, Sam would have whistled through its teeth. "Harder to get rid of those things than a wart."

Again, you get the gist of it.

"What does the smart money have to say about them? Why are they here?"

"They're waiting," said Sam. "For what, nobody knows. But only a fool would bet they're not connected to Gabriel and the rest of this mess."

"How am I the only bum to see the big picture here? Their purpose, if they even have one, is small potatoes compared to the real issue. Doesn't anybody find it strange that after umpteen-billion years we suddenly discover a previously unknown topological property of the Pleroma?"

Sam's shrug sent tendrils of ash eddying through the diner. The salesman tried to cover his cup, but too late. He scowled at us. "Hey, watch it, bub."

"Ignore the sourpuss," I said.

Sam said, "Gabriel's death changed the topology of the Pleroma. It swirled through all our Magisteria. A cold wind, Bayliss. A cold, cold wind. Who knows what detritus those deep currents dredged up?"

I rubbed out my last pill. I wasn't out of matches, though, so I struck one on my thumbnail. The flame burned down while I checked the room. Nobody seemed to be paying us any wise, so I asked, "Fine, then. What's the word on Gabriel? And no baloney here. Don't drag me into it."

"As to what happened? A few theories. Nothing concrete. Most folks don't like to linger on it."

I remembered a silvery snowfall, remembered how the friction heat of conflicting Magisteria crumbled Gabby's wings to ash. "I've never met anybody who punches in that weight class. Wouldn't care to."

"Don't pretend the Nephilim don't top your list, too."

"Yeah, well. You can't make a killing on the ponies if you don't bet the long shot once in a while."

Sam took a long sip of its coffee, but declined when I offered the last drops from my flask. I treated myself.

"When's the last time you took a trip to Earth?" I asked.

"That's your playground," said Sam. "Never understood how you could stand it down there."

"It ain't so bad. You like this joint, don't you?"

Sam didn't exactly say, in that rasp of burning sapphires, "I like a free meal."

"Who doesn't?"

Since Sam hadn't been down Earth-way in a millennium of Sundays, I took a minute to tell it about the *penitentes.* I described the surgically sculpted wounds, the dancing, the mortal attempts to evoke shorn wings and stigmata. I described the mugg I'd caught leaving the confessional right after somebody had rubbed Father Santorelli. Flo brought its order of toast. Sam chewed while I recited the headlines.

I finished. "Any thoughts?"

"On Earth as it is in Heaven," it said.

"Yeah," I said. "My thoughts were running down the same tracks. Let me save you some time: they don't lead anywhere."

"Maybe. Maybe not." Sam scribbled on its napkin with a feathery quill pen of lightning. "Funny, the stuff you can find if you keep your eyes peeled. Everybody has their dirty secrets."

Sam knew a few of mine, too, but I didn't remind it. The note it slid down the counter stank of a forest fire. I took the napkin and squinted at the chicken scratches. Powers don't have much in the way of penmanship; maybe it comes from being insubstantial all the time. I realized, after the nimbus of Saint Elmo's fire faded, that Sam had scribbled down an address.

"Thanks, Sam. You're a champ."

"Anybody asks, you didn't get that from me."

"Get what? I don't know what this is."

I had to shout to get that last part out, because just then Sam erupted like Krakatoa. It became a roiling plume of ash and sulfurous fumes, inky blackness shot through with blazing talons of lightning. Thunder shook the diner. The fry cook's radio fuzzed out and gave up the ghost. Flo dropped the coffeepot. It sent up a fountain of burned coffee when it shattered on the linoleum. She said something unladylike. So did I.

The salesman said, "Hey, rummy, I think your pal there is choking."

I threw a plate of toast at him. "Shove off, grifter."

Over in the window booth, the sheik came up for air. He and his girl glanced at Sam, looked at each other, shrugged, and went back to necking. She was built for it, long and lean.

To Sam, I said, "Maybe this is the wrong time to mention it, but if you're having an ing-bing, you should know they took my medical license away."

If earlier Sam's voice had been the rasp of burning sapphires, now those jewels were naught but plasma. It got the eruption under control just enough to rumble a stream of concepts so blue they hadn't been heard since before the universe had begun to expand. From the torrent of prime numbers and indignation I picked out just enough to know what had it doing figure eights. Another Nephil had just manifested in the Pleroma. It had slipped right past the Powers' patrols.

"Where's the fire, pal?" I reached for its arm, or what would have been an arm had it had one just then. But Sam disappeared with a thunderclap.

Flo said, "What's eating your friend?"

"Case of the jitters. Too much coffee."

Flo sighed. "Rats. He looked like a swell tipper, too."

I guess I wasn't dressed for that part.

*F*ollowing the address took me down, down, down. I expected to find some dingy joint in the Pleroma, or some love nest tucked far from prying eyes in the ontological hinterlands. But Sam's lead took me to Earth, and below it, thousands of furlongs beneath the Mohorovičić discontinuity. It was dark, and close, and streamers of mantle kept dripping onto my hat. The dry cleaners would charge extra to get the magnesium and silicon stains out; I should have brought an umbrella. Maybe a flashlight, too. Nights are full of shadow, I learned, three hundred miles beneath the surface of the Earth. It's the kind of darkness you don't see anymore, outside of solid rock and certain very dense molecular clouds. Not since we lit the fuses on those first fast firecracker stars. But the deeper I went, in search of Sam's elusive address, the greater the concentration of heavy elements in the surrounding rocks, the greater the residual radioactivity, and the brighter the surroundings. Nuclear decay lent the neighborhood a cozy glow.

I figured maybe Sam had given me a lead on some buried treasure. Compromising photos. A cask of ambrosia wine lost in a Phoenician shipwreck, dragged to the depths by a thirsty tentacled leviathan, and subsequently absorbed into a subduction zone. A shoebox full of shiny dimes. A shoebox full of tarnished dimes. I'm not particular in these matters. I forged ahead, looking forward to celebrating my not-so-ill-gotten gains with a San Francisco joy girl or two. The way I saw it, I owed myself a pretty little send-off before my luck caught up to me and the Nephilim took it upon themselves to rub out me and flame-top.

Such were my thoughts as I oozed, like soft candle wax, into a fissure shot through the heart of an olivine polymorph. I'd sunk deeper than I realized; most of the surrounding minerals were coming unstable, flowing and separating into their component compounds as plastic deformation stretched their crystals apart like taffy. The weight of the earth caused their lattices to buckle.

So I'll admit to a moment of surprise when I found the shelves. Somebody had embedded an austere Pleromatic overlay down in the upper mantle. It looked a bit like a bank vault lit with the greasy yellow light of thorium decay. At first I thought the shelves held human memory fragments—another illicit collection like the one I'd found in Gabby's Magisterium. You would have thought so, too, if you'd sniffed the mortality coming off those things. But I'd never seen such a sedate collection. And when I ran my hands over the shelves no disjointed scenes of mayfly mortal life leapt to my senses. Inert, the lot of them. Colorless and dull as the world's most closely guarded collection of lead bricks.

And yet, alive. If I listened, I could just make out the hummingbird buzz of truncated mortality. The vault fairly thrummed with it. And I knew why.

These were monkey splinters: pieces of *penitentes.*

When those loonybirds went under the knife to add wounds and pinfeathers and dripping stigmata to their mortal bodies, somebody was also *removing* something from them. I wondered if the *penitentes* knew somebody had lopped off pieces of their souls, hollowed out secret hidey-holes in their pneuma. Maybe that was part of the attraction. I didn't see it, myself, but it does take all kinds.

I scratched my head, wondering who had done this, and why, and how. It takes a special kind of scalpel to carry out surgery like that. Not the sort of thing for which any old quack will do. They don't teach this stuff in med school. Yet there were plenty of clinics where you could slap down some of the folding and limp out a few hours later lacerated with all the antiseptically sculpted metaphors for metaphysical angst your pain tolerance could handle. Somebody in the Choir had a busy little hobby. Why bother? Easier to collect stamps. Some people watch birds. I'd once known a Virtue who went around collecting the fading reverberations of cosmic strings. But pieces of mortal souls? Oh, brother.

I plucked a fragment from a shelf. I rolled it between my fingers. It had all the gravity of dandelion fluff and all the pizzazz of a dead trombone player. Mortal souls are like that. Don't let the poets tell you otherwise.

Somewhere, deep inside me, there resided a fragment similar to this: the mortal epsilon. METATRON had crammed it there. We all had them, every member of the Choir. Ours were finer, smaller, and the product of a Trumpet rather than a dull metaphysical scalpel. Compared to METATRON's handiwork this was spiritual butchery of the basest sort. But to what end? I'd managed to flick a fleck of glamour into Molly's dying eyes to make her one of a kind, and I hadn't needed to chop out part of her soul to do it.

I stuck the fragment in my eye.

And suddenly I wasn't riding currents of plastic flow through the upper mantle any longer. I was on Earth, in a mortal body, wrapped in a cloud of sweat and sex and nihilistic desperation. We wore no shirt while we danced; humid, sticky air wafted across damp spots on our back. The seeping wounds in our shoulders throbbed with pain. Infrasound backbeats ruffled our matted pinfeathers. We weren't alone on the dance floor. The woman gyrating against us had a surgically implanted eyelid in the center of her forehead, and it fluttered in time to the beat as though trapped in REM sleep. She was empty, too. Somebody had scooped a parcel from her soul, and so, too, from the souls of our fellow *penitentes* gamboling to old trip-hop samples of Gregorian chants. A collection of capering vessels, us, and none the wiser for it. The mind within the body I rode didn't sense the shade peering through its eyes.

We reached to pull the splinter from our eye. It meant grasping at our face with untrimmed nails, cuticles caked with black flecks of blood from the gashes in our palms. I flinched, and so did he. Together we stumbled through the crowd on the dance floor, herky-jerky marionette movements controlled by an epileptic puppeteer. We glimpsed an untended drink on the bar. My human host reached for it, splashed it into his eye—

—And I was back in the Pleromatic vault beneath the surface of the Earth, the fragment dangling from my eyelashes. I swatted it aside, eager to get that dingus away from my face. It rolled across a shelf, still lacking in luster and vim. This entire vault was just a little bit bent. If there were such a thing, I'd have said it was just a little bit evil.

What did the *penitentes* see in their deepest unguarded dreams? Did they dream of darkness and fire? Did they dream of eternal imprisonment in the depths of the earth?

Were they beset by nightmares of hell?

The psychic miasma of accidental voyeurism clung to me like the reek of an oversexed chain-smoking bonobo. I needed a shower. I needed quality time inside a steam cleaner.

This vault begged deeper investigation. But I wasn't keen on making another trek into the bowels of the Earth. So I worked down the aisles, scooping the *penitentes'* soul fragments into my pockets. Only when the shelves were empty and my pockets full did I head for my Magisterium.

I think I set a speed record.

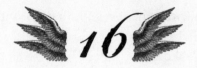

DINNER, DREAMS, AND DEATH

Molly rummaged through the kitchen cabinets of her Magisterium, searching for a clear memory of the bottle of excellent red wine she had shared with Ria on a Christmas Eve three or four years earlier. Memories and cracker crumbs accumulated on the counter and floor until she found a green glass bottle shaped like a wyvern, the label's golden script luminous on an emerald-green label. Then she sprinted upstairs to brush her teeth. She checked her hair and face in the bathroom mirror while she brushed. There was a blemish on her temple; she imagined it healed, and it disappeared. She checked her nose for anything embarrassing, and contemplated her eyebrows, but decided against plucking. Next, she hurried into the bedroom and flickered through several outfits before the full-length mirror. She chose a denim jacket, changed her mind, changed the denim to leather, decided against a jacket at all, started to leave, decided she looked better in a jacket, and donned the leather again. She cupped her hands before her mouth, exhaled, tried to catch the scent of her own breath. It was toothpaste sweet. She checked the mirror again, inspecting her nose for clogged pores.

And noticed the baleful cyclopean glare of Bayliss's cigarette burn on the floorboards behind her.

"Asshole," she muttered. With the mental equivalent of a flicked wrist she wished the burn away, imagining a floor whole and unblemished.

It didn't budge. The burn persisted.

Molly turned. The spot rippled in response to her frown, but didn't shrink. She concentrated until the precursor of a piercing headache circled in the spot between her eyes like a dog tamping down a favorite rug.

"To hell with it," she said. "Later."

*T*wo doors flanked the entrance to a hardware store. The slip of paper taped above one mailbox read, ANNE MUELLER. The narrow door opened on a narrow staircase. A steep climb took Molly to Anne's door, but it took an extra minute of nervous fidgeting before she remembered how self-confidence felt.

She knocked. The scents of spaghetti sauce, garlic bread, and vinegar wafted into the hallway when Anne opened the door. She shimmered within an aura of happy anxiety.

"Hi," she said, hummingbird quick. She looked down to hide a bashful blushing smile.

"Hey," said Molly. And fidgeted. Lost for words, she raised the wine bottle. "I brought . . ." The self-confidence left her. "Crap. Do you even drink wine?"

Anne said, "Only on special occasions." Smiling again, she ushered Molly inside.

For somebody living in a lousy one-horse town, Anne had managed to find a cute apartment. The building must have been old: high ceilings, lots of exposed brick, wrought-iron bannisters along the spiral staircase and loft. The wooden floors still carried the scuff marks where, a century earlier, machinery had rumbled and shrieked twenty hours a day. Molly could still hear the residual echoes if she closed her eyes and concentrated. The kitchen had a central island under a metal ring covered with hooks for hanging pots and pans. Most of the hooks were empty.

Anne followed her gaze. "It would be cooler if I owned more than two pots," she admitted.

"It's very cool," said Molly. She set the wine bottle on the island. "Thanks for letting me come over. Especially after I came off so bizarre the other day."

Anne blushed again. If she kept it up, soon her face would match the color of her ringlets. "We kind of got off on the wrong foot. I'm sorry I told you to fuck off."

"I deserved it," said Molly. She clapped, rubbed her palms together. "So. What can I do to help?"

"Keep me company while I toss a salad?"

She did. It was easy.

*T*earing apart a piece of garlic bread, her fingers shiny with butter, Anne asked, "So how's the mystery of the stupid fat priest coming along, Nancy Drew?"

Molly blinked. "Um. You lost me."

"Nancy Drew?" Anne shrugged, shook her head. "Just something from old books. She was a girl detective." The bridge of her nose crinkled above a soft smirk. "Like you."

Molly laughed. Anne worked in a library. It showed. She read a great deal more than Molly did. Molly wondered if that would become a problem. She wondered if she'd have a chance to find out.

"Yeah, I guess so. Never thought about it that way."

Not much of a detective, though. She was no closer to understanding the significance of Father Santorelli's Plenary Indulgences. Visiting his rectory had proved a dead end. The diocese had already crated up his few belongings in preparation for the arrival of a new parish priest. Whether intentional or not—how high did the Earthly side of this go?—they'd left behind no hints about the PIs. All that remained of Santorelli's work was a three-ring binder filled with printouts of his sermons. The later, newer entries looked like the diary of a madman: every bit of blank space, from the backs of the pages to the narrow margins on the printed sides, were filled with sketches similar to those in Anne's dream journal. He'd lacked her talent, but the contents were unmistakable. Image after image of a being with four faces, golden wings, a flaming sword. Like Anne, Santorelli had been having visions of Gabriel, too. But his were of the Seraph prior to his murder.

Each pen stroke quivered with desperation. The sketches fairly vibrated with the tension of a tilted worldview. Molly could read in those unskilled renderings the reversal of a long, slow, sad acceptance of the temporal world's boundaries. The existence of the divine, of the incorporeal realm, had long receded into the abstract realm of philosophy, as had the spiritual underpinnings of Santorelli's pastoral work in the community. His faith had slipped away from him an inch at a time.

Until an angel revealed itself to him.

Unlike Molly, who still hadn't revealed her true nature to Anne. It felt good to be regarded as a human woman again. Far better than it felt when the more responsible part of Molly wondered how long she could maintain the charade. Anne hadn't yet asked her where she lived, but she would eventually. Wouldn't *that* be an awkward conversation.

Sooner than later she'd have to come out to Anne. How in the world would she do that? *Have I mentioned I'm not entirely human?* Sure. Or maybe she could break the ice with some small talk first. *Hey, you know that afterlife your folks are always going on about? Well, the joke's on them. . . .*

And the more she considered it, the more uncomfortable it became to frame this as a traditional question of coming out. This situation was so extreme that lumping it in with the human experience seemed dismissive of all the people who had ever endured the fear and anxiety of coming out to family and friends. Molly's previous experience was no guide.

Still, for now, she was closeted, hiding her true nature. Pretending to be something she wasn't. Lying about who and what she was because she feared how the people around her would greet the truth.

Would it be anger? Fear? Disgust? Would it be the end of this tentative relationship? The cold and cruel severance of their budding friendship? Or would Anne take the news in graceful stride as Dad had done?

It hurt to deny her true self. But a violent rejection would hurt even more. This was the first normal relationship, the first friendly interaction, Molly had enjoyed since dying. She wanted to pretend it could last. She wanted to experience life as it had been before Bayliss came along.

So she masqueraded as human, choosing to stay in the closet just a little bit longer. And hating herself for it. Hating her selfishness. Hating her cowardice.

Anne was staring at her. Molly shook her head. "No progress. But you helped me a ton the other day. Honest."

"No joking?" Molly nodded. Anne said, "That's nice. It makes me feel good."

She concentrated on her food. With exaggerated care, she spun another noodle around the tines of her fork. With equally exaggerated nonchalance, Anne said, "I'm glad you called."

"Me, too," said Molly. Her voice squeaked. Her face felt hot. She looked away.

You're not human, said her nosy bastard conscience. *Anne is the victim of something vast and terrible. And you're flirting with her like it's no big deal. You scheming self-absorbed rat.*

Molly cleared her throat, but the extra space didn't make the words flow any more easily. "You probably should know that my last relationship ended badly."

Anne chewed a mouthful of salad. Swallowed. "How badly?"

Ria's a drooling vegetable now. Because I touched her.

Anne flinched from something she saw in Molly's eyes. "I'm sorry. That was rude."

"No, it wasn't. I brought it up." Molly fortified herself with a sip of wine. "Really badly. Terribly. I'm sort of still dealing with it."

"Oh. I see." Gently, silently, Anne set down her fork. "If I've misinterpreted this dinner—"

Shit. "Oh, no. No, no, no, that's not what I meant. That came out wrong. I just meant, if I seem a little skittish or if I seem to be easing into this slowly, it's not because of you, okay? I promise. It's because I'm dealing with some crazy stuff going on in my life right now." *You lying-by-omission, conveniently understating bitch,* she told herself. "But I really want to be here right now." *Well, at least that part is true.*

She couldn't read the look on Anne's face. Molly realized what she'd said. "I mean, I don't know, if there even is a 'this.' I'm not assuming there is."

Anne's cryptic expression resolved into a quirked eyebrow. The corner of her mouth followed suit a moment later. "Crazy stuff. Sure, I can see that. You've got that whole Nancy Drew thing going on." She dipped a fingertip in her ice water, playfully flicked a few beads at Molly. "I'll bet that's a full-time job."

"You have no idea."

* * *

*M*olly sat at the end of the couch. She cradled her glass, taking care not to spill wine on the artistically distressed tobacco-colored upholstery. Anne placed the bottle on the coffee table and settled on the middle cushion with one leg curled beneath her. She draped an arm over the back of the couch, extending her free leg until her foot rested on the table. Relaxed and comfortable as a cat, she took a sip of wine. So did Molly, though her stomach churned with what felt like hundreds of butterflies.

The sketchbook lay atop a pile of magazines on the coffee table. Molly debated with herself for a moment, then asked, "Do you mind if I ask if you're still having the dreams?"

"No. Yes."

"That sucks."

Anne shrugged, looking sad. "It is what it is." She shook her head, as if flicking off a cobweb that had fallen in her hair. "You told me about your one brother. Any other siblings?"

The small talk came easily. It was even fun. They talked about family, movies, music, how Nancy Drew kindled Anne's love of detective stories. Later, they kissed.

Later still, Anne dozed off with her head on Molly's shoulder. Gently, carefully, Molly inched forward until she was off the couch, then eased Anne down until she lay on her side, breathing deeply. Molly took the blanket from the back of a chair and pulled it over Anne.

Anne whimpered. Her face twisted into a thick, slow frown. A flickering aura of alarm settled over her, the emotions sharp and sour as a razor-edged lemon. The air around her tasted of the Pleroma, like ozone and iron and stale starlight. She clenched her eyes. Her head rocked back and forth as though denying something inescapable.

"Shhh." Molly knelt beside the couch. She pressed her lips to Anne's forehead. "Shhh. No dreams tonight," she whispered.

Anne's breathing relaxed into a deep, even susurration. Her face relaxed. The air around her no longer coated the back of Molly's throat with the taste of bile and tingle of hot metal.

Molly stood. "Back soon," she whispered.

She tiptoed across the room to make it appear as though she were heading for the bathroom, just in case Anne woke up at the wrong moment. Molly tossed a loop of memory around her thumb, stitched a passage to Chicago into the bathroom door frame, and stepped from Anne's apartment into a moonless night intermittently brightened by meteor streaks of burning orbital debris. She hadn't traveled far, less than one time zone; it was still late here. Late enough that most people should be asleep still. Dreaming, still. She came here because she wondered: was Anne the only PI recipient tormented by dreams of the Pleroma?

It seemed unlikely. And she was indeed dreaming of the Pleroma— if the sketches weren't enough to convince Molly, the bitter ruffled edges of her sleep did it. Molly remembered how Bayliss had first appeared to her inside her own memories. Molly might have tried something similar with Anne to catch a glimpse of the roiling dreamscape that caused her to twitch and whimper in her sleep like a dog dreaming of squirrels. But unlike Bayliss, Molly wasn't an obnoxious voyeuristic prick. She hoped.

Pacholczyk lived in a gated community with walls high enough to insulate those on the inside from the worst times on the outside, when the oceans died and the satellites burned. High enough to withstand roving bands of barbarians; surely there were more than a few of those at the gate when times were at their toughest. The houses here were larger than any two houses Molly's family had ever owned, sprawling confections of brick, nanodiamond, and ivy. Pacholczyk's house evoked the style of a seventeenth-century English manor house, though built to a (slightly) smaller scale. Molly wondered if he actually kept servants to maintain the jumbled monstrosity of cornices, oriel windows, and dripping gray stone. It was far too large for a single person; she bet half the rooms had been empty even before his divorce.

Molly rode the split-second flash of vaporized space junk through the stained-glass window of a Dutch gable. She landed on the second-floor landing of a dark and fusty house. Her arrival displaced stale still air, kicking up eddies of dust and radon. It fizzed in her lungs and tasted like moldy bread. But she had been, for a microsecond eternity while speaking with the Virtue, a luminous figure wrought of naught but thought: she no longer needed lungs, no longer needed to breathe. But if she stopped, she might forget to start again. It could prove the tip of the slippery slope to losing the connection to her human life. If that happened, might she forget Martin and Ria entirely before figuring out how to fix them? A scary thought. So Molly chose to endure the musty environment of an obnoxiously wealthy depressed divorcé rather than lose a piece of herself. If she were being honest with herself, she had to admit she also worried that she might slip up and forget to breathe in a situation where Anne might notice.

No snoring, no heavy breathing disturbed the air currents in Pacholczyk's house. But for Molly's sudden arrival, there were no stray air currents at all, nothing but the thermal noise of Brownian randomization. No drafts from the windows, no eddies from the fireplace flues. Just the aggrieved sloshing of molecules shoved aside by Molly's appearance.

The floorboards didn't creak under Molly's feet. The deep pile of the runner along the landing betrayed no footsteps. Shadows fled from her, twirling around the balusters to hide from the faint glow emanating from Molly's body. She crept through Pacholczyk's house wreathed in her own tarnished halo, an intangible angel shining with invisible holy light.

She guessed, rightly, that the master bedroom would be upstairs. Pacholczyk slept in a four-poster bed with silk sheets. One side of the massive bed lay perfectly made, the pillow undented, ready for an occupant who would never return. A duvet in a froofy satin cover lay crumpled on the floor at the foot of the bed. Lingering evidence of the former wife? There was a framed photo on the bedside table, facing the bed such that Pacholczyk could fall asleep gazing at it if he lay on his side. Sentimental old goat. Too bad he was such a leg-humper at the office.

A crucifix hung on the wall over the headboard. Even in sleep his posture was pious, with hands clasped over his breast as though praying. Something glinted between Pacholczyk's curled fingers; it took Molly a moment to realize he slept with rosary beads on his person.

Aside from the duvet, and the photo, the bedroom looked like the bedroom of a very wealthy bachelor who had always lived on his own.

It was boring. Unremarkable. So, too, his sleep, which didn't fill the room with the clicking aura of sweaty dread as Anne's did. His dreams, if he had any, were benign. So calm was his untroubled subconscious mind that Molly struggled to sense anything from him.

Which is how she noticed he wasn't breathing. The silence she'd noticed upon her arrival wasn't the silence of an empty, shuttered house. It was the silence of a still heart. The reluctant silence of the dead.

Molly had never seen a dead body before, other than her own. And that she'd glimpsed only as meaty fragments scattered across thin snow. This was much cleaner. There was no blood, no viscera, no bones, no smell. Just a pale empty shell of a man losing its residual body heat. When Molly held out her hands, she could feel the fading whisper of infrared radiation coming from the sheets. Talis Pacholczyk had died earlier in the evening. And, from the look of things, in the middle of a peaceful sleep. If his heart gave out or he'd had a stroke, it had happened so fast he didn't have time to wake up for a final gasp or a few seconds of terrified scrabbling at the pillows. Not outwardly, anyway. But Molly, who had been through death, knew that no matter how sudden, how surprising, how unexpected it came, there was plenty of room for fear in that final split second.

The drawers of the bedside table were empty. Pacholczyk didn't keep a dream journal, or if he did, it wasn't in the bedroom. There was, unsurprisingly, no sketchbook left behind to describe his dreams for the benefit of nosy angelic passersby at the scene of his death.

The adjoining en suite bathroom made the master bath in Molly's old apartment look like a decrepit shit pit from the days before indoor plumbing. She'd never seen so many nozzles in a single shower. But the bathroom was equally lopsided as the bedroom. Beard stubble, soap scum, and a long smear of spilled toothpaste caked one sink. The porcelain in the other sink basin held nothing but a thin coat of dust. Orange plastic pill bottles cascaded to the marble tiles when Molly opened the medicine cabinet.

She glanced at a few labels. She didn't recognize the names of the medications, but based on the pharmacist's instructions Pacholczyk kept enough heavy-duty sleep medication handy to put half of Chicago into a coma. The vanity held still more pills. These she recognized by virtue of long experience wresting similar chemicals from Martin at one time or another. Amphetamines.

Molly looked at the dead man again. Looked at the rosary cupped to his chest.

First, he had tried to prevent himself from sleeping. When that didn't work, he tried dosing himself so heavily that either he'd not dream at all, or not remember the dreams he did have. It worked. He'd never dream again.

He hadn't embraced sleep in a posture of pious relaxation, she realized. He'd clutched the rosary for succor. Knowing what to listen for, she used her practice from the concert hall to pick out the fading whispers of slurred prayer that had trickled through the dying man's lips as an overdose of medication dragged him into everlasting sleep. Pacholczyk had been terrified of the night, so much so that he died with the Lord's Prayer on his lips. Whether it was accidental or not was beside the point: the dreams had driven him to kill himself. Asleep or awake, no mortal mind could glimpse the Pleroma and remain unchanged.

She wondered when he had received his Plenary Indulgence. Before Anne, or after her? Did Anne face a similar fate? Molly couldn't say for certain that he'd suffered from dreams similar to Anne's, but he'd been pretty damn frightened to fall asleep.

Molly slid a hand into her pocket, fingering memories from Gabriel's special Plenary Indulgence recipients.

*T*hui Nguyen taught history at a community college about halfway between Pacholczyk's place and Santorelli's church. Months earlier, her husband had walked out on her and their preteen sons. At first, she had wished him dead. Later, when the realization sank in that he wasn't bound to return, she gave in to despair, doing and saying things she regretted. The Plenary Indulgence had been a chance at a fresh start.

But now she muttered in her sleep. Molly—invisible, intangible—watched the frantic fluttering of Nguyen's eyelids, like a pair of moths trapped in a glass jar. Beneath the sheets and skin and bone, her heart beat a deafening tattoo. Her perspiration salted the close air of her bedroom with the tang of a primordial sea. Her bathroom closet was full of prescription sleep medication.

Molly kissed her on the forehead, as she'd done for Martin and Anne. "No dreams tonight," she whispered.

Nguyen's incoherent mumbling trailed away into light snoring. Her heart rate fell; she stopped sweating.

*M*oira Parks had attended the same church for over thirty years, and had missed only a handful of Sunday masses in all that time. Her memory fragment, of the evening she received her Indulgence, fairly radiated with cloyingly sincere piety. It made Molly's teeth ache. It also made her feel a little bit ashamed that she had never believed in anything with conviction.

But the fragment itself made a paltry divining rod. Feeling and following the feeble tugs took much of Molly's concentration. When she did, the fragment led her to a cemetery.

*R*obert Jemelik's fragment was even more difficult to follow. It sent Molly up and down the shore of Lake Michigan, and across the waters, and under it, and wheeling through the nighttime sky.

He'd been cremated. His widow had spread his ashes in the lake, per the request in his suicide note.

*T*hough it was so late at night as to be early morning when Molly tracked her down, Wendy Bavin was engaged in a screaming fight with her husband. Wasn't hard to see why: she was more strung out than Martin. The pent-up weight of unrealized sleep lay so heavy upon the woman that it seemed a wonder the floor didn't collapse under her.

The husband pleaded for counseling. Bavin snatched a lamp and cocked her arm back, wheeling up for a good throw.

Molly stepped between them, touched a fingertip to Bavin's forehead. "No dreams," she said.

The woman staggered. The lamp shattered at her feet. Molly slowed her fall until her husband could catch her.

*   *   *

*M*olly found herself standing in another cemetery, this one just a few blocks from Santorelli's church, as the eastern sky turned gray, then pink. When all was said and done, four of the dozen parishioners had died in the months since receiving their Indulgences. The rest lived in constant fear of falling asleep. For some, it was a low-level dread. For others, a shrieking drug-fueled anxiety. But they all had it. They whimpered in their sleep. They sweat and cried and twisted the sheets. They cowered from something they had glimpsed but could not understand. Just as Molly's touch had broken Ria's mind, a fleeting brush with the Pleroma had warped their psyches. The dreams were the mind's futile attempt to make sense of something incomprehensible.

Molly wondered—had this happened in the past? Had there been a time when angels moved freely among humans, unconcerned with the consequences? Was the genesis of religion a desperate need to make sense of a cosmos bestrode by terrifying alien beings? To find comfort in the incomprehensible? The nightmare visions varied a little bit among the Plenary Indulgence recipients though they shared a belief system. Which begged the question of how Molly might have perceived the Choir if she'd grown up elsewhere, surrounded with very different cultural expectations. What if she had lived in ancient Egypt? Or India?

Unlike the most abstruse details of the underlying physical structure of the MOC, the answers didn't unpack themselves when Molly asked these questions. Vast as it was, the knowledge the Virtue had pumped into her mind came up short on this front. Because the angels were indifferent about how people perceived them. Bastards.

Meanwhile, people were dying.

What did you do to these people, Santorelli? Did you know what your Indulgences would bring into their lives? Or were you forced into this, like Bayliss?

Gabriel must have known about this. But . . . had he caused it, or was he trying to prevent it? Or was he watching out of idle curiosity? Had knowing about it gotten him killed? Or had somebody been trying to stop him? And what was the point of all this? What did it achieve for anybody?

Sunlight glinted off Lake Michigan. Molly rode it west, back to Anne's apartment. Anne had shifted in her sleep, tossing the blanket off, but had not awoken. The apartment still smelled of dinner, but no sweat, no stress, no fear. Molly had banished the nightmares. All it took was an angel's touch. An angel had put them in Anne's mind, via the Indulgences, and another angel took them away.

She pulled the blanket back over Anne's shoulders. Then she curled up in a ratty armchair, watching Anne snore in dreamless sleep. But Molly was too deep in thought to notice when the light of dawn ricocheted from the pot rack in the kitchen. Sunlight flitted across Anne's eyes. She stirred.

"Hey." The words came out heavy, slurred by passage through undissipated sleep. "You're still here."

"I'm still here."

"What are you doing?"

"Watching you," said Molly, because it was true and she didn't know what else to say. Then she winced. But Anne was sleepy and didn't seem to notice how creepy it sounded.

Anne smiled, a long wide grin, slow and unstoppable as the rising sun. "That's sweet." She yawned, rubbed her eyes. "Have you been sitting there all night?"

"Nah." The yawn was contagious. Molly's jaw popped. She asked, "You seemed to be sleeping pretty well. Did you have the dreams again?"

Anne stretched, kinking and unkinking each leg and arm in sequence. She blinked. "No. You know what? I don't think I dreamed about anything last night. Not that I remember." Another yawn. "Wow. This is the hardest I've slept in I don't know how long."

"Thank heaven for small miracles," said Molly.

SIZING UP THE COMPETITION

*J*kept the soul fragments in a coffee can. The dull little din-
guses were nearly indistinguishable from the grounds. I gave
the can a few shakes for good measure. Then I returned the
coffee to the kitchen cabinet, and added an extra lock to the door to
my apartment.

It used to be that things were quiet and simple. The way I liked it.
But then Gabby had gone and gotten himself scratched, and I had gotten tangled up with flametop, and it had been one damn thing after
another ever since. Trouble was her business. That cluck had me
wrapped up so tight I spent most of my time staring at the back of my
own head. Much more of that and I'd save a small fortune on cork-
screws.

I had to clear my head. I needed friendly company. I needed to get
shellacked. A willing girl and an open bottle can cure a host of ills.

The telephone rang while I brushed my teeth. But I was too busy
spitting in the sink to pay it any heed. I rinsed, spat again, scraped my
face. Seemed like forever since I'd had some quality time with a joy girl.
But I took my time; I'm not some lowly skirt chasing tomcat. Happy
ladies take a shine to the fellas who clean up nice. Fellas like me.

I slipped my best unopened bottle of rye into the pocket of my overcoat. Didn't bother with tumblers and ice; we'd ring room service.
Maybe we'd put the house chef to work, too. Surf and turf if the wren
could tuck in or maybe a salad niçoise, hold the anchovies, if she
couldn't. I still had a few leaves of cabbage left over from hocking Gabriel's feather so I wasn't on the market for some fleabag joint with a
revolving door and hourly rates. The occasion, and my mood, called
for something flossier than my usual haunts. Ladies enjoy a night on

the town with a high roller. I departed my Magisterium and shook the dust of the Pleroma from my heels.

I went with a soft-spoken brunette dish. Recent events had put me off redheads and their wicked jaws. She was a nice girl with big eyes, a tiny mouth, and a long slender neck just begging for a string of pearls. But I wasn't feeling *that* flush. She told me her name was Violet. It was the best kind of lie, the kind you wanted to believe because it matched her eyes. I lied in kind, and told her my name was Bayliss.

We took the bottle to the Blue Room. I knew a guy there. He rolled the eyes when he saw I'd brought my own, but gave me a break on the corkage and treated my date like a lady. She liked that. Liked to dance, too. And wasn't I pleased to see she could flow to the old stuff. Sometimes you pick a good one. I was overdue for a run of good luck.

"How's a girl like you familiar with music like this?"

The music was slow, her body warm, her dancing slower and warmer still.

"Aww. Half this job is role playing," she said. "You meet all sorts in this line of work. Lots of freaks and creeps." She swayed, shimmied, and did something to my insides.

"Which one am I?"

She chanced a look at my eyes but flinched away. Hid it well, though, by laying her head on my shoulder. "You, I can't figure. You didn't climb all over me the minute we met." I'm a gentleman. I don't paw. "Usually that means you're looking to pretend I'm a real date, willing to pay anything just so I'll gasp out an 'I love you' or two when you heave yourself on top of me. But I don't get that sense from you, either. You're a strange one."

I drank my rye. Violet was a gimlet girl. She nibbled the lime and didn't make a face. I liked that.

We danced, and drank, and never pretended it wasn't a business relationship. She danced like somebody who listened to the music, nothing like the full-body grand mal seizures that passed for hoofing it these days. She had genuine rhythm. That boded well for the rest of the evening. Dancing with Violet, I could almost forget what it had been like to ride in one of the *penitentes'* close sweaty bodies. Almost.

"You ever step out with a *penitente*?"

What an old-fashioned twist: she blew a raspberry. "Those kooks? They give me the willies."

"You and me both, sister. You and me both."

We turned some heads on the dance floor. She was a cut above the usual bims and frills that passed through a place like this. Violet lined up more business while I settled the tab. Solid work ethic, that girl.

She took my arm. I'd picked a hotel along the waterfront, so we blunted the sharpest edges of the hooch with a slow stroll along the bay. Not too slow, though; I was paying by the hour, and her old-fashioned dancing left me with an antique case of the hot pants. The gimlets had her pie-eyed just enough that I chanced stitching together a few shortcuts through the Pleroma. If she did notice anything off-kilter, she didn't squawk. What a trooper.

Our room had a wardrobe with real wooden hangers. A bed, too. I helped Violet out of her coat, hung it in the former, and tried not to look too obviously at the latter. I called down to room service for a bucket of ice and a bowl of strawberries. Violet kicked off her heels and sidled into the bathroom like she'd never stopped dancing.

A bellhop delivered the ice before it had melted, and for that he earned a decent tip, but nothing extravagant. He would have understood had he seen the dish. He wished me good night and bowed out. But I'd just enough time to set down the ice and the strawberries when he knocked again. I figured he'd taken a closer look at his tip.

I opened the door. Molly said, "Miss me?"

Inwardly, I moaned. Outwardly, I groaned. Molly stepped around me. The ice and the strawberries earned a quirked eyebrow; her lips settled into a little moue of disapproval when she saw the heels and the closed bathroom door. She doesn't miss a trick, flametop.

I held the door open, hoping she'd take the hint. Take it outside. No soap. "Not that it ain't a pleasure to see you again, but what say you we put this on hold until tomorrow? It's late and I'm wrecked."

She sniffed the air between our faces. "You've been drinking, I see. Having a good time?"

"Don't get sore, angel. One snootful of rye doesn't make a fella tight."

My date emerged from the bathroom, a sylph in silk. That long graceful neck continued all the way down her pipe stems. She wore a postage stamp and not enough ribbon to hold it in place. I feared she'd catch pneumonia from the icy scowls flametop flung at us.

She struck a pose and gave me a smile that should have melted the ice. Then she noticed Molly.

Violet wilted.

Molly said, "Wow, Bayliss. And here I thought you couldn't get any classier."

Violet asked, in a tone of bored and idle curiosity, "Are you the wife or the girlfriend?"

Bored because she'd probably seen this scene a dozen times before. Idle because it was no skin off her nose either way; she'd already made most of her green for the evening, and did it all without taking off her shoes. A banner night.

Molly hiked a thumb over her shoulder. "Put your clothes on and get lost," she said.

Violet gave a bored shrug and disappeared into the bathroom again. The lock clicked.

Molly wheeled on me. "You unbelievable jerk," she said. And then socked me in the kisser. I toppled backward over the ottoman, hands pressed to my face.

"Ouch! What gives, you damn cuckoo frail?" My voice sounded like it was trying to wriggle through a soda straw.

"That's for not telling me the truth about METATRON and the MOC."

She loomed over me. I inched backward. Soft carpet in this joint.

"What are you yapping about? I told you all about it. Maybe some details slipped my mind, but so what? I gave you the headlines."

"Details? You call the Jericho Event a *detail*?"

Oh. That.

Flametop wound up for a swift kick with her pointed boots. I was getting a little tired of playing punching bag for all the crazy dames in my life. Careful, Bayliss. It's becoming a habit with you.

My date emerged from the bathroom again, looking like she'd only ever gone in there to powder her nose in the first place. Looking like a nice, respectable girl a guy could take for dancing and drinks. Took her all of two seconds to survey the situation. She'd seen this scene a few times before, too. I'd wager the argument was usually about infidelity rather than the teleological origins of reality, but, you know, details. Molly paused in her abuse long enough for me to say good night to my date. She was the heart of kindness.

I helped Violet into her coat. As she stepped into her shoes, I kissed her on the cheek and said, "It was swell."

"Sure. See ya." And then she was out the door.

I listened until the ding of the elevator told me Violet was well and truly gone. I looked around the room, looking to see if she'd left behind anything, like a handbag, or her lips. She hadn't. I sighed, then turned to flametop. "You're a real piece of work. There's no parade you can't rain on, is there?"

"Shove it. Don't play the victim card with me."

Something warm and wet tickled my nose. I put a trio of fingertips to my upper lip; they came away warm, wet, and red. Flametop had done a real number on me.

I perched at the edge of the bed and squinted at her. "You seem different. You get your hair done?"

Molly reached into the bathroom, tossed me a washcloth. I wrapped it around a handful of ice from the bucket and pressed the bundle to my face.

By way of answering my question, she set aside her human form and momentarily became something else. None too graceful, this transition: she stumbled through it like somebody hopping around late for church with one leg stuck in a new pair of trousers. But for an instant she blazed so brightly it seemed a miracle we didn't leave my silhouette scorched into the wallpaper. Maybe we did. The bruise-colored afterimages shimmying through my field of vision made it hard to tell. Afterimages of wings and things. Then she snapped back into her human form. A faint *heiligenschein* glow clung to her skin. It faded slowly away as she got it under control, like somebody turning the dimmer switch on a ceiling fan.

"Well, well, well. Look who's all grown up."

"No thanks to you, asshole. Do you even remember our agreement, or have you been spending all your time on hookers and blow?"

Well. That's gratitude for you. I said as much. "You know, I've taken a few punches for you since our last heart-to-heart. I'd just as lief let you fend for yourself from now on."

"It hasn't been a picnic for me, either," she said.

"Anybody smack you with a phone book?"

"No."

"Fancy that."

We compared notes over a bowl of strawberries. They were juicy and so was the gossip. I explained how I'd erased the evidence connecting her to Gabriel (she still pleaded innocent on that charge) and described my subsequent run-ins with the Thrones and Uriel. She told me about the PI recipients and their dreams of the Choir. I took the news well until she got to the part where the churchy types were turning up stiff. That's when I choked on a berry.

"Say that again. How many are dead?"

"Four."

"And when did you say the Pole squiffed it?"

"Last night, I think."

I cast my thoughts back to Sam's rapid departure from my diner. The timing fit. Sam and his pals detected a new Nephil right around the time Molly's pal punched out. So I told her what I'd learned about the Nephilim: what the Thrones told me; the failed attempt to evict one; and what Sam had shared. I worried she'd have another conniption when I hit the part about secret vaults and *penitente* souls. But by the end she looked like somebody had kicked her dog.

"Jesus. How complicated can this get?" Flametop rested her head in her hands, twined her fingers through that curly coppery mop. "Maybe we just caught a break."

"Are you thinking what I'm thinking?"

"I never know what you're thinking. Most of the time I can't even tell what you're talking about."

"Enough sneering, already. Your face will get stuck like that. I'm thinking Father Santorelli's prodigal sheep and the Nephilim come out of the same box. The former die on Earth and the latter pop up in the Pleroma." I whistled. "What a slick racket."

"Yeah, but what are they?"

I shrugged. She sighed.

"Somebody went to a shitload of trouble to set this up. Why? What are the Nephilim *for*? What are they doing?"

"Beats me. But I'm putting my money on nothing good."

"Well," she said, "the good news is there won't be any more. I cured the surviving recipients."

I blinked. "Come again?"

"I've been making the rounds, banishing the dreams. Glimpses of the Pleroma. Whatever they are."

I tried not to sound too condescending. "Look. Angel. I know you're feeling your oats because you've started to get the hang of things. But don't let it go to your head. I've been around the block a few times and, I have to tell you, I don't know how they're playing this trick, much less how to fix it. So what exactly did you do when you say you cured them?"

She told me. I responded by taking a long draw of rye because damn if it didn't sound like she'd put the nightmares on ice for several nights running. This dame was one quick study. Who was she?

Flametop fished a piece of ice from the bucket, inspected it for blood, and then, finding it clean, popped it in her mouth. It crunched in her teeth. "What else haven't you told me?"

"That's all I know about the Nephilim. Pretty much all anybody knows. There ain't more to tell because there ain't more to know."

"Screw the Nephilim. What else haven't you told me about Gabriel? Do you know how he died? You must have suspicions, or a theory. And what about the Choir? The Pleroma? The MOC, and METATRON, and God knows what else?"

"Anybody ever tell you you've got paranoid tendencies? I'm your strongest supporter, lady. Your only supporter, if you want to get technical about it."

"First, you accidentally shoved me under a tram. But hey, that's okay, because after all you were aiming for my *brother*. And then, after you dragged me into this whole fucking nightmare of a mess, you insinuated that my predecessor had simply chosen to move on, instead of telling me that he'd been *murdered*. You failed to warn me about METATRON, which led to all sorts of fun and made me the most popular woman in the Choir. And then, when I pressed you for details, you still somehow managed to omit the full story, and I had to learn about the Jericho Event from some freaky two-faced angel."

I should have known. Lousy Virtues. Can't keep their noses out of other people's business.

She continued, "Call me crazy, but after a while I just can't help but notice a pattern. And I just can't help but wonder what other surprises await me." She crunched another ice cube down to its component molecules.

"You know, you've got a killer case of selective memory, doll. The way I remember it, you were so wrapped up in your own issues that you barely heard two things I said when I tried to give you a rundown on the Pleroma."

"That's because I had just *died,* you shit!"

"Don't get all philosophical on me. So what if you had? You really think you'd have taken it all in if I'd laid out all the cards at once? You've been a drip since day one. You meet everything I say with weeps, frowns, and melodrama. Toss in a fainting spell and you could be gunning for a studio contract."

"Screw you, too."

"Yeah, well, I was working on that, until you showed up and scotched the whole evening."

Flametop ate more ice. She chomped the crystals down to molecules, the molecules down to atoms. She exhaled twinned jets of hydrogen and oxygen. I wondered if she was aware of what she was doing. Good thing I hadn't lit any candles for Violet.

"You've known all along that this mess was so much more than a single impossible murder. This is a schism, isn't it? A fight over something much larger than one dead angel." Molly jumped to her feet. Her halo returned, the glow soft and gentle as a solar flare. She grabbed my shoulders and flung me against the wall. The impact knocked down a painting. "When pressed, you basically came out and admitted you were acting under orders from one of these factions when you roped me into this! So don't feed me some bullshit line that you don't know any more than I do!"

This was my least favorite topic. The weight of it bowed my shoulders, forced me to the floor. I crumpled. Dead angels are heavier than broken promises.

"Look at me!" I said. "Look! You've seen Cherubim and Virtues and even yourself. What am I compared to all that? I'm the lowest of the low. I'm a shabby, two-bit nickel-grabbing twerp with no choice but to draw as little water as possible so that nobody decides to step on me. You? You've got a future. But I'm stuck in the margins. That's all I'll ever be, a cheap chiseler. And there are things out there greater and more mysterious than the best of us. So yeah, I did what I was told. What choice did I have?"

I hefted the bottle, drowned my tonsils. Stewed to the gills was old Bayliss; his tears smelled like above-average rye. My face burned with shame and embarrassment. The tears flared into sizzling flame-drops as they trickled down my face. I looked up at Molly through a smoldering veil of weak flames, like a mummer-show Cherub.

"How do you flip God the bird?" I asked. "What if it notices?"

*B*y the time I banished the weeps and returned to my senses, my dignity had fled and so had flametop. The bottle was emptier than a hobo's money clip, the air dark as my prospects. Smoke wisps curlicued from blackened spots where my burning tears had fallen on the carpet.

My hat had been draped over the doorknob. The note tucked in the band had been scratched out on the back of a room service menu with a dying ballpoint.

> *Gone to find the source of the Indulgences. Try to verify*
> *connection with the Nephilim. This is our chance.*
> *Don't fuck it up.*

It wasn't signed. It didn't have to be. I'd know that inspirational tone anywhere. She really missed her calling. I'd heard the angel of compassion was looking for an intern.

The melted-plastic stink of smoldering synthetic fibers was giving me a headache. Or maybe it was riffing on a drumbeat the last fumes of rye had set to echoing inside my skull. What a combo they had going. All they needed was a xylophone player and they'd be ready for the club circuit.

I made it to my feet with the grudging help of a chair and the wall. When I was reasonably sure the room wasn't about to pull a dipsy-doodle on me, I shuffled to the bathroom, filled the sink with cold tap water, and dipped my face. The water steamed. I nudged the bed to cover the burns in the floor. Then I grabbed my hat, planted it on my crown at a rakish angle, and headed back to my Magisterium.

The door showed no sign of disturbance. Ditto the kitchen, and the coffee can. The *penitente* soul fragments were just where I'd left them. Good thing, because what Molly told me had the gears turning. I lit my pipe, cleared away the pieces with a swipe of my arm, and emptied the can on the chessboard. I reimagined the electric dipole moment of methyl groups in the caffeine—my house, my rules—which made it a snap to separate the coffee grounds from the soul fragments: I ran a comb through my hair and used static electricity to pull out the coffee. Soon I had two piles on the chessboard. One the scorched color of French roast; the other leaden gray.

My reasoning started with the Nephilim and snaked backward through the thicket like this: Those goons were remnants of the Plenary Indulgence recipients that Gabriel had been lamping. But the PIs were tainted, such that death transformed those monkeys into immutable topological defects in the Pleroma. That was a pretty trick; whoever worked this racket carried some mean medicine in their pocket. Father Santorelli was the bagman, dishing out the special Indulgences to lucky members of the faith. Gabby must have known this, or suspected some of it, because he'd been watching Santorelli, too. Gabby's interest in the Indulgences, plus his stewardship of the Jericho Trumpet, eventually got him pinked. Meanwhile somebody—The same somebody? Or was this a different faction?—had started clipping out little hidey-holes in the souls of the *penitentes* down on Earth. So when a well-meaning dope blundered into the middle of this flop and started sniffing around, somebody took a quick jaunt down from the Pleroma to hitch a ride inside a *penitente* and silence the priest.

Why go to all that trouble? I had a hunch. The only members of the Choir with recent practice mingling with the monkeys were me and flametop. News would spread quickly if angels started appearing on Earth again, meddling in human affairs. Would it tip off the opposing faction? Would it rouse METATRON? Better to hitch a ride and avoid the risk.

Gabby had been watching Molly, too. Still didn't know how she fit into all this. But she was right about one thing. The connection

between the Nephilim and the Plenary Indulgences was our big break.
Meanwhile, whoever ran the *penitentes* was in this past the mud on
their necks. That made it past time I took a closer look at those loons.
So I pinched a soul from the top of the pile, stuck it in my eye, and—

—found ourselves sitting with head bowed at a dinner table laid
with potato casserole and cans of soda, mumbling along as our family
said grace. Our shoulders ached so severely that simply raising a fork
to our mouth was agony. The big guy at the end of the table, let's call
him Dad, noticed it, and laid in to us.

"That's what you get for joining up with those freaks," he said.
"Bet they didn't even sterilize properly. You'll get tetanus or worse,
and I'll have to take a second mortgage on the house we already can't
afford just to put your body back the way God made it in the first
place. It would serve you right if they had to amputate both your
arms." He washed down the bile with a swig of beer. His breath smelled
of potatoes and cigarettes.

The woman across from him, let's call her Mom, frowned. "Not at
the dinner table. You promised."

And then he called her a stupid bitch and told her to shut her fucking mouth, because it was her goddamned fault their worthless son
had turned out such a retard. Our eyes brimmed with tears, but we
fought them to a standstill. We wouldn't cry. Not at the table. We
reached up with as much nonchalance as any seventeen-year-old had
ever mustered to scratch an imaginary itch under our eye—

—and flicked the soul fragment into the empty coffee can. I sighed.
It was going to be a long afternoon. I picked another fragment—

—and found ourselves under a tangle of naked, sweaty bodies, doing
something very personal to somebody we didn't know while somebody
else was in the same situation with us. Every pulse of our heart sent
lightning crackling through our veins, sent pharmaceutical gold streaming across the blood-brain barrier to fill our synapses with a champagne
fizz hyperawareness of the orgiastic coupling of counterfeit fallen
angels all around us. This was dangerous and careless and we didn't
care. We saw smoke, and dancers, and so many of our fellow *penitentes*
twined together, wounds and stigmata naked to the world. A tickle on
our lip; we spat away a bloody pinfeather. A man beside us shook out
long hair, stippling our face with sweat. Salt stung our eyes—

I flicked that fragment into the can. I paused for a draw on my dying pipe before queuing up number three—

A metal collar clamped around our neck, another around our waist, two more around our forearms. The cold surgical table made gooseflesh of our naked chest. This impromptu clinic wasn't listed and it wouldn't exist tomorrow. All we could see were floor tiles with a drain in the center, and a corner of the room where two walls of mirror-bright nanodiamond came together. Through a fringe of eyelashes we caught vague reflections of the others, an unlicensed surgeon and our sponsor. Her reassuring touch pumped warmth into the small of our back.

"It doesn't hurt at all," she whispered. We sought her face in the reflections, sought more reassuring lies, sought to impress her with a confident wink. But we couldn't see her face because, just for an instant, it was obscured by starlight flickering in the burnished diamond. We blinked, looked again, but then the laser scalpel was unzipping my flesh and we were too busy trying not to scream because *penitentes* eschewed anesthetic. We bit our tongue. Tears ran freely—

Who was that? Had she seen me? Had she looked into her poor sap's eyes and realized the passenger seat wasn't empty? My pipe had smoldered out. I left it alone.

Fragment number four found us attending Mass. Fragment five found us weeping, sitting on a toilet seat, staring at a pregnancy test. Fragment six landed us in the middle of a sales meeting; we spent half the time pretending to pay attention and the other half reminiscing about the previous night. Our coworkers didn't know of our life outside of work because we hid our wounds under bland business attire. Secretly, we sneered at them.

Fragment seven put us in another club, this one lit by twisting vapor trails of luminous mist. We stood at a bar, ordering a drink. Our fellow *penitentes* wiggled on the dance floor, bodies and rhythms twinned by the mirror behind the bar. A sister *penitente* leaned backward on a stool, resting her head atop the bar, mouth agape; others held her steady while the bartender mixed a drink right in her kisser. Cute trick. One of the surrounding penitentes squeezed his stigmatic palm to dribble sterile blood into the mix. "Communion Wine," we called this drink. The bartender handed him a swizzle stick: a short piece of green plastic molded into the shape of a pirate's cutlass. But in the mirror it became a sword blazing with the fires of Creation.

We gasped. He paused in his fiery stirring to look up. We ran a hand over our eyes—

Close one, that. I paused to empty and repack the pipe after that one. It took several mouthfuls of sweet, cherry-flavored smoke until I could no longer hear the receding whistle of the bullet that had just parted my hair. I wasn't the only member of the Choir taking a ride in the hollowed-out monkeys. Bits and pieces of Pleromatic overlay followed us like pieces of a tenacious dream that refused to dissipate upon the arrival of morning. It came through stronger on the high rollers, manifesting as glimpses of ancient starlight and flaming swords and who knew what else. Resolving to keep my own weak-tea glamour on a tighter leash, I went back to work.

Around and around the world, variations on a theme: snatches of family life, snatches of work life, snatches of club life, snatches of love and hate and hunger and sorrow, woven throughout with cuckoo pseudoangelic malarkey. Here and there, but glimpsed only in the corner of the eye, my fellow *penitentes* sprouted wings of brass, and third eyes, and scorpion tails. I wondered if my hosts could see them, too. I figured they could, and that they attributed this to burgeoning religious epiphany. In striving to emulate us, to emulate their warped and limited misconceptions of us, they became us. Or so they believed. The poor saps didn't know they were possessed. What a bunch of suckers.

Such were my thoughts as I eased into my next host, who was crammed between two bulky *penitentes* in the backseat of a car. Two more *penitentes* rode up front, including the driver. We were somewhere in the Midwest, entering a one-horse town where half the storefronts had been boarded over. Our companions in that cozy little clown car had the windows rolled down. We caught a whiff of river water. It seemed familiar, this place, but I couldn't place it. This was our first visit, as Bayliss or penitent loon. The jane in the front passenger seat was speaking to the driver. We eavesdropped.

". . . the library first. If she isn't there, we'll go to the apartment." With that, she flicked one dainty bleeding palm toward the hardware store sliding past on our right. Nice manicure.

Something hard dug into our ribs. We shifted. So did the loogans to our left and right. Which is how we came to realize they were rodded; it was the bulge of a shoulder rig poking us. Odd, that. This was a first. None of my other encounters with the *penitentes* had involved iron.

I took in more scenery, tried to draw a bead on how I knew this place. That got me nowhere fast. Sunlight glinted from the storefront windows of a café that used to be something else. We glanced quickly to left and right, inspecting the loogans from the corners of our eyes while the light distracted our conscious mind. When viewed through a Pleromatic veil, the faces of the muggs to either side of me were obscured by flickering sheets of flame. No wonder we were crammed like sardines; those hard boys had wings grand enough to scrape dust from the moon.

That's when I realized how I knew this burg.

I had to warn flametop. We reached for our eye—

—but somebody grabbed our wrist.

"Going somewhere, Bayliss?"

The jane in front leaned over the back of her seat, leering at us through the ghostly flickering image of an eagle's face. Her grip was stronger than the metal shackles in the impromptu surgical clinic. She clucked her tongue. It works better in a human mouth, though; her beak turned the clucking into the hollow clacking of cheap castanets.

"Who's Bayliss?" my host asked. But then he glimpsed the things riding inside his fellow carpoolers and fell silent. A warm wet stain spread through our trousers.

"We did warn you," said the woman with the angel inside her. I wondered if that was Uriel's hand on the reins, but didn't have a chance to find out. The loogan on my right reached for his shoulder rig. We tried to block him, but the human I wore had all the reflexes of a coma patient. We managed to get an elbow in his face before he could bring the heater to bear. But all that squirming kept leftie free to show some initiative. We heard the creak of leather and tried to duck. There was little room to swing a sap in that car, but damned if leftie didn't gave it his all. He swung like a pennant race hung in the balance.

The cosh came down on the back of our head. My host's human skull did its best impression of Humpty Dumpty. I figure that made me the yolk. I landed in darkness, and it wasn't over easy.

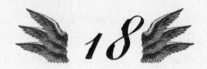

THIS ISN'T COVERED
IN THE ENCHIRIDION

*N*oontime sunlight shone on the river. A gusty wind carved ripples into the water; the ripples chopped the sunlight into glints and flashes like an old-fashioned disco ball. The flickering light tumbled up the valley to the bluff-top picnic tables behind the library. One flash contained an angel. The angel carried a picnic basket.

Molly shed her halo to emerge from behind the boxelder tree. She'd scouted the spot from inside. To a person gazing through the library windows, it would appear as though Molly had just walked around the building. She'd tried to find a balance between outright lying and giving Anne the vague impression that she was staying in another town down the road. Already the evasions and vague answers wore thin. But the longer she lied, the more frightening it became to step out of the closet regarding her true nature. The danger of rejection seemed so much greater, so much more painful. Anne wasn't a violent person, but she could hurt Molly just as much.

Like the past several, Molly had spent part of the previous night keeping an eye on Martin. Immediately after her first visit he had struck out from his apartment in search of another fix. She transmuted that, too. It was a waste of money Martin couldn't afford. Even with Molly's share, the money he inherited from their mother wouldn't last long. But if she could just keep his mind and body clear a bit longer, just a few more days, he'd be well enough to take up his old job delivering pizza. That would be a start.

Ria—well, her body—lay in a hospital bed in a much better part of Minneapolis. Her family had money. Not wealth, but more than Molly's folks had ever had. As on the past several nights, after whispering

Martin into clean, dreamless, nontoxic sleep, and after making the rounds to do the same with the PI recipients, she paced Ria's ward like a insubstantial revenant, listening. If not for the hum and beep and click of the machines quietly keeping her body alive, Ria might have been an honored stateswoman lying in repose. She shouldn't have looked so peaceful: no turbulent subconscious churned within her mind, no dreams haunted her lifeless brain. It hurt worse than anything. Worse even than what METATRON had done. Molly hadn't yet gathered the strength to approach any closer than the ward itself. Each time she tried to approach Ria's bed, to sit by her side and take her hand, Molly bounced from an impenetrable bubble of shame and guilt. It was hardest when Ria's parents came to visit. Molly fled the tears because they made the guilt so heavy it threatened to suffocate her, but told herself she withdrew to respect familial privacy. Molly wondered if her lies and evasions sounded as hollow to Anne as they did to herself. She had tamed the dreams of the Indulgence recipients; she had fought Martin's addiction to a stalemate; she hadn't done jack shit to help Ria. She was afraid to try. It was easier to hate herself than risk making it worse.

And, as she had for the past several days, she prepared lunch for two in her Magisterium, and then met Anne for lunch behind the library. The basket was an antique wicker thing with a hinged wooden flap on the top. Molly had plucked it from the memory of a photograph she'd once seen of her parents on a double date with another couple. Today she'd brought basil leaves, balsamic vinegar, sliced tomatoes, and fresh mozzarella for a caprese salad, plus blue cheese, salami, and crackers for additional snacking. For dessert, she'd rummaged childhood memories of old Christmases for a pair of perfectly ripe pears. She also packed a bottle of sparkling water. Upon reflection she decided to avoid the blue cheese because she didn't want to have bad breath if they kissed again. She hoped they would.

"This is extremely sweet of you," said Anne, taking a seat across from Molly. The bags beneath her eyes had receded since Molly banished the dreams and granted her untroubled sleep. "You don't have to do this."

"I know I don't *have* to. But it's the high point of my day. For really real." A face appeared at one of the windows. Anne's coworker. Molly tipped her head toward the library. "He's watching again."

"I think he fantasizes about watching us make out." They hadn't, not since their first date. But that was okay. It was nice, this slow unfolding of trust and connection.

Trust?

Anne continued, "My guess is that he'll go jack off in the bathroom this afternoon. Pervert."

Molly handed her a plate and the bottle of vinegar. "Drizzle this on top," she said, indicating the layered medallions of mozzarella, tomato, and basil. A cluster of whirlybird seeds from the boxelder tree cast swaying shadows across their lunch. One seed broke free. A gust of wind pushed it beyond the split-rail fence along the edge of the bluff. It spiraled down to the river, like a slow-motion helicopter crash.

"Wow. Hand-delivered gourmet lunch every day. I'm a lucky woman."

"I only know how to make three or four nice lunches. Tomorrow it's peanut butter and jelly on stale bread."

"In that case, we need to talk about our relationship."

She said it in jest, but Anne quirked her neck and shoulders like somebody finding balance on thin ice. Silently, subconsciously, her body shouted doubts and concerns. Part of her had sensed a secret.

And, as had become her habit, Molly changed the subject before those seeds of doubt took root in Anne's consciousness. It wasn't purposeful deception, she told herself. It was investigation, and possibly vital to her own survival. Plus she honestly wanted to understand Anne's experience. She said, "Can I ask you more about what it was like when you received the Indulgence?"

For each night that passed without Anne adding a new sketch to her dream journal, she opened up a little more. Which brought Molly that much closer to understanding the Plenary Indulgences. Which, she was convinced, were the key to everything. The Nephilim made her queasy: Anne might have become one of them, if Molly hadn't intervened.

Anne said, "Haven't you ever heard the phrase, 'Let sleeping dogs lay?' Lie. Whatever. My parents' priest is dead. I don't see what any of this matters."

"I'm sorry I'm always bugging you about it," said Molly. "But I'm really curious about the experience."

A boxelder bug ambled toward her plate, its red stripes almost incandescent in the sunlight. Anne shooed it away. She sighed.

"The idea behind a Plenary Indulgence is that it erases all temporal punishment for sins committed up until then. Unlike a Partial Indulgence, which just reduces the punishment. So, you know, they don't pass them out like coupons. Or they're not supposed to, anyway. It requires doing some charitable work or penance assigned specifically for the Indulgence, followed by the sacraments of confession and eucharist—you have to be in what's called a 'state of grace'—followed by prayers for the pope."

Molly splashed more vinegar on her plate. She took a sip of fizzy water, then had to suppress a burp before asking, "Was that difficult?"

"I'd been to Mass with my parents countless times. So I knew the drill. In this case we, all three of us, had been assigned to various works, including recitation of the Rosary and traveling the Stations of the Cross while spiritually penitent."

Penitent. The word sent a jolt down Molly's spine. It tingled in her teeth like a spark aimed at her fillings. Without intending to, Molly found herself drifting upstream against the current of Anne's reminiscences. She knew that if she desired it so, she could embed herself directly inside the memory Anne described. Bayliss had done something similar in the moment Molly died. But she had built their nascent relationship on misdirection and lies by omission. She refused to compound that by violating Anne's mind. She wouldn't implant herself inside Anne's reminiscences. But she could get the flow of them, ride the sensory impressions and experience the emotional currents they kicked off.

Molly closed her eyes, smelling incense. As Anne described that very long afternoon, Molly could feel a light weight descend upon each shoulder: a mother's hand on the right, a father's hand on the left. The whispering of wind through the boxelder leaves became the murmuring of prayer; the flicker of sunlight along the river became the soft glow of sunset through stained glass. Prayers scudded roughly past her lips, distorted by the mushy remnants of a communion wafer dissolving in the balsamic vinegar on her tongue. The tickle of bugs alighting on her hands became the sensation of hard glass beads wrapped through her fingers, a cold metal cross pressed into her palm. . . .

Anne's emotions shaped her own, like a magnet aligning metal filings: Molly wanted this over, but in a conflicted way also wanted it done well. She wanted to earn approval, even as she knew she didn't need it. Weary, so weary, of conflict with her parents' relentless and uncompromising worldview . . .

"My parents had to participate," said Anne, "because it was their failure that had allowed me to descend into a life of mortal sin."

"This is really pissing me off. Mortal in what sense?"

"As opposed to venial. That's forgivable. Venial sins don't lead directly to hell. Mortal sins do."

"Wow."

"Uh-huh. And by being openly gay I was committing a mortal sin, of course. I had full knowledge of what I was doing. In Santorelli's eyes, and my parents', I was making a deliberate lifestyle choice with mortal consequences."

The gentle emotional currents wafting from Anne disappeared, shredded by gale-force gusts of anger, humiliation, shame. They tossed Molly to a pew near the rear of Santorelli's church, where she knelt between Anne's parents. The bench's thin leather padding didn't ease the ache in her knees, but the discomfort helped distract her from what she was doing . . . Jesus.

"They made you pray for forgiveness? Anne, it sounds like emotional abuse to me. It's sickening."

"It wasn't fun. But that wasn't the worst part. The key thing in receiving a Plenary Indulgence, as opposed to a Partial Indulgence, is that one be absent from all attachment to sin, large and small. They say some people can strive for years, no matter how devout, and never obtain an Indulgence because of this."

"But doing that would mean—" Molly shook her head. "Doing that would have required you to renounce . . ."

Anne nodded. She took a long, shuddery breath. Behind the cosmetic eyeglasses, her eyes shone wetly. "I knew I would never do that, not in my heart. I can't be somebody else. And I know I'm not flawed or broken or evil. But I wanted so badly to make my parents happy just this one time, to show them I was doing it right. You don't know what it's like, constantly falling short of that approval." She sniffled. "Eventually I wised up and realized it was never going to happen. So I split, and cut them out."

Molly's head pounded. Her eyes watered with the tears Anne suppressed. Anne's shame clawed at her heart. Anne couldn't renounce her identity, nor did she intend to, but she wanted so badly to gain her parents' love and approval that her desperation broached some angelic breakwater, exceeded the spiritual activation energy for the tainted Indulgences. Thus was the goddamned Indulgence bestowed, setting into motion a mysterious alchemy that would have turned Anne into a revenant haunting the Pleroma if not for Molly's intervention.

Don't you see? she wanted to yell. *This thing your mom and dad claimed to be parental love was nothing of the sort. It was dark and poisonous. Love is unconditional. But theirs was not. It was an instrument they wielded to control you, to mold you into the person they wanted you to be. To change you, to transform—*

And then it hit Molly like an ice pick between the eyes.

She knew what had happened to the Jericho Trumpet.

Holy fucking shit.

It was obvious. She was a moron for not seeing it.

"Whoa." Anne rocked back as though slapped. She stared at Molly, eyes wide, lips parted. Somewhere nearby, a car hummed to a stop on the quiet street.

"What is it?"

Anne held the stare for a fraction of a second. Then she shook her head, lifted her glasses, and rubbed her eyes. "The sunlight in my eyes . . . Just for a second there you looked, I don't know, like you were glowing."

"I guess you have that effect on me," said Molly, scarcely aware of the thin words falling from her mouth. A maelstrom swept through her mind, a chaotic jumble of connections and conclusions.

METATRON had used the Trumpet to fundamentally alter the nature of the Choir. It was the tool that embedded an infinitesimal fragment of mundanity into the angels, to taint and shackle them.

Likewise, each Plenary Indulgence bestowed by Father Santorelli had changed the nature of its human recipient. Those people had become something that would, upon death, take residence within the Pleroma. But that ought to have been impossible: mortals could never perceive the divine realm, much less access it. Unless their nature had been fundamentally altered, too.

Molly had been thinking about this all wrong. The Trumpet wasn't a physical object: it was a catalyst for metaphysical transmutation. It had changed the angels, and it had changed the PI recipients.

Because the Plenary Indulgences *were* the Trumpet.

Gabriel hadn't been watching Father Santorelli. He'd hidden the Trumpet within the priest's pastoral duties, and was keeping an eye on the hiding spot. Gabriel had created the Nephilim.

The slam of a car door broke Molly's reverie. She opened her eyes. A car had parked just down the street from the library. The slam she'd heard was the sound of two *penitentes* emerging from the backseat. They were built like linebackers. To Molly's human eyes, and doubt-less Anne's, they appeared unusual only in their size. But when viewed with eyes more angelic than human, their faces burned with veils of unquenchable flame.

Anne hadn't noticed the car. She said, "It's happening again. I swear it almost looks like you're glowing."

Molly stood. Without intending to, she imparted to her voice a hint of the same power it had demonstrated in the concert hall: "Anne. Get behind me. Now."

Anne scrambled to her feet. Only then did she see the men cross-ing the street toward the library. She couldn't have seen what Molly did, and yet she gasped. The lingering touch of the Trumpet had left her faintly attuned to the Pleroma. She could sense Molly's halo, and she could sense danger in the newcomers.

Quietly, she asked, "Who are you, Molly?"

"Right now I'm the person standing between you and those ass-holes. And I'm pretty sure they don't have your best interests at heart."

"How come? Do you know those guys?"

Molly flipped her attention between the lumbering human hosts and the angels that rode within them. Overlaid faintly upon the *peni-*

tentes, like images reflected in clean window glass on a bright day, she saw faces of fire and transparent wings vast enough to enfold the sky. A pair of Cherubim approached the library.

"Yeah," said Molly. "We've met."

Stupid, stupid, stupid. Gabriel hadn't been working alone. The Cherubim had been working for him, but not fully aware of his plans. He never told them what he'd done with the Trumpet because they were just hired goons. Their jobs were simple and violent. So when Molly cured the Plenary Indulgence recipients of their deadly maddening dreams, thus indefinitely delaying the appearance of new Nephilim in the Pleroma, the Cherubim were called upon to fix the problem in a means both simple and violent.

By trying to help Anne she'd inadvertently put her in greater danger. That told Molly three things. First: Gabriel's coconspirators were still out there. Second: whatever plan they had in mind for the Nephilim, it came with a timetable, because they weren't content to wait for the remaining PI victims to die of old age. And third: it told her that she and Anne were screwed.

The *penitente* angels entered the library. Molly took a quick glance at the street. The *penitentes'* car was still there. It wasn't empty. Anne's coworker appeared at the window again, but no longer alone. He pointed to their picnic table. Shit. The window glass glowed with an ethereal fire that only Molly could see. With concentration she could even discern METATRON's gossamer tethers.

Molly turned to Anne, whose expression had become inscrutable. She spoke rapidly.

"Do you trust me?"

"I, uh, suppose, sure, except usually when people ask me that it means they're—"

"Close enough."

She laid a hand over Anne's eyes. "Look, I know this is a little confusing. But it's about to get a lot confusing. Don't open your eyes until I say so, okay?"

Anne sucked in a breath to have something to hold while making her decision. When she nodded, her eyebrows tickled Molly's hand. As did her sigh.

"Follow me," said Molly. *Hope this works . . .*

Taking Anne by the wrist, she pulled her into the shadow of the boxelder maple—

—Anne gasped—

—Molly groaned; pulling Anne into the Pleroma was like lifting a ten-pound weight with her tongue—

—and they stood in the bedroom of Molly's Magisterium apartment. The walls drooped and sagged like soft wax. Molly hadn't anticipated the supreme effort required to move a mortal body into the Magisterium. Anne kept her eyes closed, but she was rubbing her wrist where Molly had touched her. A faint red weal encircled it.

"How you doing so far?"

Anne turned toward the sound of her voice. "What was that? It burned!"

That was me. That was me losing control as I tried to yank you to safety. That was me hurting you because I don't know what I am. Didn't I tell you my last relationship ended badly?

"You're doing great. Just hold on."

Molly dialed Bayliss. As usual, he wasn't answering. "Comeon-comeoncomeonyouprick. Why aren't you ever there when I need you?"

A crash rocked the apartment, followed by a bang so heavy the displaced air ruffled Anne's hair. Anne jumped. Molly knew it was the sound of a door being ripped off the hinges and slammed to the floor. She'd hoped the Cherubim would be a little slower in figuring out where she'd taken Anne, or in making the transition from Earth to the Pleroma. She wondered, fleetingly, whether they had abandoned their human beards, or if they had dragged their hapless hosts along for the ride. Fucking angels.

Downstairs, the crashing started anew. Molly took Anne by the shoulders and gently guided her toward the closet. Not wanting to burn her again, she took an old scarf and wrapped one end around Anne's hand. "Don't let go, okay?"

She didn't wait for Anne's response. Pulling gently on the other end, Molly nudged her into the closet. She reimagined the configuration of closets in the imaginary apartment, switching the bedroom closet and the downstairs coat closet. The passage to Chicago still hung like a broken one-way mirror in the back of the coat closet. Molly hadn't gotten around to removing it. She towed Anne through the passage. Then she reimagined the coat closet as it must have been on the night the apartment burned down and closed the egress behind them. A few wisps of smoke followed them into the latticework shadows of an El pillar.

The hubbub of dozens of conversations enveloped them, the noise of traffic and trains and bicycle messengers. It was much louder and busier here, standing amidst the lunchtime crowds on a Chicago sidewalk, than where they'd been moments ago. Anne noticed.

She frowned, cocked her head. Her eyebrows slid low over her eyes, though she still hadn't opened them—a little show of faith in the midst of chaos, so endearing that Molly wanted to kiss her for it. Pedestrians flowed past them in a constant thrum, passing just inches from their spot on the leeward side of the pillar, leaving in their wake the clack of footsteps, the smells of cologne and perfume, the airborne taste of a spinach pirogi.

Anne said, her voice fluted by a rising edge of panic, "Molly?"

"Right here."

Worry strangled Anne's voice, rifled its pockets, and dumped the dead whisper in an alley. "Where are we?"

Molly scanned the crowd for *penitentes* with invisible riders. She said, "That's kind of hard to explain."

"It feels like I'm sliding back into one of my nightmares. The ones I showed you in my dream journal."

Careful not to burn her, Molly pressed her hands to Anne's face. "You're not having a nightmare. You're having a crazy nonsensical Nancy Drew adventure dream. And when you wake up, you'll look back on it with amusement."

"I'm not sure about that."

"Yeah, me neither. But hold on."

She pulled Anne into the throng, heading toward the lake. Unaware of what it was doing, the crowd parted for them. A woman stopped to take a call; two construction workers jostling for spots in line at a hotdog stand got into a fistfight, the spectacle attracting bystanders and pulling them from Molly's path; a dog slipped its owner's leash and sprinted up a side street. The world twisted itself to ease Molly's passage.

Until the lady in the turquoise serape came charging down the stairs from an El platform. The wind caught her serape and flung it behind her like a cape. Her stigmata drizzled spots of glistening crimson on the iron handrails. Invisible flames sheened her face.

The possessed *penitente* vaulted the railing. A shadow passed over the sun as the thing inside her spread its transparent wings. The Cherub had switched into a different human host. But where was its partner? Or was this a third Cherub? She landed in a crouch, hitting the concrete with a thick dry sound like the cracking of a celery stalk. One foot splayed out when she straightened. The fragments of her shattered ankle rolled like marbles in a fleshy sock as she charged Molly and Anne.

Molly yanked the scarf, put her arm around Anne's waist when she stumbled, and heaved her around the corner into the shadows beneath the stairs. Like sweeping dust under a rug, she pinched the corner of a shadow lying on the pavement and lifted the edge overhead. She ushered Anne into a nothing-space that was neither shaded nor light. The edge of the shadow twanged like a banjo string when Molly released it. They stood in the lobby of Martin's building.

Molly said, "You're doing great. How's the wrist?"

"I don't like this," said Anne. The glow of flickering biomimetic graffiti played across her face as she sniffed the fetid air. It stank of urine. "How much longer do I have to keep my eyes closed?"

This was getting absurd. Molly had thought a couple quick detours through the Pleroma would throw the Cherubim off their trail. But those asshats were too stubborn. Strange that they relied upon human hosts for dirty work like this. They seemed reluctant to show their true forms in the mortal realm. Reluctant, or unable? Or was there something else at work here? Molly remembered what Bayliss had said about his attempt to talk to Father Santorelli, and the strange confused *penitente* he had encountered. She wondered if an angel had been riding inside that poor boy, working his puppet strings when he strangled the priest.

Anne hugged herself, as though warding off the odors of piss and decay. She shivered, still waiting a response.

SOMETHING MORE THAN NIGHT

"You can look now," said Molly.

Gently, gingerly, Anne opened her eyes. She said nothing while her eyes adjusted to the gloom. The glowing graffiti illuminated debris, mildew, and a man slouched on a canvas camping chair. A hood covered the tattoos on his head. Though it was dark in the lobby, he wore wraparound sunglasses, as though he'd stared at an eclipse and damaged his eyes. Perhaps he had.

Anne said, "I don't recognize this place."

"I'd be worried if you did." Molly took her hand to examine her wrist. The burn looked superficial, yet she could see her own fingerprints marking Anne's skin. "My brother lives here."

"The one you said—"

"Yep," said Molly. "That's the one. But I need a safe place for you to hide for a while." *I don't know if this is it,* she said to herself, *but I'm running out of ideas.* Her plan—if it even counted as such—revolved around something she vaguely remembered Bayliss mentioned in passing. She wished she had time to explore it, or at the very least practice.

Anne said, "Hide from what? Who are those people? And how did we get here? Did I pass out? I'm sure I didn't."

"If I promise to answer your questions, will you trust me just a little longer? Please?"

Anne hugged herself again. It was drafty in here. Canvas creaked as the guy in the corner shifted his weight, like somebody struggling to eavesdrop and stay invisible at the same time. His chin hung low, over his chest, but his breathing and his heartbeat gave him away.

"Hey." Molly snapped her fingers under his nose. "Remember me?"

He slouched deeper into his camping chair, pulled the hood tight over his eyes. "I got nothing to say to you."

"Good. That means you can listen." She thought for a moment, remembered her mother, and produced a thin gold ring from her pocket. Crouching, she waved it under his nose. "That's a real diamond. Do something for me and it's yours. But if you try to screw me over"— Here she yanked the eyeglasses down past the tip of his nose and met his eyes. Dense circuitry in his contacts gave them a mirrored appearance.—"it's pillar of salt for you."

His gaze went to the ring. Luminous tattoos unfurled across his skull, lighting the inside of his hood like a jack-o'-lantern. He licked his lips. "What do I gotta do?"

"Anybody comes by looking for us, you haven't seen a fucking thing. If anybody happens to be a *penitente* or two, they don't get past this lobby. They'll be tougher than they look, though, so call your friends. Call your enemies. I don't care. But you hold them off." She thought a little more. "Don't kill them. But it's okay if you're rough."

The Cherubim would eat this guy alive. Good. He fed Martin's drug habit. But it might buy Anne some time.

"Deal." He reached for the diamond ring. She snatched it out of his reach.

"Nuh-uh. I come back and find everything's okay, you get this. I come back and find there's a problem, you get the other thing." Molly stuffed it back in her pocket. He pulled out an earbud as Molly rejoined Anne.

Anne asked, with forced nonchalance, "Old friend?"

Molly shook her head. "C'mon. We're almost there."

She lifted an arm to drape it over Anne's shoulders. Anne flinched. Molly swallowed hard, dropped her arm, and led her to the stairs.

*T*hey stood outside Martin's door. The elevator was out of service, so they'd had to climb twenty stories. Anne was breathing hard. The squatters in the stairwell had left them alone, concussed by the heavy awkward silence as they passed.

Molly said, "I can't go with you. I have to take care of something."

"Don't you dare abandon me in this hellhole."

"I'm not. I promise."

"You'll come back?"

"Promise." Molly nodded toward the door. "Martin's doing a little better these days." She backed into the shadows. "He'll do his best for you. Tell him you knew me, and he'll treat you like a queen."

Anne raised her hand to knock, but paused, as though reflecting upon the vagaries of the past tense.

*M*olly skipped the stairs. She stitched together shadows and returned to the lobby at the speed of thought. It was brighter and noisier than before. Light and shadow spun through the lobby as three men covered in lustrous tattoos tried to hold a line against a hulking *penitente*. The Cherub rode inside a human body that had to be at least six foot six. It towered over the men blocking its path. Pleroma-light from its inferno face diffracted through the invisible wings folded tightly around its human shell, casting a complementary dance of anti-light and un-shadow through the lobby.

The *penitente* stepped forward. Together, two men stepped forward and bulled him back. "You're not coming in," said the third.

Molly checked herself before charging in. She watched from the shadows, still wondering why the Cherubim had felt the need to carry out their errands while shrouded in a human guise. She also wondered how quickly this Cherub's patience would rub thin. In her experience they were neither subtle nor patient.

The *penitente* stepped forward again. But this time when the two tried to force him to retreat, he pressed a hand to each man's chest and shoved, hurling them across the lobby. One shattered the remains of the security door. The other slammed against the vandalized mailboxes. Both slumped to the floor, unmoving.

The tinkling echoes faded away. In the momentary silence, Molly could hear the wheezing of lungs laboring under shattered ribs. The atmosphere carried the tongue-curling salty-iron tang of aspirated blood.

The *penitente* headed for the stairs. The man to whom Molly had spoken fumbled under his shirt with trembling hands. He really wanted that ring. He couldn't hurt the angel brushing past him, had no hope of slowing it down. But there was a danger he could hurt the Cherub's human host, though.

Molly threw herself into the fray, wishing again she'd had time to practice. With thoughts focused on Bayliss's tale of sneaking into Gabriel's locked Magisterium, she revealed herself to the indomitable Cherub. The last lingering shadows abandoned the lobby. The tattooed man cowered.

"Hey, motherfucker," she said. "Remember me?"

The *penitente* didn't, but the thing inside him did. It advanced on her . . .

. . . while Molly imagined her consciousness unzipping, peeling apart like the skin of banana . . .

And then she was standing in the damaged lobby, slightly less than she had been an instant earlier, while a detached sliver of her consciousness hid in the rubble. She held the Cherub's attention, and struggled not to look at the tiny part of herself scuttling in the corners. She wondered if the Cherub could sense the hole in her.

The thing in the corner was too small and weak to move quickly. It wouldn't manage to circle around before the *penitente* attacked. Molly stepped over a fallen gang member and sidled deeper into the lobby. The possessed *penitente* kept pace, always facing her. Molly couldn't get behind him.

But the detached part of her consciousness could.

The Cherub unfurled its wings. Moondust sifted from the heavens, blazing silver-bright in the glare from the Cherub's fiery face. Behind it, something reared like a viper.

The detached fragment of her consciousness wiggled like a cat preparing to pounce. Molly grabbed the *penitente's* wrists.

"Surprise," she said, nodding to the sliver of herself.

It lunged. Molly yanked with strength both human and other,

And then she was hiding in the rubble among shards of glass and the unconscious gang members, the merest fraction of what she had been an instant earlier. When she looked up, she saw a giant version of herself facing down an angry Cherub in an ill-fitting human suit. They filled the lobby. She wondered if the Cherub could sense her.

She wormed through the grime, inching around the perimeter of the room, slowly making her way behind the *penitente*. But she was barely a wraith, a whisper of her full self. She was minuscule, the world huge. Skirting the rubble while monitoring the face-off took concentration and effort.

The *penitente* turned. It put her directly behind him.

The Cherub unfurled its wings. Moondust sifted from the heavens, blazing silver-bright in the glare from the Cherub's fiery face. She reared, impersonating a viper.

She gathered herself, pressing down like the coils of a spring. The giant Molly grabbed the *penitente's* wrists.

"Surprise," said most of Molly, and gave herself a nod.

She lunged as the rest of Molly knocked the *penitente* off bal-

pulling the *penitente* off balance, and spun him around. The other piece of her blurred into motion. The Cherub saw it, but too late. The sliver of consciousness speared into the eyes of its human disguise.

A dull sliver tinkled to the floor. The Cherub disappeared.

The *penitente* slumped against Molly, unconscious. She laid him gently to the floor. She stopped holding her breath. Then she nodded to the wispy fragment of herself. It slithered closer . . .

ance and spun him around. She crossed the gap moving at the speed of thought. The Cherub saw her. It tried to twist its human shell away, but it was too late. She hurled herself into the *penitente's* eyes.

A dull sliver tinkled to the floor. The Cherub disappeared.

The rest of Molly caught the unconscious *penitente* and laid him gently on the floor. She released a long sigh, and then gave her a shaky nod. She slithered toward the rest of herself . . .

The wormy fragment of her consciousness slurped into place like a spaghetti noodle, and then she was whole again. She gasped: assimilating the disparate experiences was even more difficult than multitasking her consciousness in the first place. She staggered under the weight of paradox. She tripped over the unconscious *penitente* and crashed against the dented and vandalized mailboxes. Molly's memory of the past few moments—her sense of identity—had acquired the eerie unreality of a photographic double exposure. Incompatible experiences churned together, an immiscible froth of oil and water.

It gave her a blinding, brain-shattering migraine. She coughed up something vinegary. She moved like an old woman when she knelt to pluck the leaden soul fragment from the floor. Her eyeballs felt ready to burst. Rather than move her eyes, she turned her entire body to face the drug dealer, who cowered in the corner.

"Hey," she said. "You got anything for a headache?"

But he was staring at his unconscious companions sprawled on the floor where the Cherub had hurled them. Then he looked at the *penitente*. "Fuck," he said.

"Now would be a good time for you to call an ambulance for your friends," she suggested. She fished in her pocket and tossed the ring.

It bounced across the filthy floor and rolled to a stop against the toe of his boot.

She shuffled closer to the unconscious *penitente*. Her headache throbbed in time to her footsteps. The fragment she had dislodged from the possessed man's eye had followed her to Earth, much as the fragments Bayliss manipulated followed him to the Pleroma. She studied it, wondering how to make the man's soul whole again.

The dealer repeated himself. "Fuck."

"Yeah," she said. But then she followed his gaze. A second *penitente* strode into the lobby.

Molly felt herself deflating like a punctured tire. She retreated into the shadows, struggling to force the pain aside, trying to focus enough to split off another piece of herself. The second Cherub saw her. It continued to look straight at Molly while, slowly and deliberately, the hollow woman's lips curled into a sneer; the glow of supernatural fire peeked through the corner of her mouth. It was wise to her trick. Rats.

Speaking through the corner of her mouth, Molly said, "Go for the eyes."

But the dealer vaulted his injured companions and ran away. He did pause just long enough to take the ring.

As the first had done, the Cherub directed its *penitente* host toward the stairs. Molly blocked her passage. The wounded woman lunged forward with arms outstretched, twisted her fingers into Molly's coat lapels, and heaved. Molly's toes left the floor. She tried to break the woman's grasp, but couldn't.

"Crap," she said, wishing she had taken Martin's offer any of the countless times he'd spoken grandly about teaching her to throw a punch.

The *penitente* flexed her arms, preparing to hurl Molly across the lobby. Molly clamped a hand around the woman's forearm. She pulled herself closer, until they were almost nose-to-nose. The searing heat of holy fire washed across her face. Instant sunburn. She squinted, peering through the blazing Pleromatic overlay to the human woman's face. Something glistened in the corner of her right eye.

Molly flicked the first *penitente's* soul fragment into the woman's left eye.

There was a scream, the death rattle of bifurcated light, and then Molly tumbled to the floor, alone. The migraine metastasized into her arms, legs, spine. She narrowly avoided choking on the contents of her stomach.

Molly was still lying there when two pairs of shoes scuffled across the floor. She opened her eyes. Anne stood in the doorway.

"Moll?"

So did Martin.

19

THE FINAL CLUE

The tunnel was long; the light at the end, warm. My *penitente* host's body felt peaceful, all hurts and worries forgotten. There was music, and the soothing voices of loved ones called to him.

We were in a clinic, lying on a gurney, staring at the ceiling. Poor sap had a bad case of tunnel vision. The mooks in the car had slugged him hard. The soothing voices said something about a subdural hematoma, and then the voices weren't soothing any longer.

Not that my host noticed. He was juiced to the gills on Class II painkillers.

So I had no choice but to listen to the whole spiel while the quacks read the headlines to a pair of sad sacks I could only assume were the parents. I was waiting for a chance to flick the fragment out of my host's eye. By the time we came around they already had him junked up nicely. He had all the conviction and muscle tone of an anorexic kitten. I could have done a mean Lindy Hop on the head of a pin with half the effort it would have taken to lift his arms just then. I managed to flutter an eyelid. They thought it was brain damage.

Somewhere in the Pleroma my essence sat at a table, staring at a pile of soul fragments. I hope it remembered to blink from time to time. Otherwise my peepers would sting like nobody's business when I made it home. Meanwhile, my focus was embedded in the *penitente* while the quacks explained how we'd been dumped on the side of the road, apparently the victim of a mugging.

What about the library, I wanted to ask. *They were headed for the library, to kill another PI recipient.*

But they didn't answer my question. They were too concerned with bad influences and brain injuries, the drips.

I kept up the fluttering, working that eyelid for all it was worth, winking and blinking at everybody in the room like a happy-time girl at her first day on the job. Eventually, a nurse noticed. I hope they gave him a raise.

He said, "He's got something in his eye," and reached forward—

—and then I was back in my Magisterium. My eyes burned. I doused them under the kitchen faucet and then went to call flametop. She beat me to the punch, though, because the telephone rang before I had it in my hands.

"Where the hell have you been?"

That's not exactly what she said. It was bluer than that. Indigo.

I arrived to find three loogans sprawled on the floor and two birds, a twist and a mugg, giving flametop a wary eye. The mugg looked like a world-class cokie. The twist, though, now she was a dish.

The mugg I'd seen before. He was the dull little monkey I'd pegged for the job opening in the Choir, before his sister went and hurled herself under that train. I wondered how things might have been different now if I'd collared the hard boy. He couldn't possibly have been more trouble than the little sister.

The dish, I gathered, was a PI recipient my partner had taken under her wing. Talk about a mother-hen complex.

Molly looked relieved to see me. That was a first, and it didn't bode well.

"What's the score, angel?" I asked.

"The Cherubim came for Anne." She nodded toward the dish. "They were riding *penitentes,* just as you said."

Cherubim? I blinked. "Can't help but notice you're still in one piece."

"Barely."

"Where are they? Our friends with the hot faces."

"They're gone. For now."

"What, they went for a powder?"

"No," she said. It wasn't a boast and it wasn't false modesty. She seemed too bushed for either. Weary as somebody who'd just fought two Cherubim to a standstill. Who, I wondered for the hundredth time, was this crazy dame?

I whistled. "Not too shabby." She swayed on her feet, like a tree in high winds. "You okay, kid?"

She cast a glance at the moping couple. Were they an item? They shared a body language that fairly jangled with wariness when they looked at flametop.

What had they witnessed? Had she shed her human disguise and given them an eyeful of the blazing form she'd unveiled in my hotel room? Well, they weren't gibbering loons, and so far METATRON hadn't reared its incorporeal head for another tongue lashing. Whatever she'd done here, flametop had managed to keep a lid on it.

"I'm tired as hell," said Molly. "I'm tired of all this shit."

"You look like you haven't slept since Teapot Dome. Dangle, why don't you. Take a breather."

"I can't. Not yet. I need to check on the others."

"You can do that after you've caught some z's."

She shook her head. Stubborn frail. "I need you to protect Anne until I return."

I could see she'd made up her mind. By now I knew the futility of arguing with her. I relented. She gathered a swirling eddy of dust in the cup of her hand, breathed on it, then blew it in my face. I inhaled knowledge of the dish's home. Then she made the introductions.

"Anne, this is Bayliss."

I tipped my hat. "How's tricks?"

The dish looked amused. Or confused. Maybe both. "Who is he?"

"Bayliss is, um, sort of a coworker. I guess."

"I like to think of myself as a mentor. A font of wisdom and experience."

The dish—Anne—said, "You guys . . . *work* . . . together?"

"Sort of," said Molly.

I said, "Partners in crime," and winked. Mine is a charming wink. Anne thought so. It broke the ice.

"Bayliss will take you home. He's annoying, and he's a sexist pig at times. Otherwise, he's okay."

"Careful, doll. You'll give me a big head."

Anne looked me over. Apparently finding the bus fare acceptable, she gave a little shrug. Then she jerked her head toward the cokie and raised her eyebrows. I don't know what the question was, but Molly's answer was, "Yeah."

Flametop spoke to me with a quiet fervor. "Do *not* leave her side. First sign of trouble, you bolt." She started to glow again. "Keep her safe. Got it?"

"Yes, I got it."

Molly said, "I'll catch up quick as I can."

I offered my arm to the dish named Anne. "Let's blow, sister."

I thought you were dead. I saw . . ." Martin's sunken eyes over-flowed with tears. "I'm so confused."

"Shhh, shhh." Molly put her arms around him, careful that her halo didn't burn him. "I know. You're not crazy." He hadn't showered in a couple of days, but nothing dodgy laced the musky scent of his sweat. "Hey, you must have known I'd always watch over you. Right?"

"Why didn't you come to me? Call me? Send me a note?"

"Because you saw me fall." She hugged him tighter. "I thought the shock of seeing me again would be too much."

"You didn't think being alone was worse?"

"I'm sorry. I was wrong."

He wiped the tears away, looked her up and down. "God, Moll. You look . . . you look like nothing happened." He frowned. "What *did* happen?"

She took his face in her hands. "That is a super long conversation. I promise we'll have it. Soon. But not now." She went up on her toes, pulled his head down, and kissed him on the forehead. It was a greet-ing and an apology, but not a benediction. "Love you, big brother."

He reached for her. "You can't go now."

"Really, really have to." She lifted Martin's hand from her shoul-der and gently pulled free. Anne was safe for the moment. But what of the others?

"But you'll come back? Promise me."

"I promise, you goon." That made him smile. "But you can do some-thing for me while I'm out."

"Yeah?" The look on Martin's face was so earnest, so puppyish, she wanted to hug him again.

"Get a job." And then he was crying and laughing at the same time, because clearly, *clearly,* this really was his sister. Molly blew him a kiss and backed into the shadows.

*H*er hot little hand warmed the crook of my arm. A humming-bird pulse fluttered in the hollow of her throat. I had to put her at ease before she squiffed out; I'd never hear the end from flametop otherwise.

"I'll have you home in two shakes." I laid a fingertip on the bridge of her eyeglasses. "Might want to close your eyes, though." I wasn't keen to watch this frail shoot her cookies.

She closed her eyes. She opened her eyes.

"Hold on," she said. "Can we go anywhere at all?"

"You hungry? I know a joint."

"Can we?"

I sighed. "Our mutual friend'll be doing figure eights if I don't get you home sooner than later. She'll blow a gasket if we lam off. Trust me, I've seen it."

This she met with a sly grin. I got the sense she was a fellow witness to flametop's sharper edges. She fixed me with the moon eyes until I caved. Never let it be said I'm immune to the charms of a helpless skirt.

"Okay, okay, just lay off, sister. One side trip. Let's keep it snappy. And no funny business."

"I've never been to France," she said.

"I know just the place," I said. "Hold tight."

*M*olly went first to check on Thui Nguyen.

The modest campus of her community college should have been full of students in the middle of the afternoon. It shouldn't have been ringed with police cars, ambulances, and flashing lights. But it was. Hordes of tearful bystanders thronged the barricades of yellow tape. The scene reminded Molly of the night she died. She tasted blood on the air, and the shattered-jam-jar tingle of anxiety.

Unseen and unheard, Molly drifted through the chaos, eavesdropping on the chatter between the cops and their incident commander. The campus was under lockdown. A student had stood up in the middle of a history lecture, whipped out a fléchette gun, and un-zipped half a dozen classmates. Plus their instructor.

Eyewitness accounts were sketchy, fragmentary, confused. He'd been a nice kid, they said. It just wasn't like him at all, they said. All agreed, though, the shooter was a *penitente*.

Molly didn't realize she'd lost her concentration until a stranger put an arm around her, offered a shoulder to catch her tears. She used it.

We shared a paper bag of roasted walnuts on the bank of the Seine, watching the tour boats drift downstream while behind us the pealing of Notre Dame's bourdon bell shook the island with an E-flat.

She leaned close, yelling to make herself heard over the ruckus. Her breath tickled my ear. "This is amazing!"

"Aw, this is nothing. You should see this place on a winter's night, with prayer and snow and soft candlelight."

She laughed. "Was that poetry?"

"It rhymed."

Anne treated me to that smile again. She reached over and rum-maged among the last walnuts. It was warm inside the bag. Our fingers touched.

I glanced up at my pal the gargoyle. He stuck his tongue at me. I took it as encouragement.

"I know a shop nearby. How are you for French wines?"

"I don't know."

"You don't drink wine?"

"Only on special occasions."

"Like this?"

"Like this."

Most days, Wendy Bavin took her lunch at one of the many shops just a few blocks from her downtown office. She was part of the lunchtime crowd that had threatened to overwhelm Molly on her first excursion to Chicago.

Most days, she navigated the traffic without incident. Most days, an illegally modified car didn't override the traffic signals and plow through a crosswalk.

Today was not most days. Four people died, including Wendy Bavin. Nobody saw the driver.

I mean it now. Enough horsing around."

My head spun. I'd forgotten just how much I enjoyed a good French red now and then. Anne did, too, judging from the unsteady rhythm of her shoes on the narrow stairs. She stumbled. I caught most of her, but fumbled the laughter. It cascaded down the stairs. The body and the laughter made a matching set, warm and soft.

She coaxed her key into the lock on the third or fourth try. The lock was a good sport and didn't make a peep about the scratches. The door eased inward when she slumped against it. I helped her to her feet before she wound up sprawled facedown halfway inside her digs.

Anne collected her rumpled dignity like a milkmaid gathering her skirts. In a voice thick with wine and affected sobriety, she said, "I promise to lock the door behind me. You can listen for it."

"Sorry, doll. Flametop will give me another swift poke in the kisser if I let you out of my sight."

"Pffff." She retreated, beckoned me to enter. I did. Ducky little place she had.

I closed the door, tossed the dead bolt and the chain. "I'll keep watch while you—"

I didn't finish because my back was pressed against the door and her lips were pressed against mine. Likewise that soft, warm body. The lips tasted of wine. I'd forgotten how much I enjoyed a good French red now and then.

We leaned against the door, chewing each other's flushed faces. This jane was more fun than Violet. She knew how to get down to brass tacks. Knew how to use her tongue, too. I guess she also enjoyed a good French red now and then.

A nother member of Santorelli's parish died on the steps of a payday loan service. He'd been mugged, then stabbed, according to witnesses. His blood stained the sidewalk. Molly knew that if anybody bothered to investigate, they'd find a smattering of sterile blood mixed with the victim's.

* * *

*W*e graduated from necking to fumbling. But she was stewed to the hat. Maybe I was, too, but I'm no tomcat. Poor Bayliss, always tripping over his tattered pride.

I took her by the elbows, gently pushed her away. She fixed me with a devilish grin, thinking that I was thinking about backing her into a mattress. Maybe I was. Ignoring the invitation in her coquettishly fluttered eyelashes, I shook my head.

"Ease off, doll," I said. "You're piffled."

"What a gentleman." Her tone spoke volumes about what she thought of gentlemen at that moment.

"It's a character flaw."

"Yeah, it is," she said, and made for the bedroom. Alone. I imagined wisps of smoke eddying in her wake, wafting from the ashes of her ardor.

A smattering of random tragedies afflicted random strangers all on the same random afternoon. And there were no survivors. Before evening fell, all the people whose nightmares Molly had banished were dead.

She had failed to protect them. All her effort for nothing. The moment she was too preoccupied to protect them . . . dead.

*N*ight had wrestled with evening, and won, by the time flametop showed her coppery mop. She didn't barge in by riding the shadows beneath the door. She knocked like a woman who'd been raised well. I tossed the lock and let her in.

"They're all dead," she said. "Those bastards killed every goddamned one of them."

Her hair fluttered in the updraft from her rage. Floorboards darkened beneath her feet. She needed to take a breather before she torched the joint.

"Take it easy, angel. Tell it to me straight."

But she didn't. Instead, she looked around the ducky apartment. "Where's Anne?"

"Relax. Your hotcha librarian is sleeping one off."

"What's that supposed to mean?"

I told her about our little misadventure, the walnuts and the wine and the fumbling. The more I spoke the more flametop looked fit to lay an egg, so I kept it short. The searing *heiligenschein* faded out. She sniffled hard enough to eject a tear.

I said, "You're looking glum, chum." But she didn't rise to the bait, so I asked, "You taking the night shift?"

"Fine." Faint, that voice, as though from a very deep well. Dames. I let myself out.

*M*olly spent the night sitting by the window, watching the empty street below. She had too many things to think about. Murders; conspiracies; the nature of reality. The way her misguided attempts to help those poor people had led to their deaths. But all she could picture was Anne and Bayliss pressed against the door with their faces mashed together. More than once she contemplated leaving, letting Anne fend for herself.

Here Molly had thought *she* was the one keeping an unconscionable secret. What the fuck, Anne?

Anne came tromping down from the bedroom loft about an hour after sunrise.

"You're back," she said. It didn't come with the slow, wide grin like the last time she awoke to find Molly there. She held the greeting at arm's length. "That's good. We need to have a long talk."

"Yeah, we do. How'd you enjoy Paris?"

Anne frowned. "Huh?"

"Bayliss told me about your side trip."

"Look. I just woke up, I didn't have any dinner, and I haven't had any coffee yet. And I was already hella confused when I went to bed. All I know is that one minute we were having lunch at the library and then the next minute we were in fucking Minneapolis," Anne said. She shuffled to the kitchen, opened the coffeemaker, and flung yesterday's grounds into the composter pail. "Oh, and then I met your brother. Who seems to believe that you died months ago."

"I'm sorry about that," said Molly. "I guess neither one of us has been completely honest with the other."

Anne dropped the coffee carafe in the sink. "How dare *you* accuse *me* of lying."

"I don't blame you for rethinking how you feel about me in light of yesterday. I honestly don't. But throwing yourself at Bayliss? That's a slap in the face."

"Wait. You think—eeeeew."

The disgust was genuine. So was Molly's confusion. "You guys didn't make out?"

Anne's face twisted up. "What? Jesus! Shit, no!"

"He said—"

"Where do you get off? I resent the implication that I don't understand my own orientation."

"He said you went to Paris, where you guys got tipsy on wine. And that you made a heavy pass at him."

Anne looked ill. "Paris?" She shook her head. Her whole body. "Even if I did like boys, which I don't, he's like a hundred years old. And he smells weird. Like cigarettes mixed with rose petals and old books."

Molly couldn't understand what she was hearing. "But Bayliss said—"

"I don't care what he said. We came straight here. No Paris, no wine, no tonsil hockey. We sat here all afternoon and evening until I got so bored with his second-rate Philip Marlowe act that I went to bed."

This was the truth; Molly felt it in her bones. Anne didn't go for men; Molly knew this. But Bayliss had been so matter of fact about it . . . What a strange thing to lie about. He must have made a pass at Anne, got shot down hard, and then lied to assuage his wounded chauvinist pride.

Molly raised her hands, palm out. "Anne? I'm genuinely sorry. I apologize."

Anne finished with the coffeemaker. She crossed her arms, leaning against the counter while the machine gurgled.

"Now that the important stuff is straightened out"—Molly winced—"I'd kinda like to know who those guys were and why we were running from them. But first, just out of curiosity, why does your brother think you're dead?"

Here it comes. Inhaled breath hissed through Molly's teeth. "Promise not to freak out?"

Anne blinked. Twice. Took a step back. "Oh my God."

Molly reached for her, but thought better of it because she couldn't handle the sight of Anne flinching away again. "I'm still the person you met. I'm still the person I told you I was. I'm just . . . a little more than that."

Molly struggled but failed to find the words that would ease an incipient spiritual crisis. Anne stared at her for the space of several heartbeats. Finally, she breathed, "This is so fucking cool."

If she weren't already dead, the whiplash might have killed Molly. "What?"

"Are you kidding? This is the coolest thing in the world." Anne paced, driven into motion by the steam pressure of ideas boiling within. "There *is* an afterlife, and it's not my parents' fucked-up homophobic cry-fest." She paused. Frowned. "You're not, like, a demon or something. Are you?"

"Uh, no."

"Didn't think so." Anne scratched her chin. "Wow. Just, wow. So we really do continue after we die."

"Uh . . ."

Molly didn't want to talk or even think about that. She was the only human to continue after death, inevitably isolated from other people by the simple fact of death. The afterlife was a vacuum. A burst balloon. Thinking about it made her dizzy, so she didn't. Not right now.

Anne said, "How did you . . ." Her question trailed off into a shrug.

"Got run over by a train."

Now it was Anne who flinched. "Yowch. Did it hurt?"

"Oh yeah."

"Did you jump?"

"No. It was an accident—"

According to Bayliss.

Bayliss, who claimed that a lesbian tried to jump his bones.

Oh, no.

Molly reeled from a sudden wave of sick dread. Something cold and oily sloshed through her gut. She dropped into a kitchen chair. It took a few steadying breaths before she could dodge the curling edge of panic.

"Anne, who is Philip Marlowe?"

* * *

*L*et me tell you a story," said Molly. "And as I go along, you tell me if it sounds familiar. Okay?"

Anne gave a confused shrug. "Sure, I guess."

Molly gathered her thoughts. *The story begins where?*

"Okay. So, there's this guy. He wears a fedora, he drinks rye whiskey, he lives on the edges. Not much connection to other people. But he's scraping by. One day, he gets a telephone call—"

"And the person on the other end offers him a job," said Anne. "He doesn't like the caller, and doesn't necessarily like the job, but he needs the work so he takes it anyway."

Molly took a steadying breath. *Please let this be a coincidence*, she thought. "You've heard this before?"

"I've read a few books that start this way."

"Huh. Does the job lead him to a woman?"

"Dame," Anne suggested. "But yeah. It either starts with a woman or leads to a woman."

"He becomes fascinated with her. But he senses that she's more than she seems. That she's harboring a big secret."

"Of course she is. These old stories aren't particularly enlightened, you know. Women are frequently a source of problems."

Molly said, "Against his better judgment, he gets involved in her life—"

Anne continued in a bored monotone, "And discovers that she's in deep trouble. In over her head."

A tingly sense of alarm raised goose pimples on the back of Molly's neck. This was not good.

She asked, "What kind of trouble?"

"Oh, it could be several things." Anne counted them off on her fingers. "The detective was hired to find her because she knows something dangerous. Or she might be on the run from a gangster ex-boyfriend. Or maybe she stole something."

"What if somebody was murdered, and something valuable went missing? And some very serious and determined people think she took it?"

Anne thought for a moment. "That works, too."

"They want it so badly that they ransack her place."

"Well, of course they do," said Anne. Then she anticipated the next beat, which sent cold sweat to pool in the small of Molly's back and trickle between her breasts. "And the detective, moved by his tarnished sense of chivalry, can't stand the sight of a damsel in distress. So he tries to intervene."

Molly remembered how Bayliss had looked after his encounter with the Cherubim. "They beat him up."

"They don't kill the detective, though," Anne said. "Just knock him around a bit."

Molly said, "But he isn't intimidated so easily. So he keeps at it. While investigating the murder victim, he finds some evidence connecting the dead guy to the woman."

"Sure he does. But he knows it's all just circumstantial, so he hides it away."

Yeah. At an old folks' home . . .

"Even though he has a sinking feeling she's more than she seems?" Molly shook her head, flailing for straws. Hoping this wasn't going where it appeared to be. "That seems like a dumb thing to do."

But Anne dashed that hope, too. "Nah, it's part of the formula. See, by this point he's starting to see her as a client, too. And the detective's personal code of honor demands that until things are resolved—either she's out of danger, or her duplicity and guilt are conclusively established—his loyalty is to his client. Even if he doesn't trust her."

Molly continued, "Okay. Anyway. So the detective investigates further. But when he goes to question somebody connected to the case, he finds—"

"A dead body. Duh."

In this case, Father Santorelli. Son of a bitch.

"Geez. Don't look so surprised," said Anne. "Philip Marlowe practically can't walk down the street without tripping over a stiff." This was a pointless conversation to her. Meanwhile, though, she was demolishing the bedrock of all Molly's experiences since she died. But what lay beneath it all?

Molly asked, dreading the answer, "What happens next?"

"Well, at some point he has a run-in with the cops. Often more than once."

"Why the cops?"

"They're interested in the woman, too. And they know he's working for her."

Molly thought about how Bayliss had described his encounter with the Thrones. "But the detective refuses to tell them anything. Why?"

"Again, that's the sense of honor at work. To share what he knows, or suspects, would be to betray his client. So he clams up. And anyway, he's hidden the evidence—"

"Or destroyed it?"

"—yeah, so there's nothing solid to connect her to whatever crime they're investigating."

What else had Bayliss told her? Uriel.

"Does he ever get warned off a case?"

"Often. For one, the cops almost always want him to drop it. They don't like him meddling in their affairs."

"Anybody else?"

"Sometimes the story involves another faction, sure. Like a club owner or something like that. Who makes a few threats to try to get the noble detective to drop the case."

"Let me guess. Because he's asking questions they don't want asked?"

"Pretty much." Anne was getting annoyed. "You know, I've been really patient. I'm still waiting for my turn to ask questions."

But it was terrifying, the way things fit the pattern Anne described. So Molly pressed on, desperate to find a contradiction.

"You have been incredibly patient. But please. Just a little more." The problem with these parallels, Molly realized, was that *she* hadn't done anything according to a script. "Tell me more about the women in these stories."

Anne sighed. "It's like I said. They're rife with the sexism of their day. The women fall into a small number of categories." Once again she ticked the points off on her fingers. "Let's see. You've got your sexy dame with a mysterious past. Then you've got your crazy, murderous sexpot. The former often turns out to be the latter, by the way. And then you've got your puppyish, virginal sylph." After a moment she counted one more finger. "Oh, almost forgot the acid-tongued harridan, too. She's more rare."

"And does he always get it on with one of them?"

"Sometimes, but not always. He has a complicated sense of honor. But there's always flirtation, sexual tension. Sometimes even a subtle invitation. Or unsubtle."

He didn't get that from me. But the story demanded it. So when the next woman came along, he pigeonholed her role in the tale to fit that demand.

That was his mistake. If he hadn't adhered so rigidly to the traditional story, Molly might never have caught on.

The raging migraine returned. It brought friends. Molly hugged herself, fought a rising tide of nausea.

If Anne was right—and the woman knew her detective stories—everything Bayliss had told Molly since the very beginning fit the elements of a noir detective novel too closely to be anything other than deliberate. This wasn't a coincidence. And it explained everything: his wardrobe . . . his sexism . . . the ancient diner in his Magisterium . . . even why Bayliss spoke like a character in an old movie.

Or, more correctly, book.

He'd cobbled together a storyline and a persona from a bunch of different detective stories. The affectations were just a side effect of that. Bayliss had absorbed the tropes of noir fiction and turned them into a framework for the tale he presented to Molly. To the extent that he held to the outline even when it blatantly contradicted the facts.

But why go to all this trouble? What did it achieve, turning himself into a hard-boiled detective pastiche in an archetypal story? Hell. Why adopt any persona at all?

What if . . . Another chilling thought. She'd never stopped to wonder why the angels were as relatable as they were. Why did some of them have any human characteristics at all? She suspected part of it had to do with cultural imprinting, or perhaps perceptual expectations carrying over from her human days. But what if the angels were far more alien, more inexplicable, than she had blindly accepted? Maybe Bayliss didn't know how to be even remotely human, much less how to interact with somebody like Molly. Perhaps he'd had to work from a template merely to have a basis for interaction. Maybe they all did. But Bayliss also needed a model for the evolving situation he wanted to convey. And for some arcane reason, the travails of an old-time gumshoe fit the bill.

And she had bought into it. She had accepted everything he told her, not realizing that he was reading from a playbook written before she was born. Bayliss had been lying to her since day one. And not just overlooking or omitting certain details, the stuff she'd called him on several times, but flat-out lying.

She didn't dare believe a single thing he had ever told her. She had to throw out everything he'd ever said.

Which meant she didn't know anything.

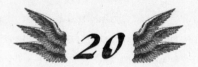

20

A FOOL (ALMOST) RUSHES IN

Not since Jericho had I seen a worse case of the jitters. When I walked the mean streets of the Pleroma, it seemed every joe and jane I passed had a raging case of floating anxiety disorder. If Gabby's death had put the Choir on edge, the popcorn proliferation of Nephilim had been the final shove. Things were tightest close to the mortal realm, where the weakest members of the Choir slid down the ontological gradient of METATRON's binding to rattle the floor with their nervous tics like a concert in the subbasement of the Pleroma. But that overarching sense of anxiety cast a long shadow. Even farther out, in the metaphysical suburbs where the sensible cars and respectable glamours could be found, it wasn't all canasta games and dinner parties. There was a strong front blowing in; we felt it in our guts. In weather like this, even the Seraphim lock their doors. Smart eggs hunker down to ride out the storm.

Not me, though. I needed words with two dumb onions.

The first of the defeated Cherubim was a blurry fractured thing. I couldn't see it well without a lot of squinting. Molly's ambush had yanked the goon apart—no mean feat, that—and now it was too busy feeling sorry for itself to zip its two halves together correctly. They didn't quite fit together, like the reflection in an imperfectly fixed mirror. What a drip. Just looking in its direction gave me a headache, so I opted to talk to its partner instead.

I thought I'd seen it all. But I'd never seen a Cherub with a black eye. That must have taken some doing because they don't even *have* eyes, the dumb lugs. Just flames. Chalk up another point in the twist's column. The poor sap held a steak to its battered face. It made the joint smell like a Fourth of July cookout. All we needed was some potato salad and tub of coleslaw.

After all, the fireworks were coming soon enough.

"One monkey," I said. "The two of you working together couldn't croak one lousy monkey."

"She was supposed to be alone."

"It wasn't supposed to matter. What a sorry wrecking crew you turned out to be."

"Sorry, boss."

"How'd she do it? How'd she get the drop on you cream puffs?"

They told me how flametop clobbered them using sleight of hand and sheer moxie. I whistled. What an item. I knew how to pick them. She was perfect.

Steak-face said, "If you wanted us to fight you shouldn't've made us wear those monkey suits. You didn't hobble us when you sent us into her Magisterium."

"Yeah," said steak-face's blurry pal. "She was no problem then."

"We should go find her, do it right this time," said the first Cherub.

The dopes. With friends like these, who needs enemies?

I said, "Listen, you thickheaded palookas. What do you think would happen if you went down to Earth for a spot of redemptive violence? If you started traipsing around the mortal realm, bumping off monkeys, letting everyone see you in your true forms?"

"She'd get what she had coming?"

"She'd be sorry? Real sorry?"

Oh, brother. I reminded myself that I hadn't hired these goons for their brains. Maybe it's the constant heat of holy fire from their faces making them feverish. Slow.

"Uh-huh," I said. "And how's about METATRON?"

There was a pause while that sank in. "Oh," said steak-face. "That."

"Yeah. That."

"You want we should go back and finish off the monkey now?"

"Nah," I said. "I'll handle it. You two lick your wounds. They must be medium rare by now."

I'd been ready to rub out Molly's girlfriend then and there when I had the chance. But as much as flametop liked to question everything I said and did, she still wasn't getting the big picture. If that cluck didn't start doing the math sooner than later, I'd have to hire a sky-writer. So it was a golden opportunity when she practically pushed that dish of a librarian into my open arms.

And besides, we could spare a stiff or two. I'd worked a little slop into the system. I wasn't born yesterday.

*O*n my way to count the Nephilim, to verify the other PI recipients had been pinked, I ran into an old acquaintance. Can't say it was a happy reunion.

"Bayliss," it said. "ssilyaB," it said.

"Think you've got me confused with somebody else." I pushed past, but not without tipping my hat. "Sorry, guy. Sorry, doll."

The Virtue raised two arms to block my passage. One lead, one gold. I sighed and, keeping one peeper on that bobbing scorpion tail, plastered a happy grin on my kisser.

"Hey, now I recognize you. Lose some weight, did you? Long time no see. You've been a stranger, eh?"

"We seek you," said its feminine aspect.

"You avoid us," said its masculine aspect.

"Seek me? Don't you kids have better things to do with your time? You should get a hobby."

"We did as you asked." ".deksa uoy sa did eW"

"Can't say I remember that." I danced out of the Virtue's reach, making for my apartment. "I'd love to stick around while you flap your gums about it, but I have a hot date with a lulu of a chess problem."

"We hold your promise. Payment is owed."

"Nuts to both of you. I'm no chiseler. Just quit squawking until I get back on my feet, how about?"

"Payment is owed." ".dewo si tnemyaP"

"Yeah, yeah. Payment. Enough with the broken record."

You'd think that given everything else I was doing, this penny-pinching sourpuss would give me a break on the tab. That's gratitude for you. But I let it slide. I'm a generous soul.

And besides. The way I figured it, all the old tabs and debts would get erased soon enough.

* * *

J returned from my errands to find an angel making coffee in my kitchen. So much for that second lock I put on the door. I couldn't wait to get out of this neighborhood. It had seen better days. So had we all.

"Please," I said, flinging my hat over the hilt of the sword in my umbrella stand, "make yourself at home."

Uriel said, "In this dive? Not likely."

She had coffee grounds and soul fragments strewn all across the counter. If I hadn't known better I might have thought she'd been struck with a recurrence of the quotidian ague while filling the percolator. But then Michael and Raguel always were the tidy ones. I decided against sharing my trick with the comb; a lousy cup of coffee was the least she deserved for breaking in to my digs again.

"Not that it ain't a pleasure, but what can I blame for this visit?"

"There's some concern," said Uriel, "over an apparent lack of progress, Bayliss."

The percolator gurgled its assent. What a sad little toady it was. It didn't even have a dog in this fight. But they had a point, the Seraph and the machine.

"Yeah, yeah. The monkey's taking it nice and slow."

"Too slow. And we've been patient."

"*You've* been patient? What am I, chopped liver?"

Uriel rummaged my cabinets for a cup. I pointed. She snagged one. "Nevertheless," she said. "We're eager to see the end of this."

As if I wasn't. That was rich. What a joker. She knew how to make a gag. I told her so.

"Cool your jets, sister. What's a few more days on top of a million millennia?"

"Every extra attosecond runs the risk METATRON will take an interest." She poured herself a cup, took one sip, made a face, dumped the coffee down the sink. I wondered how many souls went down the drain just then. "The Thrones are getting suspicious."

She had a point. The bulls were zeroing in. It had been a little uncomfortable under the bright lights. Good thing Uriel had come riding to the rescue when she did. But things were too far along now for anybody to stop it.

"They can turn blue, the lot of 'em, for all I care."

"We've already staged another attempted eviction."

"Bread and circuses. Works every time."

"We can't keep it up forever."

"Oh, brother. Like you've got it tough. I don't recall you raising so much as a pinfeather when we were rounding up a volunteer for this job."

"It was always your baby."

Well. I don't like to brag. I'm the humble type. But trust a wicked bird like Uriel to appeal to my pride. Pride was a sin, after all.

I reminded her, "Yeah, my baby. But it wasn't cheap. And in the end nobody else wanted to assume the cost."

That shut her yap. Uriel looked away. Even a lion can look chagrined from time to time.

"I miss him," she said in a voice more quiet than the hiss of the cosmic microwave background.

"Me, too," I said. "Me, too."

An awkward silence crept up on us. She staked it in the heart, changed the subject.

"What happened to the Cherubim? I hear they came back with their tails between their legs."

"Those roosters? Flametop pulled the old dipsy-doodle on them."

Uriel flapped a half-dozen wings, like a trio of opinionated pigeons. "Would you give it a rest with the slang?"

"Sorry. Hard habit to break."

"Anyway," she said, "I find that difficult to believe."

"Believe it. She's no paper flower." Uriel's ox face snorted at me again. "What? Oh. Sorry. I mean, she's tough. And she's clever."

Okay. So maybe I like to crow just a little.

"Not clever enough to piece things together."

"Trust me. She's getting there."

By slow freight, said the scowl on Uriel's human pan. The lion visage let loose with a growl.

I said, "She's the naturally suspicious type. And believe me, I just sent her one dilly of a telegram."

Uriel rolled her eyes, all eight of them. She asked, "So she's back on track now?"

"Right now"—I glanced at my watch—"I figure she and dollface are having a swell little dustup. But once they talk each other off the ceiling that nickel will drop soon enough."

"And will she do what we brought her here to do?"

I lit a pill. Tossed a smoke ring at Uriel. "Trust me. She never passes up a chance to take a swipe at me."

*T*hat son of a bitch. That unbelievable motherfucker."
Molly ran fingers through her hair while pacing the tiny confines of Anne's kitchen. Saint Elmo's fire crackled through her hair, making it snap and writhe like Medusa's asps. "That deranged piece of shit." She reversed course at the refrigerator. "Sexist two-faced asshole."

Anne said, "Molly."

"Arrogant shit-faced prick. Smug, oily, self-centered dick-licking alcoholic." About-face at the stove.

"Molly."

"That duplicitous, cocky, goat-humping, weaselly backstabbing pervert."

Anne opened a window. "Molly."

"I'll kick his ass. More than that. I'll kill him. They can die, you know. Yeah. I swear I'll take the Trumpet and—"

"Molly!"

Molly paused in her circuit, the unfinished rant piling up behind her like boxcars in a derailed train of thought. Anne looked frantic. "What?"

Anne said, "Just stop a second, would you? Look at what you're doing to my apartment."

She pointed at blistered fake linoleum left in the scorching wake of Molly's halo. Fury had energized her *heiligenschein*. The apartment reeked of melted plastic. Molly tasted a dusting of dioxin on the air, released by the smoldering polyvinyl chloride. Chlorine atoms raked fractured atomic bonds across her tongue.

"Sorry," she said.

"Some of us have security deposits, you know."

Molly knelt. She ran a hand over the damaged floor as though she were brushing the wrinkles out of a bedsheet. It became whole and unblemished under her touch.

"Well, thanks," said Anne.

"Uh-huh," said Molly, remembering the cigarette burn Bayliss had left in the floorboards of her Magisterium. The cigarette burn she had repeatedly tried and failed to fix. The blemish he'd wrought on one of her safest, warmest memories. Jesus. Her dead body had still been steaming on the snow when that son of a bitch tossed a filthy fucking *cigarette* on Ria's handiwork. She'd do so much more than kick his ass. She already knew where to find the Trumpet. Anne's Plenary Indulgence contained a piece, and the rest was scattered through the Nephilim. She could reassemble it. All she had to do was—

"Hey!" Anne shook her by the shoulders. "Enough!"

Molly blinked, shook her head, tried to see through the scarlet haze of her rage. Anne stepped back. She had donned a pair of oven mitts. They had googly eyes and were mottled black and white like Holstein cows. One cow nostril exhaled a wisp of smoke.

Anne hung them back on their magnetic hooks on the refrigerator. "Calm the hell down before you burn this place to the ground."

Molly blinked again, this time in an effort to clear away the annoying dampness in her eyes. "I can't. Don't you see? He killed me, turned me into this, this, this whatever I am, just to populate this messed-up house of cards he built. Like a, a, a fucking *toy doll*." She ran a hand across her eyes. "Like a monkey in a zoo."

Anne shook her head. "Why would he do that to you?"

"I don't *know*!"

"I'm just saying maybe it's not as bad as you think. Consider all the things you've seen and learned. We continue after we die! Isn't that something wonderful?"

"Oh, Anne, you don't understand—" Another surge of frustration killed the words in Molly's throat. Her eyes watered with the effort to muffle her exasperation; venting it with a scream would shatter the windows, knock the building off its foundation, divert the nearby river, jolt the orbit of a passing comet. But poor Anne truly didn't understand. She thought she'd be like Molly someday. Thought something would persist after her body was nothing but cold jelly.

"No, I don't. So help me understand."

Molly took a long, shuddery breath. "I'm afraid everything that happened to me since I died has been nothing but manipulation, and—"

"Uh-huh. I get that things have been kind of messed up for you. But it's not what I'm talking about. Because, and I'm gonna be really honest with you here, I'm a little less interested in your own problems than I am in understanding why those guys wanted to hurt me yesterday. I'm done with being patient. My turn."

Molly sighed. She took a chair at the kitchen table. And then a thought: "You didn't happen to ask Bayliss about it, did you?"

"He said I should ask you."

"Of course he did," Molly said to herself. "Dickwad." Then she added, "You're taking it really well."

"I was a little overwhelmed, what with the running through shadows and stepping from Chicago to Minneapolis and finding out I was dating a ghost, to have much chance to let it all sink in. But somehow all along I still felt safe with you, even when it was confusing." She crossed her arms and leaned against the counter. "That is until you decided to freak out with the realization you have no idea what you're doing. It gives a woman pause."

"Yeah. I suppose it does."

"Yeah," said Anne. She cocked her head and set her jaw, clearly waiting for an answer.

"Those *penitentes* were under the control of—sort of, like, possessed by—a pair of Cherubim." In response to Anne's frown, Molly added, "A kind of angel. They have fire where their faces should be."

Anne shivered. "And they wanted to hurt me, why?"

"Not just you. Everyone who received a Plenary Indulgence from Father Santorelli."

"My parents' dead priest."

"Dead . . . Oh, shit." An unbidden insight made Molly gasp. It was cold. She coughed. Her breath tasted like acid. She covered her mouth and said through splayed fingers, "Bayliss killed him."

"Christ! Are you serious? And you asked him to protect me?"

"Now maybe you're starting to see why I'm so angry," Molly said. "Anyway, it's complicated, but those Indulgences were metaphysically tainted. Such that when the recipients die, it has an effect on the Pleroma. Where the angels live." She made air-quotes with her fingers. " 'Heaven.' But it's misleading to call it that."

The aura of fascination still clung to Anne. Her frustration dissipated a little when she asked, her voice balanced on the edge of a reverent hush, "Is it beautiful?"

"Really weird. But don't get hung up on the angels. They're mostly assholes."

Anne looked stricken. She hadn't expected this and had probably hoped for something a little more uplifting. "Gee, don't you paint a lovely picture of the afterlife."

Molly couldn't bring herself to voice the truth: *There is no afterlife, Anne. Not for you, or Martin, or Ria, or Mom and Dad, or anybody else.* Instead she cradled her head in her hands.

"So they're doing this because they're trying to change Heaven?" Anne asked.

"I think so," said Molly.

I might have been closer than I thought when I wondered if Gabriel's murder was part of an elaborate jailbreak. But how do the Nephilim fit into that scheme? Something shivered in the back of her mind . . .

"Okay, then. No offense, but why do they need you?"

Molly said, "Because—"

But then she realized she didn't have an answer. What was Bayliss up to, and why did he need a human to do it? Merely knowing that he was a lying piece of shit provided no answers. Only questions. Molly considered trying to wring the truth from him with a liberal application of the Trumpet, but abandoned that speculation when it led her to a place that made uncovering his lies seem as innocuous as stumbling upon a surprise birthday party.

Bayliss must have figured out what had become of the Trumpet long before Molly did. After all, he'd seen the connection between the Indulgences and the Nephilim, too. More than that, though, he implicitly understood the rules of the Pleroma, the inhuman multidimensional logic of the Choir, in ways that Molly still didn't. What took her days to deduce would have been obvious to him. Intuitive. So why didn't he go retrieve it, then?

Because he wanted Molly to find it.

She cast her memory back to the conversation they'd had in the aftermath of METATRON's punishment for attempting to reverse time, when Bayliss first told her about the Trumpet. What had he called it? A tool of righteous fury.

Molly looked at Anne, to the floor, to the oven mitts.

Righteous fury. The kind that had her raring to go teach Bayliss a lesson. Like the blistering halo she wore while pacing Anne's kitchen. Like the enraged indignation she felt upon realizing she'd been a dupe.

The heat from her simmering anger instantly turned very, very cold. Cryogenic. Anne shivered again. She closed the window.

Bayliss set this whole thing in motion so that I would find and use the Trumpet.

And if not for Anne, Molly would have. If not for Anne, she'd be doing it right now.

But what's so special about me? Why is he doing this?

Anne said, "It's happening again. Your halo."

Molly concentrated on absorbing the glow into her human form. It got a little easier every time she did it, but at the same time the boundaries between her human and other loci felt blurrier. Undefined. She'd worry about that later. No choice.

She said, "I'm sorry I left you with Bayliss. I wouldn't have, if I had realized what he was doing."

Finally, Anne took a seat at the table. "Am I still in danger?"

"I doubt it. If Bayliss had wanted you . . ." Molly trailed off, unable to look Anne in the eye. "Um, dead . . . Well, it would have happened the minute I left you alone with him."

Anne scowled like somebody tasting something foul. "You really need to work on your reassurances."

"I should also be thanking you. If not for you, I would have blundered straight into whatever Bayliss has planned for me. I still don't know what that is, but at least I've opened my eyes. Thanks to you, we might have just dodged a bullet."

"Huh. Who knew reading all those detective stories would pay off someday."

"Oh, believe me, it did," said Molly. She took Anne's hand. "In fact, maybe now you can tell me this: how does the story end?"

21

FAMILY REUNION

*U*h, can I come in?"

Molly gestured toward the apartment she glimpsed behind Martin. He'd done nothing but stare since opening the door. It was awkward. And the hallway smelled like piss.

He retreated. She entered. He tackled her in a bear hug. The toes of her boots left the ground. Had she still been mortal her ribs would have creaked beneath the mountainous weight of his relief, her breath snuffed by his desperation. But she was something different now, something whose lungs were no less an affectation than her earrings.

Not that she had kept every last vestige of her human body. She hadn't had her period since she died.

"I was starting to think I imagined it," he said into her hair. He clung to tactile proof of her presence.

"Hey. Didn't I promise to come back?"

A sheepish pause. "Yeah."

"I keep my promises. Also?"

"Yeah?"

"You can put me down now."

"Oh. Sorry." He did, more gently than he'd ever done anything in her presence. More gently than when Blue, their slobbery Newfoundland, was dying of bone cancer, and had to be put down, and Mom and Dad had given them a final chance to say good-bye.

She sniffed his breath, tasted nothing more damning than beer and cigarettes on his aura. She wasn't crazy about the beer—he shouldn't be having any alcohol. But it was an acceptable compromise under the circumstances. She couldn't expect him to abandon all of his vices.

Not all at once, and not after what he'd been through. After what she'd put him through.

Martin looked her up and down. "Moll. You look . . . healthy." To his shoes, he added, "Alive." And then he blushed in embarrassment for stating something so obviously impossible. It was something a strung-out junkie might have said. Might have believed.

"I'm glad one of us does. Because you look like hell."

"I know."

His shoulders slumped, the big goof, so she chucked his chin with her thumb. "It's a huge improvement compared to what I saw when I first came to visit. After the accident."

Martin looked at her, wide-eyed, looking again like a confused and eager puppy. "You were here?"

"You were"—She started to say "out of it," but decided delicacy would do him no favors.—"stoned out of your mind. I didn't let you see me."

He closed the door. She kicked her boots into a corner and flopped onto the futon, one leg folded under her. The wooden slats of the futon frame pressed straight through the useless mattress into her shin. Martin looked ready to cry. He'd seen her do this a thousand times.

"Yes," she said. "It's really me."

"Do you want something to drink? Or eat?"

She remembered the roaches in the kitchen. A slight funk wafted from that direction, noticeable even to her human senses. "No. I want to catch up with my brother."

The futon creaked under his weight. He fidgeted, cracking his knuckles, lacing and unlacing his fingers. She let him take his time. This had to be done on his terms. Plus, she admitted to herself, the more time she spent with Martin the longer she could put off dealing with Bayliss.

Finally, Martin said, "I watched you die. The memory is so bad, so vivid . . . And it's not just that. There was a funeral. A memorial service." He reached over to pluck the program from the wall. More tactile proof that he wasn't nuts. The tape made a gentle tearing sound.

"You didn't imagine it," said Molly. "It wasn't a hallucination. It wasn't a bad trip. It happened."

It was supposed to be reassuring. Instead, it terrified him. His nostrils flared, his heart rate spiked. He was trying to be logical about this. Good for Martin.

"I'm afraid this means I've gone crazy. Or maybe I'm still high and hallucinating now."

"The fact you realize this is crazy probably means you're sane. A crazy person would think it's sane to have a conversation with his dead sister." She gave a smile that she hoped was comforting. "And you're not tripping, are you?"

He thought about it. "No. I did, a lot, right after . . . whatever it was . . . happened. But then it was like somebody pressed a button and I couldn't get a fix any longer. It hurt. I needed it so bad."

"That was me. I've been watching over you." At this, he stared again. "Please don't be mad," she added.

"I wasted a lot of money."

She touched his elbow. "Your life is worth more."

Martin scraped the back of his hand across his eyes. "Every time I close my eyes I see you falling off the platform. It's like a movie playing behind my eyelids, stuck on an endless loop I can't turn off. Your body hits the tracks, and the train skids over you, and the snow turns black, and the smell . . ."

The memory of anguish hit her in stereo, coming from both Martin and herself. Molly swallowed gorge. She tried to dodge the sensation of her body coming apart.

Desperation constricted Martin's voice. "What did happen, Moll? What's happening to us?"

"Do you remember a guy on the platform with us?"

"No."

"Well, he was there. He came up to us earlier that night, in the laneway, to bum a cigarette from you. Remember? I was looking at the sky?"

"I guess. I dunno." Martin frowned. "Maybe. Kind of a strange guy, right? He talked weird."

"That's him."

"What about him?"

"He wasn't human." Martin blinked. Molly shrugged. "I told you this was going to be a long conversation."

*   *   *

*S*he drained the last of her iced tea. Martin plucked an abandoned sliver of pepperoni from the stone platter balanced on the over-sized can of tomato paste set in the middle of their table. They had taken a taxi to Uptown, near the lakes. This had seemed a good choice: familiar surroundings; she used to cajole Martin into meeting her here every couple of months, so that they could catch up and she could keep an eye on him. Where else would they have this conversation? It would have been cheaper to take the light rail, if it served Martin's neighborhood, but even so he would have refused to stand on another train platform with her. Nor was she terribly keen on it. It was a fucked-up memory for both of them.

The pizza wasn't as good as she remembered. The neighborhood wasn't, either. She'd ruined it for herself when she'd done her best to kill Ria just a few blocks from here. She confessed to him about that. Now she was thinking about it again, wrapped in the sticky tendrils of what she'd done, and he could read it in her face because he was her brother.

It was Martin's turn to give a reassuring touch. "You didn't know."

"He did try to warn me. Bayliss. I almost did it to you, too, right after I died. Right there on the platform. That would have been it for the Pruett kids, huh?" Molly choked on a sob when she couldn't manage a laugh. "She looks so small in that hospital bed. Too small to contain the woman trapped inside."

"Ria was okay. I always thought she could have been a little nicer to you, though."

"C'mon, Martin. Don't be a creep."

"Sorry," he said, punctuating the apology with another squeeze to her elbow. He wrapped an unused straw around his ring finger, released it, watched it unspool. "You should be able to fix her. Just reach in and . . ." He touched his temple with a twisting motion of his fingertip.

"It's not that easy."

"It can't be harder than anything else you've done since Australia." *Since Australia.* That was the comfortable euphemism on which they'd settled. Because clearly, whatever Bayliss had done to her, she wasn't dead in the conventional sense.

"I understand so many things I never did before. But people are so, so complicated." Molly pressed a crumpled paper napkin to her face. It stung her eyes with pepperoni grease. With a voice like the smoke from an extinguished candle, she admitted, "I'm terrified to try. There's one way to fix it. A million ways to make it worse." She blew her nose. "Fucking entropy."

Martin said, "You use a lot of words you never used to." He changed his posture, and the topic. "Mom's lawyer arranged to have all her stuff shipped to me. But I didn't stick around in Australia to help with packing up and selling her house. I wanted to get away from there as soon as I could after . . . well, you know. So they hired a service to do it, but between that and the overseas shipping it ate a big chunk of the money she left behind."

Molly nodded. They had gone to Melbourne for their mother's funeral. Their folks had put an entire ocean between them after divorcing. Mom had fled to Australia while Dad stayed in Canada. "I'd have done the same thing. She had too much crap, anyway."

"You're entitled to half of it. Mom's crap, and the rest of the money. There's a storage unit."

Molly wondered if their mother still had those old New Age books that mentioned the Pleroma. It might have been amusing to sift through those. Not enough to justify the trouble, though. She shook her head.

"It's not like I have to pay rent anymore. Keep the stuff you really want, and sell the rest. Don't waste money on a storage unit, Martin. Put it in the bank instead. But if you even think about spending it on—"

"I know. Dad always said you were the practical one."

"I miss him. Mom, too."

"Yeah."

The sun had set by the time they emerged from the mediocre pizzeria. They walked along Lagoon toward the lakes. Molly steered them in another direction, around the block and up Hennepin. Early evening on a weekend night; the massage parlors and fast-food places did a brisk turn of business. Their stroll took them across the light-rail tracks. Both made a point of not noticing them. *Penitentes* loitered outside a former art-house theater that had been split apart and converted into a halal loan service, a police substation, and a franchise stand selling lenses and earbuds. Molly stepped warily, but none approached. None carried a secret angel.

They walked through clouds of conversation in Somali, Hmong, Hindi, Spanish, and Malay. Molly had once been told that the dining landscape in Minneapolis—in landlocked cities all over the world—had changed irrevocably after the global diaspora from what used to be coastal areas. Cold comfort to the refugees, no doubt.

Martin kept an eye on the streets. At first she thought he was trying to be chivalrous, overprotective, before she realized he was taking note of bus stops.

"Hey. When we're ready to go back," she said, "let's do it my way."

He smiled. "Can we? I'd really like that."

"Sure."

The combined glow of moon and city lights washed away the stars. But the brightest shooting stars, the most enthusiastic space debris, still etched luminous hairline fractures across the sky. A flare caught Molly's eye. She stopped on the sidewalk, looking up. She thought about Gabriel's murder, and her own. Martin turned, joined her, looked up.

"What do you see when you look up there?"

"Same as you. Moon. Night. Space junk."

"That's it?"

Molly shunted aside her human vision. She studied this evening in the city with senses that had no names.

"I feel the whisper of ionosphere slithering over the debris as it skims into the atmosphere. Hearing me say that caused you a nervous thrill; your sweat just became more alkaline. I can taste that on the air because the heightened pulse in your throat is wafting that sweat my way. The breeze—oh—the breeze sheds beautiful eddies when it breaks around your body. I wish you could see them. If I concentrate I can hear the hum and rattle of the cement mixer that produced these sidewalk slabs however many years ago. The electricity in the lights overhead and in the conduits beneath our feet is a metallic buzz flickering across my skin." A brilliant shooting star arced overhead, cleaving the night. "That was chunk of solar array. The light came from the unzipping and recombining of cadmium atoms. I just know that somehow. With concentration, I can feel the electrons peeling away one at a time like popcorn kernels going off in an air popper. If I close one eye and squint, I can see gravity, how the curvature of space and time tugs at that debris, and the moon, and you." She paused. "And I'm pretty sure that if I really tried—and didn't mind the migraine—I could probably lick the mechanism giving rise to that curvature. The stuff behind the curtain, the stuff scientists haven't yet cracked."

When she looked down again, Martin was staring at her rather than the sky. He didn't blink. It gave her goose bumps. "What?" she asked.

"Why are you even down here, Moll?"

The question, and the thready way he asked it, made her shiver. So she dodged it.

"Don't be a goof," she said.

"I mean it. Why do you bother with the rest of us?"

This was worse than losing her connection to humanity. This was humanity losing its connection to her. Her own brother didn't know what to make of her, didn't understand that she still had human emotions. Like the loneliness that pierced her through at that moment.

"Where else would I go? This is home."

She took him home via the Pleroma. It wasn't the easiest thing she'd ever done, yet it wasn't quite as difficult as when she hauled Anne through her Magisterium to elude the Cherubim. At least the walls didn't sag like candle wax while Martin marveled at the reconstructed apartment.

Molly created a door from her Magisterium to his place. Martin started to step through, but stopped.

"Wait," he said. "Before we leave, can I, um, can I see what you really look like now?"

"Doofus. I look like your sister."

"I know. But there's more now. Right?"

It was a fair question. She said, "Okay. But you have to promise not to freak out. Just remember I'm still me, regardless of what it might look like."

"I promise."

And so it was there, in the reimagined and reconstructed memory of the kitchen she once shared with Ria, that Molly set aside her human form and showed her brother what she had become. The transition went more smoothly than it had in Bayliss's hotel room. She dialed it back when Martin flinched and shielded his eyes.

"Are you okay?" she asked, momentarily consumed with a vision of bloody tears streaking Bayliss's face.

"Oh, Moll," said Martin. He was crying. Not blood, though. "They turned you into starlight."

*Y*ou have to admit," he said, sprawled on the futon, speaking with breath redolent of onions and garlic, "it's pretty fucking cool. The angels."

"That's exactly what Anne said."

"Is she the girl I met?"

"Woman. Yes. And you might feel differently if you ever met some of those jacktards."

"They really don't care about us at all?"

"No. Sort of the opposite. They're pretty resentful. They call us 'monkeys.'"

"Geez."

"Yeah."

"Still," said Martin, "it's kind of hard to swallow. I mean, I believe you, but it's like . . ."

". . . Like the entire human world is just the skin of a soap bubble filled to bursting with angels and the Voice of God and conflicting notions of reality. Yet somehow nobody has ever noticed," said Molly.

"Yeah. I mean you're here, now, and that alone is proof," Martin said. "Just by coming here and talking to me you've probably overthrown, I dunno, like, ten thousand years worth of science. And that's even before I saw a piece of the, uh, what did you call it?"

"My Magisterium."

"'Magisterium.' Wild. It's a little freaky that we're all living in the edges of this tremendous secret."

"Nobody has ever received the truth before now," said Molly, voicing the revelation as it came to her. "I guess I'm the only angel who ever bothered to share it."

After all, Martin had a point. Once Bayliss picked her (*why?*) for a peek behind the curtain, it was inevitable that part of Molly would begin see the human experience as having all the gravitas of shadow puppets capering on a cave wall. Or however it went; she vaguely remembered reading something about that in college before dropping the philosophy class. But that was beside the point. The tenuous nature of the mortal realm became obvious when seen from the proper perspective. Humanity's continual ignorance of their situation seemed almost cruel. The comforting myths of an afterlife, or reincarnation, or a plan and purpose to the universe had persisted for millennia.

But on the other hand, why should the angels bother to enlighten the monkeys? Hell, they couldn't even manifest in the mortal realm without causing permanent damage to the humans around them. It seemed the merest glimpse of an angel was enough to cause an aneurysm. Hence the *penitentes* and their hollowed-out souls. But it wasn't because they cared; it was just a dodge to avoid ticking off META-TRON. Otherwise the naked angels would have left hundreds of Rias in their wake. Except Bayliss. He didn't need a hollowed-out human to get around on Earth. Strange.

The angels couldn't care less about the human condition. *Except me*, thought Molly. She was different. She was a product of that tenuous, pointless, mortal realm. She had family, and friends, people she loved and people she hated. And she'd fought to maintain her connection to her old life. In contrast to the rest of the Choir, Molly had no reason *not* to share the truth of things. For that alone, Molly was entirely distinct from everything else in the Choir. She was unique, something quite apart from the other angels.

Another piece of the puzzle fell into place. Merciless as an avalanche, it suffocated her with a deeper understanding of Bayliss's intent. Earlier, thanks to Anne, she had realized Bayliss wanted her to use the Trumpet in a fit of anger. Now she knew why: because she differed from the other angels. Crucially.

Molly stood. Paced. She didn't have all of it yet, every single step, but she understood enough to know what she'd do next. Enough to know she had to say good-bye soon, and that it might be permanent. At least she had a chance to say it this time.

Martin said, "You look very serious all of a sudden."

"I was thinking—"

It kept coming, the avalanche. It hit her hard. Hard enough to chip a tooth, if her teeth had been breakable things not made of thought. She was thinking about good-byes, and what they meant for a creature such as her.

Regardless of what happened to her, of what happened when she confronted Bayliss, the passage of mortal time would always ensure a final, permanent good-bye. She could do almost anything, but she couldn't hold her friends and loved ones forever. Martin would die someday. Sooner than later, if his vices won. So would Ria, and Anne, and everybody she'd ever known. Every human presently alive—she'd outlive them all, if she survived the next few hours.

It was one thing to strive for connection when you had people. But what would become of Molly a hundred years from now? She wasn't fully an angel, not by their standards—she'd never be a true member of the Choir, not that she cared—and yet she wouldn't pass on like a mortal. A woman without a nation; a homeless hybrid.

Would she spend the rest of eternity constantly running up the down escalator, mourning dead connections and desperately seeking new ones? How many centuries would it take before the loneliness and loss became so great that she eschewed the last vestiges of her old human ways? When she surrendered and become something else? Would she remember Ria a hundred years from now? A thousand? Would she remember Martin a million years from now? Would she remember being a human named Molly?

Forever, she now saw with bowel-churning clarity, was a very, *very* long time. Molly stared into both barrels of an eternity spent alone, and it was fucking terrifying. It felt like a bucketful of rancid butter in her gut. She stumbled. Martin caught her elbow.

"What's up?"

"I need a hug," she sobbed. Martin obliged.

Maybe he and Ria were the lucky ones after all. They would never know a thousand years of loneliness. A million.

How long would it be, after the last of Molly's earthly connections disappeared, before she started haunting human gatherings like a ghost? Trying to thaw a frostbitten soul by holding it up to the feeble flickering of humanity? Or would she slowly become another Bayliss, a cynical shit building paper-thin simulacra of people just to have somebody to banter with?

No. Not that. She'd never be like Bayliss. Better to be alone.

Or was it? Would that lonely eternity be better than dying? Because if she failed . . . Molly wondered what it would be like to die a second time. Angels could die; she most of all. And that frightened her just as much as eternal loneliness. Maybe more.

She *knew* what it was to die. Death was cold metal, black snow, her viscera . . .

She couldn't face it a second time. It would be worse the second time. So much worse. Her first death had been unforeseen, unanticipated. What would it be like to die as an angel, perceiving the moment with ten thousand nameless senses, already knowing death intimately from her final human experience?

But those were her only choices: eternal loneliness or a second death immeasurably worse than the first.

Martin's wall display emitted a loud *zap* of static electricity. Bluish smoke wafted from a crack in the wall.

He started. "What the hell?"

"Sorry," she said. "That kind of stuff happens when I get upset."

He started at the broken display. "Wow."

"I have to go soon. I don't know when I'll be back." She pulled away, then stood. "It might be a long time." *I might end up like Gabriel.* The thought gave rise to a nagging sensation at the back of her mind. She pushed it aside for the moment. "But hey. At least we get to have a proper good-bye this time."

"You've already come back from the dead once. I don't know much about much," said Martin, "but I know better than to say good-bye."

She tried to give a reassuring laugh, but it turned into a hiccup, then another sob.

He said, "I can tell something's wrong."

"Just tired. And a little frightened about what the future might bring." She pulled him to his feet. "But that's a problem for later. Right now, I want to try to do something for you. Do you trust me?"

"You know I do."

Thanks to her interference, Martin had gone long enough without a fix that he was well on the way to recovery. But he'd always think of himself as a hopeless, broken failure unless she made a show of fixing him. She had to give him a tangible reason to believe better of himself.

"Close your eyes. I'm going to reach in and take something out of you. It won't hurt."

He knew what she meant. He didn't object.

*T*he game on the radio was just getting interesting—bases loaded, DiMaggio stepping into the box—when Sam returned. I don't know if Joltin' Joe made the grand slam because the play-by-play faded into a staticky bossa-nova rendering of the Chords of Creation.

The Powers have crummy timing. Ask anybody.

"You couldn't have waited until the end of the inning?"

Sam enveloped a stool beside me in a roiling cloud of lightning-bright ash. "You'd be more angry if I waited."

There was a hitch in its voice, a hiss or gurgle in that rasp of melting sapphires. I set down my cup. The dregs were cold anyway.

"Skim it," I said. "Just give me the cream."

"Your monkey just entered the Pleroma," said Sam. "Not her Magisterium. She's in the between-spaces, heading for the Nephilim."

I tapped a pill on the counter. Flicked a paper match into life with my thumbnail. "You sure?"

Sam said, "Whatever comes of your experiment, she isn't subtle. She leaves a wake."

Okay. So their timing is lousy. But I still have a soft spot for the Powers and their holographic ontologies. Plenty useful, these jaspers.

"What's she doing out there?"

"My guess?" A sulfurous fume roiled across the countertop. Flo swooned. "She's close to piecing it together. Suspicious."

I lit the pill and treated myself to a long draw. Savoring the taste of my instincts paying off like a long-shot trifecta, I said, modestly, "That's why I picked her."

Sam's smoke plume glowed white and blue with a constant flicker of electrical discharge. Back in the kitchen, the cook slapped the radio a couple of times. Sam said, "Don't break your arm, patting yourself on the back like that."

I tapped cigarette ashes into one of Sam's plumes. The look it gave me should have crisped my eyebrows.

"Don't worry. I haven't lost the big picture." I ground out the pill in my saucer. "Okay," I said. "The Nephilim have been stewing long enough. Let's do it. Pull the trigger."

Another flutter, this like the hiss of sizzling rubies. Sam said, "You sure?"

I mulled the angles for a microsecond. What point in a last-minute adjustment? If flametop was lamping the Nephilim, she'd received the telegram I sent courtesy of that dish librarian. Meaning any moment she'd realize she'd been played for a prize sap. And then she'd really hit the roof. I couldn't do any more without muddying the waters.

No need for corrections. She was right on course.

"I'm sure. Let's send our girl packing while she's still spitting nails."

DOING THE MATH

The raw Pleroma bore no resemblance to her expectations. How could she have anticipated this? It was exactly what Bayliss had described.

Prior to this, she'd only experienced slivers of it via those pieces encapsulated in Bayliss's Magisterium, the Virtue's, and her own. Bayliss's explanations—everything always came back to motherfucking Bayliss—cast the pure Pleroma as nothing more than a cosmic transit hub, the angelic equivalent of a Grand Central Station providing connections between the Choir's various Magisteria. He had, in his nearly incomprehensible way at times, waxed poetic about a bleak and featureless domain punctuated by the interesting regimes where individual angels imposed their will within a Magisterial sphere of influence. Having heard this, and knowing he was a lying sack of shit, Molly had taken it for granted the raw Pleroma would prove to be something entirely different. Something that would put the lie to Bayliss's affected boredom. A place of magnificence. Of blinding metaphysical grandeur.

But it wasn't a lie. The raw Pleroma had all the charm of a public school gymnasium. In fact, it reminded her of nothing so much as a cavernous gym hosting an awkward junior-high dance. Large, empty, not particularly festive, filled with scattered clumps of girls and boys too shy, or afraid, to mingle outside their immediate circle. Except here the awkward non-dancers eyeing each other were angels, and the stereo had been playing the same tune since the Big Bang. Here and there, the ghostly outlines of a shimmering Magisterium peppered the expanse.

Closer to the mortal realm, physically and ontologically, the packing of those Magisteria became tighter and tighter until they overlapped. Even here, a short conceptual distance from the boundaries of her former life, METATRON's bond tried to drag her into that resented realm where the overlapping interference fringes fuzzed into the Mantle of Ontological Consistency.

Standing in the wide-open Pleroma, outside the MOC and free of the constraints of a host Magisterium, Molly dropped her human form and turned her senses—she lost count at 1,440—across the vista, across the behind-the-scenes topology of reality. Across uncountable mutually inconsistent potential realities. Across a formless void.

The angels built their Magisteria in the Pleroma for much the same reason people used to build flour mills and sawmills alongside rivers. The Pleroma was the raw material for their whims; the supply that energized the expression of their will. The Pleroma was a superposition of every imaginable Magisterium. It was the wellspring. The foundation of everything. The subbasement of the Universe.

Her excursion did differ from what Bayliss had primed her to expect in one crucial way: nobody accosted her. No angels attacked her, no beguilingly twisted denizens of the Choir sought her out. Nobody tried to mug her. Nobody tried to rifle through her pockets for the Trumpet. Not even her friends the Cherubim.

Here and there, clusters of Archangels and Principalities harmonized like the celestial equivalent of dueling barbershop quartets. The Pleroma shivered with the high notes and reverberated with the low notes. Nearby (a mere parsec or so, by mortal reckoning) huddled a cluster of Powers, their turbulent clouds chained together by intertwined forks of lightning. Something with the wings of a bat and wearing armor that appeared to have been chiseled from an immense gemstone pulled the foamy substrate of Pleroma about itself, like a cloak, and disappeared. It had stepped into its own Magisterium, out of phase with the rest of the Choir. Maybe it wanted some peace and quiet.

She could see all these angels. They could see her. Nobody cared.

It was enough to make a woman feel unloved.

Or like a goddamned fool.

All along she had avoided the Pleroma like herpes after Bayliss convinced her it was a dangerous place. She'd believed that various factions in the Choir would seek her out; blame her for the instability and uncertainty brought about by Gabriel's murder; try to use her to obtain the missing Trumpet. So she'd stayed on Earth and followed the threads of investigation that Bayliss had spooled out for her.

But now here she was, literally stretching her wings in the milky, jewel-bright surf of a billion maybes. And nobody gave two shits.

Because, of course, it had all been a lie.

So . . . Why didn't Bayliss want her gallivanting about the Pleroma like a newborn colt? What didn't he want Molly to see?

Molly expanded her perceptions. She searched for a kink, a burr of topological imperfection in the tapestry of the divine. It came to her as a faint pulse in the fabric of the Pleroma. She visualized the murdered Plenary Indulgence recipients, imagined how the transmogrified Trumpet had wrought its spiritual alchemy on their mortal beings. Still concentrating on the Trumpet, she reimagined her form as something with pockets. From those pockets she pulled Anne's memory fragment, her resentful remembrance of receiving an Indulgence. Molly brought her new understanding of the Jericho Trumpet—a thing whose essence was its purpose, a process of metaphysical transformation—in contact with Anne's memory.

The memory changed. Like a supersaturated solution exposed to a seed crystal, it solidified. Condensed. What had been a memory of spiritual transformation was now a fragment of the catalyst: the Trumpet. Her breath caused it to chime like a tuning fork. So low was the note, so pure the melancholy, it might have been the death rattle of a dark galaxy.

Another Power scurried along on its hundred thousand legs of lightning. She hadn't seen it approaching, but it ignored her like all the others. It joined the other Powers in their huddle.

Molly waited for some distant corner of the Pleroma to resonate with sympathetic vibrations. Gently, she pinched the Trumpet fragment just enough to perturb its harmonics, then listened to the beats of slightly mismatched frequencies. It wasn't sonar, but it worked. Soon she coiled around a featureless granule embedded in the fabric of the Pleroma. Heaven's kidney stone. It was surrounded with the celestial equivalent of the yellow police tape that had cordoned the site of Molly's death. A steady stream of onlookers had etched a footpath in the surrounding Pleroma. A few loitered nearby. Mostly creepy Virtues, though one onlooker was even stranger. Bayliss's description hadn't done justice to the Thrones. Molly averted her gaze from all the eyes.

The Nephil had been wrought from a unique individual human being. Yet the Trumpet had melted and recast his or her essence, reconstituted their soul, alloyed the divine and mundane until the resulting Nephil betrayed no evidence of its progenitor.

Molly hopped the cordon. The Throne rolled to intercept. But before it could reach her, she touched the crystallized ex-memory fragment to the Nephil. The impossible wrinkle in the Pleroma shrank, while the Trumpet fragment grew. She held them together until the last hint of distortion evaporated and the underlying Pleroma thrummed like a drumhead. She tasted hoarfrost and ancient iron. The Throne skidded to a halt.

"Shit," said Molly. "How easy was that?"

Easy enough to be frightening. Because if Molly understood how to eliminate the Nephilim, surely other angels did as well. They might have lacked the catalyst memory fragment with which to begin the process, but nevertheless . . . Who among the Choir would have understood the true nature of the Nephilim? Who should have known enough about the Jericho Trumpet to recognize its work?

The Seraphim. Gabriel's comrades.

Who knew the Trumpet better than anybody? Who would have known how to pull a trick like this, stapling apparently indelible imperfections into the Pleroma?

Gabriel.

Which angels had made a big show—according to Bayliss—of trying and failing to evict the Nephilim?

The Seraphim.

And . . . prior to Molly's arrival, who in the Choir understood mortals better than anybody?

Bayliss.

Molly hopped to the next Nephil, and the next, and the next, reassembling the Trumpet as she went. The Nephilim, she came to understand, were unrealized potentials. Wave functions awaiting measurement, hovering on the brink of collapse. A superposition of the mortal and the immortal, the mundane and the divine. But the Trumpet had been used imperfectly—deliberately so—to render each Nephil a topological defect. The deceased Plenary Indulgence recipients had become monopoles where domain boundaries met, like the fractures created inside an ice cube when the water in the tray begins to freeze in several places at once and the crystals don't join up smoothly. Scars. Remnants of an imperfect phase transition.

Only, what transition? The Nephilim appeared to be effects awaiting their cause.

But that was human thinking. Time meant nothing here. It wasn't linear. It wasn't even one-dimensional.

If the Nephilim were wave functions awaiting collapse, then what was the measurement? For what observer had they been designed? Only one answer made sense. In fact—

The cluster of Powers broke apart with a mountain-cracking bang. Across the Earth, a network of robotic telescopes swiveled to document the fading glow of a newly discovered gamma ray burst. The Powers reconfigured themselves into a hypersphere. The sphere became an ontological boundary within which the Pleroma roiled and buckled. Molly tasted rank desperation, fear, illicit excitement. Nervous energy raked her like a tornado of broken glass.

The Powers' bubble grew. It rolled downhill, along the residual potential gradient embedded in the Pleroma by the Jericho Event. What the hell were they doing? Was this the angelic equivalent of bowling?

But the Powers had constructed their shared Magisterial bubble from alien mathematics. It was grossly inconsistent with the Mantle of Ontological Consistency.

It was bait.

Crap.

She looked around. The other angels had made themselves scarce.

The Powers' conflicting model of reality approached the MOC—

—Molly crouched, covered her ears—

FORBIDDEN, screamed the universe.

The Powers had rattled the cage to summon the warden. The Voice of God shook Heaven's rafters.

Yet Molly could still think, still move. METATRON paused in the midst of throttling the Powers, like an avalanche deciding halfway down the mountain to pause and consider its options.

Molly glanced at the remaining unconverted Nephilim. They were growing. One by one their wave functions collapsed in a rippling domino effect. Because METATRON was their catalyst. Their long-awaited measurer.

No longer vague and no longer inert, they took the forms for which they had been designed. The Nephilim were wooden stakes driven deep into the heart of the Pleroma. They weren't a threat to the MOC—they were a feint at the heart of the divine.

And irresistible to METATRON.

METATRON would win, of course. For the Nephilim were the work of mere angels, but METATRON was something greater, something feared by even the Choir. Even Bayliss.

But that didn't mean they couldn't bring down seven shades of shit before METATRON sorted them.

Heaven trembled. A trio of massive stars on the far side of the galaxy went off like a chain of firecrackers. One-two-three. Pop-pop-pop. If not for the obscuring bulge of the galactic center, the resulting flare of radiation might have sterilized the Earth in sixty thousand years.

As the Nephilim changed, so did the Trumpet fragment.

Molly slipped out the back.

*T*hunder and lightning shook dust from the rafters. Sheets of rain lashed the windows. We huddled in the diner to ride out the storm. Me, Flo, the shyster brush salesman, the muggs in the window booth, the sheik and his girl. It was a night for staying in and catching a show on the radio.

I sat at the counter and concentrated on providing a good home to a second plate of eggs. They looked lonely.

The next bolt of lightning hit so close the tines of my fork bristled with static electricity. I dropped it. I like my eggs as much as any bo, but I don't get hazard pay. The peal of thunder came at the same moment, so enthusiastic it knocked a pile of dishes from the shelf behind the counter. The roundheels shrieked. So did the salesman. I always knew he'd be one to melt when the heat was on.

I tapped my cup for a refill. Flo stepped over a pile of broken crockery and treated me to the dregs of the pot.

The door slammed open. Rain squalls rode a gust into the diner. The wind swirled through the diner, casing the place. But this joint wasn't worth knocking over so it hit the road. Flametop leaned against the door to close it. Nobody ever needed a new hairbrush as badly as she did at that moment.

I raised my cup in greeting. "Flametop."

"Hello, Gabriel," she said.

23

THE END

*A*bout time," said Flo. "Took her long enough."

She doffed the dish towel that had hung over her shoulder since I put it there long, long ago and headed for the kitchen. Along the way she peeled off her apron and tossed it on the counter. How glad I was to have wheedled a last refill. She wasn't coming back from this smoke break.

The brush salesman tossed a few coins on his table. Then he packed his display case, taking care that each brush fit snugly into its own slot. He followed Flo through the kitchen. So did the muggs, the tomcat, and his steady.

The cook clicked off the radio. He left it on the counter, under the wheel where Flo stuck the orders. He removed his apron, too, and joined the others where they lined up by the cellar door. He left a pile of corned beef hash and a few strips of bacon sizzling on the grill. Thoughtful guy. Flo opened the door. One by one, the constructs filed down the stairs into the cellar that had filled the space below the original diner, back in the day, but which I'd never bothered to re-create in my Magisterium.

And that was the end of that. So long, kids. Write if you find work.

After that, flametop and I had the joint all to ourselves. Maybe I should have tidied up. Thunder sifted a steady fall of dust from the ceiling. It made long, gritty streamers of the cobwebs. Lightning strobed the windows, giving everything a metallic ozone tingle, like chewing face with an electric socket. The atmosphere in the diner would have smelled of onions, bacon, and burnt coffee if not for flametop and her righteous fury. Rafter dust flared incandescent when it sprinkled into her aura, filling the joint with the odor of singed dirt.

"Your timing ain't too swell, angel. Flo just punched out. You'll have to serve yourself if you've come for a cup of joe." More thunder rattled the cups under the counter. I gestured at the rain-lashed windows. "Park the body. Watch the show."

She didn't, of course. Nobody hated me as much as she did in that moment. The heat came off her in waves, leaking from the furnace of her rage. It rippled the linoleum and sent that coppery mop writhing like Medusa's best hair day. It was a beautiful thing.

But I kept to my script. For old times' sake. "What's the score, angel? Something's got you doing figure eights."

She stepped closer. Crossed her arms. Leaned against the counter. I pretended to not notice the way her coat pocket swung with extra weight. She was rodded. Good.

"You had me believing this all started with a murdered angel on the night I died," she said. "But that wasn't true. There was no murder."

Had I been wearing my hat at the moment, I'd have tipped it to her. I felt like a proud father. "I always knew you were one brainy betty."

She rolled the tip of her tongue along the inside of her lips. Maybe she was thinking it over. Maybe she wanted me jealous of her lips. Smart money said she already knew the angles, and this was just for show. Crafty frail.

Flametop said, "But this couldn't have worked if Gabriel were still around in all his glory. Because the Seraphim truly are load-bearing members of the MOC. You had to create a hole, because you needed a cork."

"Don't leave me hanging."

"The only thing that makes sense," she said, "is if he split off a shitty little piece of himself—the tiniest, grubbiest, weakest possible fragment: *you*—and then committed suicide."

"Better get some nails, doll. Your math isn't bad but that last step is loose. Someone's going to trip on it."

"Oh, I'm sure he had help. The other Seraphim were in on it, too. How did you describe them? Thick as thieves? They throw a lot of weight—"

"Carriage trade, those swells."

"—So if Gabriel envisioned a reality built around the termination of his own existence, while the others envisioned a shared reality where Gabriel didn't exist . . ." She lifted her hand to her mouth, fingers curled over her palm. She breathed on her hand and opened her fingers, as though freeing a butterfly. "And the rest of the Choir went apeshit, because the very notion of embracing mortality was so alien, so impossible, to them. They can conceive of anything but their own deaths."

She waited for another barrage of thunder to subside; in the meantime, another drift of burning dust limned her aura. She ran a hand through that fluttering hair. Even disheveled and spitting fire, she still made the joint look suitable for a soirée with the red-carpet crowd.

She said, "But you . . . After splitting off, you came to Earth. And you spent enough time here to conceptualize mortality. Which made it possible for Gabriel and the others to do what they had to do. That's how I knew you had to be a fragment, once I saw things in the right light."

"You spin a wild yarn, kid. Don't stop just when it's getting good."

"*Penitentes.* They're the key. All the other angels doing work on Earth had to hide inside mortal shells, otherwise their unshielded glamours would drive people mad. Or break them. Even kill them. Too much of *that* would run the risk of drawing METATRON's attention. But *you* . . ." Her upper lip curled in the same way it might have done if she had found something disagreeable on the sole of her shoe. "You've spent plenty of time on Earth, elbow to elbow with mortals. And unless you made an effort, nobody would think you anything more than an eccentric prick. Which tells me you've been diminished."

I clapped. "Well done, doll. You win the wristwatch."

She frowned, then tapped herself on the forehead, something between a benediction and an admonishment. "Duh. You know, all that sexism of yours just made me realize something else. Even without the connection to Gabriel, I still should have realized you were a Seraph crumb." She crossed her arms again. "Because the Seraphim are the only angels with a definite gender. Ain't that so, wise guy?"

I fished out my flask and topped off my cup. "Sure you won't join me?" But she was too busy climbing the walls to answer. I shrugged, saluted her with my cup. "Here's mud in your eye." Rye fumes stripped the paint from my sinuses again.

Flametop said, "Why me?"

"Wrong place at the wrong time. I had to choose somebody in that alley. And you, doll, you were the head of the class." I reached over with a finger to tweak her nose. She looked ready to bite it off. I refrained. "I needed somebody with a little spark. That's you. No offense to big brother, but he wasn't exactly setting the world on fire, was he?"

"Leave him out of this."

"I did, you crazy wren. I dropped him like a week-old halibut when I saw you watching the sky. You didn't know what you were seeing, but you knew it was something special." I took a sip. "That's when I knew you were the one. Course, if you had known from the outset you were chosen for a purpose, it would have scotched the whole enterprise. So I fed you a little white lie about the accident. And, like the perfect patsy, you swallowed it. Oh, dollface, where had you been all my life?"

She didn't share in the laugh. Some twists just can't take a gag. I shrugged again.

"Relax. I'm just ribbing you. Keep sneering and your face'll get stuck like that."

Another gust of wind blew the door open. METATRON and the Nephilim were busting up the furniture. Horizontal rain sprinted across the diner to spritz my seat. I flicked my wrist; the door closed. I'd spent enough time standing in the rain on this job. While I was at it, I turned off the grill. The bacon was smelling nice and crisp. What a shame I'd never get to enjoy it.

To herself, she whispered, "Wrong place. Wrong time." Wheels turned, somewhere under all that hair. She said, "There was no memory fragment connecting me to Gabriel."

"Now you're getting sloppy. There was. I showed it to you. I lifted it in those first moments after you punched out. Your whole mayfly life was passing before your eyes. I figured you wouldn't miss a few seconds. And it did the trick, didn't it? 'Verisimilitude,' I think it's called."

"You killed Santorelli." She said it not as a question, but as a statement of fact. Which it was.

"He wasn't what you'd call a green-label bagman. Too much hand wringing, that dope. Would've botched everything, had he a chance to spill his guts at you."

Her aura blazed anew. My coffee was getting cold, so I held the cup in her direction. A few seconds in proximity to all that rage had it boiling.

"You divided the Trumpet and used it to corrupt the Plenary Indulgences. That poor priest. You took advantage of his confusion. You manipulated his failing faith to create the Nephilim."

I blew a raspberry. "Somebody sold you a bill of goods. Santorelli knew those Indulgences were more crooked than a three-dollar bill."

"You coldhearted son of a bitch. What about the people who received those crooked Indulgences? They were killed on your orders. But they had nothing to do with any of this."

I let that one slide.

The thunder was almost continuous now, one blast of lightning following close on the heels of the next as the Voice of God got down to brass tacks. So stark was the light—METATRON's light—it illuminated every strand of hair on her head like burnished copper. After all this time she still clung to her mortal form like a security blanket. But she was a superposition now, an admixture of the divine and the mundane. Like the rest of us. Somewhat.

She watched the light show. I considered lighting a pill, but she was in a right lather now, so I figured I wouldn't have time to savor it. She looked fit to sock me in the kisser. I'd known plenty of dames in my time, but never one so keen to bat me around. Any second she'd put the maulers on.

Good. I'd been waiting long enough.

But she focused on the show outside. And the battle wouldn't last forever. Even now METATRON was cleaning their clocks. What was she waiting for, an invitation? Maybe she needed one more poke, a little nudge over the cliff. They all carry it, the monkeys, that secret dark yearning for redemptive violence. Some might hide it better than others, but it's always there. Never let anybody tell you otherwise.

So I trotted out the biggest lie of all. A real lulu. I'd been waiting a billion years to toss this one out. Waiting for something sufficiently intelligent to evolve inside METATRON's precious MOC.

I said, "Thanks for the laughs, doll."

"What the fuck are you talking about?"

"Was I too quick with the praise a minute ago, or have you taken a couple to the noggin since last we talked? Spend a few billion years watching the paint dry and you'll be ready for a diversion, too. And you were the most fun we've had in millennia."

That did it. Now she was ready to fog me with that heater. Her hand snaked into her pocket. Didn't take a wise-head to know what she kept in there. Part of me wanted to smile, part of me wanted to cringe. I split the difference and gritted my teeth. This would be worth all the trouble, but wouldn't hurt any less for it.

The light show grabbed her attention. She shook her head. "If I didn't know any better," she said, "I'd think you were going out of your way to piss me off."

"Just telling it straight, angel."

"No, you're not. You pretend it was just a game, a meaningless lark, but it wasn't." Still watching the show outside, she said, "Because all that bullshit with the Plenary Indulgences was for this." She nodded toward the chaos outside our cozy little diner. "To keep METATRON distracted while I kick your ass."

I didn't like the sound of that.

*M*olly studied Bayliss's eyes, those old old eyes, and saw something new: doubt.

Outside, the thunder and lightning came so quickly, so constantly, that it was impossible to pair the flashes and rumbles together. Thunder preceded lightning, sidestepped it. The storm was becoming acausal. The ceaseless barrage shook the diner, rattled the cups and plates, set the ceiling fan swinging on its gimbals. The three-second loop of houseflies buzzing around the fan became a two-second loop, a half-second loop, and then they disappeared just as though an old-time filmstrip had jumped clear of its sprockets to escape the lamp.

Something had changed in the way Bayliss held himself. Held his Magisterium. He was rattled.

Molly let him stew. This was fun.

"You're wrong," he said.

" 'Wrong?' That's it? Don't you mean I'm all wet? Peddling my fish in the wrong market? Miscounting the trumps?"

Bayliss chewed his lip. She had the motherfucker dead to rights.

"Your mistake," she said, "was your disregard for human nature. My human nature. My desire to stay connected to other people. Because that connection spared me from blundering into your trap. And once I stepped back to tug on the loose threads, to think it through carefully, the whole thing came apart. Everything finally made sense once I accepted that you were a lying sack of shit."

Lightning struck the diner. Brighter than a nuclear flash, the light poured through the seams of Bayliss's rickety affectations. When the afterimages faded, so had one wall of the diner. And Bayliss's human form.

The thing seated before her had four faces and six wings. The wings, however, were gauzy, ghostly, insubstantial, and three of the faces—the animal faces—were more idea than fact. Only Gabriel's human visage retained solidity. The rest of him, the rest of the shattered angel, had faded into a wispy memory. He looked like a man beset by ghosts. The ghost of a lion, an eagle, and an ox, all wrapped in the vague impression of wings. Molly squinted. Deep inside the diminished Seraph, inside the husk of what had once been the grandest of angels, she glimpsed an inoperable sliver of mundanity. The dreaded mortal epsilon: legacy of the Jericho Event.

The diner shook. More plates and saucers tumbled from the shelves, disintegrating before they hit the floor. Saturnine crimson light welled up through cracks in the linoleum. This was new. META-TRON had changed.

Bayliss/Gabriel noticed it, too.

"You gonna to fog me with that heater or what, you dumb broad?"

Molly clucked her tongue. "Insults? Really? You're losing the script, Bayliss. You're supposed to be the tarnished knight. That tells me how desperate you are for me to use this."

She touched the reconstituted Trumpet in her pocket. It had grown heavier while she talked; the self-assembly had accelerated as META-TRON annealed the Pleroma. Once she reassembled the first pieces, and METATRON started evicting the Nephilim, the process had proceeded of its own accord. The wrinkles fled before the iron, but had nowhere to go.

The damn thing tended to change form when she wasn't focused. Right now she wanted something grand, something imposing. But what she fished from her pocket was a small plastic kazoo, striped pink and green, like a cheap favor from her seventh birthday. Though her soul vibrated when she touched it, the tuning fork of Creation looked like a cheap prize from a cereal box.

Oh, well, she thought. *Screw it.*

She said, "Fortunately for the Choir, I intend to. Unfortunately for you, I'm not stupid."

Soon after the Virtue had stung her, back in its Magisterial overlay of the Chicago concert hall, Molly had recognized an analogy between the confinement imposed upon the angels by METATRON and the confinement imposed upon quarks by the rules—laws of physics—within the MOC. The mundane fragments contaminating the angels in the wake of Jericho were akin to a color charge coupling them via a celestial analogy to the asymptotic freedom of quantum chromodynamics. She had mused, arguing from analogy, that the Choir remained confined because it would have taken an anti-angel to break METATRON's bonds. Which seemed nonsense at the time.

But Bayliss had created exactly that in Molly.

With Jericho, METATRON transformed the angels—purely divine beings—into beings that were mostly divine, with just a sliver of mortal imperfection to tether them. A mundanity charge. A mortal epsilon.

When Molly fell from the train platform, Bayliss had looked into her eyes—*the windows of the soul!* she mused, suppressing a laugh—and imbued upon her a quantum of divinity. But she was born of the MOC. Molly was mostly mortal, with just a sliver of the divine inside her. A mortal shell wrapped around a divine epsilon. She was, in the sense of spiritual admixtures, the opposite of the other angels. Their antithesis.

Meaning she could perform tasks with the Trumpet that no other angel could. Not even Gabriel. For in her hands it could *undo* Jericho.

Assuming, of course, she was sufficiently angry. Because, as Bayliss had said, the Trumpet was a tool of righteous fury. A tool of punishment. Thus he'd strived to ensure Molly had the means, opportunity, and motivation to unleash her fury on him when the time came.

Means: the Trumpet, which as Gabriel he had hidden on Earth, and as Bayliss he had slowly led her to rediscover.

Opportunity: the Nephilim, which even now occupied META-TRON's attention. Otherwise, the moment anybody dared touch the Trumpet to her lips, the Voice of God would have intervened.

Motive: the realization that she was the ultimate dupe, the patsy of a billion-year con job.

Hence the lies and manipulation. He wanted her—the *anti*-angel—so angry that she'd use the Trumpet indiscriminately, without pausing to think things through. He needed to piss her off so badly she wouldn't stop to realize that, rather than punishing Bayliss, her use of the Trumpet would free the angels. He needed to stoke her anger until it was searing hot.

Because above all else, he couldn't afford to let her recognize that her vengeance would destroy the Mantle of Ontological Consistency. And all of humanity along with it. Without the constancy offered by the MOC, without its sheltering bubble of causality and stable bedrock of logically consistent mathematical and physical laws, mortal biological life would become impossible. Biology would become impossible. Chemistry, physics, mathematics—likewise impossible.

Thus the plan *had* to rely on manipulation and anger, rather than a simple plea for compassion. They might have given her the divine spark, brought her to the Pleroma, explained the situation, and asked for her help. But, of course she would have refused. Because truly comprehending the bondage laid upon them by METATRON meant understanding the MOC. And the catastrophic consequences of its dissolution.

But the angels didn't give a rat's ass about any of that. Nobody ever shed tears over an anthill. To their view the MOC was a meaningless side effect of their imprisonment. The Choir just wanted to be free. And who could blame them? So Gabriel and his confederates had taken it upon themselves to arrange it. Once everything was in place, all they needed was a monkey to caper about while Bayliss the organ-grinder turned the crank on his hurdy-gurdy. The poor monkey was fungible.

But Bayliss had chosen Molly. His mistake.

"Well," she said. "Let's do what you brought me here to do."

She brought the Trumpet to her lips. Holy fire consumed the diner, the Pleroma, and Molly's mind.

* * *

olly's consciousness exploded into a trillion trillion fragments. The Trumpet was a supernova flinging the lonely atoms of her soul into the cosmic void.

She was everywhere, vibrated apart by the Platonically pure overtones of the Trumpet.

It emitted every pure note, every beginning, every point of reference, every unprovable axiom.

And it shredded her. Ground her into dust.

A dust of monopoles, of topological impossibilities, of terminated field lines and resolved expectations. The Trumpet sifted her, sieved her, renormalized her into quanta of anti-angelic admixture, into a charge/parity/time-reversed shadow of the Choir, and blew her across the thundering landscape of the Pleroma.

From a trillion simultaneous logically impossible viewpoints, she gazed upon METATRON in the final throes of eradicating the Nephilim. And when she perceived the Voice of God as it truly was, she wept. For this was the only way to know the angels' jailor: not via the agency of what it did, but as the agency of what it was.

By their acts shall you know them. You shall know them despite their acts.

It perceived her. Perceived the Trumpet at use.

FORBIDDEN, it cried.

DON'T WORRY, she said, laying a hundred million steadying hands. **I UNDERSTAND.**

She conveyed her intent. It took a protracted negotiation, long enough for light to gird a proton, but eventually METATRON let her pass.

And where Molly's anti-grace alighted upon the Pleroma, an angel's tether snapped. The angel ricocheted, Compton-scattering from the Trumpet-mediated exchange with Molly's anti-divinity. Each broken tether produced a fragment, an infinitesimal piece of debris. Like virtual particles popped free of the seething vacuum, the release of metaphysical binding energy created a sliver of the mundane. Just as Molly had expected. These were the fragments embedded into the angels by METATRON during the Jericho Event. The shackles. The mortal epsilon. They shimmered as they fell, drifting aimlessly on gyres and downdrafts of possibility, raindrops riding the edge of a storm.

It rained in heaven. Molly collected the droplets as a maiden might collect a rain of flower petals or sunflower seeds in the folds of her dress.

She had plans for these seeds. She was going to plant them anew.

*T*he first bum to slip the handcuffs was some lowly Dominion. Lucky duck. It didn't know what hit it. All it knew was that METATRON's bond had vanished; the MOC had become irrelevant. When that first Dominion raised its voice in song, the firmament rang with something that hadn't been heard in billions of years: joy.

The rest of the Choir caught on quickly. Because nobody had that kind of luck—it was all or nothing. The crystal spheres fairly rattled with the noise of 144,000 torchers crooning in triumphant relief. It was a nice little moment of harmony for a bunch of creeps, none of whom could wait to ditch the others.

Because, like I said, it was all or nothing. One small-time nickel grabber goes, we all go. Right?

*T*he sky was ablaze.
On Earth as it is in Heaven.

METATRON's rage, the cleansing fury with which it scoured the remaining Nephilim from the Pleroma, became tumultuous skies in the mortal realm.

Comets flared anew in the east, south, north, and west. New stars dotted the heavens. Ancient stars blazed with youthful vigor, shining even through the noontime sky. The Southern Cross went dark. A violent sun sent aurorae skidding all the way to the equator. The electromagnetic ripples could have, should have, toppled power grids, cities, civilizations.

But for Molly, they would have. For as the angels sifted away, escaping their eons-long bondage, the Mantle of Ontological Consistency grew weaker and weaker. Without the full weight of enforced angelic consensus to solidify and delineate them, the boundaries between possible and impossible grew hazy. Hazy enough for the entire edifice to come crumbling down.

But for Molly, it would have.

She opened her arms, shielded the Earth.

She breathed deeply. Her exhalation tugged at gravity, twisted it, gave it a minute localized *kink*. Rearranged geodesics described new trajectories for the orbital detritus that filled the underside of the sky. Metal skimmed into the upper atmosphere. It wouldn't happen overnight, but soon enough the cascade would begin, and the high frontier would become accessible once again. Humans would have to do their part, but at least she had given them an opening.

Meanwhile, the sky was ablaze.

"On Earth as it is in Heaven," said the angel who had once been Molly.

I sat on the roof of the diner, sucking hooch from my flask and watching the show. METATRON had clobbered the Nephilim— as, of course, it would—and appeared to have gone dormant again.

No, not dormant. But once that Trumpet gets going there's no stopping it; flametop disappeared the instant she touched that plastic dingus to her lips, and now she had a tiger by the tail because the Nephilim had done exactly what they were intended to do by distracting the Voice of God. METATRON hadn't stopped her in time. It was out there, I knew, watching the same show as I. And what a show it was.

The angelic diaspora made a Čerenkov light show of the Pleroma as my colleagues' various Magisteria, no longer constrained to a tight metaphysical packing, went superluminal in their quest for elbow room. Land was soon to get very cheap here on the Pleromatic side of what was once the MOC.

I wondered how long before a tumbleweed rolled past.

T he laws of physics were formless and empty, darkness fell upon the surface of mortal reality, and Molly's spirit hovered over the dead waters.

And Molly said, "Screw this."

She spread across the oceans. Dunked her hands in the water, trailed her fingernails through anaerobic silt. Felt the play of heat and salt trickle through her fingers. With practice, in her unfettered angelic form, she knew she might have eventually learned the topology by heart. But the Trumpet made it trivial.

She temporarily elbowed thermodynamics aside in order to discard ten trillion terajoules of waste heat. And then, after reestablishing the conservation of energy, she jump-started the worldwide thermohaline conveyor.

She reversed the acidification and resurrected the phytoplankton, too.

*J*oy reverberated through the Pleroma, but it sounded a little ragged as whole sections of the Choir loft fell away. Most angels didn't feel compelled to stick around singing their little wings off. The song lost its lowest registers, almost became a parody of itself, when the Principalities ducked out for parts unknown. So long, kids, it's been swell.

The diaspora was well underway now. I monitored its progress from the shattered and battered remains of my Magisterium. Part of me felt like a proud father: Uriel hadn't been blowing smoke when she said this plan had been my baby. Gabby's baby. He would've been proud to see it all grown up, had the rest of him been around to see this. And part of me did feel pride. But most of me was climbing the walls.

Unfortunately for you, I'm not stupid.

She'd said it, and I didn't like it. I kept on not liking it while the MOC fell apart and my fellow angels hit the road.

Not all of them, not right away. Sam swung by for a quick so long. A stand-up citizen, that one; pillar of the community. Raguel, Michael, and Uriel did, too. Guess they still considered me an honorary member of their little family. Seemed only fair.

"Come on, Bayliss. Time to go."

"Nah," I said, waving them ahead. "It's jake. I'm waiting on someone."

"Madness," they said.

"Somebody has to lock up and turn off the lights after the joint is empty."

Anyway, flametop wasn't finished yet.

*   *   *

*S*he was cleansing wind. She was cleansing rain. She was cleansing fire. She scrubbed the waters, the atmosphere, the sky. She spread across the surface of the Earth. The overheated, dying, used-up Earth.

"Let there be life," she said.

Molly found she didn't need the Trumpet to do these things, though it was vastly easier when she could ignore the killjoy busybody known as entropy. Yet even within the constraints of the MOC, the slow death of the planet never had to be inevitable. The merest attention from the angels, the tiniest spark of giving a shit, could have prevented it. But, of course, they were filled with too much contempt to consider how the monkeys were using the boon granted them by the Voice of God.

She swirled through the excavated bowl of the Calhoun lake bed. A terraced field of lavender sprouted in her wake. She alighted—not all of herself, but a portion of herself—alongside a bed in a Minneapolis hospital.

Someone had braided Ria's hair. It had grown since the day the ambulance took her here, and now two perfect plaits lay across her shoulders. She smelled of antiseptic soap and lemons. Molly kissed her forehead. Ria's skin was cool to the touch. It tasted of salt.

The faintest glimmer of electrical activity flickered through the nether reaches of her empty mind. Ria was there, trapped in the unrelenting grip of her damaged brain, but submerged deeper than the bottom of the sea.

"Wake up, babe," Molly whispered. She brushed a stray strand of hair from Ria's forehead.

Molly's brute-force attempt to reveal herself wasn't all that different from the way the tainted Plenary Indulgences had imbued their recipients with terrifying dreams. The tiniest sliver of the Jericho Trumpet was a peek into the Pleroma too grand for any mortal mind to comprehend. Thus it drove the recipients mad, etching their psyches, cursing them with nightmares. So, too, had Molly tried to force Ria to perceive something she could not. What Molly had done to Ria was exactly what the other angels had sought to avoid by riding inside the *penitentes*.

Ria didn't awaken straight away. It happened slowly. Like a sunrise.

Molly rescinded entropy and causality again—she had no need to fear reprisal by METATRON now—and coaxed the tattered cobweb of current to percolate through the unoccupied vault of Ria's brain.

A nearby nurses' station erupted in a chiming cacophony of alarms and monitors. Molly closed the door to soften the clangor. Ria deserved peace, not bedlam, as she regained herself.

The passage of time was a sandpapery wind whickering across Molly's skin like a cat's tongue tasting her knuckles. She curled the fingers of an upraised hand until time could do nothing but trickle through the hole she left it. She let the spare moments pool in the palm of her other hand, then flung the extra time into the hallway. That slowed things down enough to ensure nobody broke into the room while Ria recovered. She'd have a tranquil return to the living.

Molly laid her hand on Ria's forehead. She used the extra time to reach inside and carefully reassemble a billion-synapse jigsaw puzzle. One neuron at a time, always checking her progress against the picture of Ria's mind on the lid of the box.

The rippling, faintly coruscating web of electrical impulses pulsated through Ria's brain. Each puff stimulated just a few more ion exchange reactions, pushed just a few more microvolts. Slowly, gently, like the undulations of an enervated jellyfish, Ria's consciousness reclaimed its home.

Her eyelids fluttered. Molly disconnected the wires monitoring her vitals. Ria's lips parted. They were a chapped pale pink. Molly conjured a glass of water from her own Magisterium. Ria coughed. Dragged an awkward tongue across those chapped lips. Opened her eyes.

They didn't focus right away. Turning her head took more energy than she could spare. She settled for glancing blurrily about the room.

Molly knelt alongside the bed and took her hand. Part of an Édith Piaf lyric peeked from Ria's sleeve, a line of cobalt blue copperplate rendered on alabaster skin.

"Hi, babe."

It took a few seconds for Molly's voice to register. Ria croaked, "Molly?"

"How are you feeling?"

Ria coughed again. Molly touched wet fingertips to Ria's mouth. While wetting her tongue and lips, Ria studied her surroundings.

At last, she said, in a voice dusty from months of disuse, "Am I in a hospital?"

"Yes."

"I don't remember . . ."

"Shhh, shhh." Molly squeezed her hand. "You were sick for a while. But you're okay now."

Ria licked her lips again. Molly afforded her a tiny sip. "Easy," she said. "You haven't had anything in your stomach for a while."

"How long?" said Ria.

"A while." Molly stood, looked her over. "You look good. Really good."

"You look . . ." Ria squinted. Frowned. Her face moved like a glacier. But she would thaw. "Different."

"I get that a lot these days."

"How come you . . ." Ria tried to shrug, but lacked the strength. It turned into another weak cough.

"I've been stopping by. Checking on you now and then."

"Anyone else?" A moment later Ria winced in slow motion, realizing how rude that sounded. Molly smiled.

"Lots of others. You're plenty loved. Not forgotten."

"Oh. Okay." Ria's eyes slid closed. She wrenched them open again, with effort. "Thank you," she said. "I'm glad you're here."

"Me, too, kiddo. And I'm sorry."

Sorry I almost destroyed you. And that I took so long to fix it.

"Me . . ."

Ria surrendered to sleep. But it was a natural sleep this time, not the inescapable unconsciousness of a broken mind. Molly laid a hand on her face and held it there for a spare few seconds. Then she evened out the flow of time through the hospital and opened the door.

She didn't know when she'd make it back to see Ria again. Eventually, as she recovered and reestablished connections with her life, Ria would try to get in touch. She'd hear about what happened to Molly in Australia. Maybe, as time passed, she'd chalk up this interaction to a vivid dream, a sensory hallucination, her conscious mind's first gasps after being so long submerged. But even then, part of her would always know, as Martin did, that Australia wasn't the whole story.

* * *

*M*ost of the Pleroma within a few scant ontological furlongs from the mortal world had been abandoned. Stampeded, more like. The detritus left behind told the story of a mass exodus: overturned prime numbers; a broken fragment of a Lie algebra; a mutated Principle of Least Action; a smattering of energetic electrons knocked free of the Van Allen belts. Such was the trash blowing through the empty spaces of the Pleroma like Times Square confetti on New Year's morning.

The metaphysical bedrock of the MOC had fallen silent. Barren. Empty. It had become the divine reflection of what had almost been Earth's future. The Mantle of Ontological Consistency sagged. Groaned. Shifted. Without the Choir to hold it together, the notion of a logically consistent mortal reality had become untenable. Irrelevant.

Molly had to work quickly. Her clock was ticking.

Bayliss had said something very similar on the night she died. She wondered if there was some fundamental principle at work, some deep structure to the Pleroma that enforced circularity, brought endings and beginnings together like the mouth and tail of an Ouroboros. If so, it was buried deeper than anything the angels could conjure. METATRON might know. Maybe she would ask it someday.

The angels had spread far and wide. Very far. Very wide. Near Earth, the local Pleroma had become a desert. Here and there, fragments of abandoned Magisteria poked from the shifting sands like the sun-bleached ribs of an ancient Leviathan stranded a thousand miles from the modern sea.

Only one Magisterium stood even remotely intact. The diner had taken damage. So had the adjoining building that, Molly supposed, housed Bayliss's apartment. Presently, they meshed in a distinctly non-Euclidean way. Unsurprising, given all the disruptions. She was impressed he'd held it all together as well as he had.

The degraded crumb of a former Seraph sat cross-legged on the diner's roof, shading his eyes from the glare. He must have seen her coming across the sands, but didn't say or do anything until she stood just beneath the eaves.

"Figured you'd be back," he said. "Figured I'd wait for you."

"Don't you ever get tired of lying?"

Bayliss shrugged. "Force of habit."

"I'll bet."

"Any juice left in that dingus of yours?"

Molly brandished the Trumpet again. Now it looked like a silver harmonica. It glinted in the non-light. "Plenty."

"Give a guy a hand?"

Molly clapped.

"That's rich," he said.

Molly peered at him through the harmonica's air holes. META-TRON's tether was a wispy silver braid emanating from the mundane sliver buried deep inside him. Her own had been incinerated when she activated the Trumpet.

Bayliss's tether disappeared from view when she lowered the harmonica. No matter. He was still bound by the legacy of the Jericho Event.

"Gee," she said. "That looks uncomfortable."

Bayliss lifted his fedora and ran a hand through his hair. "Did you come all the way out here just to crack wise? Or do you have something in mind?"

"Why, Bayliss? You sound like you're in a hurry."

He jumped down. Wind whistled through the tattered shadows of his missing wings. The dust of desiccated realities eddied about his feet. He brushed himself off, saying, "You don't understand how long I've waited for this. Longer than you could have comprehended when you were purely mortal." He reached into a pocket, then sighed. "And my flask is empty. It makes a fellow impatient."

"I can't let you go," she said. She hadn't expected to feel a twinge of sadness.

"Sure you can, angel. Just put your lips together and blow."

"You and I are the only things holding the MOC together right now."

"I'm sure you'll do a swell job with it. But I have other plans."

"In your dreams, asshole. No, I'm planning to—" Molly tapped a finger on her chin. "How would you say it? 'I've gotta breeze, Jack.'"

"What good are you, then? Go on. Scram."

"Not yet." Molly shook her head. "I take off, the MOC collapses. You could rewrite it any way you like since there's nobody left to contradict you. Mortal reality would become what you say it is. And I'm not such a fool that I'd leave the well-being of the 'monkeys' "—she put air quotes around that— "in your hands."

"That's a shame. I'm good with my hands. Everybody says so. Consider the miracles I accomplished with you."

Molly continued, "But at the same time, I'll be damned if I spend eternity with you just to bolster the MOC."

"It's me or you, doll. Tough break."

"Actually," she said, "it isn't." Still holding the Trumpet, she slid her free hand into her pocket. "After all, I've got all these seeds to plant."

She produced the fragments left behind by the emancipated angels. Broken shackles. Slivers of the mundane. Here, in the Pleroma, they were dull as lead.

Bayliss's eyes widened. He backed away.

Even diminished, a frightened angel was a terrible thing to behold. She might have felt sorry for him. But then she remembered an excruciating death, the disorientation of waking up again, the terror of having her soul ransacked by flaming Cherubim . . . And anyway, the noir formula had a somewhat slippery notion of justice. It didn't have a lot of room for noble self-sacrifice.

"You of all people should appreciate this," she said. "Our relationship has to culminate in a tarnished moral choice. It's how these stories work."

"Hey, now, Molly. Let's not do anything hasty."

"Well, you know, I *am* a dame. I get carried away with all sorts of crazy moods." She snapped her fingers. He jumped. "Bing, I tell you."

"Okay. Point taken. Maybe I laid it on a little thick—"

"With a trowel."

"Sure, but hey, that's water under the bridge now."

He seemed so small and frightened. She felt another twinge of regret. "I wish I could have met Gabriel. All of him. Before you split off."

"You would've liked him. He would've liked you, too. Liked your fire."

"As memorials go," she said, "you're pretty cruddy."

Bayliss said, "Maybe so. But they're out there, our pals in the

Choir. They'll remember who set this in motion. Whose plan won their freedom."

"I'm sure they will."

Molly glanced at the harmonica again. Willed it into another form. Then she let the seeds run through her fingers, sifting them into the Trumpet's bell. She lifted the Trumpet to her lips.

"Don't I get a blindfold and a cigarette? I believe that's traditional."

"Shut up and try to appreciate the irony." Then she took Bayliss's advice: she put her lips together, and blew.

The note went on, and on, and on. Somebody screamed. It wasn't Molly.

When the smoke cleared, Bayliss stood at the center of a million-dimensional spiderweb. A hundred thousand gossamer threads punctured his angelic form, which was indistinguishable from his human form now. Even the ghostly hint of wings had vanished. Previously, a single mundane sliver had been enough to shackle him. Now his coupling constant was thousands of times stronger; his color charge covered the rainbow from infrared to X-ray.

He was more mundane than Molly had ever been. And just a tiny bit divine. Just enough.

The threads dragged him through the Pleroma, down the ontological gradient toward Earth and the mortal realm. He dug his heels in the sand. The tethers thrummed. He bent double with the effort to arrest his slide.

Through gritted teeth, he said, "What happens now?"

"Now you go about your very long life. Get drunk. Catch a ball game. Hire hookers. I don't care. Build another Magisterium if you have enough strength to access the Pleroma. If you do it's going to be damn close to the MOC, though, given all those hooks in you. I doubt you'll be putting much metaphysical distance between yourself and the mortal realm from now on."

Bayliss grunted with the effort to stay put. "Try . . . not to . . . sound so broken up about it."

"The MOC needs a caretaker. From now on, that's you. You've got so much mundanity crammed inside you now that the ins and outs of the mortal realm will be second nature. I bet that sooner than later you'll start finding it difficult to imagine the world as anything other than what we monkeys have always known." She clapped again. "Congratulations, Bayliss. You're a one-man Mantle of Ontological Consistency."

The tethers gave another tug. Bayliss moaned. He sank farther, through more ontological layers. "You're just ribbing me, right? Tell me this is a gag."

Molly shook her head. "Nope. And you're going to do a better job than the Choir. Those fuckwads didn't care. They let the whole thing go to hell. Uh-uh. Not anymore. You're going to keep the wheels spinning. And you're going to take your job seriously."

Bayliss slipped farther. He was waist-deep in the mortal realm now. "What about you?"

Molly brandished the empty Trumpet. "I borrowed this from somebody. I need to return it. After that, who knows? But don't worry. I'll check in from time to time."

"Like hell you will."

"Like hell I won't."

The Jericho tethers pulled him to the very edge of mundane ontology. Bayliss dangled by his fingertips. He looked like the guy in one of those ancient black-and-white silent movies, hanging from the hands of an enormous clock.

She wiped her hands on her blue jeans. "Well, I'd say it's been swell, but . . ."

She walked away. Turned. Peered down at his sweating face, his trembling fingers.

"And, Bayliss? Don't take any wooden nickels."

The view wasn't bad: Earth below, multiverse above. The Earth's onion-skin atmosphere shimmered with the incandescent flares of space junk reentry. It followed the temporary pattern Molly had imposed.

They were all down there, Molly's human connections: Anne, Martin, Ria . . . She wondered if they would ever understand how important, how crucial, their influence had been to Molly. To everything. More than connections, they were Molly's human credentials, and the world owed them. Maybe they'd look to the sky, and the sea, and read her handiwork there. Read her thanks and farewell.

She hoped so. She couldn't go down and tell them herself. Her old mortal form no longer fit.

She'd miss them. For a while.

After all, *she* hadn't died. Not really. Why should they? Though the new arrangement would keep her very busy for an extremely long time.

She could already feel it starting. A new fragment, a new divine epsilon, a new sliver of herself peeled away at a rate of just over once per second; over a hundred thousand people died every day. She had given the angels their freedom, and they had scattered to the far-flung corners of the infinite. But the diaspora wasn't for her. She couldn't roam, couldn't explore, couldn't wander. Her fate was a long, slow disintegration. Such was the deal Molly had struck with META-TRON.

There was a long-term plan at work: she'd perceived it, sizzled with the blistering truth of it, when she activated the Trumpet. The Jericho Event was merely the beginning of a greater design. But Molly had just punched a wicked dent in thirteen million millennia of preparation.

The plan wasn't ruined. Not completely. But salvaging it also meant accelerating it. After all, under the original timeline, mortals wouldn't have transcended into an afterlife for another few million years. So Molly had volunteered herself. It was the price for META-TRON's nonintervention as she freed the angels and embedded Bayliss as the MOC's sole guardian.

Thus an infinitesimal diminishment of herself each time another mortal died. But eventually, over eons, she would decay until the final sparks of her divinity transformed the last mortal humans. Martin, and Anne, and Ria, and all the others from now until humanity became something more and fulfilled its purpose—they would witness and participate in the culmination of METATRON's intent.

But Molly wouldn't get to share forever with them. Just a very, very long time. And, considering how things might have turned out, she was comfortable with that. It didn't feel like much of a sacrifice.

* * *

I landed in an alley that stank of rotting dim sum and hot dust, as though the empty corners of the world had been scorched by something moving very fast. Nobody noticed me. They were too busy ooh-ing and ahh-ing at the sky. They poured from gin mills and top-less bars, their shiny upturned eyes lit by aurorae and the flicker of antique neon. A dry night, drier than my throat; guess I no longer rated a commemorative snowfall.

I felt my age. That ain't peanuts when you're older than the universe.

I needed to dip the bill. I'd be lying if I said I didn't also feel the need for a sympathetic ear just about then. Another first, that. But the only ears who could've understood were long gone. They'd scrammed like shysters chasing a fast wagon, leaving me alone in this one-horse burg. And thanks to flametop, I was the horse.

I tried to ditch this dive for my Magisterium but came up with a double handful of nothing. It would have been easier to jitterbug in granite galoshes. The Pleroma could have been a billion miles away for all the good it did me. I loosened my collar. When did this mortal joint get so cramped?

Worst of all, worse than the desperate need to drown my tonsils, was the incessant itch at the back of my mind. My thoughts kept sliding in unwelcome directions. If this is what the monkeys called a conscience, they could keep it.

Was this how she felt after she died on the rails? Cold, alone, fearful, and lost? Or—heaven help me—was this how it always felt to be human? No thanks.

I shook my head—my *only* head now—and gave the alley a once-over. It seemed to me I knew this place. Couldn't quite place it. But then the double ding of a tram dopplered up the lane.

Nice one, angel. What a scream.

I lit a pill and settled in to watch the light show overhead. Later, if I could conjure up some cabbage, I'd wander into a watering hole. I knew a tapster who poured a mean shot of rye. And brother, did I have a story for him.

I knew that dame was trouble the minute I saw her.